Between the Covers

"You want me to find you a wife?" Paige asked in amazement

"Just hear me out." Shane squirmed in his seat. "My father went ballistic when I refused to go into the family business. I come from a long line of proctologists, and I just didn't want to go *there* if you know what I mean? My family hates the fact I'm a cop, and little has changed. Until I got this letter."

He'd forgotten about the trust fund coming due from his deceased grandfather. He'd just left his family's lawyers and had come directly to the library. Directly to Paige Turner.

"There must be plenty of women who'd be thrilled to marry you to help you receive your inheritance," Paige was saying.

"I can't marry just *any* woman. She has to fulfill the five requirements of the Huntington trust."

"*Five* requirements?" she teased. "I can hardly wait."

Shane wasn't amused.

She sighed. "Okay, I'll help you find Ms. Right." She knew it was wrong, but she was also human and very tempted. *And that was very bad.*

For more, turn to page 9

The Matchmaker's Mistake

"Liz?"

No answer. Slowly Mark opened the door. On the edge of the sink three candles flickered, and in the midst of a huge clawfoot tub that overflowed with bubbles, sat Liz.

"Mark?" she said weakly. "Say something."

He blinked, but the rest of him stayed put. He felt as if his feet had been fused to the bathroom tile.

"I'm sorry, Liz. It's just that...you look so *beautiful.*"

At those few heartfelt words, Liz's insides melted. In the dim flickering candlelight, Mark removed his suit coat and tossed it on the floor beside him, the buttons clicking softly against the tile.

He unbuttoned his slacks, then paused. "Don't laugh."

Liz froze. Those were not words a woman wanted to hear when a man was removing his pants.

Finally he took them off. It was a good thing he'd warned her not to laugh. He wore a pair of bright silky boxers in a kaleidoscope of rainbow hues.

"They were the salesclerk's idea," Mark admitted wryly.

"Very nice," Liz said. "Now, can I see how they look on the bathroom floor?"

For more, turn to page 197

HARLEQUIN DUETS

ISBN 0-373-44114-2

BETWEEN THE COVERS
Copyright © 2001 by Cathie Baumgardner

THE MATCHMAKER'S MISTAKE
Copyright © 2001 by Jane Graves

Visit us at www.eHarlequin.com

Printed in U.S.A.

Between the Covers

Cathie Linz

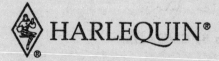

HARLEQUIN®

TORONTO • NEW YORK • LONDON
AMSTERDAM • PARIS • SYDNEY • HAMBURG
STOCKHOLM • ATHENS • TOKYO • MILAN • MADRID
PRAGUE • WARSAW • BUDAPEST • AUCKLAND

Dear Reader,

I love writing about librarians. And with a name like Paige Turner, my heroine simply had to be a librarian. I've had her in my mind for some time. She's been patient, waiting while I wrote other stories and not hers.

And then I saw George Clooney and suddenly it clicked. That sexy smile, those eyes. Oh, yes, this was definitely the man for Paige. Ah, the power of being a writer. I cast George in the role of my hero, Shane Huntington. And presto, a book was born!

Now I'd love to tell you that the rest was smooth sailing but Paige and Shane had ideas of their own. These are two people with very strong personalities and views. Paige is the one woman not taken in by Shane's sexy charm. She also ends up being the one woman who can help him.

The Huntington family home was inspired by a mansion I spotted while driving along Sheridan Road in ritzy Winnetka. Set right on the lake, it has a magnificent setting. But Paige chooses Shane over the Huntington family mansion, and I can't say I blame her one bit!

Happy reading,

Cathie Linz

Books by Cathie Linz

HARLEQUIN DUETS

For my new editor, Kathryn Lye.
Thanks for your wonderful enthusiasm for this book
and for laughing in all the right spots—
even the second time around!

1

PAIGE TURNER BLINKED at Shane Huntington in confusion. It wasn't the first time the handsome police detective had strolled into the High Grove Public Library and asked for her help as a librarian. But it was the first time she'd ever heard him mention this particular word. A word that he'd once mockingly told her he considered high up on his list of four-letter words. "You want what?" she asked him.

"A perfect...wife."

"*A Perfect Wife?* I'm not familiar with that book." Shane had been coming into the library for several months now, stopping by the Readers' Advisory desk to pick her brain about some mystery novel or another. Paige had noticed Shane that very first day, as had every other female in the building. He was pretty hard to miss with his broad shoulders and athletic grace.

And then there was his face. It wasn't a pretty boy's kind of face, it was a face that reflected the roguish charm of the man himself. His powerful jaw warned of his stubbornness while his dark brown eyes were downright intoxicating. The nice little crinkles around those eyes indicated this was a man who enjoyed laughter. The wickedly flirtatious looks he gave every woman under the age of ninety-eight indicated this was a man who enjoyed women and knew they enjoyed him.

Today he was wearing a black suit with a blue shirt and printed maroon tie. His jacket was open, but he didn't look the least bit like a rumpled TV detective. As a member of the neighboring Wentworth Police Department, he could have been the sexy poster boy for police departments across the country. Except for the fact that he was no boy, he was all MAN in big capital letters.

Frowning, Paige focused her attention on the library's computer screen as she began typing. ''The Perfect Wife,'' she repeated, determined to focus on the man's request, not the man himself. ''Do you know the author of the book?''

''I'm not talking about a book,'' Shane said, his deep-pitched voice reflecting his exasperation as he dropped into the oak armchair next to her desk. ''I'm talking about my life. I need to find a perfect wife.'' He fixed those intoxicating dark eyes directly on her.

For some reason Paige suddenly felt as if she couldn't breathe. Looking into those eyes, it was hard not to be completely swept away.

Finally ungluing her tongue from the roof of her suddenly dry mouth, she somehow managed to say, ''You're kidding, right?'' It wouldn't be the first time. In the past he'd told her numerous stories about the practical jokes he'd played on his fellow police officers.

''Do I look like I'm kidding?''

He looked too damn handsome for her comfort level…and his expression told her he felt somewhat aggravated. Okay, so he definitely wasn't kidding. "And you came to *me* because?" she asked.

"Because you always know where to find everything, so I figured you could help me with this, too."

Help him? By marrying him? Her fingers were actually shaking. She firmly clasped her hands on her lap before carefully inquiring, "By doing what exactly?"

"By helping me find a perfect wife."

When Shane had first looked at her and told her he needed a wife, for one wild moment Paige had actually thought he was talking about *her* filling that role.

The leap of excitement she'd experienced at the thought of him proposing shook her deeply, as did her current flicker of disappointment at the discovery that he merely wanted her help finding some other woman to be his perfect mate. Both emotions made her realize how far past her defenses Shane had gotten in a few months.

Not that he'd ever look at Paige and consider her to be perfect wife material. The only time the word *perfect* had been applied to her was when her ex-fiancé Quentin Abbywood had described her as perfectly dull...and that had been right before he'd run off with another woman. And not just any woman. No, Quentin had eloped with Joan Harding, the flashy mystery writer with her trademark platinum hair and miniskirts whom Paige had invited to speak at the library. Talk about rubbing salt in the wound.

That had been nearly two years ago, back in Ohio. Since then Paige had learned to keep her distance from good-looking men with sexy smiles. Men like Quentin.

Men looking for flash and fire. Men who cared more about packaging than content. It hadn't been a problem, because generally speaking that kind of man rarely gave her a second glance.

Until Shane had strolled into her library. She'd built a new life for herself here in the Chicago area, yet Shane had only to look into her eyes and murmur the word *wife* and she'd gone all weak at the knees for a moment or two. Well, forget it. She'd finally regained some measure of her self-confidence and she wasn't about to put that at risk by getting roped into another good-looking man's mishaps. No, she liked her life just as it was, thank you very much.

Finding Shane a good book to read was one thing, finding him a wife was something else again. "Do I look like I'm running a matchmaking service here?" Paige said in exasperation.

Eyeing her cautiously, he noted, "You look kind of grumpy, like you'd like to toss me out of here on my fanny."

"I don't have time for jokes." She hated the fact that she sounded like a prim librarian. Next, she'd be shaking her index finger at him and telling him to "hush." Jeez, when had she turned into a stereotype?

"I don't have time for jokes, either," he replied. "I only have a little less than a month to find a perfect wife and marry her or I don't get the million dollars."

"A million dollars?" she repeated in disbelief. "What is this?" she asked suspiciously. "Some new kind of strange TV game show?"

"No," he replied, loosening his tie before impatiently

tugging it off as if the thing was in danger of choking him. "It's my grandfather's way of making sure the Huntington name is continued."

"By paying you a million dollars to get married?"

"In a manner of speaking. And a million is a hefty chunk of money. Maybe not to the rest of the Huntington family, but it sure is to me—Shane Huntington, black sheep of the blue-blooded Huntingtons of Winnetka," he quipped but there was a sudden vulnerability in his dark gaze.

It didn't surprise her that Shane was the black sheep of his family. But the fact that he came from a wealthy family was news to her.

"Stop looking at me like that," he grumbled. "I'm just a working stiff who normally wouldn't make a million dollars in a million years."

He'd clearly mistaken her empathy at the vulnerability she'd seen in his eyes as awe at his family's connections.

"Maybe you'd better start at the beginning," she suggested.

He practically squirmed in his seat. "It's kind of a long story."

"Then you better talk fast."

"Look, under normal circumstances, this kind of money wouldn't be important to me," he assured her.

"Why? Because your family is so wealthy?"

"No, because money isn't important to me. That alone drove my father crazy. But he really went ballistic when I refused to follow in my grandfather's, uncle's and father's footsteps by going into the family business."

"Which is?"

"I come from a long line of proctologists," he admitted with a wry grin. "As I told my family, I just 'didn't want to go there' if you know what I mean."

Paige couldn't help it, she laughed.

"Yeah, well you might laugh but they didn't appreciate my humor…or my decision to become a police officer. That was almost ten years ago and little has changed since then. Until I got this."

Taking the official-looking letter from his pocket, Shane once again scanned its contents. He'd forgotten all about the trust fund from his deceased grandfather until he'd received the letter from the longtime Huntington family lawyers—Bottoms, Biggs and Bothers—requesting a meeting as soon as possible.

He'd just left that meeting ten minutes ago and had come directly here, to the public library.

This was where he came whenever he was searching for something not related to his work. He'd come to Paige Turner, a woman who'd told him that with a name like hers she was destined to work with books and become a librarian.

He knew all about being destined to do something. His family had told him from the time he was a kid that he was destined to be one of the Huntingtons of Winnetka. The fancy prep school, the Ivy League college with its sterling premed courses had all been part of the master plan.

A plan he couldn't live with.

"There must be plenty of women who'd be thrilled to marry you," Paige was saying.

"That's the problem. I can't marry just any woman." He showed her the letter. "The lawyers at the law firm of Bottoms, Biggs and Bothers informed me that if I married a woman who fulfilled the list of five requirements of the Huntington trust then I'd get the million dollars, which as I told you normally wouldn't be important to me. But there are extenuating circumstances here."

"What's the matter?" she teased him. "Did you overextend your credit cards? Bet too much on the horses at the Arlington Race Track? See a sports car you just couldn't resist?"

He wasn't amused. His jaw tightened, making it appear even more powerful than usual. She'd clearly hit a nerve here.

Putting her hand on his arm, she quietly said, "I'm sorry."

He recovered quickly, as if regretting letting her know that she'd gotten to him. The charm was back, along with his ready grin. "Okay, I admit I want the money for a female. Her name is Brittany and she's seven years old."

Did he have a child? Refusing to jump to conclusions, she said, "And your connection to Brittany is?"

"She's one of hundreds of kids that have been helped by Hope House, a place that helps families start a new life after an abusive relationship. You'd think a place that does something incredibly worthwhile like that wouldn't have a problem getting sufficient funding, but their major grant was just pulled due to a lack of money from their sponsoring agency. We were putting together a fund-raising effort, when I got this letter from the Huntington lawyers in the mail. It seemed like fate was stepping in. A million dollars would cover the funding that was pulled, and then some.''

''I don't know what to say.'' Paige felt lower than a centipede for teasing him the way she had. ''That's very generous of you, offering to help a charity that way.''

''This isn't just any charity,'' Shane quietly said. ''They saved the life of a good friend of mine. I've been involved with them ever since, as has the Wentworth Police Department. But it would take us years of pancake breakfasts and car washes to get a million dollars together.''

There was definitely more to Shane Huntington than met the eye. He wasn't just a ''hottie'' as Leslie from the circulation department put it. But the fact that he had a philanthropic side didn't change the fact that the guy was a walking minefield as far as she was concerned. Flirting was second nature to him. His charm and good looks put him a cut above other men. It also forced her to remind herself yet again that this man could never be more to her than a friendly acquaintance.

Telling herself that was all very well and good, but it didn't explain the little zing she felt each time Shane walked into the library. And it certainly didn't account for the way her heart went into overdrive when his fingers accidentally brushed hers, as they had when he'd handed over that letter to her just a few minutes ago.

She was human, and she was tempted. By Shane

Huntington. And that was bad. Because the last time she'd been tempted by a handsome charming man it had ended with her fiancé running off with that wild writer-woman and Paige having to leave town.

Getting Shane married off would be a good thing. Not only would it be for a good cause and help children in need, but it would also put Shane once and for all out of reach for her.

"You mentioned a list of requirements," she reminded him.

"Yeah, I wrote them all down." He tugged a small spiral notebook from an inside jacket pocket. "Let's see. She must fulfill the following requirements. Number one, she must be a well-bred young woman. Number two, she must come from a wealthy, well-connected and respectable family."

"I can't believe anyone would have the nerve to come up with a list like this."

"Believe it. The Huntingtons never joke. Marriages are mergers as far as my family is concerned."

"And these people are doctors?"

"They reserve their passion for their medical practice."

When she wrinkled her nose at him, he said, "I know, I know. But wait, I'm not done with the list yet. Number three, she must be capable of bearing children."

"Of all the nerve! What is she, some baby-making machine?"

Shane ignored her outburst and kept reading, "Number four, she must be a college graduate. And last but not least, number five is that she must be a redhead. A natural redhead. My grandfather had a fondness for red-heads.'' Looking at her, he murmured, ''You know, I just realized that *your* hair is sort of red.''

Sort of red? What kind of description was that? Her hair had been the bane of her existence as a kid, when the other children had nicknamed her Carrot Top and made fun of her. Now that she was in her late twenties, it had calmed down from its childhood orangy brassi-ness to what she liked to describe as auburn. That sounded much better than ''sort of red.''

''But you'd hardly be working in a library if you came from some wealthy background, right?'' When she just stared at him, he added, ''So do you know any women who'll fulfill the requirements of the Huntington list?''

''Even if I did, I have no idea how you'll convince some woman to marry you,'' she said tartly, still infu-riated on behalf of all womenkind at the way his grand-father had reduced a woman's worth to a list of require-ments, as if she were a piece of property and not a human being.

Shane gave her an adorably affronted look. ''Hey, I can be quite charming when the situation warrants it. And getting Hope House the money they need certainly warrants it. Besides I only have to stay married for one year to fulfill the requirements of the trust.''

''Does that mean you have to wait a year to get the money?'' she asked.

''No. But I do have to sign some kind of promissory note for the money so that if I don't fulfill the trust's requirements, I'd owe the trust a million bucks.''

"And what about the woman you marry? Are you going to con her into thinking you love her and want to marry her only to dump her after you get the money and the year is up?" Paige knew all about being dumped.

"Of course not!"

Even though Shane sounded and looked suitably indignant, she wasn't convinced. "Then what are you going to tell her?"

"Okay," he admitted, "so I haven't worked out all the details yet. First I have to find the right woman. I'll worry about the rest later."

"What makes you think finding a perfect wife will be easy?"

"I never said it would be easy. That's why I came to you. Because you'll tell me where to get started. Forget about my grandfather. I agree this list is insulting. But think of Brittany and all the other kids like her. I don't have a lot of time here. I have to get married before my thirtieth birthday which is less than a month away. I need to find the right woman as soon as possible and I don't know where to start," he said with a helpless shrug.

"With a roomful of rich people," Paige automatically replied. "I was reading something just the other day in *Chicago* magazine... Just a second. Let me go get it."

Shane watched Paige as she hurried over to the magazine section. She had such an elfish face that he'd always thought of her as a petite little thing, but now he realized that she was actually rather tall, probably five-seven or so. The long flowing dress she wore was blue and almost reached her ankles. But as she walked, the open flaps at the sides showed tempting glimpses of her legs.

She was one of the few women he'd met who didn't seem to be affected by his charm. Not that he was big-headed about his winning ways with women, it was just a fact of life like his dark brown hair and the bump in his nose where he'd broken it while playing hockey.

But Paige had never tried to flirt back with him. Instead she'd either laughed at him or given him one of her patented come-on-you-can't-be-serious looks. She really was kind of cute.

It was a shame she didn't have the required background or he might have had a ready-made wife right here. Not that she'd ever talked about her private life or family background. For all he knew she could have grown up on a farm in rural Iowa or come from a bad neighborhood on the south side of Chicago. Neither one of which would have bothered him, but he had that damn "Huntington list" to consider.

One thing was certain. A woman like Paige wouldn't let you get away with much.

As she reached for the magazine on the top shelf, the flowing material of her dress molded itself against the curve of her breast. Then she had the magazine in hand and was walking back toward him.

"Here's what I saw. There's a high society charity event going on downtown this weekend." She showed him the page with the information. There were photos of last year's event, showing several women smiling at the camera. They had names like Cindy and Mindy and had even white teeth that would do an orthodontist proud. One looked like she might be a strawberry-blonde, which was close enough to a redhead, maybe.

Shane immediately whipped out his cell phone to call the number listed for more information. After listening to the recorded message, he noted, "They're completely sold out of single tickets. I have to buy a set of two, and they only have one left so…" He punched in some numbers, apparently including those of his credit card number because a moment later he said, "Done. I now have the final set of tickets to the Windy City Ball, which means you have to come with me."

She looked at him as if he were crazy. "Why should I do that?"

"Because then you can help me find the best candidates for the job."

Ever the practical one, she noted, "You don't think it'll seem a little strange, you bringing a date while you're searching for your perfect bride?"

"You won't be my date. We'll say you're my cousin." He smiled as if he'd come up with a brilliant idea along the lines of Einstein's theory of relativity.

"And I'd agree to do that because…?"

"Did I show you a picture of little Brittany? This was taken last year." He drew his wallet out of his pocket and flipped it open.

Gazing at the photograph, Paige said, "She's adorable and this is emotional blackmail."

"It's for a good cause. And you'll get a free meal out of the deal."

"Oh, well, if there's a free meal involved," she said mockingly.

"Good. I knew you'd agree."

"I was being facetious."

"Too late to back out now. Put on something fancy and I'll pick you up at your place around six-thirty. Give me your address."

"No," she said quickly. Having him in her home would be allowing him to get too close. "I'll meet you there. In the hotel lobby. By the concierge desk. At seven."

"Great. Thanks for being such a good sport about this, Paige! I couldn't have found a better woman to pretend to be my cousin."

"Yes, that's me. A good sport," she muttered as Shane happily made his way out of the library. "A good sport who needs her head examined."

2

"HANDS OFF!" ESMA KINCH scolded in her very proper English accent while waving a wooden spoon at Paige. An up-and-coming caterer who looked like a supermodel with short hair, Esma had a passion for life that was downright infectious.

Paige had first met her when Esma had volunteered to cater the library's annual fund-raising event shortly after Paige had moved to Chicago. While everyone raved about her food, some of the more conservative staff members had been taken aback by Esma's outrageous love of color and bold sense of design. Since then Esma's outrageousness and expert culinary skills had made her catering business one of the most sought-after in the entire Chicago area.

Originally from London, Esma had come to Chicago by way of New York. Esma claimed that her sense of the dramatic came from her father, who was a stage actor, while her cooking skills came from her mother, a culinary chef in one of London's best hotels.

Standing there in a lime-green pullover and flowing black pants, waving her spoon with a huge grin on her face, Esma was simply the best friend Paige had ever had.

Tonight Esma had invited Paige to her loft apartment to test the new version of gumbo she'd concocted. But apparently testing the gumbo without proper authorization was a no-no.

"I only had one little taste," Paige said.

"It's not that I don't approve of a little nibble in the kitchen, but you'll ruin that new manicure of yours sticking your fingers in my cooking pots."

Frowning, Paige gazed down at her golden nails. "How long can it take for nail polish to dry?"

"Long enough. Here, sample this..." Esma held the spoon up invitingly.

Paige closed her eyes in ecstasy at the incredible explosion of flavors to her taste buds. "Mmm, I can die happy now."

"Not before you go to that Windy City Ball. I want you to taste the competition's food and tell me all about it."

"You're already the most in demand caterer in the city."

"I'm still a relative newcomer," Esma modestly said.

"Who has catered the biggest fund-raisers at both the Lyric Opera and the Art Institute this year."

"Yes, but Umberto Gerreaux is doing something special for the Windy City Ball," she pointed out, turning up the heat on her industrial stainless-steel stove. The entire kitchen was done in polished stainless steel—countertops and state-of-the-art appliances. "Now what are you going to wear to the grand event?"

"I've got a very nice black pantsuit... What?" Paige demanded as Esma made a choking sound.

"You're not wearing a pantsuit to the Windy City Ball." Esma sounded horrified at the very idea. "Absolutely not! One has to have some standards. This is your chance to shine."

"I'm not the shining type or hadn't you noticed?"

"Rubbish! You've got superb cheekbones."

"They make me look like a pixie."

"Double rubbish. You have an Audrey Hepburn kind of beauty. Wide-set eyes, those superb cheekbones and a mouth…"

"That's too big for the rest of my face," Paige inserted.

Snapping her fingers, Esma said, "I know just who to call in."

"A plastic surgeon?" she mockingly suggested.

Esma gave Paige a reprimanding look before replying, "A costume designer friend of mine. She works in the costume department of the Lyric Opera, and has a real eye for ball gowns."

"Great. I'll end up looking like something out of a Wagnerian opera."

"Your bosoms aren't big enough for Wagnerian opera heroines," Esma told her with the frankness of someone who'd known her for years. "No, you've got the grace of a ballet dancer."

"Don't I wish. I'm more likely to fall over my own two feet than do a pirouette. In fact, I'm a ballet school dropout. At the age of three I couldn't make the grade."

"You'll make the grade this time," Esma stated with her customary confidence. "Zorra will guarantee that.

And so will I. I'm not without a modicum of good taste myself.''

"I thought you knew what tasted good, not what was in good taste.''

"I have the good fortune to have been blessed with both talents.''

"And modesty as well,'' she noted dryly.

"My mum always told me, 'Esma you better learn early and learn well about the better things in life because you'll never get them unless you work hard. Or marry well.'''

Which reminded her of Shane. He had to marry well, not to get his hands on his wife's money but to get his hands on his own inheritance. And she'd agreed to help him. Well, maybe not *agreed* in so many words, exactly. But she hadn't said no.

Which was why she was standing here with golden nails and listening as Esma excitedly spoke over the small cell phone that was practically glued to her hip at all times.

Flipping her phone shut, Esma said, "Zorra is coming right over. She only lives a few blocks away.''

Zorra arrived with a dramatic flare that didn't bode well for Paige's quiet sensibility. Dressed all in black except for the colorful paisley turban she wore on her head, Zorra circled Paige, clucking her tongue at her outfit. "You look like a librarian.''

"Hey, I *am* a librarian,'' Paige replied, lifting her chin and glaring at the other woman.

Zorra was not the least bit intimidated. "There is no

need to advertise the fact by wearing sensible shoes and boring clothes.''

"I do not subscribe to the 'beauty before comfort' school of thought,'' Paige said.

Zorra held up her hand. "Quiet! I am getting an image.'' Squinting her eyes, she nodded. "Yes, something golden. Tight on top, nipped in at the waist, a ballgown skirt to dance the night away in.''

"I'm not going to be doing any dancing.''

But Zorra wasn't listening to her anymore. She was frantically sketching on the back of one of Esma's blank recipe cards. "Yes, yes, yes! It shall be brilliant. Brilliant!''

LIMOS WERE LINING UP IN FRONT of the hotel entrance, with the upper echelon of Chicago's high society stepping out and nodding to the liveried doorman. Surrounded by furs and diamonds, no one noticed Paige in her black velvet cloak. No one held any doors open for her.

She reached the concierge desk at precisely seven. There was no sign of Shane.

Maybe he'd forgotten all about it. Maybe he'd been called in to work. Maybe that was him standing on the other side of the lobby chatting up a willowy blonde.

Yep, that was him all right.

As if aware of her disapproving look, Shane suddenly turned and smiled at her. He even waved at her.

Apparently making his excuses to the woman he was talking to, he strolled across the lobby toward Paige. This gave her time to enjoy the fit of what had to be an

Armani suit. It was a charcoal-gray so dark as to be mistaken for black. The shirt he wore was the same color, as was his tie.

So he looked great. So he looked incredible. It was what was inside a man's heart that really counted.

And this man is willing to donate a million dollars to help kids in need.

"She didn't look as if she'd be a likely candidate. She's not a redhead," Paige said with a pointed look at the woman still watching him from the other side of the lobby.

"I was just practicing my charm on her," he noted with a wicked grin.

"Well, stop it. Or your real perfect wife will dump you before we even get started. Can we just stay focused on your goal here?"

"I am focused," Shane protested. "Why else do you think I'd put on designer clothes and come to a do like this?"

"I must say that they look…" She ran out of words as once again her mouth went stone-dry. It had clearly been a mistake to look at him while standing this close to him.

"They look…?" he prompted her.

She nervously swallowed and took a step away. "Suffice it to say that no one looking at you now could tell that you're a police detective."

"That's the point. So, cousin, let's go check that coat of yours and get in there because I'm starving."

"It's a cloak, not a coat," she corrected him. "And I'm not checking it."

"I'll pay for it," Shane assured her, placing his hands on her shoulders as if to help her remove her wrap.

Paige quickly stepped aside. "That's not the problem."

"Then what is the problem?"

She shrugged. "It's chilly in here. I'd rather keep it with me."

"Okay. But you're going to have to take it off at some point."

"Don't count on it," she muttered under her breath.

"What did you say?" Leaning closer, he studied her face. "And if you're chilly, why is your face flushed? Are you coming down with something?"

"Yes." She backed up until she bumped into the concierge desk. "A bad case of cold feet."

Stepping closer, he cupped her elbow with his hand. "Don't back out on me now, Paige. I'm counting on you here."

Looking into his eyes, she saw a reassurance there that helped calm her nervous butterflies.

"Come on," he coaxed her. "Let's go eat some great food and dance the night away."

The next thing she knew, she was moving with him toward the ballroom. As they passed the cloakroom, Shane paused to give her a teasing look. "All right, let's get rid of that cloak now. You don't have to be embarrassed," he earnestly assured her. "I don't expect you to have the kind of clothes these people wear. I'm sure whatever you've got on will be fine."

Did he think she'd come tonight wearing her work clothes and sensible shoes? Well, actually she had worn her comfy flats, now that she thought about it. She'd taken public transportation tonight, after which she'd had to walk a few blocks to get to the hotel. She was supposed to have changed as soon as she got into the lobby, but seeing Shane talking with that blonde had thrown her.

"Footwear is very important indeed," Esma had told her the night before, when she'd dropped off a pair of shoes for her, an early birthday present she'd said. Paige's birthday was still six months away, but Esma had waved away her protests.

"Let me stop by the ladies' room first," Paige said. Once inside, she slipped off her sensible walking shoes and replaced them with the slender gilded heels she'd put in the deep pockets of her cloak. She then tucked her walking shoes into her large purse and removed an evening bag studded with golden beads. Since she planned on checking the large purse in the cloakroom along with her velvet covering, she'd already transferred the necessary items to the evening bag.

Staring critically in the mirror, she decided her lipstick could use reapplying. Zorra had insisted that the golden undertones in this pink shade highlighted her mouth. Paige pointed out that she didn't want her mouth highlighted, it was big enough as it was. At which time Zorra had given her a fifteen-minute lecture about how women all over the country were getting special collagen treatments just to get lips that God had given Paige naturally.

Paige had to confess, the lecture and Zorra's makeup tips worked. She did look at her lips in a new way now.

Would Shane be looking at her lips in a new way now as well?

The forbidden thought raced through her mind before she quickly chased it away. She was here tonight as Shane's friend, posing as his cousin, to help him find a wife. To get him married off before he tempted her into trouble. A piece of cake.

One final check to make sure her hair was still okay, and that the glittering flea market necklace she wore was still in place. Zorra told her that in a room filled with so much of the real thing, everyone would assume her jewelry was the real thing, too.

"Ready or not, here I come," she muttered, before walking out of the ladies' room.

"You're still wearing your cloak," Shane said, apparently completely unfazed by her recent application of lipstick. "Hurry up and take it off. I missed lunch and if we don't get a move on, we're going to miss dinner, too."

She reluctantly slid the cloak off her shoulders.

When Shane's jaw dropped, she hurriedly tugged the cloak back on again.

"It's too much, isn't it," she said.

Shane blinked, as if doubting his own eyesight. Then he reached out to gently peel the cloak from her nervous clutches until she was left standing there in Zorra's creation.

"It's too much, I know." Paige plucked at the shimmering golden satin skirt nervously. "I told Zorra it was too much. Too Cinderella-ish. Just all-around too much."

Shane had her cloak completely off now and was just standing there staring at her. Unable to stand the suspense a second later, she begged him, "Say something."

"Wow." His voice was a soft murmur.

"Wow it's way too much and I look stupid?"

"Are you kidding? You look…breathtaking." Placing his hand on his heart, Shane shook his head in amazement while giving her a visual once-over from head to foot and then back again, his eyes traveling over her with heated approval. "You blow me away."

Suddenly nervous of the sensual look in his dark eyes, she said, "I'm here as your cousin, remember? And I'm not sure you should be looking at your cousin that way."

"I can't help it," he murmured, showing no sign of remorse.

"Well, get over it," she whispered. "People are staring."

"Because you look so gorgeous in that dress."

"Yeah, right," she scoffed.

"I'm serious." Turning her to face a large mirror flanking the ballroom entrance, he said, "See for yourself."

What she saw was Shane, his hands on her shoulders, his mirror image looking almost as good as he did. He had the kind of body meant for wearing expensive clothing and he had the confidence to carry it off.

And then she saw herself, her cheeks flushed, her lips glistening in the mellow light, her dress somehow seeming more appropriate in these grand surroundings. The spaghetti straps showed off her shoulders while the bodice fit her like a glove, nipping in at her waist before billowing out into a dream of a skirt that went all the way to her ankles. She almost didn't recognize herself.

Where had this Paige Turner come from? She wasn't the Readers' Advisory librarian at High Grove Public Library. She wasn't the dull woman whose fiancé had run away with a flashy mystery writer. She wasn't the woman who preferred staying in the background.

She was someone new. Someone reborn. Someone standing beside an incredibly sexy man and wondering what it would be like to go to bed with him.

She definitely was not herself!

"Call in the reality police." Paige wasn't aware that she'd actually murmured the words aloud until Shane grinned.

"No need to fear, ma'am," he drawled. "You're with me."

That's what she was afraid of. Being with him...and falling for him.

3

"SO ARE YOU GOING TO GIVE IN?" Shane asked her.

"Wha...at?" Paige practically gulped. Had he somehow read her mind? Was the powerful tug of attraction she'd felt for him written all over her face? Had her expression somehow indicated the fact that she'd just been thinking about what it would be like to go to bed with him?

"Your cloak," he said. "Are you going to give in and let me check it in the cloakroom?"

Her cloak. He was talking about her cloak. Not about her. He had her so confused she didn't know up from down, which was not a good thing. She needed to keep her wits about her to navigate this evening without getting hurt because of foolish expectations on her part. Shane had made it clear what her role was to be tonight. She was here to help him find a wife. Not to play Cinderella to his Prince Charming.

"I didn't realize it was that difficult a question to answer," Shane was saying in a teasing voice. "If keeping your cloak means that much to you, then by all means keep it."

"No." She handed him the large leather purse. "Go ahead and check this with the cloak. Thanks." She wanted to add, *And while you're at it, check my silly Cinderella fantasies in the cloakroom, too, because I certainly don't need them messing things up.*

As they entered the ballroom, Paige was still attempting to recover some measure of her customary equanimity. Her surroundings made that hard to do. The room was decorated like an illustration from some gloriously fanciful fairy tale. The ceiling glittered like a night sky filled with hundreds of stars while the ballroom walls were hidden behind a forest of greenery dotted with twinkling lights. And at the front of the room, past the dancing area, was the outline of a large castle.

It was an impressive sight. Equally impressive was the warmth being generated from Shane's hand on her arm as he guided her across the crowded ballroom to their table. There was no denying that, despite the fact that Paige had vowed to remain unaffected, Shane still had the ability to make her heart race. Again, not a good thing.

Maybe some food would make her feel better.

"Here, we are," Shane said, before pulling out a chair for her. "Table thirteen."

"It's a good thing I'm not superstitious," she murmured as she sat down and studied the calligraphied lettering of the menu listing their meal tonight. Setting that aside, she nervously selected a warm bread stick from an artful display in a small ceramic shoe set near her plate before focusing her attention on the others at their table.

The floral centerpiece of what had to be at least three dozen gorgeous peach- and lilac-colored roses was low enough not to obstruct her view. She soon realized that their tablemates were all couples in their sixties. No marriage candidates for Shane here.

A glance at Shane, who was giving her a rueful look, indicated that he'd reached the same conclusion.

"In police work, we'd widen the investigation at this point," he leaned closer to tell her.

As his warm breath bounced off her flushed cheek, she hastily reached for another bread stick. It was much better than doing something rash, like stroking his cheek with her hand to test the smoothness of his skin.

By the time the waiters, looking like royal pages dressed in their burgundy brocade vests atop downy white shirts and black slacks, whisked away their cold cucumber soup and replaced it with prime rib, Paige's heart had settled down. The silver-haired woman to her right had been particularly chatty, introducing herself as Inez O'Reilly and her husband as Frank.

"They really do up a good show, don't they," Inez said, indicating their surroundings with a wave of her hand.

Paige nodded. "We don't have anything quite this glittery back in Toledo," she ruefully acknowledged.

Inez nodded. "I remember the first time I attended this event. They had a circus theme that year, complete with a tent and elephants out in the parking lot. For a girl who grew up on the south side and was a salesgirl at Marshall Fields, it was quite an experience I can tell you. I wasn't born to this lifestyle. In fact, neither my husband nor myself was born with a silver spoon in our mouths."

"Yeah, well silver spoons aren't all they're cracked up to be," Shane leaned forward to say.

"I'm not sure that most of the people in this room would agree with you," Inez noted.

Shane's grin was unrepentant. "That doesn't bother me. I'm used to going against popular consensus."

"Ah, you must be a free thinker like my husband, Frank." Inez patted her silent husband's arm fondly before returning her attention to Shane and Paige. "I must say, you two make a lovely couple," she noted.

"Oh, we're not a couple," Paige hastily assured her. "Shane is my...cousin."

"Really?" Inez arched a perfectly plucked eyebrow at her.

For one crazy moment Paige had the wildest urge to say, *No, really I'm his mistress.*

The rebellious thought made her blink. Unlike Shane, it wasn't like her to be defiant in the face of popular consensus. And the popular consensus had always been that she was the mousy quiet one in her family, that there wasn't a flamboyant bone in her body. Which was why Quentin had run off with the flashy Joan Harding, who didn't have a thoughtful bone in her body. Joan considered the world to be her oyster, and everything was hers for the taking, including Paige's fiancé.

No, it was much safer not to get involved with another good-looking man. Someone quiet like herself would be much safer. And there was nothing quiet about Shane. "I'm his cousin," she firmly repeated.

Conversation temporarily lagged as everyone concentrated on the delicious food. Paige made a mental note to tell Esma about the tasty asparagus tips and baby carrot combination. Dessert was a white chocolate mousse in a delicate chocolate slipper topped with a fresh raspberry glaze.

With the Cinderella theme all around her, it was a constant battle not to get swept up in the magic. Once the dancing began after the meal and Shane insisted she join him for the first dance, it became downright impossible to resist.

Shane took her in his arms as if he'd done so many times before. But it was to be expected from a man as smooth as he was. He was no doubt accustomed to sweeping women off their feet.

What *was* surprising was that she didn't hesitate or falter. Maybe it was her golden dress, or her new shoes. Whatever the reason, she moved with Shane as if she were indeed Cinderella dancing at the ball. The old-fashioned Strauss waltz was written to bring a man and a woman together—her hand clasped in his, his arm encircling her waist, his body brushing hers as they swirled together.

It was so easy to forget, to pretend, to become the fantasy. Held in his arms this way, she was no longer Paige Turner—librarian. She was the mysterious Woman in Gold. She'd seen the envious looks she'd gotten from some of the other women in the room. They wanted to be her.

She wanted to be her. The woman in the awesome dress dancing with an awesome man. On their way to the dance floor she'd received several compliments of "Lovely dress, where did you get it?"

But she knew it wasn't just the dress garnering the attention. It was Shane. The sheer physical impact he had on women was unmistakable. And the suit he was wearing set off his good looks to perfection. Oh, yeah, Shane Huntington had perfection down pat.

She wished she was…more confident. More experienced. More…*everything*.

Then Shane smiled at her. It was a new kind of smile, not like any of the others he'd given her. This was the smile a man gave a woman he was interested in and it was quite devastating.

Paige forgot to breathe, forgot to move. Stumbling over her own two feet, she bumped into another couple. That quickly, the spell was broken.

"I'm so sorry," she hurriedly apologized to the young woman she'd collided with.

The music stopped and so did Paige's heart as she realized that the woman was a stunning redhead who was eyeing Shane with hungry interest. There was no ring on the woman's left hand and when she spoke, she spoke directly to Shane.

"That's what I get for dancing with a junior partner in our law firm. How about you? What's your excuse?"

Paige didn't miss the way the woman had quickly checked out Shane's ringless left hand as well as Paige's ringless left hand.

"I'm just his cousin," Paige forced herself to say.

"That's good. My name is Scarlet McKenzie. Our law firm, McKenzie, Banks and Stevenson, booked an entire table for this event."

Shane smiled at Scarlet. Paige tried to tell herself that

it wasn't the same kind of smile he'd just given her minutes before, but the truth was she couldn't be sure. She felt totally flustered, as if she'd suddenly woken from a dream to find she'd been sleepwalking and was now someplace she was unprepared to be.

"Maybe it would be better if we get out of the way and let these two trip the light fantastic," the junior lawyer suggested to Paige in an undertone.

Paige smiled and nodded her agreement. In a white backless dress, Scarlet looked lovely with Shane, like something taken from the pages of a glossy magazine. The silk jersey material of her designer outfit draped Scarlet's body to perfection and made Paige feel like an overdressed angel from the top of someone's Christmas tree.

Get out of the way. The junior lawyer's words rang in her head like the tolling of a clock at midnight. As Shane danced away with Scarlet, Paige decided that it was time she did get out of the way...completely. By leaving the ball.

Her work here was done. The party was over, at least for her. It was time she leave before everyone saw her for what she really was. Someone who didn't fit in. Someone who never seemed to fit in, at least not for very long.

After stopping by their table to make her farewells to Inez and the others, Paige hurried out of the ballroom and headed straight for the cloakroom where she retrieved her cloak and her bag. Perching on a nearby chair, she quickly removed her dainty golden shoes and replaced them with her sturdy sensible footwear.

And all the while she was silently lecturing herself. You fool! You knew what you were letting yourself in for and still you fell for it. The magic, the fantasy, the man. Well, it's over now. Time to come back to terra firma. Your magic carriage just turned back into a plain old pumpkin, Cinderella. Time to catch the bus home.

PAIGE HAD JUST RETURNED from a library budget meeting and was about to head out for lunch when Shane showed up at the Readers' Advisory desk.

"I think this belongs to you," he said, dangling one of her golden shoes from his index finger.

"Where did you find that?" She didn't even realize it was missing. She could have sworn she'd stuffed both shoes into her leather bag last night.

"Next to the cloakroom."

"It must have fallen out of my bag." She stretched her hand out for the shoe but Shane moved it out of reach.

"Or maybe I should make you try it on," he murmured, a teasing gleam in his dark eyes, "to make sure it's a perfect fit."

She refused to be swayed by his boyish charm or sexy body. Today he was wearing another of his customary dark suits, with a light blue shirt and dark gray tie. She was not impressed. She refused to be impressed. "Speaking of perfect fits, it looked like Scarlet should be a good candidate to be your perfect wife. A lawyer, a redhead, from the respected law firm of McKenzie, Banks and Stevenson."

"Is that why you left so early last night?" he countered. "Because of Scarlet?"

She shrugged. "I thought my job was done."

"Your *job?* I didn't realize being with me was such a chore," he retorted irritably.

She didn't know how to answer that, so she stayed silent and tried to look busy tidying a desk that wasn't even really hers. This desk was in the public area of the library and was the work station for anyone doing Readers' Advisory duty. Her desk was in a cubicle in the back offices. And it was already neat.

"Since it was such a chore for you to come with me last night," Shane continued, "you'll be pleased to know that Scarlet and I are going out on a date tonight."

"Pleased? I'm delighted." She was definitely getting better at this lying business. She really sounded as if she didn't care, as if she couldn't wait for him and Scarlet to set the date.

"I also got a lead on another possibility from the guy sitting next to me at our table last night. He showed me a picture of his niece, Kate O'Malley. Her family is from the north shore, in the printing business."

"Another *possibility?*" Now her voice reflected her chagrin. "Doesn't it make you even the least bit uncomfortable talking about these women as is they were stocks you were thinking of buying?"

"Hey, this list wasn't my idea. These are certainly not requirements I'd come up with for a perfect wife."

"No?" she challenged him. "Then what requirements would you be looking for?"

Grinning, he removed his ever-present notebook from

the inside pocket of his jacket. "I've started my own personal list..." he began when she boldly snatched the notebook out of his hand.

"Number one: Looks good in a thong," she read aloud in disbelief. "Number two: Minimum C-cup bra size."

Shane shrugged off her hostile glare, the beginnings of a very masculine smile tugging at the corner of his mouth. "Hey, a guy can dream, can't he."

"And apparently you dream of big-breasted small-bottomed women."

Which definitely put her out of the running. Her body attributes ran the other way around—small-breasted, bigger bottom.

"You'll note that I put an asterisk next to that second requirement," he apparently felt compelled to point out. "Which means it's just a suggestion, not a written-in-stone item."

"Women all over Chicago will no doubt be so relieved to hear that," Paige retorted. "Why, I can hear their sighs now. No, wait, forgive me. That was the sound of my stomach turning."

"Hey, I didn't tell you to read my list."

"It's like a car accident. I know I shouldn't look but I can't seem to turn away. So I'll continue. Number three: Must be a hockey fan. A hockey fan?" she repeated. "It's not exactly a high society sport."

"Yeah, I know," he said glumly. "Still a guy can dream..."

Tossing his notebook back at him, she said, "*You* must be dreaming if you think you're going to find any

woman willing to put up with you! Good luck with
Scarlet. I have a feeling you're going to need it.''

"I LOVE WHAT YOU'VE DONE with this place," Esma
told her as she did each time she came over to Paige's
apartment.

Paige studied her surroundings with a sense of ac-
complishment. She'd worked hard to get things right.
Her couch had a loose beige slipcover with a Provençal
botanical motif that was repeated in the pillows nestling
on the comfy beige armchairs. The accent end table with
its weathered eggshell-colored paint and walnut top was
French Country in design. The matching square coffee
table had a large decorative wooden bowl on top in
which both her cats, Simon and Schuster, were curled
together like two peas in a pod.

"I've brought some tidbits for the kitties," Esma
whispered, placing her tangerine nail-polished fingertips
to her lips in a *shh* motion, knowing that Simon and
Schuster picked up on keywords that had anything to
do with food.

"You're spoiling them," Paige said, but there was no
disapproval in her voice. "I think I must have the only
pair of cats addicted to caviar."

"They're rather fond of lobster, too," Esma reminded
her, forgetting to lower her voice.

At the sound of the *L*-word, Simon raised his head
and sleepily blinked at them. Recognizing Esma, he un-
curled himself from the bowl and bent for a glorious
stretch, his gray fur glistening in the early-evening sun
pouring though the western windows. The building had

once been a warehouse and it still had the whitewashed brick walls and industrial-type large windows to prove it. Paige had placed a kitty perch near the window so that they could sit and watch the world go by when they weren't snoozing in their huge bowl.

"Mmmrrrroooow." Simon was the more talkative of the two and he wasted no time going over to Esma and ingratiating himself.

"Ooh, you sweet talker you," Esma said. "Come along now, and look what I've brought you both."

Simon obediently raced after Esma and indeed reached the kitchen first while Schuster belatedly realized there was food coming. Still blinking sleepily, the gray-and-orange cat followed at an amble.

"It's nice of you to bring them a few of the leftovers from your catering jobs," Paige said.

"I never could resist a waifish face," Esma said as Simon looked up at her with a feed-me-feed-me look.

"Which is why you like me," Paige replied as Esma cut up the bits of lobster with the efficiency of a professional chef before equally distributing it to the cats' dishes.

"I hope you notice that I did not walk in here and immediately demand to be told about last night," Esma said as she washed her hands and dried them on the kitchen towel Paige kept tucked through the fridge door handle. Unlike Esma's kitchen, here the appliances were standard beige to match the wall coloring. But Paige had added her own sense of style by displaying a trio of old wooden signs advertising flower seeds on the soffit above the cabinets.

"I did notice your restraint," Paige congratulated her friend as the two of them returned to the living room. "Please thank Zorra again for all her work. I'll get the dress dry-cleaned and get it back to her."

"Nonsense." Esma dismissed her words with a single wave of her hand. "She made it just for you."

"I did have several people ask me who designed the dress and I told them about Zorra and her Web site."

"Excellent. She told me she's already had people place a few orders for her designs." Esma curled up on the couch, a splash of color in her vivid orange jeans and purple T-shirt, and then patted the seat beside her. "Come sit. I'm dying to know all the rest of the details about the ball. How was the food? How was your date? How was the food? Did you get to dance? Oh, and how was the food?"

"I brought you a copy of the menu." Paige handed it to Esma before joining her on the couch. "Just in case you might possibly be interested in the food," she added wryly.

"Mind you, it's not that I'm obsessed with food or the fact that the caterer for that event is a chauvinist pig. Truly, I'm just as interested in hearing about how your evening went."

"It went." Paige shrugged and absently tugged at her slate-blue cardigan top, wondering if it had always made her chest look flat.

"Well, that wasn't very enlightening," Esma said. "Come on now, tell me all about it. From the moment he came to pick you up—"

"I met him at the hotel—" Paige inserted.

"To the time he brought you home."

"I took a cab."

Esma frowned her disapproval. "You met him at the hotel and you took a cab home? What kind of date is this?"

"It wasn't a date at all. I told you it wasn't a romantic evening. I was just helping Shane out, that's all. Like a friend."

"Is he gay?" Esma demanded bluntly.

Paige blinked in surprise at her question. "No, he's not gay."

"Well, he'd have to be gay not to appreciate how gorgeous you were in that dress last night."

"I was in a room filled with gorgeous people in designer gowns by designers like Versace and Vera Wang," Paige reminded her. "The women were wearing shoes that cost a thousand dollars."

Esma didn't ask Paige how she knew the price of designer shoes. Instead she quietly said, "Have you told him about your life back in Toledo?"

"No. And I have no intention of doing that. There's no looking back," she stated firmly. "I've started a new life here. Besides, there's no way I'm what he's looking for."

"Which is?"

"The perfect wife," Paige replied, pleased that her voice was tart rather than wistful. "In fact, he's on a date with a likely candidate right now."

"YOU CALL THESE ROLLS WARM?" Scarlet demanded of a clearly intimidated waitress. "Maybe they were…a decade ago. Get them out of my sight and bring me some fresh ones immediately!''

Okay, so Shane was the first to admit that Scarlet could be a little...abrasive. They'd only been in the trendy French restaurant for thirty minutes and already she'd sent two busboys and a fellow diner cowering. Now she'd brought their server to tears.

The romantically lit white-tablecloth surroundings were at odds with Scarlet's strident behavior. Even the well-dressed crowd sipping their martinis at the bar had turned to cast their disapproving looks in Scarlet's direction.

Apparently blithely indifferent, Scarlet turned and gave Shane a confident smile. ''My staff tells me I haven't developed people skills, but I tell them I don't have time for that. There are only so many hours in the day and I can't spend them rubbing the ego of someone incapable of doing a job without getting warm fuzzies and effusive compliments. I've got a plan for my life.''

He had a plan, too—to get a wife. But he wasn't sure Scarlet would fit into that mold. He doubted she liked hockey, although with an attitude like hers, she'd make one hell of a player. He could see her shoving the puck right down the goalie's throat...with her bare hands.

''Do you like children?'' she surprised him by asking. In fact, she'd been interviewing him all evening, as if he were a job applicant of some kind. Actually, he supposed that was what he should have been doing with her, if she hadn't beaten him to the punch.

''They're okay,'' he cautiously replied. ''Why? Are they in your plan?''

"Certainly. I've already picked out the nanny service I'd use. And the boarding school."

"What's the point of having kids if you're going to ship them out?"

She gave him a superior look. "Why...to continue the family line of course."

"Ah, of course."

"I thought you'd understand, your being a Huntington and all."

"I'm the black sheep in the family," Shane modestly replied.

"So I've heard. Naturally I had to do a little digging into your background before we went out tonight."

"Naturally." He toasted her with the glass of cabernet sauvignon at forty-five dollars a bottle. Scarlet had been "starved" so she'd ordered the most expensive appetizer, which she'd only picked at. Then she'd ordered a lobster entrée that just said "Market price," making it anyone's guess what the final toll would come to. At this rate, finding the perfect wife could make him go broke. Tonight's meal alone would cost almost two hundred bucks. And while that was nothing to a Huntington, it took a sizable chunk out of this Huntington's limited pay check.

As if reading his mind, Scarlet said, "I can't believe you're actually a police detective." She then gave a delicate shudder. It was the first delicate thing he'd seen her do. "Not that I don't understand about rebelling against one's family. I mean, I went to Harvard instead of my father's alma mater of Northwestern."

"How bold of you." Shane had done some research

of his own. Scarlet came from a long line of attorneys. Her father had served as a state representative before joining his father's practice. There was nothing in her family background that the Huntington attorneys could possible find fault with. In fact, they'd probably do handstands at the thought of him getting hitched to a family of lawyers.

His father would no doubt approve as well. He was always complaining about how expensive malpractice insurance was and how handy it would be to have an attorney in the family. Imagine his delight at having an entire law firm filled with attorneys.

Yeah, Scarlet McKenzie would be the perfect candidate to be the perfect wife. How depressing.

So far she'd aced requirements one and two from the list, well-bred, college graduate. Maybe her red hair came out of a bottle? One thing he knew for sure, he didn't aim on personally checking that one out. The woman did nothing for him.

Why was that? Was it her barracuda tendencies? Or the fact that her personality reminded him too much of his own family? Either way, this was not working out as he'd planned.

IT WAS A LITTLE AFTER NINE and Paige was in the middle of reading Amanda Quick's latest historical romance when the buzzer sounded. She wasn't expecting anyone. Unless it was Esma again? Pressing the intercom button, she said, "Who is it?"

"It's me, Shane. I need to talk to you."

She buzzed him up.

"Nice security," he said approvingly from the top of the stairs leading to her second-story apartment. She already had her front door open and was staring at him with unabashed surprise. "What are you doing here and how did you know where I live?"

"I'm a police detective," he reminded her, answering her last question first. "And you cursed me."

"Only under my breath," she murmured wryly as she stepped aside to allow him entry into her apartment.

"I meant you jinxed me tonight." He dropped into her favorite chair as if he'd been here many times before. "Wishing me luck with Scarlet and then saying you had a feeling I'd need it."

Sighing, she curled up on the couch across from him before giving him a resigned look. "What did you do to mess up?"

"Hey, I did not mess up," he denied, loosening his tie before tugging it off completely and stuffing it into his pocket.

"No? Then why doesn't she ever want to see you again?"

"Not want to see me again?" He arched a dark eyebrow at her. "She wanted me to spend the night at her place."

Paige felt the heat rushing to her face. "Look, if you came here expecting to give me a play-by-play description of your sexual antics with Scarlet—"

"I didn't have sex with her," Shane interrupted her to say bluntly, "she's not the one. I came here to tell you that the search isn't over yet."

"What do you mean it's not over yet?" Paige demanded, leaping to her feet to start pacing around the room. She hadn't felt the need to pace since leaving Toledo. The first time Shane showed up in her home, he had her pacing. "You've only had one date with the woman. You can't have expected to propose to her on the first date."

"I'm not proposing to her at all," he stated.

"Why not?" She abruptly stopped pacing and turned around to face him, not realizing he was standing right behind her. Had he not reached out his arms to steady her, she'd have fallen at his feet.

"Sorry," Paige said, only her voice didn't sound like her own. It sounded like a breathy Marilyn Monroe. And her body didn't feel like her own, either. Instead it was alive with sexual awareness.

Her hands rested on his shoulders, to hold him at bay or to keep him close...she wasn't sure which. Seized by a dizzying sense of pleasure, she couldn't move, she couldn't speak, she couldn't believe how much she wanted him to kiss her.

And when his lips did lower to hers she couldn't believe how incredible it was. What began as a gentle coupling of their mouths rapidly escalated into a sensual dalliance of sultry taste and touch as his tongue tempted her lips to part.

She succumbed to temptation. Oh, how she succumbed! And not only that, she savored every erotic tongue thrust, every passionate nibble. She welcomed the feel of his hands slipping beneath the hem of her cardigan to grasp her lower back.

His fingertips were warm against her bare skin and

each one created ripples of delight as they wandered at will, exploring her as his mouth explored...with expertise and skill.

A whirlpool of intense delight sucked her in, drowning her reservations as she was immersed in a sensual world where time and prudence were temporarily suspended.

4

THE CLOCK CHIMING ON THE END table sounded an alarm that abruptly brought Paige out of her passion-induced reverie.

Breaking away from Shane, she took several steps back and then glared at him. She was as angry with herself as she was with him. First, she had to regain control of the situation, which had so suddenly spiraled out of control. And that began with him. *He* was the one who'd initiated the kiss after all, even if she was the one who'd responded to it. So he was the one who got the first shot in her angry volley. "This wasn't part of the deal."

She recognized the little head tilt thing he did, his chin dipping down as his eyes dropped to the floor before looking back at her with a half grin. It was his yep-I'm-in-trouble-but-you-love-me-anyway look. "What deal?" he asked.

"The deal where I help you find the perfect wife," she said in a stern voice. "Practicing your routine on me was never part of the deal."

"You think I was just *practicing?*" Now he sounded insulted.

"I think that kissing me is not going to help you get

your inheritance.'' *And it sure wasn't going to help her any, either!* Kissing a man who was intent on marrying someone else was just asking for trouble, even if his intended wife remained unknown as yet. In any event, it wouldn't be her. It *couldn't* be her.

How could she ever hope to keep the attention of someone like Shane? He put Quentin to shame. Her ex-fiancé was just a shadowy presence when compared to Shane's edgy vitality.

And then there was that kiss. That also put Quentin to shame. She'd never shared a kiss like that with Quentin. She'd never been tempted to. She'd never known a kiss could be so…so all-encompassing that you forgot what planet you were even on.

But maybe she was the only one who felt that way. Maybe Shane experienced this explosion of emotion with every woman he kissed. He had his inscrutable cop's face on now, the one that prevented her from reading his thoughts no matter how hard she tried.

''So what do you suggest we do?'' he surprised her by saying.

''Me? Why I…'' She quickly gathered her thoughts and her composure. ''I think we should forget it ever happened.''

He gave her an intent look before agreeing. ''If that's what you want.''

For one wildly rebellious moment what she wanted was for him to be really and truly head-over-heels in love with her, for him to take her in his arms and kiss her again, telling her that she was the only woman in the world for him before they sank onto the plush carpet and made passionate love for the rest of the night. But barring that scenario, then yes, she wanted to forget how vulnerable she was to his kiss because it only served to remind her of her own shortcomings.

It would serve him right if she told him about her past. But no, she wasn't going to fall into that trap. Opening herself to him would only serve to further increase her vulnerability. It was time to get a little distance and perspective on things here.

Gazing down at her feet, Paige belatedly realized she was still wearing her fuzzy bunny slippers.

Ah, yes, there was nothing like a pair of floppy-eared footwear to drive the men crazy. Yeah, right.

The bottom line was that she was just a pair of fuzzy bunny slippers in a bold platform-shoe world. She was no femme fatale and she liked it that way. Frankly the pressure of trying to be perfect all the time was too much. She knew. She'd been there and done that—badly.

No, she needed to yet again remind herself of her role in this scenario. She wasn't the princess heroine, she was the librarian gathering information. "So if Scarlet isn't the right candidate, what other plans do you have?"

"Do you remember me telling you about the O'Malleys earlier today? They were seated next to me at the ball last night."

Had it only been last night? It felt like a lifetime ago that she'd put on that golden gown and made her way to the ball. So much had happened since then. Most of it in her own head, and in her viewpoint. Where once she'd been able to keep her distance with Shane, now that he'd danced with her, held her in his arms and kissed her, that changed everything—as much as she tried to deny it.

This had to be temporary insanity caused by Shane's wicked sex appeal.

"As I said," he continued, "I was talking to Patrick and he showed me some pictures of his grandkids—"

"You're going to date one of his grandkids?" Paige interrupted him to say, visions of him going out with a curvaceous teenager filling her mind.

"No, but he has a niece who was in one of the shots. Her name is Kate and she has red hair."

"I have to tell you this feels so weird—picking these women by the color of their hair and the size of their family's bank account."

"You should try *dating* them."

"That would definitely feel even weirder," she told him with a grin.

"Yeah, well just do what I've been doing and keep telling yourself it's for a good cause."

"Oh, I'm sure it's very hard for you to have to date such beautiful women," she commiserated with a mocking smile. "Although as I recall, nothing on the Huntington list said the woman had to be beautiful. That requirement must be coming from your own personal list. So let's see, so far you're looking for a beautiful busty redhead who looks good in a thong and loves hockey."

"And loves the Eagles."

"The national bird?"

"No. And not the football team, either. I'm talking about the group The Eagles. You know 'Hotel California.'"

"So you're looking for a beautiful busty redhead who looks good in a thong and loves watching hockey while listening to her favorite Eagles CD. Yes, I can see that dating a woman like that would be a real chore."

"Dating them isn't the hard part," Shane retorted. "Marrying them will be the hard part."

"Convincing them to marry you will be the hard part," she corrected him. The man might kiss like a dream but some women required more than that. And, yes, he was good-looking in a "real guy" rather than a "pretty boy" kind of way, but some women looked for more than surface appearances. Sure, he had a roguish charm and...

Okay, so most women might, possibly, probably definitely *would* line up to marry him.

"Convincing the right woman is a concern," he admitted. "Especially since I'm running out of time."

"We're talking about a person here, a human being, not some automobile you're going to pick up at the local dealership."

"I'm well aware of the seriousness of this matter."

"Good. Then you'll be fine on your own from now on." She didn't realize she was going to say the words until they came out.

"Hold on a minute." He gave her a startled look. "I never said that."

"No, I did." And having said it, Paige felt better. She was in way over her head here.

"Why? Because I kissed you?"

"No, because I've decided that I'm not comfortable with any of this."

"And you think I am?" Shane shoved an impatient hand through his dark hair. "Trust me, I'm not. I'm just trying to make something positive happen out of this family mess my grandfather made."

Okay, now she felt guilty. She certainly did know all about trying to make something positive out of family messes. "Have you tried talking to your parents about this?" she suggested.

"My parents would be horrified at my plans."

"Then maybe you should reconsider."

"Why? My parents have been horrified by everything I've done since I turned twenty-one. Why should I be affected by that now? No, I'm sticking to my plan. And if you won't help me I'll do it on my own."

He looked so upset that she relented a bit on her earlier stance of complete noninvolvement. "Let me know how your date goes with Kate."

"Why should you care?" he said, still a bit irritated with her.

"I have no idea," she retorted. "Attribute it to my desire to know how this story ends."

"Your desire, hmm?" His sudden slow smile made her knees wobble. "Far be it from me not to satisfy your...curiosity."

"Very good." She briskly patted him on the shoulder as she handed him his coat. "Now just smile like that at Kate and you should be married in no time at all."

"You're certainly eager to marry me off all of a sudden."

"It's not sudden at all," she assured him, feeling more like her old self again. She might not be flamboyant, but that didn't mean she was dumb. Refusing to help him at all would only make her feel guilty.

No, her best defense against his charm was to treat him like a friend and to get him married off ASAP. Before she did something stupid—like fall in love with him herself.

"I'M SORRY TO BOTHER YOU, but I'm looking for a book." The reader, a woman in her forties, looked at Paige expectantly. Sunlight poured through the large mullioned windows on the south wall of the High Grove Public Library, creating a series of sunny squares on the pale marble flooring. The woman stood in one of those sunny squares, her demeanor one of apologetic hesitance.

"You're not bothering me," Paige quickly assured her. Assisting patrons was Paige's favorite part of her job. She loved connecting a reader with special books, creating a special union. Special unions got her thinking about Shane, though, so she had to shove that thought aside and instead focus on the woman before her. Most patrons didn't just plunk down onto the chair beside the Readers' Advisory desk the way Shane did. Most stood in front of the desk, as this woman did.

"The book is set in Chicago and it's a mystery," the woman said, "but I don't remember the author's name."

"That's okay," Paige replied. "Do you remember if the author was a man or a woman?"

"I'm not sure."

"Do you remember anything else about the book?" Paige asked.

"I think the detective in it is a woman. Oh, wait, and I believe they made a movie based on the book. Kathleen Turner was in it. The movie, not the book. Although I haven't actually read the book, but I don't think Kathleen Turner is in the book, just the movie."

"You're talking about author Sara Paretsky's books about private investigator V. I. Warshawski." Paige began typing the author's name into the library's computerized database. "Did you want to read the book the movie was based on?"

"She wrote more than one book?"

Paige nodded. "Yes, there are several about this private investigator."

"Then I'd like to begin with the first one and read the rest in order."

Paige checked her computer screen. "Then you'd want to start with *Indemnity Only*. The computer is indicating that we do have a copy and that it is on the shelves. Would you like me to check for you? Or you can look for yourself if you'd rather. Our mysteries are right behind me, shelved in alphabetical order by author. The *P* section should be on the right-hand side of that bookshelf."

"I'll go check myself. Thank you so much for your help."

"That's what I'm here for," Paige told her. Like

many patrons, this woman was apologetic about asking for help. That wasn't a problem that Shane shared. He had no problem at all strolling into the library and demanding that she help him find the perfect wife.

There he was, invading her thoughts again. Normally the library was a refuge for her, a place designed for serene thought. Built in the early 1900s, the Arts and Crafts style had been designed by a student of Frank Lloyd Wright. Even the oak furniture and bookshelves reflected the Arts and Crafts style with its straight lines and lack of ostentatious ornamentation, while the tops of the many mullioned windows featured simple geometric designs of colored glass in earth-tone colors. The two-story building had an abundance of light and a shortage of space. The children's section was downstairs while the adult fiction and nonfiction departments were upstairs. This suited Paige just fine but some patrons took exception to the library's layout.

As if on cue, Mrs. Schmidt got off the elevator and marched right over to Paige's desk. The tall, thin woman was in her sixties and was known for being obstreperous. It was a reputation the older woman had been cultivating for the past twenty years. "I don't know why they put the adult books on the second floor," Mrs. Schmidt complained. "They should have put the children's department up here. Let those youngsters get the exercise. It's not right I tell you."

And tell Paige she did. Every Monday, Wednesday and Friday when she came in for another pile of the true crime books she so enjoyed, the bloodier the better. Paige wasn't sure if it was her choice of reading material or the militant gleam in her eyes, but she'd long ago decided that she did not want to get on Mrs. Schmidt's bad side.

Paige gave her what she hoped was a commiserating look, acting for all the world as if she hadn't already heard Mrs. Schmidt make this same complaint a hundred times before. "Would you like to speak to our library director about your concerns?"

Paige had learned that few people wanted to speak to their director, who could put an insomniac to sleep with his lengthy discourses on obscure topics. Mrs. Schmidt was no exception. "No, I do not want to speak to that young whippersnapper." Sniffing her disapproval of life in general, Mrs. Schmidt moved on.

During the lull, Paige began working on one of her administrative duties, signing time sheets and working out her staff schedule. As the fiction department head she had two other full-time professionals working with her and three part-timers. Sometimes working out everyone's schedule was harder than pleasing Mrs. Schmidt. But somehow things eventually worked out in the end.

Normally she did most of her paperwork in her cubbyhole of an office located in the area behind closed doors along with the technical services and cataloging departments. But she was trying to get caught up on a few things today, so she'd brought some work out to the Readers' Advisory desk with her.

She was interrupted by another patron who stopped by a few minutes later. "I just wanted to thank you for recommending that book by Susan Elizabeth Phillips. I did so enjoy it. And to think she's a local Chicago area author.''

"I'm so glad you liked it." Paige chatted for a few minutes with the young woman, telling her about an upcoming romance readers' book group discussion that would take place next month.

Once that patron left, there were a flurry of phone questions, including enquiries about an older book club selection and the waiting list on the latest Tom Clancy book.

It was midafternoon when Irene Small showed up to replace her at the desk. Irene was a fellow librarian who always spoke her mind. She looked small and dainty, with stylishly cut salt-and-pepper hair and perfectly applied makeup. So it was always a surprise when Irene made one of her customarily outrageous comments. "I heard that our sexy cop has been stopping by more than usual lately. Are you two an item?"

"Do I look like the kind of woman Shane Huntington would be interested in?" Paige retorted.

"Never judge a book by its cover."

"Not judge it perhaps, but you can certainly ascertain certain information about a book from its front and back covers. And nothing about my front or back cover says 'looks good in a thong.'"

"Why would you want it to?" Irene calmly countered.

"It's on Shane Huntington's personal list describing the perfect woman," Paige admitted.

"The man has obviously never worn a thong, although he'd probably look very good in one himself."

Paige cracked up.

"Because once you've worn a thong yourself," Irene continued, "you'd never wish that on anyone but your worst enemy. In fact, whoever invented thongs should be sued," Irene firmly declared. "My husband gave me one this past Valentine's Day and let me tell you, it's an instrument of torture. I'd be glad to inform Detective Huntington of this fact myself if you'd like. After all, they might want to use it at the police department as a way to get suspects to talk. Threaten to make the suspected perpetrator wear a thong. That ought to do the trick. Should break even the most hardened criminal's resolve."

"I don't know, Irene. That might come under the heading of undue use of force."

"Remember my offer to tell Detective Shane the true thong facts," Irene said as she took Paige's place behind the desk.

"I wouldn't trust the job to anyone else but you, Irene," Paige solemnly assured her.

SHANE WAS NOT HAVING A GOOD day. And the antics of his partner, Bill Kozlowski, otherwise known as Koz, were not helping matters any. Koz was the only one on the force, aside from the police chief, who knew that Shane was one of "those" Huntingtons, the rich ones from Winnetka. But that didn't mean that Koz didn't take great joy in needling his buddy when they were alone.

The Wentworth Police Department was located in what had once been a school and was now village hall.

Filing cabinets were jammed along the walls, filling every available space. The detective division consisted of two olive-green metal desks pushed together in a corner so that they faced each other.

Both desks had a computer, a metal gooseneck lamp and a black phone but the resemblance ended there. Koz's desk was cluttered with framed photographs of his wife and kids, a collection of small toys he claimed helped him think and a pile of papers he swore multiplied when he wasn't looking. Shane's desk had folders in a neat metal rack and his Chicago Blackhawks coffee mug on it. That was pretty much it.

Not as wealthy as neighboring High Grove, Wentworth was a middle-class community with a diverse population. Diverse and occasionally perverse as exemplified by the Cubs Flasher, so called because he appeared wearing nothing but a Cubs cap and a trench coat. He'd made his latest "appearance" at the Metra train station during this morning's commuter rush hour.

"I still say the guy went off his rocker because the Cubs are such a bad baseball team," Koz stated. "They haven't won a World Series since 1908. Frankly I'm surprised there aren't more crazed and frustrated fans out there doing the same thing."

"Yeah, that's just what we need," Shane drawled. "A dozen flashers. The chief and mayor are already prepared to blow a gasket over this guy. You know, we interviewed witnesses all morning and didn't get the same description out of any two of them."

"Except that the guy is a white male. That's it. No specifics. That college student we talked to said the perp was quite old while the accountant said he was quite young.''

"I like the substitute teacher who told him, 'Frankly my dear I don't give a damn.'''

"Well, I do give a damn," Shane said in exasperation. "So far this guy has kept away from schools and places where kids might see him, but it's only a matter of time before that happens. We've got to catch him before then."

"We will," Koz agreed. "Just not today. Our shift officially ended two hours ago you know."

Looking at the wall clock, Shane swore under his breath. "Damn it, I'm going to be late."

"Who's the lucky woman tonight?" Koz asked, well aware of Shane's search for a perfect wife and amused by it.

"You don't know her."

"I still don't know why you wouldn't date my second cousin's manicurist, Mimi. She's got red hair."

"Yeah, fire-engine red out of a bottle. And she's also got a rap sheet longer than my arm." This wasn't the first time Koz had tried to hook him up with Mimi. "Somehow I don't think the Huntington lawyers would approve."

"They might not, but I sure do," Koz said with a deliberately lascivious look.

"Then you date her," Shane retorted.

"Somehow I don't think my wife would approve of that."

"I'm sure you're right. Meanwhile, I'm outta here."

Tonight's candidate, Kate O'Malley, had suggested

they meet at a new north shore restaurant that had apparently been getting rave reviews. The silvery-blue and black interior was trendy and the dim light made finding Kate a little harder. Then he heard her voice. He'd thought it must have been something to do with the speakerphone she'd used when she'd spoken to him earlier, but apparently not.

It wasn't until they were seated that he truly realized how piercing Kate's voice actually was. It sounded like fingernails on a chalkboard and had a whiny quality that a parent would no doubt recognize. Even the waiter was wincing as she placed her order.

And Kate wasn't brief about it. She couldn't just point at her menu. No, she had to go on and on. "I can't decide whether to have the Hawaiian spearfish or the grilled ostrich with the black-eye peas, brussels sprouts, bacon and melted Brie in a clove-accented zinfandel reduction," Kate said.

After much discussion, which made his ears hurt, Kate went with the ostrich. She then launched into a twenty-minute monologue about Alsatian varietals versus Italian reds at a wine bar she'd visited last night.

Propping his chin in the palm of one hand allowed him to use his fingers to cover one ear, but even so there was no drowning out the shrill sound of Kate's voice. Maybe this is why ostriches were known for shoving their heads in the ground. To avoid hearing Kate drone on and on about food and how she was a gourmand and he wasn't.

Shane closed his eyes and imagined himself standing at the altar, wearing a pair of industrial-strength headphones to drown out the piercing stridency of Kate's voice. He groaned, but no one heard him.

PAIGE HAD JUST SETTLED IN her favorite chair to finish the latest Amanda Quick book when her phone rang. It was Friday night, almost ten at night, but she'd told Esma to call as soon as she got home from her catering job.

"Hey, Esma," she began only to be interrupted by a decidedly male voice.

"It's not Esma, it's me, Shane, following your orders."

"Excuse me?"

"You told me to let you know how my date with Kate went. But I can't tell you over the phone. I'd rather tell you in person. I'm only about ten minutes away. Can I stop by?"

She meant to say no but somehow the word *yes* was out of her mouth before she could stop it.

"Thanks." He sounded relieved. "See you soon."

If the mere sound of his voice was enough to turn her no into a yes, Paige knew she needed some help here. So she immediately rushed into her bedroom.

This was her sanctuary. The cozy ivory chenille comforter went well with the soft peach tones of the vintage floral-patterned pillows and sheets on her queen-size bed, which was piled high with matching pillows— the look capturing the romance of Paris. The aged wooden headboard was draped on both sides by a pair of ecru Battenburg lace curtains. On the bedside table made of antique-looking pine was a pile of books to be read.

Bending down, she lifted up the ruffled floral bedskirt and scrounged under the bed for her fuzzy bunny slippers. Slipping them on, she stared at herself in the full-length mirror in the corner.

Wiggling the silly footwear at her own reflection, she told herself, "That's to remind you that you're no glass-slippered Cinderella. As if Cinderella would ever be caught dead in this outfit," she added, tugging on the elastic waistband of her drawstring cotton pants. Although the chocolate-brown color of the pants and matching top went well with her auburn hair, it was hardly a fashionable outfit. It was something you wore when you were home alone.

But she refused to change clothes. To change would mean that Shane had more power over her than she was willing to accept. No, she was the mistress of her wardrobe. She wasn't about to pretty herself up for him.

Having said that she still quickly swiped some lipstick on; a demure rose color. While she had no intention of dressing up for him, Paige still had her pride and she didn't want him seeing her at her worst. The bunny slippers would be sufficient to keep her fantasies from running away with her common sense.

When she let Shane into her apartment he showed no signs of noticing either her slippers or her lipstick.

"Well, the good news," he announced, "is that I found several new candidates in addition to Kate. I met up with them earlier in the week. I met Claudia Richards for lunch only to discover she's a chain-smoker as well as someone whose perfume gave me a migraine. I joined Sandra Benson for drinks last night. That's when she told me that she's already living with a guy but might be interested in a threesome. And then there was Kate, tonight. You know the screeching sound of fingernails on a blackboard? Well, amplify that by ten and you've got the sound of Kate's voice. And she never stopped talking. About food like grilled ostrich and Alsatian wines. After a week like this one, I could write a book on the dates from hell," he said morosely.

"I think not," she replied. "That's one book I could write myself. Where shall I begin? Let's see, how about with Gil who brought his dog on our first date. And not only that, he insisted she sit at the dinner table with us."

Shane smiled, just as she'd intended. It was a pretty empowering feeling, the notion that she could make him smile. "And then there was Andy," she continued, "who talked about his sinusitis all night. Or how about Ron the doctor who described the colonoscopy he performed that day."

"You forget, I come from a long line of proctologists," Shane said. "I'm accustomed to gruesome medical discussions over the dinner table."

"And after that upbringing, you're letting a little thing like someone's voice throw you? I find that very hard to believe. And what was wrong with your first date, Scarlet? You never did get around to telling me." She belatedly realized that was because he'd kissed her instead.

"Scarlet was a barracuda."

"I don't think this is about Scarlet being a barracuda,

or Kate's voice, or Leslie's perfume giving you a head-ache. I don't think it's the women at all. I think it's *you*."

He frowned at her. "What are you talking about?"

"You. You don't really want to get married at all. You never did. And by finding fault with every woman you go out with, then you're off the hook. Presto, you don't have to get married."

"And then Hope House doesn't get the money it des-perately needs and I desperately want to get for them. Yeah, right," he scoffed. "Your scenario makes lots of sense."

"You're a man," she retorted, aggravated by his mocking response to her comments. "You don't have to make sense. It's not your job."

"Well, your job was to help me find a wife."

His words stung. "My job is to help library patrons with their fiction needs. There's absolutely nothing in the job description about helping stubborn police detec-tives find perfect society wives."

"You said you'd help me," he reminded her.

"And so I have. But there's not much I can do if you refuse to be helped."

"I haven't refused," he denied, looking suitably af-fronted. "I've gone out with all these women."

"And found something stupidly wrong with every one of them."

Shoving an impatient hand through his dark hair, he growled, "A woman who fits the requirements of the list is practically impossible to find—"

"That's not true," she interrupted him. "Any of

those women would have fit the requirements from the Huntington list. Heck, even I would fit the requirements. It's your stupid personal list that's the problem.''

"What did you say?'' he demanded.

"That it's your stupid personal list that's the problem—''

"No, before that. You said *you'd* fit the requirements of the Huntington list.'' Shane pinned her with a challenging look. "Is that true?''

5

Oops. Now she'd done it. How could she have let something like that slip out? Wearing her fuzzy bunny slippers didn't seem to be working at keeping her practical.

"Is it true?" Shane repeated, giving her an I-mean-business look that probably worked well during his interrogations of suspects. It worked equally well on her.

"All right," she confessed, "so I'd sort of fit the requirements. That doesn't mean—"

"Sort of?" he interrupted her. "There's no *sort of* about any of this. Do you come from a well-connected and respectable family?" Now he definitely sounded like a cop.

"I...I..." she stammered.

"Just answer the question. Do you come from a well-connected and respectable family. Yes or no?"

"Yes."

"And you're a natural-redheaded college graduate capable of bearing children?"

"The last time I checked, yes," she replied tartly, irritated by his questions, his tone of voice, not to mention his expression. "My family is wealthy, okay? You don't have to look so stunned. What, you figured I'm a mousy librarian with two cats and no life?''

He blinked at her non sequitur. ''Where did that come from?''

''You know the stereotype,'' she muttered, feeling like a fool for revealing some of her insecurities. At times like these she felt like the ugly duckling back at Godden's School for Girls, the one the other girls had made fun of because of her brilliant hair or because she always had her nose in a book. The girl who hadn't fit in. Quentin's defection had resurrected those self-doubts big time.

''I know that you don't fit any stereotype,'' Shane said. His expression turned rueful as he admitted, ''As for cats, well I have a dark confession to make here. I've got one of my own. A scrawny orange tomcat who was hanging around the alley behind Hope House. I took him to the vet, got him cleaned up and intended to give him to the animal shelter for them to find a home for him but somehow he ended up coming home with me. He's called Puck.''

''You named him after the character in Shakespeare's *A Midsummer Night's Dream?*''

''No, he's named after a hockey puck. He eats so much he's gotten big and round like a puck.''

''I see.''

''Well, I'm glad someone sees, because frankly I'm still in the dark as to why you'd let me go through all this ridiculous searching when you qualify.'' He was back on his high horse again.

"You said you were looking for a perfect wife," Paige reminded him. "Believe me, I'm not perfect."

"If you fulfill the qualifications of the Huntington list, then you're perfect in my family's attorneys' eyes."

"Any of the women you've been dating would be perfect in their eyes."

"Yeah," he replied, "but you don't bother me the way they did."

"You're really too kind. It's long been my lifetime goal not to be a bother to some man," she retorted tartly.

"You know what I mean."

Unfortunately she did. He was right. She wasn't the sort of woman who made a man sit up and take notice. She was the kind who blended into the background until needed. And then he'd only needed her to help him find another woman, one who was perfect for him.

Damn it she was tired of being Ms. Fuzzy Bunny Slippers. That golden dress Zorra had made proved that Paige could look as sexy as the next woman. All she needed was the self-confidence to go with it.

She was tempted to go into her bedroom and put on that sexy black lace peignoir set she'd bought on a dare from Esma. Maybe that would get Shane's attention, make him think twice about her being a woman who didn't bother men. Hah!

She tried to imagine herself strolling out of her bedroom dressed in the lacy black silk nightgown. But in her mental picture all she saw was Shane, his jaw hanging open—not from awe but from embarrassment.

Okay, scrap that idea. No way was she abandoning her bunny slippers tonight.

"I'm still stunned that you didn't mention anything about your background until now," Shane was saying. "How long were you intending to keep this a secret?"

"As long as possible," she muttered. She started to pace before remembering that she'd ended up kissing Shane the last time she'd done that. So she sat down and slung her legs over the arm of her chair instead, letting her bunny slippers dangle partway off her feet.

Shane frowned at her in bewilderment. "But why? Why keep your past a secret?"

"Because I wanted to make a name for myself without using my family's influence." She shot him a challenging look. "Surely you of all people can understand that."

"Sure, I can understand that. What I can't understand is why you'd let me stumble around in a frantic effort to find the right woman to make the Hungtingon lawyers happy when you had the power to stop it all by simply telling me the truth."

"I may fulfill all the requirements on the list, but I don't even come close on any of the requirements you put on your personal list," she pointed out. Unable to sit still a moment longer, she leaped to her feet and advanced on him, jabbing her index finger at his broad chest. "*You* want a woman who looks good in a thong and loves the Eagles. Well, I donate money to protect eagles in Alaska and as for the thong, well that's never going to happen. You want a woman who shares your passion for hockey and the only thing I know about hockey is that a bunch of guys skate around with sticks pausing occasionally to punch each other. Oh, yeah, I can see where I'd be exactly the kind of woman you were looking for.''

"You just need to be the kind of woman the Huntington lawyers are looking for. Do you think they'd approve of your family?''

"The Turners of Toledo have been one of Ohio's leading families since my great-great-great-great grandfather came to Ohio in the late 1700s,'' she loftily informed him. "The question would be, would my family approve of the Huntingtons.''

"I love it!'' he said in delight. "Marry me.''

"Absolutely not,'' she said with firm matter-of-factness.

"Why not?''

"Because I don't want to.''

"Well, I don't really want to get married, either, but you don't see that stopping me, do you?''

She glared at him. "Listen, my ex-fiancé pretended to care for me because of my family background—''

He interrupted her. "You were engaged?''

His disbelieving tone of voice sparked her anger. "Again, let me say that you don't have to sound so surprised that I was engaged.''

"I'm not surprised you were engaged. Again,'' he deliberately repeated her terminology, "I'm merely surprised that you didn't tell me you were engaged.''

"The subject never came up.''

"Well, it's come up now. Tell me about it.''

"Why should I?'' she countered, not at all eager to

share the fact that she'd been dumped and labeled dull by her ex-fiancé.

"Because I want to know and because I'm your friend."

"My friend, huh? Is that what you are?" she muttered.

"Then tell me as the guy who's trying to be your next fiancé."

She decided to tell him as both a warning and a lesson about why she wanted no part of his scheme. "Quentin was like you—charming, good-looking and self-confident. I met him at a social function and we seemed to hit it off right away. Although I didn't realize it at the time, he was looking for a woman to marry that would please his family, bankers from Pennsylvania. I fit the bill so he asked me to be his wife and I said yes because I was in love with him and he'd told me he was in love with me. Both our families were delighted. Even my grandmother approved of him, and she doesn't like anyone. Two days before the formal announcement of our engagement, Quentin ran away with Joan Harding, a flamboyantly wild mystery writer I'd booked to speak at the library where I was working in Ohio. I'm sure she'd look good in a thong, Shane."

"You're never going to let me hear the end of that, are you?" he noted wryly. "Okay, so you were right. Maybe I was using that personal list of what I wanted in a woman as a way to avoid getting married."

"Or maybe you are a shallow idiot who judges women by their appearance in a thong."

"Well, there always is that possibility," he acknowledged with such teasing humor that she had to smile.

"How do you do that?" she grumbled.

"Do what?" he asked innocently.

"Diffuse my anger. Just when I'm ready to say that's it, I don't want any part of this cockeyed plan of yours, you somehow draw me back in again."

"It's my irresistible charm," he said with fake humility.

"And your modesty."

"That, too." He hung his head and gave her one of those but-you-love-me-anyway looks that were so hard to resist. "So when do we get married?"

"Does the phrase when hell freezes over ring a bell for you?"

"So you want a winter wedding? We can't wait that long. My thirtieth birthday is in less than two weeks and I've got to be married by then. I think we should get married next week."

"And I think you should have your head examined."

"Come on," he coaxed her, using all his considerable charm. "What would be so bad about being married to me?"

"Do you have an hour or two?" she retorted, refusing to succumb.

"Sure." Dropping onto her couch, he leaned back and made himself comfortable. "I've got all night. Talk to me."

"It's simply not a good idea."

"Talking to you?"

"Marrying you." Not that talking to him was all that

great an idea, either, because the man had a way of making her forget her good intentions.

"We actually do have a lot more in common than we have differences," he told her. "We've both got cats. We both come from families that had expectations of us that we somehow didn't fulfill. We've both chosen to work for a living in a path that's far different from our family. Unless you come from a long line of librarians?"

She shook her head. "No, my family made their money in manufacturing and my father increased it by investing in computer technology early on."

"So your father is a businessman?"

"My father isn't easy to classify nor is he easy to explain." He hadn't always been easy to live with, either, but she didn't feel like sharing that bit of information at this point. "He's a great storyteller with a unique sense of humor. He's the one who named me Paige."

"What about your mother? What's she like?"

"My mother died when I was nine. She was quiet and calm. She let my father have the limelight, which he relishes. After her death, my grandmother arranged for me to go to a prestigious girls' school in New England."

"Ah, yes, shipped off to boarding school." Shane nodded knowingly. "A trait of the ridiculously rich. Have kids but don't bother raising them yourself. Why bother when you can hire someone else to do it?"

She didn't want him thinking badly of her relatives. "I get along fine with my family. The only reason I left

Ohio was because of Quentin. I wanted a fresh start, where friends wouldn't look at me in pity because my fiancé ran off with another woman only forty-eight hours before our engagement was printed in all the newspapers.''

"I'm not Quentin," he quietly told her. "When I make a promise, I keep it. I wouldn't run off with another woman."

"How do you know that?"

"Because I know myself."

"But you don't know *me*." Her voice was thick with emotion. "Quentin said I was dull and boring. That's why he ran off with that wild writer-woman Joan."

"He ran off because he was a jerk." Shane reached out to tug her down to the couch beside him. "There is no way you are dull." He tipped her chin up and brushed his lips against hers. "Or boring." His mouth settled on hers, this time lingering at the corner of her mouth, tasting and testing with creative temptation. "No woman who kisses the way you do is dull or boring." He trailed his fingers along her cheek as his mouth once again slowly descended toward hers.

This time the kiss rapidly escalated with passionate heat. Dipping his tongue into the warm depths of her mouth, he introduced her to a new level of pleasure. Meanwhile his hands held her and caressed her, doing wickedly delightful things that made her catch her breath, that made her catch on fire.

"You have no idea how you make me feel," he whispered against her skin as he kissed his way to the baggy neckline of her top. "Let me show you…"

She didn't know how she said yes. If she spoke the words aloud, or if her body melting against his was the signal. She only knew that she didn't want this to stop, she didn't want to think, she just wanted Shane.

He said he wanted to show her how she made him feel, and she wanted to be shown. Badly. Intensely.

He lowered her to the couch, so that she was resting beneath him. Now she could feel the muscles of his thighs flexing against her own as he fit his body to hers, producing an intimately electric contact where male met female.

Her desire was propelled into a new dimension, one rich with sensual abandonment where clothes got in the way and bare flesh was meant to be licked and kissed and tasted. He was driving her wild. She seemed to be having a similar effect on him if the slam of his heart-beat and the throbbing hardness of his body were any indication.

The concept that he wanted her was almost beyond grasping. But his body wasn't beyond grasping, hugging, hanging on to. Quentin had never treated her this way. He'd never made her feel this way. He'd never indicated he wanted her more than he wanted air. Yet Shane did all that and more. Without saying a word. Using his touch, his hands, his lips. And using them so incredibly well that she thought she'd died and gone to heaven.

Alive with excitement, she was reeling drunkenly in a world where time and prudence no longer existed. His tie was gone, his shirt opened. Her slippers were long gone and her T-shirt had somehow disappeared. The bare skin of his chest was fused against hers, the sides of the shirt he still wore draping down and sealed the connection of flesh to flesh. Was he rubbing against her or was she rubbing against him? It felt so good. The silky material of her bra magnified his touch, intensified the friction.

Threading her hands through his hair she lifted his wandering lips back to hers, greeting his tongue with a few provocative moves of her own.

The thin material of his slacks and her pants did little to hide his burgeoning need. Her feet were bare and her body was crying out, crying out…

"*Mrrroooow!*" Her cat Simon was the one crying out, standing on the arm of the couch yodeling right in their ears, demanding his supper.

Startled by the deafening intensity of the feline's demands, Shane almost fell off the couch. Showing no remorse for having interrupted them, Simon proceeded to walk across them as if stepping on them would get their attention. It did.

Tugging her T-shirt back on, Paige scooted off the couch as Shane sat up, Simon perched upon his lap.

"Step carefully there, big fella," Shane cautioned the cat. "You damage the goods and I might not have any heirs."

"I'm so sorry," Paige said, smoothing a hand over her mussed up hair. "Simon is hungry and wants his supper."

"I know how it feels to be hungry and wanting," Shane told her, looking at her mouth in a way that made her heart race. "If you're really sorry, go feed your cat and we can always pick up where we left off."

"I don't think that's a good idea."

Closing his eyes and groaning, he said, "How did I know you were going to say that?"

She desperately grabbed her fuzzy bunny slippers and hugged them to her. This wasn't supposed to have happened. He was supposed to find someone else to be his wife. He wasn't supposed to ask her to marry him. And she wasn't supposed to be tempted to say yes.

"You're hanging on to those slippers as if they were garlic intended to ward off evil vampires," he noted, his masculine voice caressing her as his hands and mouth had done not so long ago.

"No one can be sexy in fuzzy bunny slippers." She said the words as if they were a mantra.

"Apparently you can be," he replied, getting to his feet. "We will continue this." The softly spoken words were a promise. "Maybe not tonight, but we will continue this. You can count on it."

And then he was gone, leaving her standing there clutching her bunny slippers while her cat wound around her bare feet and ankles.

6

"HE ASKED YOU TO DO WHAT?" Esma exclaimed, pausing in the midst of making spicy crab rolls to stare at Paige in amazement.

"To marry him," Paige replied, glad they were at Esma's place rather than hers. The memory of Shane almost seducing her on the couch permeated Paige's apartment. She saw him everywhere she looked—even places he'd never been before, like her bedroom. She hadn't been able to get the thought of Shane out of her mind.

She'd hoped that the no-nonsense surroundings of Esma's stainless-steel kitchen would prevent her from dwelling on Shane, obsessing over what had almost happened last night. But even here she was still talking about him.

"I thought you were just supposed to be helping him find a bride," Esma said, wiping her hands on a fire-engine-red kitchen towel that matched the apron she wore along with a lemon-yellow T-shirt and black pants. "When did you *become* the bride?"

Paige nibbled on a delicious artichoke canapé Esma had made earlier before replying, "I haven't said yes yet."

"Yet." Esma picked up on the qualifier right away. "Which means you're considering it. *Ooh,* but it would be lovely to have a wedding to cater."

"You already have more catering jobs than you know what to do with."

"Yes, but your wedding would be special." Esma was all dreamy-eyed. Paige recognized the look as her "envisioning expression." Esma wore it whenever she was planning a special do. "And Zorra could do up a wedding dress for you! *Ooh,* I'm getting excited and goose-bumpy just thinking about it."

"Well, I'm not."

"Why ever not?"

"Because we're talking about a man who doesn't love me." A man who makes me all excited and goose-bumpy, Paige thought to herself. "We're talking about a marriage that wouldn't really be a marriage."

Esma frowned in confusion. "Then what would it be?"

"More like a business arrangement."

"Sounds like monkey business to me," Esma said, returning to her spicy crab roll preparation while keeping an eagle eye on Paige. "So you'd be stuck in a marriage with a man you have no feelings for."

"I didn't say that," Paige protested.

"Then what are your feelings for him?"

Paige sighed and reached for another artichoke canapé. "That's the million-dollar question. Literally. If he marries the right woman, he gets a million dollars, which he plans on donating to Hope House, which helps kids start a new life after leaving an abusive situation."

"What's to keep this Shane from pocketing the one million himself once he marries you?"

"His sense of ethics." Paige's reply was firm and without hesitation. "If he'd just wanted money for himself, he'd have gone back to his family and toed the line."

"Maybe he wants the money without having to deal with his family," Esma pointed out, playing devil's advocate.

Paige shook her head. "He's not like that."

"Then tell me what he is like. Or better yet, arrange for me to meet the man myself. That way I can get a fix on him."

"You don't need to meet him because I have no intention of marrying him."

"That may be what you say, but you get a certain look on your face when you speak about him that says something else entirely."

"That look is hunger," Paige firmly stated. "When are we going to eat?"

But Esma wasn't convinced. "That is not your hungry look, unless it's hunger for Shane."

"Don't you know any natural redheaded women who come from a wealthy background that Shane could marry?" Paige said with a hint of desperation. "I sort of agreed to help him find a perfect wife, that's how this whole thing started."

"The guy has a fetish for redheads?"

"It's a requirement of his grandfather's will that in order for Shane to get his inheritance he has to find a woman who fulfills the requirements on the Huntington list.''

"There's actually a list?'' Esma's voice relayed her astonishment.

Paige nodded before adding, "But don't tell anyone about this. I don't want to be gossiping about Shane's private business.''

"The man just asked you to marry him. I don't think telling me about him is gossiping.''

"He only asked me because I fulfill the requirements of the list and he's just found that out.''

Esma's expression turned serious as she realized the consequences of that statement. "Which means you told him about your family back in Toledo.''

Paige nodded. She'd told Esma about her past but no one else knew. "It just sort of slipped out.''

"And he responded by asking you to marry him.''

"Yes. He said I didn't bother him like the other red-heads he'd tried dating. He has to get married before his thirtieth birthday and that's coming up soon.''

"He just cold-bloodedly came out and proposed to you? That's it? Oh my, you're blushing. Come on now.'' Esma hopped onto the kitchen stool next to Paige's and nudged her with a friendly elbow. "Tell me everything.''

"Let's just say that Shane tried to charm me into saying yes.''

"He tried to seduce you, you mean. Oh my.'' She picked up a recipe card and fanned herself. "And was he successful?''

"Clearly not as I did not say I'd marry him.''

Esma smacked Paige's arm with friendly camaraderie. "I meant did he succeed in seducing you?"

"Not quite. We were on the couch and Simon jumped on us and broke things up."

"Saved by your cat, were you? Well, there's a first. How was Shane with your cats? Did he throw a fit about being interrupted?"

"Actually he was a good sport about it. He's got a cat of his own named Puck."

"So this Shane of yours likes Shakespeare, does he?"

"Actually he likes hockey. He named the cat after a hockey puck."

"Hockey, eh? One of those North American sports I haven't come to understand yet. Give me a good game of cricket any day. I must say that I'm intrigued by this Shane of yours. We should get together for dinner and I'll check him out."

"Inviting him to dinner would only give him the false impression that I might weaken and agree to marry him."

"Given the way you talk about him, I'd say that your agreeing to marry him is more a probability than a false impression," Esma stated with a knowing nod of her head. "Never mind. If you don't want to invite him to dinner we won't invite him to dinner. Now try one of these crab rolls."

"So you're the infamous Detective Shane Huntington."

Shane looked up from the computer keyboard where he was writing up a case report to find a gorgeous woman towering over his desk. She was dressed in form-fitting black jeans and a lime-green tank top. Her English accent was sexy but the look she was giving him was no come-on.

"And you are?" he enquired.

"Esma Kinch. Paige's dear friend."

"Ah, the caterer." He nodded and smiled. "Paige has mentioned you."

"She's done more than mention you," Esma said. "Which is why I'm here. To check you out for myself. Is that chair clean?" she added, eyeing the metal chair beside his desk with suspicion.

"It's clean enough," he replied, watching her as she gingerly sat down. "Does Paige know you're here?"

"No, and I'd like to keep it that way."

Now she was making him nervous. "What can I do for you?"

"Tell me why you asked Paige to marry you," she said bluntly. "Don't look so surprised. Surely you didn't think she'd keep a thing like that private? Well, she might have tried, but I've got excellent interrogation techniques."

"I'll keep that in mind should we need any new detectives here," Shane noted dryly.

"I don't believe I'd enjoy working in such a drab place," Esma replied before suggesting, "A bit of paint would brighten up the place, you know. A splash of tangerine color here, a dab of lemon-yellow accents there would work wonders."

"We don't actually decorate the police department."

"I can tell." She returned her attention to him. "Your

parents are having a bit of a do at their estate sometime soon, aren't they? They asked if I'd cater the event, but I didn't have time really.''

"Trust me, you don't ever want to cater one of their do's. My mother would drive you crazy.''

"Well, actually that's why I turned them down,'' Esma leaned forward to confess. "I thought they fell under the life-is-too-short-to-deal-with-this category.''

"You've got that right.''

"There is something *you* haven't gotten right,'' Esma said. "And that's your handling of Paige.''

Shane tried to look calm while frantically wondering if Paige had told Esma about last night, specifically about them making out on her couch. Had Paige complained about the quality of his caresses?

"You do realize that you've taken all these other candidates out to dinner and you haven't even done that much with Paige.''

On the one hand he felt relief that Paige hadn't complained about his lovemaking. On the other hand he felt guilt as he realized Esma was absolutely right. "I invited her to the Windy City Ball.''

Esma waved his words away, drawing his attention to the large ring on her hand—a peridot if he wasn't mistaken. "As your cousin not your date. That doesn't count.''

"You're right. I should invite her out. I'll do that right away.''

"Only if *you* think it's a good idea.'' Her visual message added *Don't mess up.*

He nodded to indicate that her message was received

and understood. ''I think Paige is very lucky to have a great friend like you.''

Esma gracefully got up and nodded right back at him. Then she smiled as if he'd just passed some kind of important final exam. ''And I think she could do worse in the husband department than choosing you.''

SHANE HAD NO IDEA HOW MANY women he'd invited out in his lifetime. But he was sure he'd never been this nervous about it before. Not even when he'd asked Melody Dumbowski to kiss him when they were both seven years old. Not even then had he suffered this pang of uncertainty.

The uncertainty wasn't about Paige. He knew he wanted to ask her out. He knew she deserved that much and more. He knew he wanted her to be his wife. He knew he wanted her, period. He also knew he did not want to make any mistakes. Too much was riding on this. The kids at Hope House were counting on him. He couldn't let them down.

At first he'd thought that bringing Paige to his favorite Italian restaurant had been a brilliant idea. But now that they were here, he was worried that he should have taken her someplace fancier. After all, he'd taken Scarlet and Kate someplace fancy. And Paige was certainly more deserving than either Scarlet or Kate.

She looked great tonight, in that simple quiet elegant way she had. She wasn't a shout, she was a whisper. And she captured his attention with her smile. Her mouth looked unusually soft and vulnerable in the candlelight.

At the library, when he'd first asked for her help in finding him the perfect wife, he described her hair as sort of red. He didn't know if it was his imagination or the lighting in here or if she'd done something different with her hair—but her hair was like liquid fire. Not harsh, not garish, just silky curls shot with color brushing her face. Paige had the kind of hair that moved when she turned her head and as she talked to him she was turning her head a lot. She was turning his head as well.

"I really think you shouldn't give up your search for the perfect wife just yet," she was saying with a quiet earnestness that made him want to lean across the table and kiss her.

"I've already found the perfect wife," he replied. "I'm sitting here looking at her and wondering what took me so long to really see her."

"You're still not really seeing me," she said in exasperation. "You're seeing what you want to see."

"Not at all." His voice was like a caress. "If I was seeing what I wanted to see, you'd be wearing that silky black bra you had on last night. And those fuzzy bunny slippers. I'm a sucker for a woman in fuzzy bunny slippers."

"Now you tell me."

"You mean you weren't wearing them for my benefit?" he said, as if knowing exactly what she'd been thinking when she'd deliberately put those slippers on each time he'd come to her apartment.

"I think I'll take the fifth amendment on that one," she replied, "and not answer on the grounds that I might incriminate myself.'' Lifting the menu in front of her flushed face, she hid behind it. ''What's good here?''

''You are.''

She lowered the menu enough to give him a look. No other woman gave him that look. That you-must-be-kidding look. It made him hot for her, despite the fact that he knew that wasn't her intention. Far from it. She was trying to put him in his place. The problem was his place was next to her, preferably with both of them naked and rolling between silk sheets. He just had to convince her of that.

Paige tried to read Shane's thoughts, certain she was overreacting to his flirtatious ways. This was a man who flirted with every woman under the age of ninety-eight. This was a man who enjoyed available women. This was a man who'd kissed her senseless last night. This was a man who'd shuddered with desire in her arms.

She fanned herself with the menu. The fact that he got to her wasn't reason to marry him. It was reason to run in the other direction. Fast. Because it meant that Shane had the ability to hurt her as she'd never been hurt before. Not even by Quentin.

''Want me to order for you?'' Shane asked.

Flustered, she nodded. When the food came it was delicious, but she couldn't even say what it was. Pasta and a creamy sauce with fresh prawns. Beyond that she didn't have a clue. She was too distracted watching him eat. There was something incredibly sensual about the way he'd drawn that last bit of angel hair pasta into his mouth. Had he done that on purpose? Was he trying to drive her crazy?

Well two could play at that game. Spearing a prawn, she lifted her fork to her mouth and nibbled at the plump seafood. Was that a groan she heard from him? "Did you say something?" she paused midnibble to ask him.

"No." His voice sounded hoarse and his eyes were glued to her mouth.

She smiled, amazed at the feeling of power she experienced. Getting to a man as experienced as Shane was a real confidence builder.

After dessert of a delicious tiramisu, they left the restaurant. Shane opened his car door for her. He drove a black car that looked fast and sleek. She was no automotive junkie. Plus she didn't like hockey or know much about the Eagles' music. Some of her earlier confidence evaporated, which is why she didn't ask where they were going until he pulled into an empty parking lot.

She looked at the large building in surprise. "This is an ice skating arena."

"It certainly is." He got out and came around the hood of the car to open her door for her. Holding out his hand, he helped her out. The evening was unusually warm for mid-May, but then Chicago was known for its changeable weather. And Shane, she reminded herself, was known for the practical jokes he'd played on his fellow police officers. She hoped he wasn't about to pull a stunt on her like those he'd told her about.

"We're not going to a hockey game, are we?"

"Certainly not," he said but then opened the car trunk to remove a well-worn pair of men's ice skates. Clearly they were his.

"Then why are we here?" she asked. "The place doesn't look open," she added, even as she followed him to the entrance. It was hard not to when he held her hand, his fingers entwined with hers.

"It isn't open. But I know the manager and he lets me come in to practice a few moves."

She could imagine Shane making all kinds of moves, all of them erotic. Her face became flushed again. An ice rink might be a good thing, might cool her down.

"Do you know how to skate?" he asked her as he escorted her to the door where a man with a goatee and a big smile undid the lock and let them in.

"A bit," she cautiously replied. "Is this why you told me to wear something comfortable to dinner tonight, something I could move around in?"

"Yeah. I thought we could have some fun."

"On the ice?" She sounded skeptical.

"On the ice." He arched a dark eyebrow at her. "It's not like I'm planning to seduce you in the middle of the rink."

Why not? she wanted to say. Because he didn't think she was a wild woman like fiancé-stealer Joan Harding. Not that she wanted to be a fiancé-stealer, she had her ethics. But being a wild woman had a certain appeal to a woman who'd been labeled as quiet and dull. After all, how many people heard librarian and immediately thought wild woman? Not many.

Well, Paige had a few surprises up her own sleeve.

"Do you need my help getting those skates on?" he asked after getting a pair in the right size for her from Bernie, the rink manager.

"Sure," she said, sitting down and holding out her foot as he knelt before her to slip the skates on.

The Cinderella imagery wasn't lost on her. She half expected him to say "Ah the shoe, or in this case the skate, fits. You are the woman I shall marry." But apparently her imagery wasn't his because he said nothing as he efficiently laced up her skates.

"Is this another little item from your personal list?" she asked him. "The perfect wife must know how to ice skate?"

He paused to give her a reproachful look. "I told you I stopped adding to that list."

"After looks good in a thong and loves the Eagles, I guess there's not much left to add, is there?"

"Forget about my stupid list. Do you think you can stand up now?"

"I'll try." She nibbled on her bottom lip as she cautiously got to her feet.

"Hang on to me," Shane said, keeping his arm around her waist to steady her as he guided her onto the ice rink. "Okay, now just get your balance, get a feel for the ice. We'll go slow." Turning so that he was facing her and skating backward, he took hold of both her hands and pulled her along. "There, you're doing fine."

They made it halfway around the rink when she said, "Let me try it on my own now."

He appeared uncertain. "Are you sure?"

She nodded. "I think I can do it."

"Okay. Now remember..." The rest of his words faded away as Paige did a perfect pirouette in front of him before gracefully skating away from him in a move that would have made a figure skater proud. "Uh, just a guess here, but you've done this before, haven't you?"

"Done what? Conned a cop? Who me?" She swirled close enough to him to bat her eyes at him before sailing away. "As if I'd ever do such a thing."

"There's still a lot about you I don't know, isn't there."

"My point exactly," she said triumphantly.

"That doesn't mean I can't like what I already do know," he noted, catching her in his arms before she skated away.

"I know I like this," he murmured against her mouth before skating her backward so that she was pinned between the ice rink's side rails and his warm body. The ice beneath her emanated cold but his body against her radiated heat.

And as for his kiss...well, that was a flame that drew her in and consumed her in its passionate fire. He parted her lips with hungry accuracy, his tongue seeking hers. Again her good intentions went up in smoke. Again she responded to his every move, adding creatively sexy moves of her own. Again...they were interrupted.

This time it was the sound of childish laughter that brought her back to earth—childish laughter coming from more than one child. Breaking away from him she realized they were surrounded by kids.

"I thought you said this place was closed," she said to Shane, feeling like an R-rated wanton woman making out in front of children.

"It's closed except for my special friends," he replied.

"I'm special!" a little girl with her black hair in braids exclaimed.

Paige recognized her as Brittany, the little girl whose picture Shane had shown her that day he'd first asked for her help.

"You sure are," Shane agreed, taking Brittany by the hand and skating with her.

"Me next," another little girl said while a shy child next to her stood by and gazed at them.

"Want me to help you skate?" Paige asked both girls. The shy one nodded. The next thing Paige knew, she was surrounded by other kids eager to learn more about skating. She tried to give the shy little girl, whose name was Leah, some additional special attention, knowing as she did how being the quiet one wasn't always easy.

It wasn't until Shane formed a conga line on the ice, with everyone holding on to the waist of the person in front of them that Paige had the chance to stand aside and watch Shane interact with the kids. He was a natural with them. Even shy little Leah. Her thoughts were spoken aloud by the woman beside her.

"He's great with them, isn't he? I'm sorry about the kids interrupting you that way. By the way, my name is Sheila. Sheila Romerez. I'm the director of Hope House." Wearing jeans and a T-shirt that said Hope Heals, Sheila was the kind of woman that emanated goodwill, a natural earth mother. Her long dark hair streaked with gray was gathered in a single braid down her back. "My husband is the awkward-looking man at the end of the conga line. He helps me run Hope House. And Shane, well, he helps us all. He's arranged for the kids to use this rink once a week when it's not open to the public. Some of them are still nervous around a lot of strangers and a rink filled with rowdy kids they don't know would be a stressful, rather than a fun, experience for them."

"I can understand that." Holding out her hand, she said, "I'm Paige Turner."

"I figured as much." Sheila's handshake was firm. "Shane's told us about you."

"He has?"

"Sure. He calls you the book goddess. Says you know everything there is to know about books."

Paige might know about books, but she clearly had a lot to learn about men. She knew Shane wanted his inheritance to help the families and kids at Hope House, but somehow she'd never gotten a firm grasp of that concept. She'd been distracted by the sexiness of the man. She hadn't concentrated on the soul of the person beneath the handsome facade.

"He's actually talked about you a lot over the past few months," Sheila was saying.

"You mean the past few weeks, don't you?"

"No. It's been months," Sheila stated. "I figured that it would just be a matter of time before the two of you got romantically involved. But then I believe in happy endings."

"Despite all you've seen to the contrary?"

"*Because* of all I've seen to the contrary. Sometimes

we get off the path to happiness, sometimes we take a wrong turn. But with help we can always find our way back again.''

Keeping her eyes on a laughing Shane, Paige unsteadily said, ''What if you're too frightened of making a mistake to move?''

''Then you have to pinpoint what you're afraid of and you have to decide if doing nothing would be worse than making a mistake. We all make mistakes, we all fail. But once you've made that bold move, you know that you've done something, you know that at least you've given it a try.''

A bold move. That's certainly what agreeing to marry Shane would be. But seeing him there, interacting with the kids, the fear slipped away. And in its place was the knowledge that regardless of the ultimate outcome, Paige was going to make this bold move.

Waiting until he was alone and the kids had headed off for snacks and sodas, Paige skated right up to him and said, ''Yes.''

He blinked at her. ''Yes what?''

''Yes, I'll marry you.'' And she sealed her bold move with an equally bold kiss.

7

"YES?" SHANE REPEATED as if he couldn't have heard her correctly.

"Yes. Yes, I'll marry you. Isn't that what you wanted?" Now Paige was the uncertain one.

"Absolutely," he quickly assured her. "It's just…I thought you'd need more."

Need more? she thought to herself. More what? Love? Or that she'd need to hear him declare he had feelings for her beyond the fact that she "didn't bother" him? That she'd need to hear that he wanted her? That he maybe even loved her? "More what?" she breathlessly asked.

"More time," he said.

She tried not to be disappointed. Shane might find her moderately attractive, but that was it. And the practical part of her knew that. Besides, this engagement wasn't really about her or about Shane. It was about these kids and Hope House. The moment she'd seen the kids and interacted with them, seen the way Shane related to them and they related to him, she'd been a goner. "You said time was running out," she reminded him.

"It is. I'm so glad you said yes. This is great!" Shane took her in his arms to give her a big bear hug. "Hey, kids!'' he shouted over her head. "I'm getting married and you're all invited to the celebration!''

As they were surrounded by cheering children, Paige vowed to be happy with what she had and not to long for more. She was marrying Shane to help these children and to help him. Her reasons were the same as when she'd gone with him to the Windy City Ball. He'd asked for her help.

The cause was a noble one. The fact that she found him incredibly sexy should play no part in the matter. This wasn't about sex or about the awesome way Shane made her feel when he kissed her.

Yeah, right. Who was she kidding? She was kidding herself. And she planned on continuing to kid herself right through this engagement.

"I'M MEETING HIS PARENTS,'' Paige told Esma, her voice frantic, as she yanked her friend into her apartment. She'd called Esma over right after Shane had phoned her to announce that their appearance was required at his mother's birthday party tomorrow night. Paige had only been engaged to Shane for barely twenty-four hours and already he was making her crazy. "I need a dress.''

"What's the occasion?''

"Aside from the fact that I agreed to marry him, you mean?''

"Yes, aside from…'' Esma gave her a classic double take. *"You what?''*

"I said I'd marry him.''

"Ooh! I'm so happy for you.'' Her vibrant face was

alive with excitement and happiness, Esma rushed forward to give Paige a huge hug. "I knew he was good husband material when I—" she broke off.

"When you what?" Paige asked suspiciously.

"When I went to see him. I wasn't going to tell you…"

"You saw him?" Paige dropped into her favorite chair. She had a feeling she'd need to be sitting down for this story. "When was this?"

"After he asked you to marry him." Seeing Paige's stunned expression, Esma defended her actions. "Well, I had to check him out, didn't I? I couldn't very well let you marry him without my checking him out first, now could I?" Kicking off her clogs, Esma curled up on the couch within arm's reach.

"And what did you think?"

Esma's smile was almost as brilliant as her fuchsia tank dress. "He's lovely, as me mum would say."

"Lovely, huh?" Paige had to smile at the British term. "I'll bet that's a new description for him. I doubt he's been called lovely before."

"And he's quite sexy as well, isn't he, you lucky girl."

"Luck had nothing to do with it," Paige retorted, trying to keep her feet on the ground, figuratively speaking if not literally. She shifted in her seat to a more comfortable position, but her discomfort was also due to the subject matter they were discussing. "I told you before about his needing to be married in order to get his inheritance."

Esma nodded. "Which he plans on giving to that charity, what was the name again?"

"Hope House," Paige replied. "I met some of the kids from there last night at the ice rink."

"Shane took you to an ice rink? That was his idea of a romantic date?" Esma sounded disappointed.

"It actually was very special," Paige said with a slightly dreamy smile, remembering their kisses—the one he'd given her before the kids had arrived and the one she'd given him when she'd accepted his proposal.

"Special, eh?" Esma teased her. "Well, I'm glad to hear that. Now tell me all about the wedding," she ordered, rubbing her hands together in anticipation. "Have you set a date yet?"

"Next weekend."

Esma shrieked. "Next weekend! Crikey! We'll have to call Zorra right away about your wedding dress. Hmm—" Esma gave Paige a speculative look "—if she used the same design as that golden dress for the ball only in white satin that should work. I'll give her a call right now. And of course I'll cater the reception. Where are you having it?"

"I don't have a clue. Everything has happened so fast. And I want you to be my maid of honor," Paige said, reaching out to grab Esma's arm as if searching for a safe anchor in a rocky ocean. "You can't cater the reception and be my maid of honor, too."

"I most certainly can. Now don't you worry about a thing." Esma patted her hand. "I'll make all the arrangements. The High Grove Country Club is right on the lake and has a lovely view. So does the Huntington estate. Are you going to get married there?"

"I think I'd prefer neutral ground."

"Then the country club it is." Removing the tiny cell phone from her hot-pink straw bag, Esma immediately called Zorra and then the country club. Five minutes later it was all settled.

"Zorra has a dress already done, in a lovely shade of purple that will be perfect for this birthday-do at the Huntington estate tomorrow. And I called in a few favors to get the country club booked for a week from Saturday. Now how many will be attending?"

"I...uh...don't know...uh...everything is happening so fast," Paige gasped.

"Here put your head down over your knees," Esma instructed her, placing a reassuring hand on Paige's back. "You're just hyperventilating. I do it all the time before a big job. Just take slow breaths. In. Out. In. Out."

Paige followed her advice and the light-headedness soon passed. Slowly sitting back up, she said, "Do you think I'm crazy?"

"I think you'd be crazy to miss an opportunity like this."

"An opportunity to do what?" Paige countered nervously. "Make a fool of myself?"

Esma gave her a reprimanding look. "Now what makes you say that?"

"This isn't a real marriage," Paige reminded her. "I mean Shane is only doing this to get his inheritance. In a year we'll get an annulment or a divorce."

"Has Shane said he doesn't consider this to be a real marriage?" Esma demanded.

"When he first told me about the plan and asked for my help in finding him the perfect wife, he said that the marriage only had to last for a year in order for him to get his inheritance."

"And during that time the two of you won't be...?"

Paige blushed. One of the curses of being a redhead. "I don't know," she mumbled.

"I can't believe Shane actually told you he has no intention of sleeping with you while you're married."

"He never said that," Paige had to admit.

"Then you're the one putting words in his mouth. Is the idea of having sex with him so bad that you don't want to sleep with him?"

Paige's blush deepened. "No, the idea of having sex with him isn't *bad* at all. Naughty, maybe," she added with a grin. "And downright, seductively wicked, for sure."

"So what's the problem?" Esma asked.

"I don't look good in a thong."

Esma blinked at her. "Excuse me?"

"He likes women who look good in a thong."

"I look good in a thong," Esma declared without a bit of reticence, "but I don't see him asking me to marry him."

"Because you don't fit the other requirements on the Huntington list. If you did, then he probably would be marrying you."

"I doubt that. Look at all those women he dated,"

Esma reminded her. "Yet you told me he didn't want to marry any of them. He asked you instead."

"Because I don't bother him. He told me so."

Esma smiled knowingly. "Well, that little purple dress Zorra is bringing over should fix that. Shane better prepare to be bothered—big time!"

THE PROSPECT OF MEETING Shane's parents tonight had Paige as nervous as her cat Schuster when it was time to go to the vet. No doubt Shane would be delighted that she likened his parents to a vet visit, although he himself had described it in terms of getting his teeth drilled.

What if they didn't like her? She'd already asked Shane that question about a dozen times. She'd just asked him again on the phone.

"My parents don't really like anyone, not even me," he replied with his customary wry humor. "And we both know how lovable I am."

"In that case, tell me again why we're going to see them?"

"Because it's my mother's fiftieth birthday. And I'd rather face a firing squad than the wrath that missing my mother's birthday would incur."

"I thought you were the black sheep of the family," she reminded him. "The one who didn't get along with anyone."

"Well, actually I get along pretty well with my younger brother."

"A brother? I didn't know you have a brother," she said in dismay. "You never told me that before. As your fiancée, I think it's something I should know, don't you? I mean, aren't your parents going to think it's strange that you're marring a woman who doesn't even know you have a younger brother? Or do they already know why you're marrying me? Sure they do. They're your family. They'll take one look at the color of my hair and figure that's why you're marrying me.'' She was hyperventilating again. Remembering Esma's advice, she leaned forward until her forehead was touching her knees.

''Even if they do know why I'm marrying you, they're much too well-bred to say anything about it,'' Shane assured her. ''That is one advantage of being from a family like mine. Certain things simply are not done.''

''I'd think marrying a woman to get your hands on a million dollars would be one of the things that simply isn't done,'' she muttered.

''Stop worrying,'' he said. ''I'll be there in an hour to pick you up. Will you be ready then?''

''I'll be ready,'' she replied, before hanging up the phone. ''But I don't know if you will be.'' Sitting up, she focused her gaze on the infamous purple dress hanging on her closet door. She'd already tried it on. Several times. And each time she was amazed at the magic that Zorra had wrought.

The material was silk, but it was the fit that was the real secret. The dress draped her perfectly. Paige had never been one to wear a vibrant color like purple, fearing it might clash with her hair. But it instead complemented her coloring in a way she'd never imagined.

She'd already used a curling iron on her hair. The wispy spirals also gave her an entirely new look as did the new shade of eye shadow which brought out a hint of violet in her blue eyes. Looking at herself in the mirror, even *she'd* been amazed. Surely Shane would be, too?

Paige was ready at the appointed time. Shane arrived at the appointed time. Everything was going according to plan.

Except there was no way to plan for his reaction. Opening the door to him, she stood back and waited. And waited.

Shane didn't say a word.

"Say something!" she finally burst out in exasperation.

"I'm speechless. You take my breath away. Here." Shane reached for her hand and placed it on his chest. She could feel his heart beating through the fine cotton of his dark blue shirt. "Feel that? That's my heart on the verge of stopping at the mere sight of you."

"Heart stopping can be a bad thing."

"It can be," he agreed. "But it isn't in this case. It's not a bad thing at all. It's an incredibly exciting thing."

Incredibly exciting? Her? "So you think this dress is okay?" She nervously ran a hand down the material. "I wasn't sure what to wear...."

He placed the index finger of his free hand on her lips to quiet her words. "You'll be the most beautiful woman there."

Her look was very skeptical. "I find that hard to believe."

"I know you do. Why is that?" he quietly asked. "Because of the number Quentin did on you?"

"Because the truth is I'm not beautiful, although this dress does make me look better than usual," she had to admit.

"Hey, if I say you're beautiful then you're beautiful. I have more experience in these matters than you do."

"You have more experience than I do in most matters," she muttered.

"I'm willing to teach you everything I know," Shane whispered, leaning closer to kiss her cheek. "But not right now. If we're late my mother will have my hide."

"I can't believe you're afraid of her." Paige's amusement was evident in her voice. "I mean, you went off and became a cop, so you've certainly done more things to anger your mother than being late."

"I'm not afraid of her," he denied. "I just have a healthy respect for the damage she can do."

"Oh, gee, that makes me feel much better," Paige said. "Now I really can't wait to meet her."

"She'll probably like you. And she'll want every detail about where you got that dress. Don't tell her. Keep her guessing, it'll drive her crazy."

"You're bad."

"Yeah, I am," Shane readily agreed with that tilt of his head she was coming to recognize along with the but-you-love-me-anyway look. "Uh, there's something I have to do before we leave."

Misunderstanding him, she said, "The washroom is down the hall."

"No, I meant this." He pulled a velvet ring box from

the inside pocket of his jacket. "I'm hoping it'll fit you, but if not we can have it sized. It belonged to my grandmother."

"Oh, Shane, it's beautiful." The princess-cut diamond in a platinum setting was breathtaking in its simplicity and ageless elegance.

"Here put it on." He handed her the ring.

Traditionally her fiancé would place the ring on her finger for her. But there was nothing traditional about her agreement with Shane, and she'd do well to remember that.

"HAVE YOU TOLD YOUR PARENTS that you're getting married?" Paige asked Shane as they drove along Sheridan Road.

"Not really."

She frowned. "I don't understand how the question could have a not really answer. Either you've told them or you haven't."

"I haven't actually spoken with them directly. I left a message on my mother's voice mail saying I'd be coming to her birthday party and that I'd be bringing you with me."

"Do you bring many women home with you?" she couldn't resist asking.

"No." He didn't elaborate.

"When do you plan on telling them that we're getting married? I mean, the wedding is only a week away from tomorrow."

"I'll tell them after the party tonight. My mother likes having the limelight to herself on her birthday."

"Then I think you should keep the ring until then."
She slipped it off her finger and retrieved the ring box
from the inside pocket of his jacket while he drove.
"How do you think they'll react when you tell them?"

"They're Huntingtons. They don't react. It would be
crass to do so. Ah, here we are." He pulled into a gated
entryway. Punching a set of numbers into the security
box, he noted, "Home sweet home," as the intricate
black wrought-iron gates slowly opened to let them in.

Paige had gotten glimpses of some of the palatial es-
tates perched between Sheridan Road and Lake Michigan. And she'd certainly seen her fair share of mansions.
But even so, this was impressive and just a tad intimi-
dating. The long curving driveway was flanked by a
broad sweep of lawn and meticulously trimmed hedges.
With its crisp white shutters and gray stone, the house
itself was vast and possessed a stately magnificence that
was intended to convey class and power. The setting
May sunshine on the stone facade made it sparkle and
shimmer as if it were specially chosen by divine inter-
vention.

The Turner house in Toledo, while large, could not
compare. The home where she'd grown up was a whim-
sical Queen Anne filled with turrets, pillars and unexpected roof peaks. It had a welcoming rather than an
imposing presence.

"Now remember," Shane was saying as he stopped
the car in front of the impressive entrance and tossed
the keys to a uniformed valet for parking, "my mother
has two expressions. Positive and negative. They're hard
to tell apart so you have to look closely. Her positive

expression is indicated by a slight lifting of the left side of her mouth. Her negative expression is indicated by a slight frown, not enough to cause wrinkles, of course.'' Opening the car door for Paige, Shane added, ''My mother does not argue. She does not emote.''

''I think I know the type,'' Paige said. ''Proctology must pay better than I thought,'' she noted with a wry nod toward the huge house.

Shane laughed. ''The Huntingtons had piles of money from investing in the railroads back in the mid-1800s.''

''The house is that old?''

''No. This was built in the 1920s by my great-great-grandfather. He had ten kids. There are thirteen bedrooms and at least as many baths. There are lots of carved wooden beams and stained-glass windows throughout the place. The windows in the formal dining room actually portray food. The fireplace in the living room has carvings of knights jousting.''

Knights jousting? Maybe there was hope for the house after all.

As they passed through the huge front foyer and a grand staircase that could have come from the movie set of *Gone with the Wind,* Shane said, ''The parquet flooring and carved library door are from an eighteenth-century Norman palace.''

''The door looks like it weighs a ton.''

''It does. Literally.'' He paused, as if hearing himself for the first time. ''Jeez, I just walked in the house and I sound just like my mother.''

''I certainly hope not,'' she teased him. ''While your

voice is modestly attractive in a guy, I don't think it would be equally attractive coming from a woman.''

''Only modestly attractive?'' Shane said in a pseudo-outraged voice.

''I'm afraid so.'' She patted his arm in commiseration before offering, ''But I am very impressed by the size of your...library door, if that makes you feel any better.''

His laughter made her heart sing.

''I think you'll do okay tonight,'' he noted in admiration while guiding her through a pair of open French doors to a huge multilevel stone terrace that was crowded with guests. From here they had a breathtaking view of velvety green lawn leading down to Lake Michigan. Over the discordant sound of conversation and crystal wineglasses being filled, Paige could actually hear the waves on the lake hitting the shore. A shore the Huntingtons owned, along with this huge mansion that looked as beautiful from the back as it did from the front.

''My mother is out here someplace. Can you pick her out?'' Shane asked her as he snared a pair of wineglasses from the tray of a passing waiter. ''I'll give you a hint, she loves gold—as in gold credit cards, a gold Lexus, gold hair, gold-plated bathroom fixtures, gold goblets.'' He lifted his glass, which was rimmed with gold.

''If I had to guess, I'd say that's her over in the far corner by the bar setup.''

''You're good.'' Shane raised his glass to Paige in a show of respect. ''Yes, that's her. Charlotte

Huntington—birthday girl.'' Paige studied her for a moment. She'd met the type many times before. Although Charlotte was petite, she had a regal bearing, her posture so upright it was as if she had a board for a spine. Her hair, golden-blond as Shane had said, was perfectly coiffed and her designer suit a subtle shade of ivory. The discreet necklace around her throat was no doubt eighteen-carat gold and had a canary-yellow diamond in it large enough to shine clear across the terrace but small enough not to be ostentatious.

The curious looks they were getting as Shane led her over to his parents would have made Paige feel self-conscious were it not for the fact that along with the curiosity was also admiration. Again Zorra's dress design had saved the day for Paige. She'd tried to buy the dress from Zorra, but she'd insisted that Paige have it, provided she tell everyone who designed it.

''You're a walking advertisement,'' Zorra had stated with a snap of her fingers.

And so this walking advertisement was walking across a terrace filled with people she didn't know to meet a woman that was eyeing her with open curiosity. ''I thought your mother only had two expressions,'' Paige murmured out of the side of her mouth.

''I thought she did.'' Shane sounded surprised. ''Even S.F. looks interested in our approach.''

''S.F.?'' she repeated in confusion.

''My father. Samuel Franklin Huntington.''

Paige shifted her attention from Shane's mother to his father. With his thick head of silver hair and tall car-

riage, he was the epitome of upper-class wealth and reserve.

"Happy birthday, Mother." With a devilish grin,
Shane swept her up in a big bear hug. "Did the male
stripper I hired to jump out of your birthday cake arrive
yet?"

8

"SHANE, BEHAVE YOURSELF," Charlotte demanded, discreetly batting at his arms until he set her back on her feet. Her earlier look of curiosity had disappeared, replaced by a "negative" look. Paige wouldn't have noticed it had Shane not warned her ahead of time to look for the slight frown on his mother's face.

"What?" Shane said, stepping away from her. "You don't think I'd hire a male stripper for your birthday?"

"Even you would have more sense than that," his mother replied.

Paige winced at the emphasis placed on the "even you."

"What about you, Dad?" Shane countered. "What do you think?"

"Nothing you'd do would surprise me," S.F. declared.

Instead of looking hurt, Shane nodded as if he'd expected no less from his father.

Even so, Paige ached for him. Reaching out, she placed her hand in his as a show of support. Her actions got his parents' attention once again.

His mother gave Paige an efficient head-to-toe visual once-over that registered everything from the color of

Paige's eye shadow to the price of her Italian leather shoes. Then she calmly said, "Ah, you must be the woman Shane is going to marry."

Shane looked as surprised at his mother's words as Paige was. Paige wasn't wearing the engagement ring Shane had given her; it was still safely tucked in the ring box in his jacket. Did the older woman have X-ray vision or something?

"Close your mouth, dear," she chastised her son. "People are watching."

"How did you find out?" he demanded.

"I was speaking to our family attorney this morning and—"

"He spilled the beans," Shane inserted.

"Really, Shane." The slight frown had returned. "Must you use such vulgar slang?"

"Really, Mother," he said in return. "Most people wouldn't consider beans to be vulgar."

"The Huntingtons are not—"

"—most people," Shane completed the sentence for her. "I know. Believe me, I know. Most families would not have a list of requirements for a suitable wife."

"Your father didn't require a list. He already knew what was suitable and what was not. And he was already married with a son by the time he was your age. You, on the other hand, have proved to be especially stubborn and intractable where these matters are concerned. But that's all water under the bridge. Come along, dear." This time her attention was focused on Paige as the older woman placed her cool hand on Paige's arm and drew her aside. "I want to hear all about your family."

''Paige stays with me,'' Shane stated, placing a firm arm around her shoulders.

''Are you afraid I'll scare your little fiancée?'' Charlotte's voice was laced with an amusement that didn't sound real.

''Actually Shane is so much in love with me that he can't bear to leave my side,'' Paige boldly stated. ''Isn't that so, darling?''

''Absolutely true, sweetheart.'' Leaning down to kiss her, he whispered ''good move'' before his lips covered hers.

Talk about a good move, the way his tongue tangled with hers was downright seductive. Paige forgot his mother was standing a few feet away, forgot that this wasn't real, forgot everything as the powerful magic of his touch swept her away.

''Here now, that's enough of that,'' Shane's father said with gruff disapproval.

Embarrassed, Paige pulled away.

Angered that his father had made Paige feel uncomfortable, Shane drawled, ''What's the matter, Dad? You don't remember what it's like to be young and in love?''

''I do remember what behavior is appropriate at a function of this sort and what behavior is not,'' S.F. retorted.

''That's enough,'' Charlotte said. ''It's my birthday and I refuse to allow my son and my husband to ruin it.''

Both men turned to her with a male ''What did I do?'' expression.

Holding up her hand, Charlotte quieted their protests.

"We are going to have a good time this evening," she ordered them both. "Is that understood?"

Both men nodded, reluctantly.

"Good. Now I believe the wedding is next Saturday. Not much time to prepare."

"We're having a small wedding and Paige has already made all the arrangements," Shane stated, hoping to head off his mother before she got into grandiose planning mode. "She's got her dress and the caterer."

"You already had a wedding dress all picked out?" Charlotte noted. "My, you must have been eager to be married."

"Actually," Paige demurely replied, "I have some wonderful friends who are very talented."

"Friends? Surely you're not planning on having a friend sew your dress for you?" Charlotte sounded as if she imagined Paige showing up in something horrible.

Shane was about to jump to Paige's defense when she did so herself. "My wedding dress is being designed by a very talented new designer. The dress I'm wearing today is one of her creations."

Shane knew his mother well enough to know that she was dying to ask who the designer was but much too proud to do so.

"And the reception is being handled by a very good friend of mine in the catering business. You may have heard of her. Esma Kinch."

"Esma Kinch!" This time his mother couldn't hide her jealousy. "Why I tried to get her to cater this party, but there was a scheduling conflict and she was unable to do it."

Shane remembered Esma telling him that working with his mother fell under the life-is-too-short category. Not that he didn't love his mother. He did. Not that she ever made it easy to love her. She didn't. But she was the only mother he had.

That didn't mean he was prepared to let her manipulate him into doing things her way. Her tactics hadn't worked in getting him to change his choice of careers, much to her dismay and continual consternation. You'd think she'd be happy that Shane's youngest brother, Robert, had gone into the family's medical practice as had both of his cousins. But, no, that hadn't been enough.

Now there was his marriage. His mother hadn't seemed at all surprised at the news. Of course, she had started dropping hints about wanting a grandchild for the last year or two, clearly indicating she wanted him married. He had a hard time believing she was really eager to be called grandma. He suspected it had more to do with her wanting to make Shane's father happy— and continuing the Huntington family line for another generation would do that.

Paige noticed that Shane was unusually quiet as his mother went on and on about the difficulty in finding a good caterer. She wondered what he was thinking. Was he sorry he'd brought her here today? Was he regretting his decision to marry in order to get his inheritance? He didn't seem like the kind of man who had regrets. He seemed like the kind of man who made up his mind and stuck to it, come hell or high water.

His parents weren't quite as bad as she'd expected.

Sure, they were snobs and cliquish in their interactions with others. And, yes, neither one of them possessed exactly what you'd call a warm and loving personality. But the deep-seated animosity she'd feared might be present wasn't.

Actually they reminded her a great deal of her own grandmother. Only her grandmother was even worse.

"So what do your parents have to say about your marriage to our son?" Charlotte asked. "Were they surprised by your haste in having the ceremony so quickly?"

In fact, Paige hadn't told her family yet because they were on a three-week trip to Europe—a blessing in disguise. Because her grandmother would surely disapprove of Paige's hasty nuptials and Paige had enough mayhem in her life right now without dealing with either her disapproving grandmother or her eccentric father.

Luckily Paige didn't have to answer as Charlotte was distracted by the arrival of a new group of guests.

But Shane had noticed something amiss because once they were alone in a quiet corner of the patio, he said, "You haven't told your family yet, have you?"

"No."

"Are you going to tell them?"

"They're in Europe now and aren't coming back for another two weeks."

"If you want them at our wedding, I'm sure you can reach them in Europe."

"I don't have their itinerary so I'm not even sure where they are staying. I'll tell them after the fact. It'll work out better that way anyway. My grandmother can be…rather a handful when she wants to be.''

"As can my mother. We should put the two of them together. But are you sure about not having your family there? Don't most brides dream of having their fathers walk them down the aisle?''

"I'm not most brides and this isn't exactly going to be a normal marriage.''

"Define normal,'' he said. "If by normal, you mean a marriage like my parents, then you're right. Our marriage won't be like that. But we do have some pretty strong things going for us. Like the fact that you know me better than you think. And then there's the attraction between us…'' He ran his index finger down her bare arm and she shivered with awareness. "I don't know where it came from…''

"I know where it's coming from,'' she said tartly with a meaningful look at the placket of his slacks.

He burst out laughing.

"I may have auburn hair, but that doesn't mean I don't have a redhead's temper on occasion,'' she informed him, peeved at his earlier comment. Did he have to make it plain that he saw no obvious reason why there would be an attraction between them?

Still smiling, Shane reached out to gently caress a short lock of her hair between his fingers. "Your hair is the exact color of an Irish setter I had as a kid.''

"Gee, you're too kind,'' Paige noted mockingly. "Comparing my looks to your dog. I'm flattered.''

"You know, from the moment we met, you never cut

me any slack. You never let me get away with anything. When I smile at other women, they smile back.''

"Instantly charmed, the poor fools," she said.

"See?" His grin was immediate. "That's what I mean. I can't pull anything over on you. You're on to me, and you always have been. I find that very appealing."

"Right," she scoffed.

"I'm serious," he said even as he removed the ring box from his jacket pocket and slid the engagement ring on her finger.

"You're never serious," she countered.

"Never?" he murmured, fixing his gaze on her mouth. "I'm very serious when I'm kissing you. And you seem very…serious then, too."

Unable to sustain the visual caress he was giving her, she had to look away. "You're much better at this flirting routine than I am," she had to acknowledge, gazing down at the ring on her finger.

"I'm not so sure about that," Shane retorted. "Look at that dress you're wearing. I sure have been. Looking. Admiring. I'm not sure exactly what makes it so sexy. But it just is."

"I'm still a librarian just dressed up in fancy clothes," Paige warned him. "I'll never look good in a thong."

"Forget about the thong," he murmured. "Much too obvious. I'm finding I'm much more intrigued by the unknown, by the enigmatic."

She looked at him in surprise. "I thought I was an open book."

He shook his head. "No way. You're like one of those mysteries that's full of twists."

"So not only do I resemble your faithful old Irish setter but I'm twisted as well, hmm?" She was teasing him now.

"Calling your fiancée twisted already, big brother?"

"Eavesdropping again, little brother?" Shane returned, giving him a hearty thump on the back. "How are things?"

"Things are fine," Robert replied. "Mother tells me you're getting married next Saturday."

"I sure am. Feel like coming?"

"I have two operations scheduled that day."

"Well, then, who am I to stand in the way of some hearty soul getting new plumbing."

"But they're early in the morning," Robert added. "What time is the wedding?"

"Three in the afternoon," Paige replied.

"Then I should be able to fit it in."

"Hey, don't put yourself out on my account," Shane said.

"As if I would. No, I just want to see this for myself. My big brother, the one who vowed he'd never settle with just one woman, the one who claimed wife was a four-letter word. My brother tying the knot. This I've got to see." Robert laughed gleefully. "Of course, there is grandfather's will to consider. Your thirtieth birthday is coming up, isn't it. A week from Tuesday I believe."

"Laugh all you want," Shane said darkly. "But you're next. I'll bet the same provisions apply to you getting your inheritance from grandfather."

"No, they don't. Because Grandfather knew I went into the family business before he died. Only the black sheep son has to jump through hoops, although I must say that she's a very good-looking hoop."

"You're the first one to call me a hoop," Paige replied, her anger showing through.

"Does that mean you're going to toss that artichoke canapé at me?" Robert said cautiously.

"No, but it does mean that you're going to have to work big time to make it up to me."

"Would expensive chocolates do the trick?" Robert asked with a slight smile.

"As if I could be bought with chocolates," she loftily replied before asking, "Dark chocolate or milk?"

"Dark," he instantly replied. "Truffles. Five-pound box."

"Well," she pretended to consider his offer. "It's a beginning, I suppose. Send it and a check made out for the same amount as the cost of the chocolates to Hope House and you've got a deal."

"You're smart." Robert sounded surprised by the discovery.

"Yes, I am," Paige readily agreed. "So you'd better be on your best behavior around me."

"Does that warning apply to my big brother Shane as well?"

"Shane's best behavior is good…but his bad behavior is even better," she drawled in her own adaptation of Mae West's saying.

Robert laughed before advising, "Just don't tell our mother that."

THE SIT-DOWN DINNER WAS SET out on the far side of the lawn in a huge white tent. The one hundred guests were seated at tables lined with golden damask tablecloths and white china. Bowls of white roses adorned the center of each table. It wasn't the Windy City Ball but it was an impressive display.

The embossed card in front of Paige said In Honor Of Charlotte Huntington's Birthday and listed the upcoming menu. She gave herself a mental reminder to discreetly snitch the card before the end of the meal to give it to Esma. That might be hard to do since Shane's mother had seated them at her table.

Beluga caviar on melba toast was awaiting them when they sat down. Salad with foie gras and asparagus tips with artichoke truffle vinaigrette was promised as the next course, followed by breast of duck with grape sauce and wild rice along with baby turnips and zucchini. Dessert was gratin of berries with a champagne sabayon sauce.

No chocolate. No cake. Too bad. Paige had been looking forward to watching Charlotte blow out the candles. But that would no doubt require too much effort and not look ladylike.

At least Paige knew which fork to use for which course. She also knew she would have been a lot more nervous had this been a real engagement. Then she would have been worried about Shane's parents liking her. This way she could keep her distance and watch the proceedings from afar.

It wasn't as though she and Shane were really going

to spend a lifetime together. It wasn't as if they were madly in love.

Unlike her last engagement, this time she had her eyes open to reality from the very beginning. Shane didn't love her. She knew that going in.

That's what made this experience different than her time with Quentin. Then she'd believed the fantasy. Now she knew she was only playing a role, like an actress in a play. Paige knew it wouldn't last, so she'd enjoy it for what it was while it was instead of wishing for what it wasn't.

Still, she did wish they'd had chocolate for dessert. The meal went by quickly and without incident. Paige was just starting to relax when Charlotte stood up as dessert was being cleared.

"I want to thank you all for coming to my party this evening," Shane's mother said in her cultured voice. "I have some good news to share."

"Oh, no," Shane said, but it was too late.

"My son Shane is getting married this Saturday at the High Grove Country Club. Naturally you're all invited."

"Oh, no," Shane repeated. So much for their plans of a small wedding. "When did I start to lose control over the situation?" Shane muttered in dismay.

"The minute you walked through the front door," his brother cheerfully replied. "Welcome home, big brother."

"I DIDN'T KNOW, I SWEAR." Shane sounded frantic as he drove Paige home. It was the first chance they'd had to be alone since his mother had made her announcement. "I didn't know she was going to invite everyone there to our wedding."

Paige wondered if she should put him out of his misery yet and tell him that she knew all about relatives doing things beyond your control. Her father was a prime example of that. Thank heavens he was in Europe.

"You're mad, aren't you?" he said with resignation. "That's why you aren't saying anything."

She really didn't have the heart to string him along, although he did deserve it for dragging her to this party tonight with barely twenty-four hours warning.

"Why didn't you tell me about tonight's party sooner?" she demanded.

He blinked. "Are you crazy? There's no way I was having you meet my parents until you'd already agreed to marry me. There was no way you'd ever say yes after realizing what you were getting into."

"And you weren't afraid I'd back out after meeting them?"

"No," he said quietly. "You're not the kind of woman who goes back on her word."

What kind of woman am I? she wanted to ask him. *The kind you could ever fall in love with? The kind who could love you in return? Or the kind who needs her head examined for agreeing to this crazy scheme in the first place, no matter how noble the cause?*

She wished she knew. But Shane was right about one thing. She wasn't the kind of woman to go back on her word. She'd said she'd marry him and she would.

9

"I KNEW IT!" IRENE EXCLAIMED after Paige told her on Monday that she and Shane were getting married. "I knew the two of you were an item. And I knew he'd come to his senses about the thong thing."

"The thong thing?" Leslie from the circulation department repeated. "Do tell."

They were all seated in the staff room, eating lunch. Paige thought this would be an appropriate time to tell her co-workers about her wedding and hand out invitations, which Esma had miraculously arranged for already.

"Shane told Paige he wanted to marry a woman who looked good in a thong," Irene answered Leslie's request for more information.

"He's such a hottie," Leslie said. "I noticed him the first time he walked into the library."

"We all noticed him," Irene agreed.

"And he's asked you to marry him. How romantic." Leslie gazed at Paige in awe. "Congratulations!"

"Thanks." She was infinitely appreciative that none of her co-workers had looked at her with disbelief when she'd made her announcement. If they were surprised that Shane wanted to marry her, none of them showed it. Instead they received the news with a hurray-for-our-team attitude that made her feel good.

After lunch, Paige worked at the Readers' Advisory desk. For some reason Leslie's comment about Shane being a hottie was sticking with her, as was the memory of that kiss they'd shared on his family's patio. She got warm just thinking about it. And then there was that sensual kiss on the ice rink, when Shane had pressed her against the Plexiglas, his body warm against hers as he seduced her with his hands and his tongue…

"Can you help me?" a middle-aged woman asked. "I'm looking for a book by Sue Grafton. It's a mystery and I think it's called *A is for Abstinence*."

Abstinence. Shane was definitely tempting her to give that up in favor of the promised passion in his arms.

Blinking, Paige forced her R-rated thoughts about Shane out of her mind and concentrated on helping the patron. Paige said, "I think the title of the book you're looking for is *A is for Alibi*."

"Yes, that's it," the woman agreed.

After sending the patron on her way with several other mysteries as well as the one she'd requested, Paige turned her attention to reworking the schedule so that she could take Thursday and Friday off as vacation days to prepare for her wedding this weekend without leaving the department understaffed.

"What a stupid concept!" a man standing in front of her declared.

Taken aback, it took Paige a second or two to realize he was pointing to the sign on the desk that said Never

Apologize For Your Reading Tastes rather than the rescheduling she was doing.

"There's good stuff to read and then there's junk," the man, whom Paige had never seen before, stated. "And you *should* apologize for reading junk."

"Everyone has different tastes," Paige began when he interrupted her.

"And if their tastes run to junk, they should apologize for having bad taste."

Clearly the man felt he was the high priest of good taste. It was made all the more amusing by the fact that he was wearing a plaid shirt with a brown bow tie and his glasses were held together with a piece of orange wire at the hinge.

Still, Paige was polite. "We all read different things for different reasons," she began, when he interrupted her for a second time.

"There's no reason to read junk," he barked.

Paige failed to see why the man was so irritated. Unfazed, the man continued on his diatribe.

Paige let him rant on until eventually the man ran out of steam and simply stomped off.

"Mondays are usually quiet around here," Irene noted as she joined Paige, shaking her head at the departing troublemaker. "The news of your wedding sure changed that. We weren't looking for anything wild to happen until the full moon on Friday. The strange man who just lectured you about good taste shouldn't have shown up until then."

"The full moon does seem to increase the number of

peculiar patrons,'' Paige acknowledged. ''Everyone seems to get crabbier or more on edge.''

''Except for the library staff, of course,'' Irene said with a grin.

''Of course,'' Paige agreed with matching amusement. ''We here at the High Grove Public Library are always courteous and kind. Even to crabby patrons who think they know it all.''

''Yes, well at least we don't have to worry about the Cubs Flasher showing up in the library like they do over in Wentworth,'' Irene said. ''I heard that the library board there is considering putting up security cameras in the more remote corners of the library so that if he does show up again, they can catch him on tape and identify him.''

''If he shows up *again?*'' Paige repeated.

''That's right,'' Iris said. ''Didn't you hear? He showed up at the library over the weekend. He actually had the gall to ask the reference librarian there if she had any books on flashing. Then he whipped open his trench coat. Luckily Mrs. Bergmeister was on duty that day and she'd just misplaced her glasses so she couldn't see a thing. But someone behind the man saw what was going on and shouted. Even so, the flasher still got away. I'll bet your Shane is involved in the investigation.''

It was only then that Paige realized that Shane rarely talked about his work. In fact, he rarely talked about himself at all unless she forced him to, as was the case with the information about his family.

He also never talked about what he was doing at

Hope House, even though Paige knew through her earlier contact with Sheila that he visited there at least twice a week. Paige planned on stopping by Hope House sometime soon to learn more about the mysterious man she was marrying in six days.

But first Paige had to see Zorra about a wedding dress.

"Ow!" PAIGE EXCLAIMED.

"Stop wiggling!" Zorra said around a mouthful of pins as she pinched Paige's waist suspiciously before almost piercing her with another straight pin. "Have you gained weight?" Zorra sniffed. "Perhaps it would be best if you stopped inhaling this candy." She reached as if to pull away the bowl of licorice bits that Paige held clutched to her breast, but Paige refused to let go.

"Don't touch my candy!"

"It's not wise to come between Paige and her candy," Esma advised Zorra, who wisely retreated.

Walking around Paige, she said, "Something is wrong with the way the material in the skirt is falling. You are wearing the proper shoes, correct? The ones you will be wearing at the wedding?"

"No, I forgot." Lifting her skirt with a guilty expression, Paige displayed her fuzzy bunny slippers.

"Here." Esma quickly handed her the shoe box with the proper shoes.

Once Paige had the heels on, Zorra was happier with the drape of the material, but now was circling her with a critical eye toward the waist. "We could take out the waist a bit and create a basque design with a fitted bodice and a downward pointing V at the waist. It makes the stomach look smaller." She inserted another pin.

"Ouch! Look you are not helping here," Paige said irritably. "I already feel self-conscious as it is. I don't need you telling me I have a big stomach. All my other clothes seem to still fit me just fine." Paige picked out two of the licorice candies, one pink and one white, and ate them. "Maybe I should just wear the gold dress instead of having you make up another one," Paige suggested, starting to feel like a voodoo doll from all the pins that Zorra had mistakenly stuck in her instead of the soft satin material of her dress. "What?" she demanded as Zorra and Esma both looked at her in disapproval.

"You do not wear a ball gown to your own wedding."

"But this dress is practically the same design as that one," Paige pointed out.

"You and I know this," Zorra replied. "And Esma, too. But the others will not. They will see you as a vision and the dress as divine. And I will be as inundated with the rich and richer wanting me to design their dresses."

"I did mention your name to a number of the guests at the Huntingtons' party on Friday night. The purple dress was a work of art."

Zorra nodded, like a queen. "And this dress will be even better."

"It will be ready by Saturday?" Paige asked hesitantly, seeking reassurance as she once again paired a white candy with a pink one. She only craved the licorice candy when she was under extreme stress, and pairing the candies the way she did was a good luck trick from her childhood days.

"But of course." Zorra placed the last of the pins she'd had in her mouth along the waistband of the dress and fixed Paige with a regal stare. "What is the point of making your dress if it is not ready in time for the wedding?"

"It's just that, well…" Paige fluttered her free hand at the pinned-together dress. "It looks like there's still a lot to be done on it yet."

"You do not have a trained eye for these matters. Tell her, Esma."

"Not to worry," Esma cheerfully told Paige as she helped her out of the dress, which was now as prickly as a porcupine.

Esma had been her Rock of Gibraltar the past few days. Her friend hadn't even flinched when Paige had told her what Charlotte Huntington had done, inviting all her friends without consulting with either Shane or Paige and thereby upping the guest list from the 25 that Paige had wanted to 125.

"How can you be so calm?" Paige asked her as she tugged a knit cotton T-shirt dress over her head. Ah, the relief of soft material without anything jabbing at her. Too bad she couldn't get married in this.

Yeah, that would look very nice, she silently mocked herself. You walking up the aisle in your bunny slippers and a cream-colored T-shirt dress. Carrying dark purple petunias from the window boxes on her deck. Yes, that would make quite an impression on the society bigwigs attending.

Paige sighed. She needed this dress, the one Zorra was making. She needed it to boost her morale and self-confidence the way the golden ball gown had.

"I can be calm because I'm not the one getting married this weekend. Here, what do you think?" Esma asked. "Should I wear the peach-colored dress or do you think the passion-fruit color is better?" Since Esma was her only attendant, there were no bridesmaids dresses to contend with. Instead there Esma was holding up two of the many stunning dresses in her wardrobe. "Both colors are being featured in your flowers. Your wedding bouquet will be a nosegay of white and peach-colored roses, lilies of the valley and baby's breath as you requested, while the flowers decorating the Palmer Room where you're having the ceremony will be full-blown peach-colored roses, white hydrangeas and peonies."

"I would never have been able to get this all together if you didn't have such valuable contacts, like the florist."

"In a case like this, it pays to have a caterer as your best friend," Esma agreed.

Zorra interrupted them to say, "Please inform your animal that this ribbon is for your dress and not for her to play with."

"Actually Simon is a *he*," Paige said as she stepped forward to scoop her cat up in her arms. Schuster, meanwhile, was watching the goings-on from the large dec-

orative bowl on the weathered coffee table, unwilling to
move when he had the bowl all to himself for a change.

Zorra, all dressed in black as was her trademark look,
brushed the cat hair from her baggy slacks.

After deciding on the peach-colored dress for Esma
and the rosebud design lace for Zorra to put on the bodice of the dress, Paige was relieved when the fitting was
over.

Left on her own, with Simon purring on her lap, she
reminded herself that she was only playing a role, that
her engagement to Shane wasn't the real thing. Although Shane had agreed that their marriage wouldn't
be normal, he had seemed to indicate at his parents'
house that theirs would not be a marriage in name only.

The prospect filled her with nervous anticipation and
an achy kind of yearning. Or maybe she just needed
more candy.

As IT TURNED OUT, the press of work and wedding prep-
arations prevented Paige from visiting Hope House until
Thursday afternoon. She'd only seen Shane briefly over
the past few days as he was working overtime to get
Friday and the weekend off. Sure, she'd talked to him
on the phone, but she still felt no closer to learning more
about the man she was soon to marry than she had earlier. She was hoping this visit today would change that.

"I'm so glad you stopped by," Sheila Romerez said.
"And congratulations again on your upcoming wedding," she added, getting up from her desk to give Paige
a quick hug. "I thought there were sparks between the
two of you when we saw you at the ice rink."

Shane hadn't told them that the reason he was marrying Paige was to gain access to the million dollars so that he could give it to Hope House. "I don't want them to feel awkward about it," he'd said when she'd asked him about the omission. "They know about the million dollars, but they don't know about the details of my grandfather's will and I want to keep it that way." Paige was more than glad to honor his wishes, although it did make her feel a tad dishonest to go along with the charade.

"It was so kind of you and Shane to invite us all to the wedding," Sheila said, clearing a straight-back chair of a pile of folders and indicating that Paige should sit down.

"Hope House means a great deal to Shane."

"And you're okay with that?" Sheila asked, returning to her side of the desk and placing the folders on stacks of others.

"Absolutely." Paige was surprised by the question. "Why wouldn't I be?"

"Some women might be jealous of the time he spends here, not to mention the huge sum of money he's donating. It will make such a difference in so many people's lives." Sheila then went on to show Paige the new blueprints for a new addition out of the back of the house that would allow more children and their families to stay at the facility. "We can also buy the property next door to us, allowing for the expansion of the playground facility. Shane coaches the kids in basketball and softball as well as teaching them to skate at the ice rink. He's such a positive influence in the lives of these kids, many of whom have never had a sympathetic male figure in their lives before.''

"You don't have to convince me," Paige assured her. "I know that Shane's doing the right thing donating his time and money to Hope House."

"He's also doing the right thing marrying you," Sheila said.

Paige nervously nibbled on her bottom lip. "I hope he thinks so."

"Of course he does." Sheila smiled at her reassuringly. "Shane is a smart guy. And a compassionate and honorable guy."

Paige nodded. "Yes, I know."

"Did you know he's got musical talent as well?"

"No, that I did not know."

"He's in the playroom right now. Go on and see for yourself. It's the big room at the end of the hall, past the middle stairwell." The house had at one time been a large Victorian mansion, with a dozen bedrooms on three floors as well as front and back parlors. The floor plan resembled a bit of a maze as Paige went down the hallway, around the middle set of stairs, and down another hallway. The wallpaper was old and fading and the floor was scuffed although clean. And the air was filled with the sound of music. "Old McDonald's Farm" to be exact.

At the end of the hallway ahead of her, Paige could see a large sunny room filled with children. And she could see one corner of a somewhat battered upright piano.

Quietly moving closer, she saw that Shane was sitting

at the piano, cheerfully banging out the music. At the appropriate time he'd point to a child to provide the name of the animal they'd sing about next. She listened as they went through pig and cow and horse. Then he pointed to little Leah, the shy little girl whom Paige remembered from that evening at the ice rink. "Llama!" she yelled out with a big grin.

Without missing a beat, Shane sang, the familiar refrain using a llama.

And standing there watching him, Paige could feel the last of her defenses against Shane crumbling away.

SHANE FOLLOWED PAIGE as she drove back to her apartment. They'd stopped for dinner earlier and then she'd invited him to her home for a nightcap. All evening the sensual messages had been passing back and forth between them, the sexual tension building with every minute that went by.

They barely made it in the door of her apartment before Shane took her in his arms.

"I've been wanting to do this all night," he murmured against her mouth. The kiss was passionate and exciting, but it wasn't enough.

"And I've been wanting..."

"What?" he prompted her, nibbling on her lower lip. "Tell me."

"More," she whispered.

He arched an eyebrow at her. "More?"

She nodded.

"As in more kissing or as in making love?" he enquired.

"Both of the above."

"Thank God." He held her against him, letting her feel how much he wanted her. "I wasn't going to press you."

"Mmm, press me," she whispered, moving against him.

"First we need to open a can of tuna."

She blinked at him. "Tuna?" She'd heard of whipping cream being used to liven up a love scene, but a can of tuna?

"For the cats," he explained, striding into her kitchen and popping the top on a tuna can he'd found in her cupboard. "I don't aim on being interrupted again," he said, dumping the contents into the two cats' dishes as both Simon and Schuster raced into the kitchen. They recognized the sound of a tuna can opening and were soon totally engrossed in eating.

Meanwhile, Shane was totally engrossed in kissing her again as he led her back into the living room. This time, when his mouth covered hers, he held nothing back as his tongue boldly tangled with hers in a rhythmic thrust that foretold of things to come. Excitement coursed through her body like wildfire, making her hot, making her ache, making her moist.

"I want to do this right," he murmured, his hand already sliding between the buttons of her denim blouse he'd miraculously undone in record time to hold her breast in the palm of one hand. Using his other hand, he cupped her bottom and held her against his throbbing masculinity.

"It's right," she huskily assured him, lifting her bent

knee to gain closer access between the part of him that was eager to fill the aching part of her.

An instant later he'd lifted her up so that she could wrap her legs around his waist. Her arms were around his neck as he kissed her yet again with wild passion. Breaking away, he gasped, "Not here. Not against a wall. In bed. Your bed."

He gentled the kiss as he carried her to her bedroom, carefully depositing her on the softness of her bed before quickly following her down. Her blouse had slid halfway off, so he removed it completely before staring down at her with brown eyes smoldering with the darkness of desire.

"You do realize," he murmured in a low, sexy voice, "that as a detective I am a trained investigator."

"And just what are you planning on investigating here, Detective?"

"You. I plan on investigating you. And all your physical...evidence." He trailed his fingertips from the hollow at the base of her throat down to her waist. "As a trained investigator, I look for physical evidence like this bra. This bra is a tangible item that proves you are an incredibly sexy woman."

"It proves that, huh?" She looked down at his hands on her skin and felt her temperature rising.

"Sure does. This lace..." He traced the tip of his index finger along the edge of the material cupping her breasts. "Why, its sole purpose is to drive a man wild."

"I had wondered why it was there," she murmured.

"Well, now you know."

"I also know that you're wearing more clothes than I am," she said.

"We can fix that," Shane replied with a sexy smile.

"I should hope so."

Leaning away from her, Shane whipped off his black T-shirt. "Is that better?"

"It's a beginning. It's a crime to cover this up," she noted, running her hands over the muscular contours of his chest with playful appreciation.

"It's a crime to cover this up, too," he replied, releasing the front clasp of her bra to free her breasts. "And since you're the person who perpetrated this crime, I'm going to have to interrogate you."

"Should I have a lawyer present?" she teased him as he tossed her bra across the room.

"I don't think that will be necessary," he said, splitting his attention between her face and her breasts. "You can answer these questions on your own."

Was he going to ask her why she'd decided to make love with him? Or why she'd agreed to marry him? How could she answer such questions when she wasn't completely sure of the reasons herself?

"Now, Ms. Turner," he began in his cop voice, "are you aware that it's a crime to cover up breasts as luscious as these are?"

"They're not very big," she said almost apologetically.

"I'll be the judge of that. Hmm." He curved his hand over her bare skin, brushing his thumb against her nipple. "They feel mighty nice to me. Mighty nice, indeed. Now I'm going to have to ask you a few questions, ma'am. Do you prefer this...?'' He caressed her right breast with his seductive hands. ''Or do you prefer this...?'' Lowering his head, he kissed his way across the creamy slope of her left breast.

''Oh!'' She arched her back as blissful pleasure raced through her body.

''Or maybe this is better?'' he murmured against her skin before swirling his wet tongue around the aroused rosy peak.

''Yes!'' she gasped, spearing her fingers through his silky dark hair to hold his head in place against her. ''Yes!''

He took his time, working his seductive magic on her, removing her khaki skirt and his jeans before moving down her body as he asked her what she liked, what brought her the most pleasure. After peeling away her underwear, he erotically mined her inner treasures, building her need until she was lost in a hazy world of sensual pleasure.

Nothing mattered but his hands, his lips and the mounting pressure growing deep within her. He'd lift her to one peak of joy only to lead her on to larger crests of bliss...upward, upward, tightening, tightening...

Frightened by the intensity of her response, she gripped handfuls of her chenille comforter and gasped Shane's name.

''Easy,'' he soothed her. ''Just let go, let it happen. Come on,'' he coaxed her with both his roughly whispered words and his secretly erotic moves, culminating with his thumb brushing against the dewy nub hidden within the folds of her femininity.

The explosion of her climax held her in its grip as waves of unbelievable delight spiraled through her.

And then he was there, sheathed in a condom—hot, heavy, and ready for her as he slid his way home. The friction of his thrusts aroused nerve endings already vibrating with sensory overload as once again her body shifted in anticipation of the glorious release to come. Lifting her knees, she held on to him as her body welcomed him with the most intimate of embraces, drawing him in deeper and then holding him there with a delicate orgasmic grip that created its own brand of heavenly satisfaction.

Shouting her name, Shane froze above her reveling in the splendor, before joining her in the wanton slide to completion.

PAIGE OPENED HER EYES TO SEE sunshine streaming through her bedroom window. Disoriented for a second, she wondered at the delicious feeling of warmth against her back, wondering if it was Simon or Schuster before she realized that it was Shane. His arm rested around her bare waist.

Lifting his arm, she gave in to the urge to kiss the pulse at his wrist before carefully sliding out of bed and replacing his arm on the rumpled sheets. A glance at the bedside clock had already told her that it was late, almost eleven. Normally her cats would have woken her earlier, but they must still be satiated from the huge can of tuna Shane had given them last night.

Paige knew how it felt to be satisfied beyond your wildest dreams. Only in her case it had been Shane, not tuna, that had brought about these feelings.

And what feelings they were, she noted as she tiptoed to the bathroom, not wanting to wake Shane just yet. After spending the entire night making wild passionate love to him, she needed to regain some composure before seeing him again. It wasn't until she was in the shower, that she allowed herself to reflect on what had happened. And it hit her with the force of the massaging water.

She loved Shane. The soap fell from her hands. She was in love with Shane. Fallen as surely as the soap she'd just dropped. Fallen hard and with utter abandonment, holding nothing back.

Suddenly shaky, she leaned against the back wall of the shower stall. How had this happened? When had the attraction between them turned into something else, something bigger and deeper?

Had it happened when she'd seen him singing to the kids at Hope House last night? Had it happened when he'd sensuously interrogated her last night? No, she remembered being unsure even then of her feelings. Or had she just been denying the inevitable? Had she loved Shane from the moment he'd walked into the library that first time? Was that why she'd always had that special bond with him? Had her defenses prevented her from seeing it?

So many questions, so few answers. Except for this one. She loved Shane.

The water turned cold and so did she. Shane had

never claimed to love her. He'd made his reasons for marrying her clear from the start. She wasn't supposed to fall for the fantasy. She was supposed to enjoy the role of being his fiancée and then his wife. But she wasn't supposed to open her heart up this way.

Stepping out of the shower and wrapping her robe around her, she stood there staring at herself in the steamy bathroom mirror. Yes, her expression looked as stunned as she felt.

What if Shane had woken to a similar discovery? What if last night had transformed him as it had her? What if even now he was in her bed, preparing to declare his love for her?

She hurried back to her bedroom only to find Shane already halfway dressed.

And instead of proclaiming his emotions, he said, "Did I tell you I'm not going to be able to join you for lunch with the attorneys today?"

"Lunch?" she repeated in confusion, her hopes of an immediate declaration of love dashed. "You didn't tell me about any lunch today."

"Sure I did. I wanted to come with you when you sit down with the family lawyer, but the chief beepered me while you were in the shower."

While she was in the shower, where she'd just made the life-altering discovery that she loved him.

"And I've got to head back to the police station right away," he continued, "because they've got a lead on the Cubs Flasher. Hey, don't look so scared."

Easy for you to say, she thought to herself. *You're not the one who just discovered you love some-one…someone who doesn't love you back.*

10

"THE GUYS FROM BOTTOMS, Biggs and Bothers aren't so bad," Shane reassured her. He was wearing the jeans he'd had on last night, but had yet to put on his black T-shirt. "You'll charm the socks off of them, I'm sure."

The only thing Paige was sure of was that she was in big trouble. Loving Shane had never been part of the deal. She hadn't signed up for that and neither had he.

"Hey, are you okay?" Shane asked in concern. "You look awfully pale all of a sudden. Here, come sit down." He led her to the bed.

She gingerly perched on the edge of the mattress and thought maybe it was just the sex. The incredibly mind-blowing sex she'd had with Shane on this very mattress last night. Maybe her mind was still clouded by passion. Maybe it wasn't love after all.

And maybe pigs could fly.

No, it was love all right.

Mere lust wouldn't make her this shaky, wouldn't make her feel as if the very foundation on which she'd based her life had shifted beneath her feet.

Shane was rubbing her hands as if dealing with someone in shock. She certainly qualified because she was in shock big time over being in love with Shane.

Did he love her in return? She stared at him intently, as if hoping to read the answer in his eyes.

But they seemed no different than before. Yes, they looked at her with concern. Yes, they were incredibly attractive eyes. She especially loved those little laugh lines at the corners. She almost reached out to touch them before stopping herself. She had to because she could find no indication of a similar awareness in his gaze, no sign of his having a life-altering experience like love.

Maybe he was just real good at hiding his emotions? Or maybe he just didn't feel the way she did. If she were a betting woman, she'd have to put money on the latter.

"You'll be fine," he was telling her in an atta-girl bracing voice. "You're a Turner of Toledo. You eat lawyers for breakfast. You're a librarian. You..."

He paused and her heart raced in anticipation. "Yes?"

"Look really sexy." He leaned forward to lick a droplet of water from the shadowy valley between her breasts. She was wearing a plush terry-cloth robe and a blush that covered her from head to toe caused by the tantalizing magic of his tongue on her skin. He had one arm braced around her waist, which was a good thing because otherwise she might have melted right there and then.

"Um, what...mmm..." Her head was tilted back, allowing him greater access as she moaned her pleasure. Her voice was throaty and sexy. "What time am I supposed to meet...mmm...the lawyers?"

"Noon," he murmured against her skin.

"What?" She leaped off the bed, almost knocking Shane back on his fanny. "But that's in half an hour!"

"You're right. And I have to get down to the station or the chief will have my hide." He paused long enough to give her one quick awesome kiss before grabbing his T-shirt and walking out of her bedroom.

"Wait!" she frantically called out. "Where am I supposed to meet the lawyers?"

He popped his head around the door frame. "At the High Grove Country Club."

Great. The same place she was getting married tomorrow and having the wedding rehearsal tonight. "Don't forget the rehearsal is tonight at five," she said. "I am not going through that alone so you'd better be there."

"I'll be there," he promised, giving her a wink and a sexy smile before leaving.

She didn't even have time to stand around and appreciate how good he looked on the threshold to her bedroom. She had to get a move on.

What to wear, what to wear? Paige made a mad dash to her closet seeking out the answer.

A suit. A suit would be good. She had to own a suit. Yes, there it was pushed to the back corner of the closet. For good reason. It had a stain on the jacket.

Another suit. She had to have another suit. She did. Her black pantsuit, but that was too fancy for day wear.

What about this suit? She pulled it out of the closet. Her funeral suit. At least that's what she called it. It was black and fit her well. Once it was on, she studied her reflection in the full-length mirror.

Who wore a skirt this short to a funeral? She tugged on the hem but to no avail. Had the dry cleaners shrunk it? Would the Huntington lawyers think she was a shameless hussy who showed her knees...and several inches of thigh?

Closing her eyes as she fought off panic, she wondered how she could have gone from dull to shameless hussy in two days? Why hadn't Shane given her more warning about this lunch? Was he deliberately trying to drive her crazy?

If so, he was succeeding.

She sat on the bed and pulled on panty hose and shoes. Of course, Schuster took it into his head to jump onto the bed and her lap right at that moment. Great. Now she had cat fur on her black suit.

Scooting Schuster off her lap, she grabbed a lint brush and removed the fur from her skirt. Then, because the cat was giving her such a reproachful look, she got all weepy-eyed and had to give him a hug and murmur her apologies at being so curt with him. After which she had to reach for the lint brush again.

Paige was still doing her makeup after she'd parked in the fancy lot at the country club, powdering her nose and touching up her lipstick. For some reason her hair was acting perverse today and refused to fall into place the way it usually did. One particular lock kept sticking up, making her feel like some cartoon character.

She certainly had the hair color for it. Red, just like

a rooster's. Or "sort of red" to quote Shane. The man had such a way with words.

But he'd made up for it last night. Her body still tingled just thinking about what they'd done last night. And how many times they'd done it. And in such a variety of angles and poses.

Her face turned brilliant red. Great. She was blushing again. And, peering into her rearview mirror, she discovered she had stubble burn along the upper curve of her breast. Doing up another button of her suit took care of that, but not the matching redness at the base of her neck.

Reaching into the back seat, she grabbed a silk paisley scarf and wrapped it around her neck. She was all thumbs and had to do it three times before it looked halfway decent.

It was now ten minutes after twelve. She was late. Jumping out of the car, she almost slipped out of her shoes as she hustled toward the entrance. There she was told that Mr. Biggs was waiting for her in the Oak Room for their private luncheon.

The Oak Room should have been called The Dark Room because the dark green draperies shut out most of the light while someone had dimmed the elegant chandelier. Compared to the bright sunshine outside, the place was a cave.

Blinking, she saw a man come forward. He was tall and thin, with the kind of hawkish legal-looking face she'd expect from a villain in a Dickensian novel. Aside from his modern-day suit, he could have just stepped out of a "Masterpiece Theatre" episode. "Ah, you must be Ms. Turner. Welcome. I'm Timothy Biggs. And this is my associate Jonathan Bottoms.'' Mr. Bottoms could have been Mr. Biggs's twin brother, so alike did they look to her nervous eyes. Both men were tall, had silvery hair and beady eyes. ''We're so glad you could join us today,'' Mr. Biggs told her, cupping her elbow with his hand and leading her farther into the room.

''I'm so sorry I'm late,'' she said in a breathless rush.

''That's quite all right,'' Mr. Biggs said. ''We have a surprise for you. Look, who's joined us.''

Her heart leaped with hope. Had Shane come riding to her rescue? But no... She blinked. No, it couldn't be...

''Well, Paige, what do you have to say for yourself?'' her grandmother demanded with a thump of her ebony cane.

''THIS STINKS,'' SHANE GROUCHED as he sat beside his partner at the bar of Al's Tavern.

''So you've said at least ten times before,'' Koz replied as he grabbed a handful of bar nuts.

''I was supposed to be eating lunch with Paige and the Huntington lawyers right now.''

''Yep,'' Koz nodded and tossed a peanut into his mouth. Crunching it, he noted, ''You've said that at least ten times before, too.''

''I don't know why the chief called me out today in the first place. There's nothing going on here.'' Shane looked around at the deserted bar with impatience. A neon light advertising a popular brand of beer flashed in the window. The jukebox in the far corner was silent.

Even the barkeeper was quiet, wiping glasses clean. "The place is a morgue. The Cubs Flasher has no history of showing up in bars."

"Now *that* line you've said at least twenty times."

"Well, it's true. We've already followed up on all this material." Shane jabbed an impatient finger at the file with his notes in it, sitting atop the bar. "These so-called leads are all lame."

"They may be lame," Koz drawled, "but *she's* sure not."

"Who?" Shane looked around and saw her. She was hard to miss.

"Hi there, big boy," a voluptuous young woman with breasts the size of Dolly Parton's purred as she sidled up really close to him. "My name is Bitsy and I hear you're getting married. That's a real crime." She was wearing a police uniform, but Shane doubted that was her real profession.

Sure enough, a second later Bitsy boldly ripped off her blouse and skirt to reveal very little clothing underneath them. The leopard-skin print thong she wore was so small there was barely enough room for two leopard spots.

As for her breasts, well, they were barely within the legal limit of...anything. And now she was standing so close, his nose was practically pressed up against the mighty silicone-enhanced mounds.

"Welcome to your bachelor party!" Koz shouted with glee as a crowd of his fellow police officers poured through the door into Al's Tavern.

"I can't breathe," Shane gasped, leaning back to try

to get some oxygen. Thankfully Bitsy let go of her death grip on him and sauntered off, giving him an eyeful of her cheeky bottom.

"Isn't she great!" Koz shouted, thumping Shane on the back. "She was recommended by Mimi. You remember, my second cousin's manicurist."

"With the rap sheet, yeah, I remember. So this was all a setup?" Shane shook his head, unable to believe what he was seeing. Al's Tavern was no longer a morgue. The place was jumping now. "The chief was in on this, too?"

Koz nodded. "He gave his approval. And he gave his okay for a few of us to swap shifts so we could be here this afternoon."

"I can't believe you did this," Shane muttered, as Bitsy came closer to loop a black feather boa around his neck as the Rolling Stone's song "Satisfaction" blared from the corner jukebox. "Paige is going to kill me," he said, only to get a mouthful of feathers.

"Where do you think you're going?" Koz demanded as Shane slid off the bar stool and headed to the exit.

"Out of here," Shane replied over the din of the pounding music. "You don't understand, I sent Paige off into the Bottoms, Biggs, and Bothers lion den of a lunch all alone."

"No, you don't understand," Koz stated as he whipped out a pair of cuffs and chained Shane to...Bitsy. "This is your bachelor party. We went through a lot of trouble to set this up, so we could enjoy...I mean so *you* could enjoy it."

"Hit it, boys," Bitsy instructed. A minute later the

deafening sound of "Hey, Big Spender" filled the air. Removing her fake police cap with a quick flick of one hand, Bitsy let her long hair fall down around her ample bosom as she strutted her stuff on four-inch heels, dragging him along and rolling her hips with the talent of a belly dancer.

Talk about a captive audience. Shane was stuck. And Bitsy was good. So why wasn't he interested? Why did he wish that he was having lunch with Paige instead of watching a nearly naked woman do some pretty incredible contortions?

She shoved him onto a bar stool, but even her lap-dance wasn't getting much of a rise out of him. Smiling at her apologetically, he scooched her up and off his thighs before she did any damage to his private parts. He'd need them later tonight…with Paige. Provided she didn't kill him first.

"GRANDMA." Paige leaned closer to kiss the papery-thin skin of her cheek. At eighty-one, her grandmother was a cross between Queen Victoria and the French designer Coco Channel, for whom she'd been named. Being engulfed in the designer's perfume that her grandmother loved and hearing the clatter of her long pearl necklace was like being transported back to her teenage years. Her grandmother only fingered her pearls when she was about to deliver a lecture on Turner decorum. "What are you doing here?" Paige asked, trying not to sound as dismayed as she felt. "I thought you were in Europe with Dad."

Paige had no sooner said the words than she heard her father's rich baritone voice. "Hi there, kitten."

"Dad," she said weakly. "You're here, too." A stupid observation but she wasn't working on much sleep here. Instead of getting a good night's rest to prepare herself for surprises like this, she'd been making mad passionate love with Shane.

"Of course I'm here," her father boomed. "I wouldn't miss my daughter's wedding for the world."

"We tracked down your family in Europe and had them fly in as a surprise for you," Mr. Biggs said.

"Well, I am surprised," Paige acknowledged brightly.

"I can't believe you didn't contact us yourself," Coco Turner said with a disapproving sniff and another rattle of her pearls.

"I didn't want to ruin your trip abroad. I knew how much you were looking forward to it." And since they hadn't left her an itinerary, Paige wasn't even sure what part of Europe they were in.

"When these lawyers phoned, we were staying at the Palazzio Hotel in Venice, which I was just as happy to leave," Coco said. "It's not what it used to be. They're letting all sorts in these days. When I was a girl we dressed for meals. Don't slouch, Paige," she said almost as an aside. "You know it makes you look unattractive. Now where was I? Oh, yes, in my day there was a certain code of behavior. You wore gloves for afternoon teas and you never wore white before Memorial Day. A girl would never dream of showing up in shorts at anything but a private gathering. And now, why they're actually wearing shorts on the airplanes.'' Coco shuddered and her pearls rattled. ''It's a disgrace I say.'' She thumped her cane for emphasis. ''A disgrace. Paige would never dream of wearing shorts on an airplane. Isn't that correct, Paige?''

''That's correct, Grandmama.'' But then Paige wouldn't wear shorts anyplace. With her pale skin, she never tanned and after being taunted by the other girls at Godden's School for Girls with chants of albino, she'd taken to covering up her legs. Not that the skirt she was wearing today gave that indication. But even it was conservative by many women's standards.

But then other people's standards had never been important to her grandmother. Only Coco Turner's own strict standards mattered in her book. And Coco was eyeing Paige's nylon-clad knees with disapproval.

Tugging Paige closer, her grandmother whispered, ''Isn't that skirt a little short, dear?''

''My other suit was still at the cleaners.'' It was the best excuse Paige could come up with and she could tell by her grandmother's frown that it didn't cut much slack with her.

''An organized woman always has her wardrobe prepared so that she has the proper attire for the proper occasion.'' With that reprimand she let Paige go and fixed her eagle eye on the lawyers. ''Where is your client?''

''Shane had to work,'' Paige answered on their behalf.

''You said he's in law enforcement?'' Again Coco directed her question to the attorneys.

Again Paige answered on their behalf. "Shane is a detective with the Wentworth Police Department."

"I was speaking to Mr. Biggs," Coco said, a hint of reprimand in her voice.

"Sorry, Grandmama."

"So I'm not to meet the man you're going to marry tomorrow until he shows up at the church?"

"Actually we're not getting married in a church."

The clatter of her grandmother's pearls was almost deafening. "Not getting married in a church?" Coco slowly repeated, as if certain she must have heard incorrectly.

"We're getting married here, at the High Grove Country Club tomorrow," Paige said.

"Not getting married in a church?" Coco said again.

Paige could feel the sweat collecting. Or perspiration, as her grandmother would say. Not that money or perspiration was something one talked about. She tried to daintily wipe away the bead of...perspiration trickling down the back of her neck. Had Paige known her family would be here, she would have powdered her entire body, not just her face. They had a way of making her nervous. "The churches were all booked."

"Why are you getting married so quickly?" her father suddenly said. "You're not pregnant, are you?"

"Bertrand, that's enough!" Coco fixed him with a steely stare.

"I am not pregnant," Paige hastily assured her father, and the Huntington lawyers just in case they were wondering. "We moved up the wedding date because of Shane's grandfather's will." She hoped that wasn't revealing too much. After all, she hadn't said they were marrying because of the will, although the look Mr. Biggs and Mr. Bottoms were giving her said that they already knew that much.

Mr. Biggs took it upon himself to explain. "Mr. Huntington has to marry before his thirtieth birthday next Tuesday or he won't receive his one million dollar inheritance."

Coco was not impressed. "Talking about money is so uncouth, don't you agree?"

"Well, I..." Mr. Biggs was at a loss for words. Paige had a feeling it wasn't an occurrence that happened very often.

"Did I tell you about the South African diamond mine I once invested in?" Paige's father asked the two attorneys with a hearty laugh. "The government called me in to help them get things in order."

"Now, Dad, you don't want to go telling that story," Paige inserted with a nervous laugh of her own. For one thing, the story wasn't true. But then her father, a natural storyteller, saw no reason why the truth should ever be allowed to get in the way of a good yarn.

As if aware of her reticence, and curious as to the reason for it, Mr. Biggs immediately said, "I'd love to hear this story."

"Let's eat lunch first," Paige suggested, reaching for a menu and handing one to her father and then her grandmother. "What are you going to have? I'm starving." Paige could tell by her grandmother's frown that talking about hunger was also uncouth. "Sorry, Grandmama. But I didn't have a chance to eat breakfast this morning.'' Paige fidgeted with the scarf around her neck, remembering how she'd spent her morning instead. In bed. With Shane.

"You're slouching again, Paige. And your scarf is coming undone. Perhaps you should retire and fix it." Coco's suggestion was more like an order.

"No!" There was no way Paige was leaving her family and Shane's attorneys here alone. There was no fixing this situation. The best she could hope for was damage control and she could only do that if she was present. She tightened her scarf, feeling as if it were a noose around her throat. Returning her attention to the menu, she said, "The grilled tuna sounds good, don't you think?"

"Mr. Turner, you were about to tell us about your experiences with the diamond mines," Mr. Biggs reminded her father.

"Call me Bertie," her father replied.

"You know I don't like that nickname," Coco said.

Meanwhile Paige was trying to give her father some kind of discreet sign that he was to be on his best behavior. But her father was too wrapped up in the prospect of telling one of his stories to pay her much attention.

"Maybe the veal would be better," Paige said, still trying to get everyone's attention on to the menu.

"Better than my diamond mine story?" her father said. "Not likely."

"Would you care for a drink?" their waiter enquired. Paige was so relieved at the interruption she almost jumped up and kissed him.

"Yes, I'll have a Bloody Mary."

"It's the middle of the day," her grandmother said, looking at Paige as if she'd lost her mind. "Since when have you started drinking in the middle of the day?"

Great. Now the Huntington lawyers would think she was a drunk. "I don't usually drink at all. That is, naturally I drink. Everyone drinks. Water, fruit juices, tea, that sort of thing. I don't drink a lot of alcohol."

"What would you consider to be a lot?" Mr. Bottoms enquired.

Sure, *now* the quiet partner had to speak up. "I don't know." How much was a lot? "A bottle a day?"

"So you drink less than a bottle of alcohol a day?"

That didn't sound too good. "I only have a glass once or twice a week, that's all," she hurriedly assured him.

"My dear, you're sounding very defensive," her grandmother informed her.

"Why is that?" Mr. Bottoms asked Paige.

"Because you're making me feel as if I were on the witness stand," Paige said, getting even more flustered.

"And why is that a bad thing?" Mr. Bottoms enquired. "If you have nothing to hide…?"

You're a Turner of Toledo, Shane had told her this morning. You eat lawyers for breakfast. Yeah, right. "I have nothing to hide." Except for the stubble burns on her throat and breasts. Paige placed a guilty hand on the silk scarf.

Mr. Bottoms noted her body language. "So you don't have a drinking problem, is that what you're saying?"

Paige nodded. "Yes."

"Yes, you do have a drinking problem?" the attorney pressed.

"No, I mean yes, I'm saying I don't have a drinking problem."

In unison, everyone at the table frowned at Paige's bumbling statement.

Panic-stricken, she felt as if she'd stumbled into a *Saturday Night Live* sketch where everyone knew the script but her.

"Did you have a drink before you came here today?" Mr. Biggs asked her gently.

"No, I most certainly did not!" Although if I'd known I was coming here or that my family would be here, I might have, she thought to herself.

"Can we get back to my diamond mine story?" her father demanded, unhappy at being left out of the limelight so long.

"Doesn't anyone else want a drink?" Paige asked, tilting her head at the still-waiting waiter.

"You know I never partake of alcoholic beverages until after five in the evening," her grandmother stated.

"If it will make you feel better, I'll have a gin and tonic on the rocks," her father said.

"No!" Page exclaimed. Her father did not handle alcohol well. Get one drink in him and his stories became even more outrageous than usual. "No, that's okay. I'll have an iced tea instead of that Bloody Mary," Paige decided.

"Wise move," her grandmother congratulated her.

"So," her father said, his blue eyes gleaming, "I'm in South Africa, speaking to the mining minister when..."

"I'M GOING TO KILL HIM," Paige told Esma. Her voice was calm and filled with conviction as they stood on the terrace outside the country club's elegant Palmer Room where the wedding was to take place tomorrow. "There's no need to have this wedding rehearsal because I'm going to kill Shane. He's fifteen minutes late already, you know. His family's attorneys kept me at lunch so long that I didn't even have time to go home and change. I don't think it bodes well that I'm wearing my black funeral suit to my own wedding rehearsal, do you?"

"There now, stay calm." Esma patted her shoulder. "Would you like a sip of my wine?"

"I'd like to drink an entire bottle, but the Huntington family attorneys already think I'm a drunk."

Esma stared at her in disbelief. "Where would they get a wild idea like that?"

"From my bumbling performance at lunch."

Esma frowned in confusion. "You were performing at lunch?"

"They were grilling me and I got nervous."

"Come on, how bad could it be?"

"An hour ago my father claimed he personally found the largest blue diamond in the world."

Esma's eyes widened. "You didn't tell me your father did that."

"Because he didn't," Paige returned in an agitated undertone. "He loves to tell stories and he tends to exaggerate. He reads an article in *National Geographic* and presto he's a diamond expert. He read about archeology in the Smithsonian and suddenly he's telling people he's a consultant to the museum in Cairo."

"Oh, my." Esma's expression turned sympathetic.

"Oh, my is right. That's why I was so relieved that he was with my grandmother in Europe and wouldn't be here for all of this."

"You didn't want your family here for the wedding?"

"I would have if it was a normal wedding, but it's not." She stared out at the rest of the gathering—her father and grandmother and Shane's lawyers—with sleep-deprived eyes. "Nothing about this day has been normal."

As if on cue a man wearing a trench coat and a Cubs baseball cap suddenly popped out from behind one of the large potted schleffera that edged the terrace.

"Here now, young man," Paige's grandmother called out. "That trench coat is not proper attire for a gathering of this sort." Marching over, she said, "Paige, is this the man you're about to marry? He not only shows up late for his wedding rehearsal, but he shows up naked as well? Oh, do cover yourself up," she impatiently told the flasher. "You've got nothing there to be proud of."

"That is not Shane," Paige said, hurrying to protect her grandmother as a group of police officers suddenly swarmed the veranda. "*That's* Shane." She pointed to him as he slapped a pair of handcuffs on the man in the trenchcoat.

"Hi, honey," Shane called out to her with one of his trademark smiles. "Sorry I'm late."

Not as sorry as you're going to be, Paige vowed after seeing the smudge of brilliant red lipstick on his cheek.

11

PAIGE HAD TO GET AWAY before she did something crazy, like take the bowl of fruit punch from the terrace and dump it over Shane's head. She could feel the rate of her breathing escalating. Asking Esma to take care of things, she bolted for the relative peace and security of the ladies' room.

It was a lovely space, all pink marble and gilded mirrors and tasteful floral arrangements. Maybe she'd stay here permanently.

Sinking onto one of the velvet-covered stools, she covered her face with her hands and wondered when her life had gotten so wild? The answer was simple. The moment Shane had walked into it.

"I heard you were hyperventilating in the ladies' room."

It was Shane's voice and it sounded very close. Surely he hadn't...

Her eyes flew open. But he had. He'd invaded the inner sanctity of the High Grove Country Club ladies' room.

Her gaze darted around the room to see if there were any other women present. There weren't. At least not yet. "You can't be in here!" she said in a scandalized voice.

"Sure I can," he said, strolling over to her.

"What if someone walks in?"

"I've got Koz stationed right outside the door with instructions not to let anyone past him. He's a cop, he can handle the assignment." He came closer to rub her back soothingly. "You want to talk to me, tell me what's going on?"

"You know," she said in an unsteady voice, "I thought I left Toledo to get away from the embarrassment of my broken engagement, but now I realize that I also left to get away from my family. I'm too quiet for my father and too wild for my grandmother. Remember how in *Goldilocks and the Three Bears* one bed was too big and one was too small but one was just right?"

"Okay, I was with you in the beginning," he admitted, "but now I have no idea what you're talking about."

Of course he didn't know. He'd never longed to be somebody's "just right." He was born perfect. She socked his arm as anger rocketed through her. "You have no idea what you've put me through today!" she shouted at him. "And then you have the nerve to show up late for your own wedding rehearsal! Or did you only show up to arrest that naked man in the trench coat?"

"Do you know how long we've been after the Cubs Flasher?"

"Look at me," she said somewhat hysterically. "Do I look like I care? Trust me, I've got bigger problems right now than some stupid flasher. My family showed up."

"I know."

Her eyes narrowed dangerously, her redheaded anger skyrocketing. "You knew your family's attorneys were flying my family in, and you didn't warn me?"

"No," he said, quickly stepping back and holding up his hands as if to ward off an attack. "I just meant that I saw them out on the terrace. Your grandmother and father, right?"

"Right. And we just went through the lunch from hell with your Big Bottom attorneys."

His lips twitched. "Actually the firm's name is Bottoms, Biggs and Bothers," Shane said, trying to keep a straight face.

"Well, they certainly bothered me all right," Paige muttered. "They think I'm an alcoholic."

"Where would they get a crazy idea like that?"

"From me."

He frowned in confusion. "Why would you tell them you were an alcoholic?"

"I didn't tell them that," she said in exasperation. "They just assumed it because I ordered a Bloody Mary at lunch."

"Look," he began in that tone that men have been using against irrational women since the beginning of time, "I know this must have been a rough day for you…"

"You have no idea. And don't go using that condescending male voice on me." She angrily jabbed her index finger at his chest. "Where did you get that smear of lipstick on your face?"

Looking into the mirror, Shane swore and grabbed a paper towel to wipe the incriminating evidence away. Somehow he didn't think it would help matters to tell Paige that while she was being grilled by the Huntington attorneys, he was being given a lap-dance by an exotic dancer for his bachelor party.

"It was police business," he said. Which was sort of true. The party hadn't been his idea. He'd thought he was at Al's Tavern for police business.

"More like monkey business, it seems to me." Arms akimbo, she stood and glared at him. "I heard your friend Koz asking you if you liked Bitsy's performance. Did she look good in a thong?"

"Would you get over this thong thing?" Shane demanded in exasperation. "Okay, if you must know the guys from the station threw me a surprise bachelor party. I had no idea they were going to do that. I really thought I was being called in because of the Cubs Flasher case, just like I told you this morning. Then Bitsy showed up. I tried to tell Koz that this wasn't a good time for me to have a bachelor party, but he cuffed me and I was stuck."

"You poor thing," she cooed sharply. "Stuck with an exotic dancer named Bitsy. What color was her thong?"

"Actually it was leopard print, but..."

"Too bad she didn't have red hair or you could have married her tomorrow. No, wait, your lawyers probably wouldn't approve of a stripper, now would they? Too bad.''

"Are you jealous of Bitsy? I swear I never met the woman before today. And I want you to know that I did not enjoy her performance."

"How sad for you." Her voice was distinctly sarcastic.

"I kept wishing I was with you."

Shane's husky words hit her like a sucker punch. There he was giving her that I'm-in-trouble-but-you-love-me-anyway look, tilting his head down and then smiling slowly as his gaze met hers.

She started hyperventilating again. What had she gotten herself into here? She'd fallen in love with a charmer. She was supposed to be marrying him to help the kids at Hope House, not because she wanted him in her bed. And what about that? Whose bed would they be sleeping in after tomorrow? They'd never even gotten around to discussing the practical details.

"Where will we live?" she demanded, her voice unsteady and thready and thick with panic. "We're getting married tomorrow and we never even talked about where we'll live."

"Wherever you want. I'm not picky."

Not picky? She stared at him in dismay and felt her oxygen supply depleting even further. Was that why Shane was marrying her? Because he wasn't picky, even if his grandfather's will was?

But if that was the case, she silently reminded herself, then he could have chosen Scarlet or Kate or the other women he'd dated. The ones who *bothered* him.

"Now what are you thinking?" Shane asked cautiously.

She wasn't about to confront him about his feelings for her at this point. She was already feeling vulnerable enough as it was. But there were plenty of things she was worrying about, so she easily picked one of them. "Our cats. Our cats might fight if we move in together."

"Puck is too lazy to fight. He gets along with everyone. Come on, this isn't really about our cats is it? Tell me what's wrong? Are you getting cold feet?"

"And hands." She held them out to him. "Here, feel."

Her fingers were indeed ice-cold. But they didn't remain that way for long as Shane lifted them to his mouth and kissed them, warming them with his breath.

"Are you getting warmer?" he murmured against her skin as his tongue flicked the sensitive pulse at the inside of her wrist.

"A little."

He slid his mouth up her arm, kissing the inside juncture of her elbow before moving on to the top of her arm, moving swiftly now to undo the silk scarf around her neck in order to caress the base of her throat before focusing on her lips. It seemed like ages since he'd kissed her that morning.

He must have felt the same way because he was kissing her as if he hadn't seen her in decades, as if he were a soldier returning from war, as if he needed her as much as he needed air or water. His touch evoked a remembered intimacy of moments shared last night and sparked a firestorm of passion.

Before Paige knew what had happened, she found herself perched on the edge of the marble counter, her legs parted as Shane pressed against her. Turning her head to the side to allow him better access to the curve of her throat, she saw their reflections in the huge lighted mirror behind her. She was surprised that the mirror wasn't all fogged up from the steamy passion they were generating. Then he was kissing her parted lips again and all thought ceased, replaced by pure sensation.

The marble beneath her thighs was cold and hard, Shane's body was hot and hard. His hand was sliding beneath the hem of her short black skirt—she hadn't had time to change from her funeral suit.

Then she heard the one sound that could have distracted her from the depths of desire. The sound of her grandmother's raised voice right outside the door.

"What do you mean I can't go into the ladies' room? Move aside, young man. My granddaughter is in there, and I'm going in whether you like it or not!" This declaration was followed by a decisive thump.

"Oh, no!" Paige gasped as she scooted away from Shane. "My grandmother has decked your best friend with her cane."

"I've done no such thing," Coco declared from inside the spacious ladies' room. "And I won't even ask what you're doing sitting on that countertop, Paige. But whatever it is, it can wait. You and I clearly have to have a little talk about wedding rehearsal decorum."

Shane stepped forward and gallantly took all the

blame by saying, "Mrs. Turner, I'm Shane Huntington and this is all my fault."

"Tell me something I don't know," Coco retorted, not the least bit impressed by his charming smile.

"I'm so sorry for being late for the rehearsal and for not being able to join you at lunch," Shane said apologetically.

"I understand you were being entertained by a stripper at the time," Coco retorted.

Shane vowed that he was going to kill Koz. "Well, actually she was an exotic dancer and the guys at the department were responsible for that."

"For her being an exotic dancer?" Coco asked.

"No. For my being there. They'd thrown me a surprise bachelor party."

"And the man in the trench coat at your rehearsal?" Coco demanded. "Was he a friend of yours?"

"No, ma'am. I'm very sorry you were exposed to that."

Coco sniffed disapprovingly. "In my day men didn't go around is such a state of undress."

"In this day, it's illegal to go around in such a state."

Thumping her cane, Coca said, "Well, young man, why should I let you marry my granddaughter tomorrow?"

"Grandmama," Paige protested, a blush reddening her face.

"Be quiet, Paige. I'm speaking to your fiancé. I've spoken to his attorneys, so I believe I have the right to get an answer from him directly. So, young man, I'll ask you again. Why should I let you marry my granddaughter tomorrow?''

"Because it's the right thing to do."

She thumped her cane again, this time in approval. "And rightly so. If you'd gotten all maudlin and vowed you loved her, I would have dismissed your words as I should have dismissed her last fiancé's words."

"My *last* fiancé?" Paige said. "You make it sound like I've had a dozen. And why shouldn't he love me?" The question was out of her mouth before she could stop it.

"Because love doesn't last. Honor does. Remember that, Paige, and you'll lead a productive life." Coco patted her cheek. "Now come along, we've got a rehearsal to complete. What is it those theater people say? A bad rehearsal means a good opening performance? Let's certainly hope so."

It had to be the full moon, Paige decided as she followed her grandmother. There was no other explanation for the craziness of today.

Maybe it also explained why she thought she loved Shane. Maybe she'd wake up tomorrow and be over it, be over him.

It could happen.

In a million years...maybe.

"TELL ME AGAIN WHY WE CAN'T elope?" Paige leaned close to desperately whisper to Shane as they sat at a long table in the upscale La Traviata restaurant where his parents were hosting the rehearsal dinner. Everyone from the wedding party was there, including a flower girl and ring bearer that Paige had never seen before and had no prior knowledge of.

Her family was there, her father speaking to Shane's father, telling him his Etruscan gold story while Shane's mother was listening intently to Paige's grandmother talk about heaven knew what. Paige wasn't close enough to hear, she only knew she was becoming increasingly filled with dread.

"We can't elope because the guys at Bottoms, Biggs and Bothers probably wouldn't consider an elopement to be a proper wedding and it might put the inheritance at risk," Shane replied. "We certainly don't want to do anything to mess things up at this late date."

"Listen, I'm really worried about how that meeting with the attorneys went earlier today," she confessed, her voice anxious. "I'm telling you, it was a disaster. My father tends to...uh...exaggerate his roles in the stories he tells. That makes him the life of all the parties back in Toledo, but those two attorneys did not look amused. I tried to let my father know that this wasn't the time nor place for his storytelling antics, but that didn't work. What if I messed everything up?"

"So your dad never worked for the FBI as he told me on the way over here?" Shane said with a teasing smile.

"Only for a month and only on a consulting basis regarding their computerized payroll system."

"There's no law against embellishing the truth a little. You worry too much." Shane squeezed her shoulders reassuringly. "I think our families are getting along amazingly well. I've never seen my mother bond with anyone the way she has with your grandmother,'' he noted, his voice reflecting his amazement and relief. ''It's really quite incredible.''

So he thought her grandmother was incredible? Nice. Too bad he couldn't say the same thing about her.

Remembering a question she'd been meaning to ask him, she said, ''Do your parents know what you plan on doing with the money once you get it?''

He shook his head. ''I haven't told them, and they haven't asked. I suspect that they're so glad their oldest son in marrying someone suitable—''

''As opposed to someone who looks good in a thong,'' she interjected.

''—that they don't care about the details,'' he continued. ''When are you going to let go of that thong thing?''

''When you do. Did I tell you that your mother mentioned her concerns about you at her birthday party?''

Shane rolled his eyes. ''Did she try to get you to pressure me to leave the police department?''

''Sure, but she saw that wasn't going to work. She did tell me that she feared you'd end up marrying a stripper someday.''

''Jeez, thanks, Mom,'' he said with a wry shake of his head. ''I don't believe her. And I sure hope you didn't believe her.''

''Sometimes I don't know what to believe,'' Paige admitted before a yawn caught her by surprise. Today's events combined with last night's lack of sleep was catching up to her and she was having a hard time keeping her eyes open.

"So where are you two going on your honeymoon?" her father asked them.

"To bed," Shane replied. "In fact, I think we should all head to our own beds right now. We've all had a long day."

To which her father said, "The longest day I ever had was on a trip I once took to Madagascar..."

"MMM," PAIGE MOANED, "I think I've died and gone to heaven."

"I told you it was a good idea for you to have a massage this morning," Esma said from beyond the curtain separating her booth from the one where Paige was having her massage. "Every bride should start her wedding day at the ritzy High Grove Health Spa."

"So should every maid of honor," Paige replied.

"Which is why we're both here this morning. This way we can start out relaxed instead of stressed and tired."

Last night Paige had been so exhausted that she'd fallen asleep as soon as her head hit the pillow. Shane had not stayed the night and they hadn't made love again.

"You're tensing up again," the masseuse told Paige.

"Sorry," she murmured. And she was. Sorry that she and Shane hadn't been able to spend the night together. It might have helped to lessen her fears. On the other hand, a second night without sleep would have left her looking like a zombie walking down the aisle today.

Ah, but what a way to go. The wicked thought crossed her mind and made her smile.

The beauty routine continued back at Paige's apartment, where Zorra was waiting with a suitcase filled with makeup.

Seeing the huge array of pots and colors, Paige became nervous. "Uh, it's nice of you to offer to do this for me, Zorra, but…"

"She's afraid you're going to do her up with enough stage makeup to look like Madam Butterfly," Esma cheerfully inserted, munching on a celery stick.

Zorra frowned. "Why would I want to do that? You have no faith," she reprimanded Paige. "You need to trust that things will be beautiful and they will be."

If only it were that easy, Paige thought to herself. But she vowed to try to have more faith that today would go smoothly. It seems that was all it took to make it come true. The makeup was perfect and the swirly curls Zorra created made Paige's hair more beautiful than she'd ever seen it.

And then there was the dress—a vision in white satin and tulle. It was a dream come true. The wide satin straps showed off her pale shoulders while the fitted bodice accentuated her breasts. The ball-gown skirt cascaded down to her ankles with billowy perfection.

Zorra and Esma hadn't let Paige look in a mirror until they were completely done with their magic. Staring at herself, she almost couldn't believe her own eyes. Paige actually reached out to touch her mirror image, as if to confirm that this really was her.

"I don't know what to say," she whispered.

"Say you're happy."

Turning to Zorra, she said, "I'm ecstatic. And awe-struck by your talent."

Zorra beamed then frowned. "Now let's just hope we can leave without your animals ruining this dress."

"Now you're the one without any faith," Paige teased her. "I fed Simon and Schuster tuna, and they're camped out on the living room couch for their daylong nap."

Looking out the window, Esma said, "The limo is here." She looked elegantly gorgeous in her peach-colored bias-cut chiffon gown.

"Do you have everything?" Zorra asked. "The shoes?"

"Check," Paige confirmed, sticking out her foot.

"Jewelry?"

Paige fingered the choker pearl necklace and match-ing earrings her grandmother had given her last night before leaving the restaurant. "Check."

"Gloves?"

"Check," Paige and Esma both said, as they held up the elbow length white gloves they planned on wearing for the ceremony.

"I'm missing something," Zorra fretted. "I know, the veil!"

"I'm already wearing it," Paige reminded her. The short veil, aptly named a blusher veil, would be worn over her face as she walked down the aisle and lifted by Shane during the ceremony. For now it was already raised away from her face.

"We'd best be off," Esma said. "See you there, Zorra."

As Paige left her apartment, it hit her that this was the last time she'd be doing so as a single woman. Then there was no time to think at all as the white stretch limo whisked them off to the High Grove Country Club. Once there, Paige got a quick peek at the Palmer Room, now transformed with rows of white slip-covered chairs and floral swags of full-blown peach-colored roses, white hydrangeas and peonies. A string quartet, Shane's mother's idea, was quietly playing at the front of the room. Guests were already arriving, so Paige and Esma quickly moved down the hallway to the small anteroom set aside for the use of the bridal party.

Esma saw Paige safely ensconced there, then hurried off for a quick check with her staff on the food for the reception afterward, being held in the neighboring Masters Ballroom. "I'll only be a moment," Esma promised before leaving. "You'll be all right without me for that long, won't you?"

"I'll be fine," Paige assured her.

And she was. For the first few minutes. Then the sound of raised voices caught her attention. Especially once she recognized one of the voices belonged to Shane.

Moving closer to the far wall, she could hear them clearly—Shane and his father. In the room next door. Talking about *her*.

"What do you mean the attorneys won't accept Paige?" Shane yelled angrily. "She fulfills every one of those stupid requirements on the damn Huntington list!"

"Apparently Biggs and Bottoms didn't agree. They

don't regard her family, although wealthy and well-connected, as being respectable enough. They thought
you'd take the news better coming from me.''

''You mean they were afraid to tell me the news
themselves, the cowards. I can't believe you're telling
me this now. The wedding is only a few minutes away.''

''Do you want me to tell Paige…?''

''Tell her what?'' Shane interrupted. ''I don't care
what the lawyers say, I'm not going to stand her up now.
To hell with Biggs and Bottoms, I'm marrying Paige
anyway. I'm not walking out on her.''

No, he wouldn't. Shane was an honorable man. She
heard the door slam and then silence.

Paige felt strangely calm. Once again she was the one
who didn't fit in, the one who was judged and somehow
found lacking. She knew what had to be done. And she
knew that she had to do it. Because she wasn't going
to make Shane go through with this marriage. It meant
she'd have to walk out on him, but not without an explanation. She'd act bright and cheerful, as if her heart
wasn't breaking, as if none of this mattered to her.

''There now, that didn't take long, did it,'' Esma said
in a breathless rush as she returned to Paige's side. ''The
ballroom looks wonderful, lined with greenery twinkling
with fairy lights. Shane had them copy the decorating
theme from the Windy City Ball. Wait until you see it.''

''I'm not going to see it,'' Paige said, her voice crack-
ing with strain. ''I'm canceling this wedding.''

''What?'' Esma gasped. ''What are you talking
about?''

"I just heard Shane and his father talking in the room next door. The family attorneys didn't approve of me."

"Not approve of you?" Esma repeated in disbelief. "Are they crazy?"

"I don't have time to argue about this, Esma. I have to call a halt to this wedding before it's too late."

"But it's already too late. The guests are already all gathered in the Palmer Room. Shane and his best man are already there. Your dad's right outside, waiting to escort you down the aisle. Do you want me to send him in, so he can have a word with you?"

"No, he'd just tell me about the time he attended Prince Andrew and Fergie's wedding, which is actually one of his true stories."

"What are you going to do?" Esma demanded as Paige strode toward the door.

"I already told you. I'm going to call this thing off right now, while I've still got the nerve."

"Wait," Esma urged her. "Think about this a minute or two…"

"No!" Paige's voice trembled before she quickly regained control. "If I do that, I might be tempted to take advantage of the fact that Shane is an honorable man who won't go back on his promise and ignore the fact that he doesn't love me. No, I've got to do this and I've got to do it now!"

Freeing herself from Esma's hold, Paige breezed right on past her father. "Hold on," he boomed. "Aren't I supposed to be walking with you for this bit?"

As Esma explained the change of plans to Paige's father, Paige headed straight for the entrance leading to the Palmer Room and her wedding. A wedding that wasn't to be.

Opening the door just enough so that she could pop her head through, she nervously said, "Hi, everyone. Could I have your attention, please?" No one heard her above the sound of the string quartet. Raising her voice, she shouted, "Could you stop the music please?" Dead silence. Blind panic on her part. *Stay calm. Be cheerful.* "Thank you. Hi, everyone," she said in an artificially bright voice as every face in the room turned to stare at her. Her face was flushed, no doubt beet-red by now. "I'm sorry you all had to come out here for nothing today, but the wedding is off and you...you should all go home."

There was an immediate murmur of curious voices and several people restlessly got to their feet when Shane ordered in his best cop voice, "Nobody move!"

12

PAIGE TRIED TO MAKE A QUICK getaway, but somehow she'd hooked her veil on something along the doorframe. While she frantically tried to free it, Shane came marching down the aisle until he was only a few feet away. "What's going on here?" he demanded, his hands on his hips, his usually laughing brown eyes glaring at her.

How dare he be mad at her. She was trying to do him a favor here. Couldn't the blockhead see that? "I *know*," she said, trying to convey her awareness of the situation without giving more fodder for gossip to the high society crowd watching and listening in.

"Know what?" he said.

"About the situation. With the attorneys," she added in an undertone. "I know you don't have to marry me."

"I know I don't have to marry you." He gave her his patented but-you-love-me-anyway look. "I *want* to marry you."

She nodded understandingly. "Because you're an honorable man."

"Because I love you," he quietly said with one of his most charming smiles.

She sighed. "Now you're just being nice."

Completely engrossed, the guests watched and listened with unabashed curiosity.

"Nice?" Shane repeated in amazement. "I finally declare my love for you and you say I'm being nice?"

"He doesn't really love me." Paige felt compelled to tell the guests.

They nodded understandingly, at least the women did.

"I do so love her," Shane told them, and her. "I realize that I should have told you earlier."

"That might have been a good idea," Esma said from behind Paige, her acerbic British accent delighting the crowd.

"Hey, it's not easy for me to reveal my emotions," Shane growled. "And, trust me, doing so in front of all these stuffed shirts is not my idea of a good time. But I'm doing it because I love you."

"Shane, you really don't have to do this." Paige patted his arm reassuringly before telling the woman seated on the aisle in the last row, "It's because he has an overdeveloped sense of responsibility. You might not realize that, Mr. and Mrs. Huntington," she said, addressing her comments now to his stunned parents at the front of the room. "But your son is a very honorable man. Do you know what he was going to do with that million dollars he would have inherited if the attorneys had approved of me? He was going to donate it, all of it, to a place called Hope House. Hi, Sheila," Paige added, spotting the director in the third row. "I'm sorry this didn't work out. Maybe there's still a way we can raise the money…"

"I've already arranged to raise the money," he said, interrupting her.

"You did? How?"

"I'm giving it to him," S.F. said. "His inheritance money reverts back into the family estate. When my son finally had the sense to talk to me about his plans, I pointed that fact out to him. The family agrees that in our opinion you would make Shane a wonderful wife and the attorneys are misguided for not giving their approval. We also agree that Hope House is a worthy project. So Shane will still get the money, and it will still go to that charity."

"That's great," Paige said, glad that some good was still coming out of this mess. "But he doesn't have to marry me to get the money if you're giving it to him."

"I could make that a requirement if you like," S.F. said.

"No," Paige immediately and forcefully replied. "I would not like that, thank you. Well, if you'll all excuse me, I really must be going now…"

"I'm telling you, Paige Turner, I'm not marrying you because I have to," Shane shouted in exasperation. "I'm marrying you because I love you. Really. I'm not being nice here. When have you ever known me to be nice?"

"You're nice most of the time," she replied. "Isn't that right, Sheila?"

"I'd have to agree," Sheila said. "Only the nicest of men would donate a million dollars to helping others."

"Okay forget nice." Shane's voice had gone from

exasperated to panicked. "Just listen to me, Paige. I love you because you wear fuzzy bunny slippers and have no idea how adorable they make you look. I love you because of your generous heart and your luscious mouth. I love you despite the fact that you don't like hockey. And don't you dare even mention the thong thing. Remember how in *Goldilocks and the Three Bears* one bed is too small and one is too big and one is just right? Well, I finally get it, okay? To me you're just right. You've got to marry me!"

His almost incoherent tumble of words went straight to her heart. Finally! Finally she believed him. This wasn't her smooth-talking charmer here. This was Shane, really telling her that she was just right, that he really loved her. She wasn't dreaming this, this was really, really, *really* happening to her!

It was only as she threw her arms around Shane to kiss him and say yes she would marry him that she realized what he'd done. Her husband-to-be, the man who loved her, had just handcuffed her to him!

"I'm not letting you get away," Shane warned her. "You're the best thing that's ever happened to me and I want to be the best thing that's ever happened to you."

"I thought you were supposed to save the handcuffs for the honeymoon," her father mockingly called out from the doorway behind them. "Are we going to have a wedding here today or not?"

"Yes, we're having a wedding," Paige said, blinking away the tears of happiness from her eyes. "A wedding between two people who love each other. Because I love you, too, Shane.''

"Save the kissing for after the ceremony," her father said. "And undo these handcuffs while you're at it."

Smiling at Paige as if she were his reason for living, Shane reached into his pocket for the key. It wasn't there. Turning to his best friend and best man, he said, "Okay, Koz, the joke is over. Hand over the key."

"Hey, I may have given you the handcuffs as a joke, but when I did I also gave you the key. I don't have it."

"You're joking, right?"

"I'm serious," Koz maintained.

Thumping her cane imperiously, Paige's grandmother proclaimed, "Let's get this show on the road. At this rate I'll be a hundred before you two say your I do's."

And so it was that Shane and Paige were married, bound together not only by their vows to each other but also by a pair of handcuffs.

It wasn't until they were at the reception afterward that Coco finally came forward with the missing key. "I wasn't taking any chances on any more delays in that wedding," the older woman regally declared.

"Life is filled with chances," Paige told her grandmother, kissing her cheek. "I've finally learned that sometimes it's worth the risk you take."

"You still think loving me is a risk?" Shane protested as he slipped his arm around Paige's waist. Tipping her chin up so that he could gaze into her eyes, he murmured, "Don't you know that my love for you is a sure thing?"

She smiled at him. "I thought I'd give you the next thirty years to convince me."

"Thirty years, hmm? That's not much time. I better start convincing you right now." And he did, by kissing her.

The Matchmaker's Mistake

Jane Sullivan

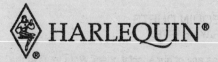

TORONTO • NEW YORK • LONDON
AMSTERDAM • PARIS • SYDNEY • HAMBURG
STOCKHOLM • ATHENS • TOKYO • MILAN • MADRID
PRAGUE • WARSAW • BUDAPEST • AUCKLAND

Dear Reader,

I've always loved transformation stories: The superhero
hiding behind the horn-rimmed glasses, Eliza Dolittle
blossoming into My Fair Lady, Cinderella rising from
oppressed stepsister to the object of Prince Charming's
affection.

The Matchmaker's Mistake is such a story—with a twist.
What if a woman with matchmaking tendencies helped
an ambitious professional man make the transformation
from ordinary to extraordinary so he could attract the
woman of his dreams? What if she then realized that
she'd fallen in love with the man she'd created? Would
he ever see that the matchmaker herself might be his
perfect match?

I hope you enjoy *The Matchmaker's Mistake*. Please
visit me at my Web site at www.janesullivan.com, or
write to me at jane@janesullivan.com. I'd love to hear
from you!

Best regards,

Jane Sullivan

Books by Jane Sullivan

HARLEQUIN DUETS
33—STRAY HEARTS

For my beautiful daughter, Charlotte
Kanga and Roo forever!

1

"HEY, MCALISTER. Did you hear the news?"

Mark McAlister looked up from the balance sheets scattered across his desk. When he saw Jared Sloan swaggering into his office, he wished he'd locked the door and booby-trapped it for good measure. Monday mornings were bad enough for Mark without being subjected to Sloan before he'd even had his second cup of coffee.

Sloan stopped in front of Mark's desk, folding his arms across his chest in the casual yet commanding pose of a man who thought he ruled the world. Mark had no time for gossip, but if he didn't ask, Sloan would never leave.

"What news is that?"

"Carson Industries. They're signing with us this morning."

It took every ounce of self-control Mark had to keep his shock from showing on his face. Last Friday he'd given Jack Carson a presentation to show how Carson Industries was needlessly throwing away hundreds of thousands of dollars every year in taxes. He'd approached the issue with logic and reason, but Carson had frowned his way through most of the presentation, then left the office with a noncommittal "I'll get back to you." Mark had been around long enough to know what that meant: *Don't call me. I'll call you.*

Had he read Carson wrong? Had he finally won a client through a clear, concise presentation of the facts? He felt a rush of satisfaction, his heart beating double time.

"That's good," he told Sloan, trying not to let his relief show. "Of course, I assumed Carson would say yes after he had a chance to think about the numbers. We can save him a bundle with those tax credits I proposed, and that environmental loophole—"

"The numbers? Are you kidding?" Sloan burst into laughter. "Any accounting firm in Dallas can throw numbers on a page, McAlister. I took a different approach."

Mark froze, dread washing over him. Not again. This couldn't be happening *again*. He could barely spit out the words. "*You* got him to sign?"

"Yeah. With a little help from Tiffany, of course. Turns out she and Carson's wife were both Tri-Delts at Southern Methodist University, so Tiffany invited her and Carson to join us in Aspen for the weekend. It took my lovely wife less than an hour to find out that Carson's wife makes all the decisions in that family." Sloan gave him a superior smile. "It was all downhill from there."

Sloan's secret weapon. The Tiffany Connection.

Tiffany was the daughter of one of Dallas's most prominent neurosurgeons. She had a master's degree in anthropology. She belonged to the Junior League, and she was on the board of the Dallas Symphony. She was acquainted with movers and shakers all over the state of Texas, and she'd used that influence more than once to snag her husband a client.

Sloan gave Mark a big, phony grin. "I think this calls for a celebration, don't you? There'll be a bottle of bubbly floating around my office later on. Be sure to drop by."

At that moment it was all Mark could do not to vault over his desk, take Sloan by the throat and squeeze all that mocking condescension right out of him. It was bad enough that he horned in on every client Mark tried to sign. What was worse, he gloated about it—incessantly— then made Mark look like a bad sport for taking it personally.

"I've got work to do, Sloan. If you want to spend your day guzzling champagne, that's up to you."

"Aw, come on, McAlister! It's not important who's actually getting Carson to sign on the dotted line. This is a team effort, right?"

Team effort? What a joke. The day Sloan became a team player was the day hell became a winter wonderland.

"Don't worry," Sloan added. "I'm sure your contribution will be considered as much as mine when the new partnership is announced in a few months. After all, somebody's got to crunch those numbers, right?" He gave Mark an irritating little chuckle, then strolled out of his office.

Anger and resentment tore through Mark. He wanted that partnership so badly he could taste it, but it was going to be a damned hard thing to accomplish if Sloan continued to one-up him every step of the way. How was he ever going to outshine a phony ex-frat boy, who'd written the book on corporate ladder climbing, and his savvy, ambitious wife?

He strode out of his office to his secretary's desk. Tina Boyd had her hands on her computer keyboard, her fingers flying like mad. Her short, spiky blond hair and long pink fingernails made her a striking standout among her peers, but Mark wouldn't have traded her for anyone. She was a hundred pounds of pure secretarial dynamite, which left her plenty of time for her volunteer job as officer-in-charge of the rumor mill at Nichols, Marbury & White.

"Tina, can I ask you a question?"

"Sure, boss," she said, her fingers never ceasing their frantic tapping. "Shoot."

Mark lowered his voice. "The partnership. What's the grapevine telling you?"

Tina's fingers froze on the keyboard. She paused a moment, then lifted them off. She turned around in her chair to face him, her mouth falling into a sympathetic frown. "It doesn't look good for you."

That was exactly what he'd expected to hear, but still the words felt like an anvil settling on his chest.

"Almost everyone knows you're the best candidate," Tina added. "But that nasty Jared Sloan and his prissy wife won't get out of the way long enough for the big boys to see that."

Another fact he was painfully aware of.

"Actually," Tina continued, "from what I've been able to see, it's easy to become a partner at this company. All you have to do is turn yourself into a pushy, arrogant jerk and get yourself a woman who knows how to play the corporate social game, and you'll move right to the top of the list."

Mark gave her a wry smile. "Thanks for the tip. I'll get to work on it right away."

"You do, and you can find yourself another secretary."

"What? You don't want to be partner's secretary?"

"Not if the partner's a jerk." She stared at him a long time, her admonishing expression melting into concern. "You're a nice guy, Mark. Best boss I've ever had. Don't lose that for anything, okay?"

Yeah, and he knew exactly where nice guys finished. Dead last.

He went back into his office and shut the door. He leaned against it, his eyes closed, as that familiar wave of insecurity washed over him again—the one that told him a kid raised in a trailer park in Waldon Springs, Texas, population 937, couldn't possibly ascend to a partnership in one of the most prestigious accounting firms in the country.

But a guy like Sloan could.

Sloan came in late. He left early. He shoved work off on every other accountant in the firm, including the partners themselves. He was a lousy manager, driving most of his people to eventually hate the sight of him, and he routinely took credit for other people's accomplishments. But all of it was tolerated, because Sloan had one talent Mark had never been able to master.

He brought clients to the firm in droves.

As Mark stood in the quiet of his office, the echoes of his childhood vibrated inside his head. As one of the "poor folks" in town, he'd spent most of his early years ducking his head in shame, but as he grew older, he turned that shame into a motivating force that drove him to graduate near the top of his class. That had helped land him a college scholarship that paid part of his tuition. But still he'd had to work to pay the rest, leaving him no time for the social life his classmates took for granted. When he'd graduated and gone to work for Nichols, Marbury & White, he'd naturally assumed that hard work would have its reward. He neglected his social life to the point where he'd pretty much become a workaholic recluse.

How could he have been so blind?

At this firm, professional excellence meant more than being a good accountant. It meant poise and polish, wining and dining, and the man who made it to the very top of the ladder was not the one who masterminded the financial strategy that saved the client thousands in taxes, but the man who brought that client to the firm in the first place.

All these years while Mark had been working himself to death, guys with half his expertise, guys like Sloan, had been using his shoulders as a stepping stone to success. At the same time, they'd learned how to attract the right kind of women, women who were at their sides right now, helping push them to the top. Mark had never had anyone but himself to rely on when it came to playing the social game, and he wasn't even sure he knew the rules.

Then Tina's words popped into his mind again. *Turn*

yourself into a pushy, arrogant jerk and get yourself a woman who knows how to play the corporate social game....

Mark felt a jolt of sudden realization. Maybe Tina had been more right than she realized. He had no plans of turning into a pushy, arrogant jerk any time soon, but the woman thing...

Why hadn't he seen it before?

He froze for a moment as the thought took hold, then crossed to his window and looked down seven stories to the rush-hour crowd swirling along the busy downtown street.

She was out there somewhere. The woman who could help him meet every professional goal he had, and then some. A woman with elegance and refinement, who could mesmerize clients just by being in the same room. A woman would put him on the same plane as Sloan and every other guy at the firm who minored in accounting and majored in schmoozing.

Unfortunately, he had no idea how to go about attracting such a woman.

In Waldon Springs, you were considered a social success if you drank wine that didn't have a screw top and didn't pick your teeth at the dinner table. Mark's knowledge of the social graces had ascended a step or two above that over the years, but he still got queasy at the very thought of approaching a poised, confident, cultured woman.

Well, as of today, that was going to change.

The firm's annual dinner dance was in three weeks. If he showed up with a woman who glowed so brightly that she made his image skyrocket just by standing next to him, then the partners would start to see him as something other than a pencil-pushing number cruncher. They'd see him not as a guy in the trenches, but as a guy at the top. Partner material.

But first he had to find her.

Faced with that seemingly impossible task, his resolve should have wavered, but with each passing moment it only grew stronger. He hadn't gotten this far in life without plowing through insurmountable odds, and now that he realized the source of his problem, he wasn't about to turn down this challenge.

One way or another, he'd find the right woman. And when he did, he'd have every bit of the success he'd been striving for. And the memory of that boy he'd been in Waldon Springs so many years ago, the one who couldn't possibly cross to the right side of the tracks and make something out of his life, would never come back to haunt him again.

"I'LL BET YOU TEN BUCKS he doesn't go through with it."

Liz Prescott plunked olives into a pair of martinis and set the glasses onto Sherri's drink tray. "No way. I might as well *give* you ten bucks and call it quits. He's not going anywhere."

"Even if he did speak to her," Sherri said, grabbing a stack of cocktail napkins, "I doubt he'd get to first base."

Liz nodded. "A woman like that wouldn't even let him into the ballpark."

For the past thirty minutes, a guy sitting on the left side of the bar had been watching a pristine, wool-suited blonde sitting on the right side. Her manicure was perfect, her hair upswept in one of those sophisticated twists, and, even at the end of the day, her makeup still had that fresh, dewy finish Liz couldn't even manage to get first thing in the morning. Ms. Perfect chatted with the woman beside her in that haughty, cosmopolitan way that Liz hated, punctuating her conversation with the latest buzzwords and radiating an aura of arrogance a man would have to use a machete to whack his way through. Still, the guy couldn't take his eyes off her. He wore that hypervigilant expression that dated all the way back to prehistoric man—the one that said he'd found a woman worth slaying a mastodon for if only he could work up the nerve to say hello.

Simon's Bar and Grille attracted upwardly mobile young professionals who came here at happy hour to meet other upwardly mobile young professionals. Tending bar in this place was like being in the middle of one gigantic mating ritual, but apparently no one had let this guy in on how to play the game.

He was so unassuming that he practically melted into the wall, leaving Liz to wonder if he might get lost in a crowd of two. His suit was a nondescript gray, styleless and ultraconservative, that was further drabbed-down by a starched white shirt and solid burgundy tie. But it wasn't as if he had a pocket protector for his pens, or high-water pants or anything like that. He was actually okay-looking, with nice brown eyes behind those glasses, and thick, dark hair that would look great in the hands of the right stylist. But the women here could smell a lack of confidence at a hundred paces, and that blonde was no exception.

"He's kind of cute, though," Liz said. "Don't you think?"

"Yeah, but around here, cute doesn't cut it," Sherri answered. "Now, if he'd let her browse his financial portfolio first, or maybe wave the keys to a Jaguar under her nose, he might just have a chance."

Sherri's assessment of the situation was right on target. When Liz first started working here, the yuppie overload had just about driven her nuts. Every time a cell phone rang, a bunch of people dove into purses, pockets and planners. If the night was a little slow, she could count on doing her job by the hazy glow of a dozen laptop screens. And she'd never seen such a variety of credit cards in her life. Gold cards. Silver cards. Platinum cards. Photo cards. Holographic image cards. If someone had hauled out a card encrusted in diamonds with blinking neon lights, she wouldn't have been surprised.

But while the people here were not the type Liz would hang out with if she had a choice, they still fascinated her because people fascinated her, period. She was only a bartender now, but this fall she was starting college to pursue a degree in psychology. At twenty-seven she'd be a bit old to be a freshman, but it was better late than never.

Excitement burst through her at the very thought of becoming a clinical psychologist. Listening to people talk about their problems all day long and offering them sage and wonderful advice to put their lives back on track—did it get any better than that? In the meantime, what better place to practice her future profession than behind a bar?

"How many drinks does that make for him?" Sherri asked, as the subject of their prospective wager sucked down what was left of his scotch and water in one huge gulp.

"Two. Think it's enough to get him moving?"

"Nope."

But this time, when he set his glass down, a flicker of determination came over his face. Liz felt a glimmer of hope. Maybe he was finally going to make a move. Could this mean money in her pocket after all?

"I won't go ten," she told Sherri. "But I've got five that says he at least gets off the stool."

"Okay. You're on."

They watched furtively as Mr. Conservative straightened his tie, then patted his lapels. He placed his hands on the bar, his chest rising and falling as if he were inhaling a few deep breaths. Then he swung a leg to the side to rise from the stool.

"Ha!" Liz whispered. "There he goes. You owe me—"

But right in the middle of Liz's premature celebration, the guy froze. Liz turned a quick eye to the other end of the bar. Larry the Lounge Lizard had approached the blonde and was taking the stool beside her.

Larry, whose real name was Howard Something-or-Other, had earned his nickname by hitting on every living, breathing female who ventured through the door. Actually, breathing wasn't even a prerequisite. If someone were to bring an unconscious woman into the club, Larry would perform CPR, *then* hit on her. Liz had no doubt the blonde would eventually chew him up and spit him out, but right now, he was really screwing things up for the guy at the other end of the bar.

Liz turned back to the man she had her money on, and her worst fears were confirmed. As the guy watched Larry put the moves on the blonde, he glared at him for a few moments, then sat back down on the bar stool with what was clearly a muttered curse.

"Nope," Sherri said, flashing Liz a triumphant smile. "Looks like you owe *me*. Five bucks."

"But Larry got in the way!"

"Yeah, and the track was muddy, the blackjack dealer was crooked, and the referee made a bad call. So sad. Now, pay up."

Liz pulled five one-dollar bills from her apron pocket and slapped them into her friend's hand. "You're heartless, you know that?"

Sherri plucked out one of the bills and tucked it back into Liz's pocket. "Here. Play the lottery. But if you win, you'll have to split the millions with me, since I gave you—"

"Your customers are waiting for their drinks. Go!"

Sherri smiled. "Sore loser."

Liz grinned as Sherri scooped up the tray and headed to table six, where she dropped off another round of drinks to a pair of impeccably dressed twenty-something males. They were scanning the club nonstop, looking for those special women who could bear them two-point-five children without all that embarrassing weight gain.

"Miss?"

Liz turned to see Mr. Conservative holding up his empty highball glass. She poured him another scotch and water and set it down on the bar in front of him. He downed half of it and didn't even blink.

"Rough night?" Liz asked.

"You might say that."

She nodded over her shoulder. "You want to talk to that blonde at the end of the bar. Is that right?"

His eyes narrowed with suspicion, as if he thought she'd crawled inside his head and gone rummaging around. The truth was that anyone this side of blind could have read his I-gotta-have-her expression from halfway across the room.

He turned away. "No. I don't want to talk to anyone."

Liz leaned closer and lowered her voice. "Ignore that guy who's hitting on her right now. He talks a good game, but we don't call him Larry the Lounge Lizard for nothing. His mother dresses him from the department store where she works, and the only reason he drives a Mercedes is because his uncle owns a dealership."

"Why are you telling me this?"

"Because I don't want you to think he's competition."

He stared down at his drink. "Competition?"

Liz rolled her eyes. Denying his interest in that blonde was like Donald Trump denying his interest in real estate. She rested her forearms on the bar and looked him in the eye.

"Look. You've sat on that stool for the past thirty minutes, checking out that woman. If you don't make a move pretty soon, I'm gonna have to start charging you rent."

He shot her a look of irritation. "This is none of your business."

Liz smiled impishly. "Sure it is. You're sitting at my bar. Everything that goes on here is my business." She inched closer, raising her eyebrows expectantly. "So do you want to meet her or not?"

He gazed at the blonde. A look of longing entered his eyes, and Liz wondered if any man had ever looked at *her* like that. Finally he let out a breath of resignation. "Yes. I want to meet her. But she's occupied."

Liz glanced over her shoulder and saw Larry leaning closer to the blonde. While his drunken look practically screamed *Hey, baby, how about you and me doing the horizontal tango?* the blonde's expression said he was on the verge of getting a knee in the groin.

"I told you that guy's not a problem. Watch."

Right on cue, the blonde turned on her bar stool and met Larry face-to-face. She smiled sweetly with a cutesy, Barbie doll expression, but while Liz couldn't hear what she was saying, the look on Larry's face said her words were pure venom. Larry generally took rejection like a real trooper, but this time his eyes widened with surprise. He backed away one step, then two, then turned in a huff and stalked off. Liz had seen it coming, but, still, she was impressed. Most women had to whip out their cell phones and dial 911 to get rid of Larry.

Mr. Conservative gave Liz a look of total astonishment. "How did you know that?"

"Gosh, I don't know." She gave him a teasing smile. "I guess I must be psychic."

"Then why don't you look into the future and tell me what *my* chances are with her?"

Liz winced. If that blonde could make Larry turn tail and run, she probably had claws she hadn't even sharpened yet. This guy seemed nice. Why would he want to subject himself to a woman like that? Sure, she was beautiful, but it was a phony, put-on kind of beauty that was swimming in arrogance. Were men really that blind? Or did they truly not care what was inside the package as long as the wrapping was pretty?

Liz had never had any delusions about her own beauty, or sometimes, she thought, *lack* of beauty, but at least she'd never tried to be something she wasn't. She knew her bright auburn hair was too curly and wild, always sneaking out of the knot she gathered it in and cascading in ringlets around her face. Her figure, with breasts and hips a supermodel would run screaming from, was way too curvy to be fashionable. On the plus side, though, she had a pair of long, shapely legs that had stopped more than a few men in their tracks, and a smile that rivaled Julia Roberts's. She'd learned a long time ago to minimize her liabilities and play up her assets, which meant incarcerating her hair, wearing control-top panty hose, hemming her skirts another inch or two and smiling as often as possible.

"Why are you so fixated on her?" Liz asked.

"Her name is Gwen Adams. She manages a high-class art gallery on Ashworth Avenue. She went to Vassar, and she speaks three languages. And look at her. Not a hair out of place."

Liz automatically reached up to smooth down a few of her own more rebellious curls. "Then you already know her?"

"Not really. She's a friend of a friend."

"So you haven't actually spoken to her?"

"No. But trust me. She's perfect for me."

Oh, boy. This guy was a goner. Liz had seen infatuation before, but this was ridiculous.

One of the waitresses slapped a drink order on the bar. Liz held up a finger, telling the guy she wasn't through with him yet. She drew two beers and grabbed a sparkling water from the fridge, wondering what she could say to get it through to him that his dream woman was really a nightmare in disguise.

Oh, hell. Who was she to decide who belonged with whom? Even though she wouldn't have put the two of them together in a thousand years, love was a funny thing. She'd dated a string of men who'd looked really, really good, then turned out to be bums. Couldn't it work the other way, too? Maybe deep down, he and the Ice Princess were soul mates. If so, Liz had never been one to stand in the way of true love.

She put the mugs of beer and the bottle of glorified tap water on the tray and the waitress took them away. She returned to where the guy sat swirling his drink around in his glass.

Looking at him now, she decided she'd been a little hasty before in her assessment of him. He was more than just okay-looking. He had nice, broad shoulders that made his dull, boring suit look not so dull and boring. A pair of utilitarian horn-rimmed glasses dominated his face, but if he ever took them off, his strong facial features—a firm jaw, bold cheekbones and full, almost sensuous lips— could easily take center stage. And if he ever smiled, which he certainly hadn't tonight, she had the feeling it would light up the room brighter than a Vegas casino. If Gwen had any foresight at all, she just might be getting a diamond in the rough.

"So you want to know what your chances are with her?" Liz asked.

"Yes."

"Exactly zero if you don't get up off that stool, walk over there and introduce yourself."

"I will."

"Good."

"Just let me finish this drink first."

As exasperated as Liz was over his reluctance to take action, at the same time she couldn't ignore the tiny thrill that swept through her. The longer he sat there, the more obvious it became that if he wanted to get that woman's attention, he was going to need some help.

Her help.

People's problems naturally piqued Liz's interest, hence her interest in psychology. It was in her genetic makeup, just as her auburn hair and her green eyes were. Decades ago, her grandmother, Norma Prescott, had run a soda shop in Grand Rapids, Michigan, where she addressed typical problems on a daily basis. Family legend had it that after the stock market crash, she'd actually prevented one distraught customer from climbing the top of the ten-story building next door and taking one of those much-publicized free falls.

And then there was her mother, Laura Lee Prescott, who owned a hair salon in Big Fork, Texas. Even as a child, Liz had realized that the people who patronized her mother's place of business generally wanted more than a cut or a perm.

"I told him exactly what you said last week, Laura Lee. I told him it was time to poop or get off the pot. And guess what? We're getting married in June!"

"I kept my mouth shut about the twenty dollars she owed me, just like you said. Then I found out she'd stuck it into the pocket of my purse last week at bingo and forgot to tell me!"

"I thought you were nuts, Laura Lee. But I gave her a new clothes dryer on her birthday instead of perfume and flowers, and she said it was about time I gave her something to help out around the house instead of something silly and useless."

To Liz and everyone else in town, Laura Lee Prescott had been Dr. Joyce Brothers, Ann Landers and Sigmund Freud all rolled into one. Even as a child, Liz had stood in awe of the way people respected every word her mother uttered. And as Liz eased into womanhood, the tingle she felt inside every time she sensed a problem in her vicinity told her, without a doubt, that she was now the keeper of the family heritage. She was even taking things one step further than her mother and grandmother by getting a degree in psychology. Best of all, she intended to specialize in couples therapy. She couldn't imagine anything more satisfying than being an interim matchmaker, spending her days repairing broken relationships and bringing people back together again.

But right now, she had a different kind of matchmaking to attend to.

"Give me one of your business cards," she told the guy.

He looked at her warily. "Why?"

"Just do it."

He reached into the breast pocket of his coat and produced a business card. Liz took it from him, then tilted it slightly to read it in the dim light. Mark McAlister. Tax Accounting Manager. Nichols, Marbury & White, Certified Public Accountants. She sighed. Did it get any more boring than that?

Oh, well. She had to play the hand she was dealt. She stuck the card into her apron pocket and started toward the fridge.

"Wait," Mark said. "What are you doing?"

"Trust me," she said over her shoulder. "I'll get the door open, but you've got to walk through it. Now, pay attention."

"Hey!" he said. "Wait a minute! Get back here!"

Liz ignored his protests. She pulled a bottle of the ridiculously overpriced white wine Ms. High-and-Mighty was drinking from the fridge, poured a glass, then strolled over and placed it in front of her. Gwen looked at her questioningly.

"It's from the gentleman at the other end of the bar,"

Liz said, handing her Mark's business card. Gwen scanned the card briefly, then zeroed in on Mark.

When Mark realized Gwen was looking at him, his eyes widened. He sat up from his dejected slump and tried to look cool and nonchalant. But as Gwen's gaze flicked up and down appraisingly, he ended up giving her a shaky smile and a tiny wave with his fingertips. Liz sighed inwardly. Was he the only man on earth who hadn't seen a James Bond movie?

"Him?" Gwen said, crinkling her nose as if she'd smelled something rotten.

"Yes. The handsome dark-haired man. I talked to him for a moment." Liz gave the blonde a conspiratorial, woman-to-woman wiggle of the eyebrows. "He's *very* intriguing."

"Yes. Well. I'm sure you'd think so."

Because you're a low-class, drink-slinging barmaid, Liz said to herself, filling in the rest of that unspoken thought. She wondered how Gwen would like to stop drinking her wine and start wearing it.

Very deliberately, Gwen pushed the glass of wine to the back of the bar. Then, with her fingertip alone, she slid Mark's business card away from her until it came to rest against a bowl of peanuts an arm's length away, ensuring that no one, under any circumstances, would even think of associating her with it. Then she resumed her conversation with the woman next to her, as if Liz hadn't just offered her an introduction to a man who might be willing to worship the ground she walked on.

Liz couldn't believe it. She thought her ploy would at least give Mark a chance to say hello, but no such luck. And now that Princess Gwen had banished him to the dungeon for eternity, he was going to feel embarrassed. Mortified. Humiliated.

But to Liz's surprise, when she turned back around, he

didn't appear to be any of those things. He was something worse. And that something was directed right at her.

She watched, with mounting apprehension, as he tossed down the rest of his drink, then slammed the glass down on the bar, glaring at her with a narrow-eyed, tight-lipped expression that told her it was a really good thing he wasn't armed. His face actually started to turn red, and if smoke came out his ears she wouldn't have been surprised. He skewered her with his angry gaze for a full five seconds, then rose from his stool, tossed money on the bar, and stalked out of the club.

2

MARK STRODE through the parking lot toward the sanctuary of his gray Volvo, hauling his keys out of his pocket as he walked. He wanted to put as much distance between himself and the Humiliation Zone as possible. Gwen Adams, the woman he needed, the woman who could solve all his problems, the woman whose grace and refinement would make Tiffany Sloan look like a guest on the "Jerry Springer Show," had just regarded him as if he were something disgusting growing on the underside of a rock. What had ever made him think she'd give him the time of day?

He reached his car and jammed the key into the door lock. Actually, he might have had a chance with Gwen, if only a certain redheaded bartender hadn't gotten in the way. How could she have done that to him? How could she have screwed up his one chance at meeting the woman who could help him reach every goal he'd ever had?

"Mark! Wait!"

He spun around, stunned to see the bartender in question hoofing it down the sidewalk. Her denim skirt was too short, her heels too tall, and as she hurried toward him, several strands of her hair came loose from the bun at the crown of her head and trailed behind her in streaks of red.

He ignored her and got into his car. She circled his Volvo and skidded to a halt beside the passenger door.

She knocked on the window. He shook his head and started the engine. She knocked again, more urgently this time, jabbing her finger toward the lock.

Oh, boy. He did *not* need this.

With a heavy sigh, Mark reached to the panel beside him and flipped open the lock. She yanked the car door open and slid into the passenger seat, closing it behind her with a definitive *thunk*. She turned and stared at him with soft green eyes—eyes that might have seemed really innocent if he hadn't known about the pushy, presumptuous brain that lurked behind them.

He glared at her. "What do you want?"

"Well," she said, shifting around to face him. "I just wanted to tell you that I don't think things are as bad as they look. We haven't done any permanent damage where Gwen is concerned. I think if we—"

"Wait a minute. What's this *we* stuff?"

"I'm not going to lie to you. That woman is wrong for you. I'd hate to think of the man she'd be right for. But if you're determined to go after her, I suppose—" she paused "—I suppose I'd be willing to help you."

Mark couldn't believe it. This woman was loony. "Help me? Haven't you *helped* me enough already?"

"I know I was a bit hasty," she admitted. "But if you'll just give me a chance, I'll show you how we can—"

"You keep saying *we*. This is not a *we* thing."

"I admit she's going to be a tougher sell than I thought. But when it comes to getting a woman's attention, I'm an expert."

"Experts get things right. You missed this one by a mile."

"Okay," she admitted. "Maybe I did this time. But at least I took action. Were you ever going to get off that stool and go talk to her? Or were you going to spend the

whole evening staring at her, then go home and kick yourself for not approaching her?''

He hated to admit it, but she was right. Gwen had paralyzed him, making him feel like the unsophisticated
small-town guy he was. Still, did that give this woman
the right to butt in?

"I just miscalculated a little," she continued. "That's
all. But if you'll give me another chance, I know I can
help you."

"I don't get it. Why do you want to help me?"

She smiled. "Practice. See, I'm going to be a clinical
psychologist some day. Couples therapy. Helping people
is my destiny."

Destiny? What in the *hell* was she talking about? "No.
You can't help me. You don't even know me."

"Of course I know you. I've known you for—" she
checked her watch "—eighteen minutes now."

"No," he corrected, pointing an accusing finger at her,
"you don't know me at all. And still you ran out here
and jumped right into my car. That's a very dangerous
thing to do. That's how women get abducted and mur-
dered. By being careless. Don't you ever read the news-
paper?"

Her mouth turned up in an amused grin. "So you're a
dangerous man?"

Mark sighed inwardly. Dangerous man? God, just once
he'd love to have a woman think so. Instead, he'd always
been the kind of shy, unassuming guy that would make
overprotective fathers put their shotguns away on prom
night and forget all about curfews.

"Oh, yeah. Give me the tax code and a calculator, and
I'm the most dangerous man you've ever met."

She smiled again. "I'll keep that in mind next April."

Yeah, he could spin circles around a tax return, all
right. And right now he'd trade the majority of that
knowledge for the ability to utter one charming, sophis-

ticated sentence to a charming, sophisticated woman without feeling as if she saw Waldon Springs plastered across his forehead in neon lights.

She leaned toward him, a conspiratorial look on her face. "What if I told you I know a way that you can get Gwen's undivided attention for at least fifteen minutes and be a hero in her eyes at the same time?"

Yeah, and pigs were going to sprout wings and head for the treetops. "I'd say you're nuts. Now, would you mind getting out of my car?"

"I'm serious! I can tell you how to do it!"

Mark let out an exasperated sigh. It appeared that if he wanted her out of his car, he was going to have to do one of two things: Forcibly remove her, or listen to her crazy advice.

"Okay," he said, glancing at his watch. "You've got two minutes. Tell me."

"It's kind of complicated. Two minutes is not enough—"

"Sorry. It's all I've got." He leaned over to open her door.

"No! Wait!"

He turned and glared at her, the engine idling softly.

"It's just that I'm supposed to be in there working," she explained, "not out here chatting, and it will take a little time to tell you what I have in mind. Gwen's a regular. She usually comes in about six-thirty. If you'll come by about six o'clock tomorrow night, I'll explain everything."

"Don't you have to *work* when you're at work?"

"It's okay. I can get someone to cover for me."

Mark started to tell her for the third time that their conversation was over, only to find her looking at him with such a hopeful, expectant gaze that his resolve wavered. A curly strand of hair fell across her face, which she brushed away, only to have it fall against her cheek again. She had three piercings in each ear filled with an assortment of silver stars and moons. Her form-fitting knit top was cut a bit too low, her skirt a bit too high, and he'd be willing to bet that somewhere on her voluptuous body she had a tattoo. Just a small, unobtrusive one that said "body ornament" without saying "biker chick." He could see her lounging in a tattoo parlor, selected parts of her body exposed, as some guy named Vinny permanently etched a happy face on her hip, or maybe a rosebud on the swell of her breast....

Good, God, what was wrong with him? What was he doing taking a mental tour of her body in search of tattoos? For all he cared, she could have the U.S.S. *Constitution* slapped across her chest.

"There's no point in going any further with this," he told her. "You can't help me. Gwen's different. She's—"

"No. That's where you're wrong. When it gets right down to it, she's no different from any other woman. If you know which buttons to push, she's yours."

She's yours. Mark fought to quell the tiny rush of excitement he felt when he heard those words, as if this strange woman really were offering him the key to his career success. She made it sound so easy. Just a little button pushing.

No. You know it won't be that easy. This woman is nuts. Run. Save yourself while you still can.

"No," he said. "I'm not coming back here tomorrow night."

"Are you sure about that?"

He opened his mouth to say, again, that of *course* he was sure, when all at once he thought about Gwen, and about how bright his future would be if she were by his side. But there wasn't a thing this woman could do to make it happen.

"Of course I'm sure. I'm not coming."

She smiled.

"I *said* I'm not coming."

Her smile widened even more. Did she have a hearing problem?

"Did you hear me? I will *not* be here!"

Her smile grew so bright she could have put the sun out of business. "I'll see you at six o'clock."

She pushed open the passenger door and stepped out, only to stick her head back in the car again. "Oh, by the way, I'm Liz. Liz Prescott. It was nice to meet you, Mark."

She gave him yet another big smile, then shut the door and trotted off, leaving Mark sitting behind the wheel of his car, his teeth clenched in frustration. She dodged a black Mercedes coming into the parking lot, then hopped onto the sidewalk and scurried toward the door of the club, her short denim skirt swishing back and forth in rhythm with her high-heeled strides.

If audacity were a crime, he'd certainly collected enough evidence to convict her of it now. She actually expected him to come back here tomorrow night for his first class in Attracting the Opposite Sex. What did she think he was? Crazy? Desperate? Even more off-the-wall than she was?

If you know which buttons to push, she's yours.

Mark froze, his hands on the steering wheel, and stared at the dashboard. Liz's words echoed around in his head, taunting him with the possibilities, and just for a moment he thought maybe…

No. He had no business having anything to do with a pushy, underdressed bartender who undoubtedly watched soap operas, drank beer from a bottle and painted her toenails purple. A woman like that wouldn't have the slightest idea how to attract a woman like Gwen. She'd screwed up his life enough already. Why give her the opportunity to add insult to injury?

He headed toward home, telling himself that his situation would have to get a whole lot more desperate before he'd even think about accepting help from a crazy woman. There was no way he was coming back here tomorrow night.

No way.

"LET'S GET SOMETHING straight right off the bat," Mark said, as he slid onto a seat at the bar the next evening at precisely six o'clock. "I'm here to listen. That's all. If you tell me to do anything that sounds ineffective or just plain weird, I'm outta here."

Liz gave him one of her ultrabright smiles. "Hello, Mark. It's good to see you, too. Can I get you a drink?"

I was insane to come here, Mark told himself. *Totally and completely insane.*

All day long at work he'd stuck to his guns, telling himself he was *not* going to come here tonight. Then before Sloan left for the day, he stopped by Mark's office to rub his nose in the fact that he and Tiffany were meeting one of the partners and his wife for dinner after work. As he walked away with that annoying little chuckle of his, Tina made a highly inappropriate gesture behind his back that highlighted one of her long, pink fingernails. Mark wished his frustration could have been as easily soothed. Desperate to find a way to beat Sloan at his own game, he'd headed for Simon's Bar & Grille again in spite of his vow to avoid it at all costs.

"No," he told Liz. "I don't want a drink. I want to get down to business."

Liz inched closer and rested her forearms against the bar in front of him, a conspiratorial grin on her face. "Wait till you hear my plan. It'll knock your socks off."

If he emerged from this experience minus only a pair of socks, he'd consider himself lucky.

"Okay," Mark said, hoping for the best and preparing for the worst. "Tell me what you have in mind."

"I CAN'T BELIEVE I let you talk me into this," Mark muttered as he strode through Simon's parking lot alongside Liz, berating himself with every step. "What if somebody catches us?"

"That's why you're going to be my lookout," Liz said. "Just tell me if somebody comes."

"What if a cop drives by?"

Liz rolled her eyes. "A cop's not going to drive by. You're not going to jail, and you're not going to hell. Didn't you ever do this when you were a teenager?"

"God, no."

"Did you ever toilet paper a house?"

"Nope."

"Egg a few windows?"

"Of course not."

"What *did* you do?"

Mark shot her an irritated look. "Where I went to school, vandalism was not a prerequisite for graduation."

"Yeah. That's the problem with education these days. They don't teach real-world skills."

Mark had always wondered what teenage vandals were like when they grew up. Now he knew. They grew into adult vandals.

"There it is," Liz said, pointing toward a dark blue BMW at the back of the parking lot.

"You're sure it's her car?"

"I'm sure."

Mark was glad Gwen had arrived late this evening. She'd been relegated to the back of the lot next to a very large Cadillac, which, thankfully, would help shield them from sight. Little did she know, though, that while she sat inside sipping a glass of wine, her car was becoming a crime statistic.

When they reached the car, Liz looked left and right for witnesses, then ducked down beside the rear tire. A few seconds later Mark heard the hiss of air escaping.

"This is crazy," he whispered.

"Will you lighten up? I'm letting air out of a tire, not bombing a major metropolitan airport."

The hissing seemed to go on for hours, but the only people Mark saw were on the other side of the lot, filtering in and out of the club. Her mission finally accomplished, Liz stood up and gave Mark a big grin. "It's a perfect plan, isn't it? No woman can ignore a man who comes to her rescue. Even Gwen."

As they hurried back across the parking lot, Mark had to admit Liz's plan had possibilities. Gwen would find her flat tire, become understandably distressed, and then he'd just happen to come along to change it for her, thereby rescuing her, thereby earning her gratitude and goodwill, and—

"Wait a minute!" Mark grabbed Liz's arm and pulled her to a halt. "This is never going to work. She's going to remember me from last night!"

Liz dismissed his concern with a wave of her hand. "Nah. Guys hit on her all the time. She won't remember."

"I think she will."

"If you're worried, just take your glasses off. She won't recognize you then."

"If I can't see, I won't recognize her, either."

Liz held out her hand. "Give them to me."

"No! I'm not going to—"

"You're right, Mark. She might recognize you. Do you want one strike against you before you even get started?"

Mark glared at Liz, then yanked his glasses off and put them in her hand. She stepped back five paces and held up two fingers.

"How many?"

Mark squinted. "Two."

"Right."

"Plus the two beside them makes four."

Liz folded his glasses and tucked them into her apron pocket. "No problem. Whatever you see, just divide it in half. You're an accountant. You can probably do the math in your head."

He stared at her, dumbfounded. "Don't take this wrong, Liz. But you're nuts."

"Now, I resent that," she said, a smile playing across her lips. "I'm not nuts. Sometimes I just...think outside the box."

No kidding. This woman was so far out of the box that no force in the universe could stuff her back inside.

"Now, do you remember what I told you to do?" she asked.

"I can handle it, Liz."

"I know you can." She smoothed his jacket lapels, then gave his cheek a friendly pat. He blinked with surprise, then reminded himself that Liz was just one of those overly friendly, touchy-feely types and it didn't mean a thing. Still, he noted how warm her hand felt, and he had the fleeting thought that he wouldn't mind if it stayed there a little longer.

"But it might be a good idea to get that uptight look off your face," Liz added.

Mark closed his eyes and took a deep breath, trying to relax. Why was this so hard?

Because you're from the Lucky Seven Trailer Park in Waldon Springs, Texas—a place women like Gwen would only see in their worst nightmares. And she's going to know right away, just as she did last night, that you're not the kind of guy for her.

"How many psychologists does it take to change a lightbulb?" Liz asked.

Mark blinked. "Is this a joke?"

"No, I'm from the Society of American Psychologists and I'm taking a poll. Of *course* it's a joke."

"Then spare me, will you? I can do without humor right now."

"Wrong. I think you need all the humor you can get."

She continued to stare at him until he sighed with resignation. "Okay. I'll bite. How many psychologists does it take to change a lightbulb?"

"Only one. But it has to really want to change."

In spite of the fact that the joke barely registered on the comedy meter, Mark couldn't help smiling. If Gwen were as easy to talk to as Liz, his communication problems would be solved.

"Bad joke," he said.

"The worst," Liz agreed. She put her hand against his arm, then leaned toward him and dropped her voice. "Rule number one for attracting the opposite sex. Do that more often."

"Do what more often?"

"Smile. Just the way you did right there. Women can't resist it."

Her voice was soft and breathy, and as he glanced down to where her hand rested against his arm, he felt an unexpected tingle, his senses suddenly on red alert. He jerked his gaze back up, only to have it waylayed by Liz's body-hugging emerald-green top. Odd or not, she had some obvious physical assets only a man in a coma would miss.

Finally Mark managed to tear his gaze away from her blouse and what lay beneath it, but when he met her soft green eyes, he froze all over again. Caught in her gaze, his heart missed a beat or two, and the flush he'd felt moments earlier magnified, multiplying the heat of the Texas twilight. As she continued to stare at him with a playful, engaging smile, he could see now that, despite her strange wardrobe, her wild, untamed hair and her bizarre thought process, she really was attractive.

Very attractive.

"Mark? Are you okay?"

All at once his neurons woke up and sent a distress signal to his brain. *What do you think you're doing? Gwen's the one you need to be thinking about. Remember her? The beautiful, sophisticated woman who's the key to that partnership you desperately want?*

"Yeah. I'm fine."

She patted his arm. "Good. I thought I'd lost you there for a minute."

He'd been without a woman way too long. That was the problem. But he was at a crisis point in his life right now, and not just any woman would do. He needed someone like Gwen, who was willowy, graceful and model-thin, with a gossamer beauty that oozed elegance. A caviar-and-champagne kind of woman. Liz, on the other hand, was the kind of practical, down-to-earth woman you could share nachos with at a baseball game.

"Uh-oh," Liz said, staring past his shoulder.

"What?"

"She's coming out."

Mark spun around to see a person-shaped blob moving out the door of the club. At least he thought it was the door of the club. Without his glasses, it could have been the gates of heaven for all he knew.

"Gwen?" he said. "What's she doing leaving so early?"

"I don't know."

Mark grabbed Liz's arm and pulled her around the back of the building. He peered back around the corner to see Gwen walking briskly across the parking lot. Now that she was closer, he could see her well enough to admire her confident, long-legged strides and the regal set of her chin—a woman who clearly commanded her surroundings.

When Gwen saw her car, she stopped and stared for a moment, as if taking in the fact that it was leaning perceptibly to the right. She circled the car and stopped beside the right rear tire, then planted her fists on her hips and glared down at it.

Liz tapped Mark's arm. "That's your cue. I'm going back inside. Let me know what happens."

It was now or never.

Mark took a deep breath and started across the parking lot, zeroing in on the out-of-focus woman by the blurry blue BMW. He came up behind her, trying to act nonchalant.

"Excuse me. You seem to be having a problem."

Gwen spun around, her lips set in a firm line of irritation, her ice-blue eyes brimming with annoyance. Even in a state of total disgust she managed to look stunningly beautiful.

"Of course something's wrong," she muttered, staring at him as though he were blind. "I have a flat tire."

Mark leaned over and eyed the pancaked tire as if seeing it for the first time. "Well, look at that. You sure do."

"It's a brand-new tire," she said, exasperation flooding her voice. "There's no reason for it to go flat." She checked her watch, looking dismayed. "I'm meeting a girlfriend at the theater tonight for an eight-fifteen curtain. I'll *never* make it now!"

"I'd be happy to change your tire for you."

Gwen stared at him blankly. "You what?"

"I said I'll change your tire."

It was as if he'd spoken Swahili. "You mean *you?* You'll change my tire?"

"Uh…yeah."

"Personally?"

Mark felt a glimmer of apprehension. What was it about his offer that she didn't understand?

Then it struck him. He'd just offered to do what she considered to be manual labor. She now pegged him as one of those people who did their own laundry and cleaned their own toilets. He *was* one of those people, but he desperately wanted her *not* to think that. He wanted to come across as a wealthy, cultured professional who would never consider getting his hands dirty, unless, of course, he had to come to the rescue of a woman in distress.

He thought quickly. "I'd call my people to come over and take care of this," he said, not bothering to identify precisely who his "people" were since he didn't have any, "but since you're short on time, why don't I roll up my sleeves and try to get it done a little faster?"

"You actually know how to change a tire?"

"Uh...I watched my mechanic once," Mark told her. "I think I remember how to do it."

Or maybe it was those summers he spent working at Fred's Chevron in Waldon Springs for minimum wage so he could save money for college. Maybe that's what had imparted him with such broad-based knowledge. One or the other.

"How long will it take?" Gwen asked.

"Ten or fifteen minutes."

"Oh?" She checked her watch. "Well, then. I might be able to make that curtain after all. By all means, go ahead."

Mark let out the breath he'd been holding. So far, so good. "If you'll give me the keys to your trunk, I'll get the spare."

"Yes. Of course."

He took her keys, his mind spinning. He knew what Liz had told him to say next, but now as he played the words over in his mind, they sounded desperately dumb and hopelessly contrived. Still, silence wasn't going to get him anywhere, and he certainly couldn't think of anything else to say. He had no choice but to open his mouth and hope for the best.

"I know this flat tire is rather unlucky for you," he told her. "But it's *very* lucky for me."

Gwen raised her eyebrows. "Oh?"

Mark's chest felt so tight he could barely breathe. *She's not going to buy this.... She's not going to buy this....*

"Yes. If you hadn't had a flat tire, I might never have had the opportunity to meet such a beautiful woman."

Gwen blinked with surprise. Mark struggled to maintain the friendly, easygoing smile Liz had counseled him on. *Patience,* she'd told him. *Say the line, then shut up. Keep looking at her, though, as if she's the only woman on earth. If you can do that, whatever she says next won't be a brush-off.*

The silence between them seemed to stretch out for an eternity. For an instant he imagined strangling a certain redhead for her goofy advice. Then the most wonderful thing happened.

Gwen smiled.

"Well," she said, actually looking a little flustered. "I guess I'm lucky, too. I don't know what I'd have done without you."

Mark felt as if the elephant that had been sitting on his chest had headed off to the watering hole. *It's working. Liz's advice is actually working.*

"If you hadn't come along, I'd have had to call the auto club," Gwen said, "and I'm afraid I've never felt comfortable around mechanics." She put a palm against her chest and crinkled her forehead oh-so slightly, as if the memory made her feel faint. "Their manner, their dress, their personal hygiene—they always leave a bit to be desired."

Mark made a mental note. Buy extra-strength deodorant, shave twice a day, and never, ever, have his name embroidered on his shirt pocket.

He took off his suit coat and held it out to Gwen. "Would you mind holding this while I change the tire?"

"Certainly."

Gwen took it and draped it over her arm. At the same time Mark caught the faint scent of a warm, exotic, *expensive* perfume. He would have expected nothing less.

He rolled up his sleeves, then turned to open the trunk. Since Liz's advice had been right on the money so far, he decided he'd stick to it like glue. She'd told him that under no circumstances should he ask Gwen out tonight, because it would look as if he expected something in return for helping her. Tomorrow night at the club, though, he could strike up a conversation, and she'd remember him as that nice guy who'd come to her rescue. Then maybe after a date or two, he'd feel comfortable asking her to the firm's dinner dance.

Gwen checked her watch, a look of consternation passing over her face. "Oh, my, I really *do* need to make that eight-fifteen curtain…"

"No problem. I'll have you on the road before you know it."

She smiled at him again, and in that moment he decided he'd push her car all the way to the theater if that's what it took to get her there on time.

Gwen was everything he needed in a woman, and sooner or later she was going to be his.

LIZ DIDN'T REALIZE how much her mind had wandered from her job until she put a cherry in a martini and an olive in a daiquiri. She caught the mistake as soon as she saw her customers' perplexed expressions. She swept the drinks away with a sincere apology and made new ones, checking her watch every thirty seconds or so. What was going on with Mark and Gwen? She thought of going to the window to watch, but the tables by the windows along that side were occupied.

Things had to be going well. How could they not? Gwen might be snooty and condescending, but could she really give the cold shoulder to a guy who was kind enough to change a flat for her?

Just about the time Liz decided to grab a broom from the supply closet because she was sure the sidewalk out front needed sweeping, Mark came back into the club. As he wove through the Friday crowd, her heart pounded with anticipation. She searched his face for some indication of what might have happened between him and Gwen, but as he approached the bar, he gave her nothing but a deadpan stare. Her stomach did a nervous flip-flop. He'd be smiling, wouldn't he, if everything had worked out okay?

"Mark? What happened?"

"I need my glasses back."

"Oh! Of course." She patted her apron pockets, pulled his glasses out and handed them to him. He put them on, then turned and walked away from the bar. Where was he going?

"Mark! Wait!"

He kept walking. Liz hurried down to the end of the bar, ducked beneath it and took off after him. She caught up with him as he reached the front door.

"Hey! Wait a minute! You have to tell me what happened! Did my plan work?"

"I don't want to talk about it."

Something had gone dreadfully wrong. But what?

"Did you say what I told you to say?"

"Liz—"

"Please tell me."

Mark took a deep, silent breath, then let it out slowly. "Yes. I did."

"And?"

"It worked just fine."

"You're saying it was fine, but obviously—" Liz stopped short. "Oh, God. Don't tell me she's married!"

"No, Liz. She's not married."

"Boyfriend?"

"I don't think so. She was on her way to the theater with a girlfriend."

"She's a *lesbian?*"

Mark gave her an admonishing look. "I said *a* girlfriend, not *her* girlfriend."

"You didn't try to ask her out, did you?"

"No. Of course not."

"Well, it's pretty clear that *something* went wrong. Was it something I told you to do?"

"Liz. It's okay. Your advice was perfect. Everything you suggested worked just as you said it would."

Liz was completely befuddled. "Then what?"

"It doesn't matter now. I need to get home."

She inched closer to him and dropped her voice. "Mark, if I did anything to hurt you—anything—I'm sorry. I'm really, really sorry." She was surprised at how deeply she felt that, and how desperately she wanted him to believe it.

He laid his hand gently on her shoulder. "It wasn't your fault," he said softly. "And it wasn't Gwen's. It was nobody's fault but mine."

He slid his hand down her arm, then closed his fingers around her wrist and gave it a gentle squeeze. "Thanks for trying."

With that, he turned and left the club.

3

HOURS LATER, Mark sat on the tiny, cramped balcony of
his apartment, beer number two in hand, staring out across
the city lights of North Dallas. Even though it was approaching midnight, the oppressive July heat seemed to
ooze up from the pavement below, enveloping him in
heavy, saunalike air. It was cool inside his apartment, but
right now he preferred the heat. It suited the way he felt
right now.

He slapped at a Texas-size mosquito making a lazy
figure eight around his head, then took another swig of
beer, feeling it burn all the way down his throat. Ever
since he'd left Simon's tonight, a sick feeling had twisted
around in his stomach—a feeling of utter and complete
defeat. Just when he'd mustered up a little bit of hope,
everything had fallen apart.

About the time beer number three started to sound
pretty good, he heard a car door slam in the parking lot
below his balcony. He peered over the iron railing.

He squeezed his eyes closed, then opened them again,
praying he'd had one beer too many and he was seeing
things. Redheaded things. A specific redheaded thing that
looked way too much like Liz Prescott, trotting along the
sidewalk, heading toward the stairs in the breezeway leading up to his apartment.

He rose quickly from his chair and went back through
the sliding-glass door into his living room, which was
illuminated only by a single lamp turned on low. He heard

the distinctive clicking of high-heeled shoes hitting the stairs outside, and when the knock on his door came, he groaned. He did *not* need this.

He waited.

Another knock.

Then...silence? He felt a rush of hope. If he just ignored her, would she go away?

"Mark! I know you're in there!"

Go away? What had he been thinking? This woman had more tenacity than peanut butter stuck to the roof of your mouth.

"Come on, Mark! I saw you on your balcony!"

He flipped the dead bolt and yanked open the door. "Will you keep it down? It's almost midnight!"

"Sorry. My shift wasn't over until eleven. I couldn't get here any sooner."

"I don't understand why you're here at all!"

"Aren't you going to invite me in?"

Mark wished he had a choice in the matter. But knowing Liz, if he didn't let her in, she'd probably crawl through the window or pick the lock.

She stepped into his apartment, and he closed the door behind her. "How did you know where I live?"

"It wasn't too tough to figure out. You're in the book."

"But there must be other Mark McAlisters. How many doors did you have to knock on before you found me?"

"Zero. I doubted you lived with the drug dealers in the sleazy part of South Dallas, or the twenty-somethings in The Village, or the blue-bloods in Highland Park. I picked the average North Dallas apartment address, and darned if I wasn't right." She nodded at the beer can he held. "Aren't you going to offer me a beer?"

Mark couldn't believe her audacity. Contrary to what she might believe, this was *not* a social occasion.

"Never mind," she said. "I'll get one myself."

To his utter disbelief, she strode through his dining

room, tossed her purse on the table, then went into his kitchen. She opened the fridge and started rummaging around, her denim-clad derriere sticking out beyond the door. Beneath that derriere were those mile-long legs, on which his gaze instantly locked. A great big *wow* formed in his brain that came within a centimeter of gushing out his mouth.

She stood up and closed the refrigerator door. He stuffed his eyeballs back into his head and transferred his gaze to the back of a dining room chair. It was late, and he'd had a couple of beers. That's why he'd stared at her like some kind of junior-high kid on hormone overload. That, and the fact that it had been an eternity since he'd seen any woman's body sticking out of his fridge, much less a body as gifted as Liz's.

She came back into the living room. "It's kinda dark in here, isn't it?"

Brushing past him, she went to the lamp on the end table and jacked up the three-way bulb, making his living room brighter than a landing strip at the airport. Then she picked up a framed photograph from his end table.

"Is this your mother?"

"Yes."

"Nice house. Is that where you grew up?"

"No. She moved there later." *And why are you asking?*

Liz set the picture down and plopped herself onto his sofa, kicked off her shoes and tucked her legs beneath her. After popping the top on the can, she stared up at him questioningly.

"Aren't you going to sit down?"

Mark felt as if he'd just intruded into her house, rather than the other way around. He didn't want her here. He wanted to wallow in his misery all by himself, and Liz's presence only reminded him once again of everything that had gone wrong tonight—and in the rest of his life, as well.

"I know why you're here. I do *not* want to talk about Gwen."

"Good. Neither do I."

He blinked. "You don't?"

"No. I mean, what's to discuss? I worked hard to come up with the flat tire thing, and you messed it up. Case closed."

Mark's mouth fell open. "I did *not* mess it up! I followed your instructions to the letter!"

Liz raised an eyebrow.

He glared at her.

She shrugged offhandedly. "Whatever."

"And I *said* I don't want to talk about Gwen!"

"Fine. I won't." She paused, taking a sip of beer, then eyed him critically. "Except to say that if you don't know how to change a tire, you should have said so."

His mouth fell open again. "What do you mean, I don't know how to change a tire?"

"You don't have to be embarrassed, Mark. A lot of men—"

"For your information," he said, angrily pointing a finger at her, "I've been changing tires since I was twelve years old! And I don't want to talk about *that*, either!"

She gave him another one of those infuriating shrugs. "Fine. We won't talk about it. It's just as well, anyway. I mean, I can't imagine where you ever got the idea that a woman like Gwen would be interested in a guy like you."

Liz might as well have socked him one right in the stomach. He stared at her, speechless, his face growing hot with humiliation. Is that what she really thought? Had she known all along he had no chance with Gwen and had just been humoring him?

He swallowed hard, feeling as if she were seeing the real Mark McAlister, the backward, small-town guy who had deluded himself into thinking he'd ever be a match for a woman like Gwen Adams.

He sat down on the sofa, his elbows on his knees, holding his beer in both hands. He let out a breath of resignation.

"Well?" Liz said.

"Well, what? You're right."

Liz sat up suddenly, her cavalier expression vanishing. "What did you say?"

"I said you're right. A guy like me—"

"A guy like *you,*" she said, slapping her beer down on the coffee table, "is worth *ten* women like her. And don't you *ever* forget that!"

"But you just said—"

"I know what I just said! But you weren't supposed to agree with me!"

Mark stared at her incredulously.

"You were supposed to tell me she's the one who's not good enough for you, and if she can't see that, then it's her loss. *That's* what you were supposed to tell me!"

Mark was silent. Right about now, he couldn't have uttered those words if his life depended on it.

"Is that what this is about?" Liz asked. "You think you're not good enough for Gwen Adams?"

"No. Gwen's the one doing the thinking. And for the third time, I *don't* want to talk about it!"

Another shrug. "Fine. I'll wait."

"For what?"

"For you to change your mind."

"Liz—"

"Did I tell you I like your sofa?" she said, settling against a sofa pillow with a comfortable sigh. "Very cozy. I mean, I could stay here for *hours.*"

"Now, just a minute—"

"You won't throw me out the door. You won't toss me over the balcony. And no matter how irritated you get, you won't call 911 and have me escorted from the premises. And since I have no plans to leave of my own accord..."

She leaned forward, rested her hand against his arm and gave it a gentle squeeze, her expression becoming solemn and sincere. "Why don't you tell me what happened between you and Gwen?"

A long silence stretched between them. He stared down at his beer can, all the while aware of Liz's green eyes fixed on him, those eyes that teased him and challenged him and never took no for an answer. She had a talent for insinuating herself into his life as if she'd known him forever. And the longer her hand remained on his arm as if it belonged there, the more he felt as if he *had* known her forever, and in a way, that was more than friendly.

Wait a minute. What are you thinking?

Touchy-feely, he reminded himself, as he slid his arm from beneath her hand. Making overt gestures of familiarity with near-strangers was second nature to Liz. She was simply that kind of person, and it didn't mean a thing. She was also the kind of person who would never leave unless he spilled his guts.

"Okay," he said finally. "I'll tell you. But you have to promise not to laugh."

"Laugh? Why would I laugh?"

"You'll know in a minute." He blew out a long breath. "I gave Gwen my suit coat to hold while I changed the tire."

"Yeah?"

"She read the tag inside the collar."

"And...?"

Mark closed his eyes. *Just spit it out.* "Have you ever heard of Zoltan the Suit Man?"

"Sure. That big, ugly, bald guy who advertises on TV. At the top of his lungs."

Mark was silent.

"That's where you buy your suits?"

He cringed, waiting for the gales of laughter he knew were coming. Instead, Liz just shrugged.

"So what's the matter with that? From what I hear, most of the suits he sells are designer seconds or last year's overstock. He buys them in big lots and puts his own label in. You get a nice suit at about half the price you'd normally pay. Right?"

"Right. But Gwen didn't feel that way about it."

"She brushed you off because of the label in your suit?"

"Essentially, yes."

"She actually said, 'I never want to see you again because you wear inferior clothing'?"

"No. Of course not. But I'm happy to know her maid's husband looked really spiffy in his Zoltan suit at his grandson's christening, and the gardener at her condo complex got a bargain there when he had to have a suit for his grandmother's funeral."

"But she didn't really blow you off."

"Come on, Liz! What more did she have to say?"

Liz held up her palms. "Wait a minute. Let me get this straight. You're telling me that the only thing standing between you and your dream woman is a suit label?"

"No! Don't you understand? It's what the label represents!"

"What it represents is a smart buying decision. It represents a guy who doesn't waste money. It represents—"

"No!" Mark clunked his drink down on the coffee table. "What it represents is a guy who comes from *nothing,* who's so used to being broke that he's a tightwad about *everything,* a guy who was too dumb to figure out that you can have it on the inside, but if you don't show it on the outside, it won't do you a damned bit of good. A guy a sharp, sophisticated woman would *never* be interested in. And the fact that you can't see that, Liz, means you're not half as smart about people as you think you are!''

He let out a harsh, disgusted breath, rose from the sofa, then strode to the balcony. He yanked the sliding-glass door open and went outside, then closed it behind him so hard it rattled in its frame. He walked to the balcony railing and gripped it tightly, his head bowed, frustration racing through him like a runaway train.

Well, now there was no question about it. Gwen wasn't the only one who knew what a backward nobody he really was. He'd just filled Liz in on that fact, too. How could she possibly have missed it? He'd yelled it loud enough to wake the dead.

What in the *hell* had made him say all that?

Frustration, that's what. And a lot of it. But why had he taken it out on her when all she'd ever done was try to help him?

A minute or two passed. Mark played over a dozen different ways to apologize in his head, and they all sounded as dumb as his outburst had. Then he heard the patio door slide open softly in its tracks and close again with a gentle click.

Liz came up beside him, her arms folded, and stared out at the city lights. He didn't know what to say. Maybe something like, *After I yelled at you like that, why are you still here?*

"Feel better now?"

"Oh, yeah. I always feel better after loud, moronic outbursts.''

"Hey, you're not the only one, you know.''

"I was the only one who shouted like an idiot.''

"No. I mean that you're not the only one who came from nothing.'' She leaned her forearms against the railing next to him. "Most of the time I was growing up, it was just me and my mom. We lived in Big Fork, Texas. Ever hear of it?''

"Can't say I have."

"Doesn't surprise me. The only people who have heard of it are the two thousand people who live there."

"Where was your dad?"

"He died when I was nine. He was on the roof of our house, replacing a few bad shingles. He fell." She shook her head. "He didn't have any life insurance, and without his income, my mom had a hard time making ends meet. She was a hairdresser, and in a town that small, she didn't bring in much money." Liz laughed softly. "To this day I still can't stand the sight of rice and beans."

Mark concentrated not on Liz's words, but on the carefree tone of her voice. Despite financial difficulties, she clearly remembered her childhood with fondness. All he remembered was shame and humiliation.

"How about you?" Liz said. "Do you come from a small town, too?"

"Oh, yeah," he said. "Waldon Springs, Texas. A real thriving metropolis."

"Tell me about it."

"Nothing to tell. It was your average microscopic backwoods town full of narrow-minded people. I left almost twelve years ago, and I don't much like going back."

Liz looked at him with surprise. "Come on, Mark. There must have been something good about living there."

"I grew up in a trailer park three miles outside Waldon Springs that was so shabby I was ashamed that people knew I lived there. My mother was a maid at a motel in a nearby town. She did the best she could. Without a high school diploma, though, she didn't have a lot of options."

"Where was your father?"

"I never knew my father. He took off before I was even born. We were the local charity case. So you see,

Liz, there was really nothing good about living there. Not a single blessed thing.''

He had no idea what made him tell her all that. Maybe it was because she was basically a stranger and it really didn't matter. Or maybe it was because even though he'd known her such a short time, she felt less like a stranger than some people he'd known for years.

But there was still plenty she didn't know. He hadn't told her about working odd jobs from the time he was ten years old just to help put food on the table. He hadn't told her about kids laughing at his tattered clothes, his rusted-out secondhand bicycle, his shoes with holes in the soles. He hadn't told her about most of his teachers looking right through him as if he weren't there, assuming that any kid with his background couldn't possibly have the ambition it took to make something of himself.

He hadn't told her any of those things. Yet when she turned and met his gaze, the look of understanding in her eyes spoke louder than any words could possibly have, as if she knew every bit of the heartache he felt without him saying a word.

"This is Dallas, Mark," Liz said softly. "Not Waldon Springs. Whatever your life was like then, it's over now. You're clearly a successful guy. I think it's time you dumped Zoltan and got yourself another wardrobe consultant.''

He shook his head. "It's more than just the suit, Liz."

"I know. But that's a good start, isn't it? If you work on the outside, the inside will follow." She gave him a tiny smile. "And I can help you."

Mark felt an instant sense of foreboding. Since meeting Liz, the words that he'd grown to fear the most were *I can help you.*

"See, I have this friend who works at Bergman's, that upscale department store at the Galleria," she explained. "He can advise you on picking out a new suit. Or a couple of new suits." She paused, her eyes brightening. "And shoes. And shirts. And accessory stuff like ties and belts. And casual things, too. Everything. You could get a whole new wardrobe!"

"No. No way. I don't shop at places like that."

"My friend can get you a thirty-percent discount."

"I said no. I have no intention of spending that kind of money, discount or not."

Liz gave him a skeptical look. "You may have been broke once, Mark. But you're not anymore, are you?"

He opened his mouth to protest, then snapped it shut again. What was this woman, anyway? A human lie detector?

She was right. He wasn't broke anymore. But all at once he realized that he still thought of himself that way. Why else would he wear suits sold by the King of Bad Advertising, live in a dinky apartment and drive an eight-year-old car, despite making more money in a year than he ever thought he'd see in a lifetime?

"You're a manager at that big ol' accounting firm," Liz went on. "You've got money out the wazoo, don't you?"

"No," he protested. "Probably not as much as you think. I mean, it *is* a lot, but it's not all liquid. Stock, mutual funds, retirement plan—"

"And a healthy checking account, and a huge line of credit, and—correct me if I'm wrong—at least two hundred bucks in your pocket right now."

Mark blinked. "How did you—"

"Because I'm smart about people, Mark. That's how I knew."

He deserved that. Big time. And whatever else she wanted to throw at him. When it came to people smarts, Liz Prescott was at the head of the class.

"That house in the photograph on your end table," Liz said. "You bought it for your mother, didn't you?"

He jerked his head around, and she met his gaze without blinking. He looked away again.

"It's not all that big. I wish I could have done more."

"She looks pretty happy in the picture."

Mark nodded. Remembering the look of delight on his mother's face when he'd given it to her made *him* happy every time he thought about it.

"You're clearly very successful, Mark. Don't you think it's time you did something for yourself?"

"Liz—"

"Go to Bergman's. See my friend, Eddie. I've known him for years. He's a genius with clothes. He'll have you looking like a million bucks in no time."

"Yeah, and that's just about what it would cost me."

"Nah, it'll only be…well, okay. Maybe half a million. But trust me—you can take Bergman's labels anywhere."

After Gwen had seen that Zoltan label, Mark had no hope of impressing her no matter what clothes he wore. Still, he knew now that his image needed a complete overhaul, and Liz was offering him the means to do it. He'd be a fool not to listen to her.

"Okay," he said suddenly. "I'll do it."

"You will?"

Mark had that weird feeling that his mouth was moving but somebody else's words were coming out of it. "Yeah. I will. Whatever it takes."

Liz beamed. "Great! We'll get you all kinds of clothes. And a new haircut wouldn't hurt, either. And maybe new glasses, too, or even contacts. What do you think?"

He closed his eyes, dollar signs and decimal points floating around in his mind, wishing for the first time in his life that he wasn't so adept at math.

"Okay," he said, that disembodied voice talking again. "Whatever you think."

"This is going to be such *fun!*" she exclaimed, then rose to her tiptoes and threw her arms around his neck in a quick, enthusiastic hug. In a reflex action, his arms went around her, returning the embrace even though he really wasn't a "huggy" kind of person. But Liz made wild outbursts of affection seem like the most natural thing in the world, especially when she felt so soft and so warm and exuded more bubbly effervescence than a bottle of champagne. She then took his face in her hands and planted a quick, definitive kiss right on his lips.

He stared down at her, his lips still tingling. For a split second their gazes locked, and he was so close to her he could see sparkles of light reflecting in her eyes. Then she patted his cheek, slipped out of his arms and grabbed her purse from his dining room table.

Touchy-feely, he reminded himself, as Liz tossed her purse over her shoulder. *She does that with everyone. Doesn't she?*

He followed her to the front door. She put her hand on the doorknob, then turned back.

"This really is going to be fun. You'll see."

Fun? Just the thought of knocking the cobwebs off his platinum credit card made him break out in a cold sweat.

No. He had to stop this broke thinking. Those thoughts had helped him keep Zoltan in business and kept him looking like a loser. And he wasn't going to tolerate that anymore.

"I've never even been to the Galleria," Mark said. "Don't they charge you just to breathe the air in there?"

Liz smiled. "Don't worry. Eddie will give you his discount on that, too."

4

THE MOMENT Mark followed Liz into the extravagant four-story expanse of the Galleria, he decided he hated it and that feeling only grew stronger with every passing minute. The other Saturday afternoon shoppers seemed perfectly content to stroll beneath the massive glass atrium ceiling, sip a cappuccino beside the indoor ice-skating rink, or pause at a kiosk to buy a gold-plated dog collar. But to Mark, the whole thing was just too big and glitzy.

Liz had insisted on coming by to pick him up this afternoon, and he knew it was because she was afraid he was going to back out at the last minute. And he might have, if he'd known it was going to be like this. Every inch of the place breathed *money, money, money*, like some glass-and-steel monster waiting to suck up cash, credit cards and loose jewelry from every human being who came through the doors. And judging from the looks of the people who shopped here, this particular mall monster had a smorgasbord of potential victims to choose from.

Mark looked down at the clothes he wore—faded jeans, a Texas Rangers T-shirt, beat-up sneakers—then surveyed the rest of the mall patrons. He passed a woman wearing a navy business suit and crisp white shirt, then a man in a sport coat and slacks. A couple of women wore jeans, but they looked like the hundred-dollar-a-pair kind, topped with expensive-looking blouses.

He turned to Liz. "Why didn't you warn me that people dress up to shop here?"

Liz looked around. "Not everybody is dressed up. I'm not."

She wore a pair of jeans, just as he did. Formfitting denims she filled out as only Liz could, accompanied by hot-pink flip-flops and a straw handbag tossed over her shoulder. She wore a T-shirt, too, only hers read, We've Got Enough Youth. How About a Fountain of Smart? But that was Liz. He wouldn't have expected her to wear anything else.

"Then we're both out of place."

"Mark, dressing up to go clothes shopping is like cleaning up before the maid comes. Oh, look! There's the hair salon." She checked her watch. "We're right on time."

"For what?"

"Your appointment. I called them this morning after I talked to Eddie."

"Now, wait a minute. I know we talked about a haircut, but—"

"Come on. They're waiting for you."

Liz took him by the arm and led him into the salon, where a spaghetti-thin woman with buzz-cut black hair sat behind the counter wearing a heavy-lidded look of sheer boredom. Glancing around, Mark saw that every stylist was clothed in black from head to toe, each sporting a head of hair that was frizzed, colored, spiked or otherwise mutilated. It looked like a casting call for a horror movie.

"This place is bizarre," he whispered to Liz.

"It's supposed to be chic."

"Chic? A few broomsticks and pumpkins and they'd be ready for Halloween."

"That's just for show. They don't actually do that to customers' hair."

"How much is this trip to the dark side going to cost me?"

"How much does a haircut usually cost you?"

"Twenty bucks."

"Uh...it'll probably be a little more than that."

Worried, he looked around for a sign like the one in the shop where he usually went, one that said exactly what you would have to pay for a shampoo, cut and blow-dry. But there wasn't any such sign here.

Oh, hell. When was he going to stop worrying about every little dollar and start living a little? Successful people didn't pinch pennies, and they certainly didn't worry about paying for a stupid haircut.

How much could one haircut cost, anyway?

"SIXTY-FIVE DOLLARS? *Sixty-five dollars? For this?*"

Mark ran a hand through his newly cut hair, and for a moment, Liz wondered if his eyeballs were going to pop right out of his head. The receptionist sat paralyzed on her stool, staring at Mark as if he were only one healthy brain cell away from being totally deranged. At the same time, all five stylists and their customers sat frozen in time, every one of them wearing a wide-eyed expression of disbelief that such an acutely uncivilized man had been allowed on the premises. A man who had just broken the cardinal rule of high-class establishments: One does not mention the price of anything, and certainly not at the top of one's lungs.

Liz clamped her hand onto Mark's arm and pulled him aside. He dropped his voice, but his expression was still crazed.

"Did you hear that, Liz? Sixty-five dollars?"

"Mark, please—"

"No way, Liz. I am *not* going to pay—"

"You have to!"

"That's *three times* what a haircut usually costs me!"

"You don't have any choice! What do you expect them to do? Glue your hair back on?"

Mark narrowed his eyes in an I'll-get-you-for-this stare, then muttered something that sounded like four-letter words in a rare and unusual combination. Finally he yanked his wallet out of his pocket and turned back to the receptionist. While his back was turned, Liz pulled a ten from her purse and slipped it to the stylist. Under the circumstances, reminding Mark to leave a tip would be the equivalent of squirting gasoline on a fire.

A few minutes later they were heading down the mall again, Liz taking two hurried steps to every one of Mark's. She put on a cheery smile, hoping her little bit of sunshine would chase away the thunderclouds building on his horizon.

"See," she said, "now that wasn't so bad, was it?"

He screeched to a halt and spun around. "I could have stuck my head in a blender and gotten the same effect, and it wouldn't have cost me a dime!"

"No! It looks great! Now, I know the woman who cut it was a little weird, but—"

"Woman? I thought it was a man!"

Liz rolled her eyes. "Whatever. It doesn't matter. Weird or not, that *person* did a fabulous job. I'm not kidding, Mark. You look wonderful."

"You're just saying that so I don't go back to him, or her, or *whatever,* and demand my money back!"

"Trust me, will you? It's a great haircut. Here. Have another look."

She took him by the shoulders and turned him until he caught his reflection in a shop window. He groaned. "Good God, I look like I got struck by lightning!"

"Oh, will you stop? It's got a lot of style to it, but it's still conservative, right?"

He patted his hair, then made a face of disgust. "It's got that mouse stuff in it."

Liz smiled. "That's 'mousse.'"

"Whatever. It feels like Styrofoam."

"It's trendy."

"It's stupid."

Liz sighed. "Look again. Are you *sure* you don't like it?"

Mark returned his gaze to the shop window. Liz stood beside him and eyed his reflection, too. She noticed not just his hair, but how tall and long-legged he was, wearing a pair of jeans just the way she liked to see them on a man—faded and formfitting, as if they'd spent years molding themselves to him. And he had nice, broad shoulders that filled out his Rangers T-shirt equally well. The glasses he wore still made him look like Clark Kent, but she was pretty sure there was a superhero in there somewhere. With luck, before the day was out she'd have him in contact lenses.

He poked at his hair a moment more, then dropped his hand to his side. "Okay. Maybe it's not so bad. Or at least it won't be, once it grows out a little."

Liz breathed a silent sigh of relief. Mission accomplished. Now that they were past the hair hurdle, hopefully things would be downhill from here.

THE MOMENT they stepped into Bergman's, Mark felt a twinge of foreboding, and the feeling grew more intense with every step he took. Its overly elegant, deathly quiet atmosphere made him think twice about actually touching anything. The walls were a muted beige, and in lieu of harsh overhead fluorescent lights, the store was lit with wall sconces and crystal chandeliers. The flooring consisted of wide oak planks polished to a high gloss, and brass and glass sparkled like precious gems everywhere. In an alcove by the escalator, to Mark's utter disbelief, a guy in a tux was playing a baby grand piano.

He and Liz made their way around the cosmetics section of the store, past the shoes, then came alongside the women's department. They passed a display of dresses, and Mark stopped long enough to glance furtively at a price tag, trying to get some idea of what he might be in for. Relief flooded through him.

"Eighty-nine dollars," he said to Liz. "That's not so bad for a dress, right?"

"Uh…you're looking at the wrong tag. That's for the matching scarf."

Mark dropped the price tag as if it had suddenly caught fire. He did a rough mental calculation: A woman's scarf equals a man's tie equals…

Oh, God.

"May I help you, sir?"

He turned to see a salesgirl wearing a stark black suit and white blouse, her hair drawn into a tight bun at the nape of her neck. She was one of three identical women he saw working in the same department. Same hair, same clothes, same colors. The Stepford Salesgirls. And all of them were so bone-thin that Mark wondered if having an eating disorder was a prerequisite for employment.

"No," he replied to the salesgirl. "We're just looking."

She gave him a skimpy smile, as if she'd already used up her quota for the day. "Let me know if I can help you in any way."

Yeah. Be sure to call me when you have a ninety-percent-off sale.

As the woman strolled away, Mark leaned toward Liz and whispered, "Has anyone considered feeding those women?"

"Thin is in," she whispered back.

"*That* thin is pathological. The Halloween crew at the hair place we just left could use a few skeletons. They'd be perfect for the job."

Liz laughed. "You just don't know chic when you see it."

"No, but I do know emaciation when I see it."

"I wouldn't mind being that thin."

"You've got to be kidding. You've got a great body. Why would you want to trade it for one of those?"

The words were out of Mark's mouth before he realized it, and immediately he wished he could take them back. He'd admired Liz's physical attributes more than once since he'd met her, but he hadn't intended to blurt it out.

"Really?" Her eyes widened with disbelief. Then she smiled hopefully. "You really think I look better than they do?"

How could she even ask that? It was as if she were offering him a choice between a starvation victim and Marilyn Monroe.

"Of course you do. A lot better." He couldn't stop his gaze from traveling furtively down her body, taking in all those curves he'd been admiring. "Don't tell me you're one of those women who puts a lettuce leaf on a plate and calls it dinner."

"Are you kidding? I eat anything. Which is why I look like me and not like them."

"So if, say, we were to go for a pizza after shopping, you'd actually eat some of it?"

"Mark, if you put a pizza with everything in front of me, you'll lose a finger if you reach for a slice."

"I take my pizza pretty seriously, too. You might be the one minus a few digits."

"Then let's do it. And I know just the place—Gino's down on Lower Greenville. But you have to let me pick up the tab. After today your credit card might be a little out of breath."

They started toward the men's department again, and it wasn't until they were within smelling distance of the leather accessories that it suddenly dawned on Mark what he'd just done.

He'd asked Liz out.

No. It wasn't really like a date or anything. It was just a quick pizza. But would *she* think it was something else?

He gave Liz a sidelong glance, and decided she wouldn't think that for a minute. She'd horned in on his love life, shown up at his house at midnight uninvited, then coerced him into a million-dollar shopping trip, and all of it had been totally platonic. Asking her to share a pizza was nothing to worry about.

But if it *had* been a date...

He couldn't believe how easy it had been. He'd always been so immersed in his work that he hadn't dated much, and he'd always gotten a little tongue-tied when asking a woman out. But Liz—Liz was something else. Liz was friendly. Liz was comfortable. Liz was easy to be around. Liz was—

"Liz, darling!"

From between two racks of suits, a man emerged who was barely taller than the racks themselves. His build was so insubstantial that a good, solid wind would blow him over. He wore one of those weird three-button suit coats in an odd shade of olive-green, a geometric-patterned tie, and a bright, cantaloupe-colored shirt. Mark never would have thought to put those particular clothes on the same body, but he had to admit that somehow it all looked good together.

Eddie kissed Liz on either cheek, then turned to Mark. "Is this your friend?"

"Yes. This is Mark."

Eddie put his hand on his chin thoughtfully, then began a slow stroll around Mark, eyeing him up and down. He turned back to Liz with a single raised eyebrow. "Well, as I told you, I do love a challenge." His gaze shifted back to Mark, then traveled up to his hair. "Hmm. Nice haircut, though."

Liz beamed at Mark, giving him an I-told-you-so look, and he rolled his eyes.

Eddie made a shooing sign at Liz with his hands. "Now, darling, why don't you go find a sale somewhere and come back in an hour? I have things under control here."

"Thanks, Eddie. I knew I could count on you."

"Wait a minute!" Mark said. "You're not staying?"

"You can trust Eddie," Liz said. "If he recommends something, spend the money. It'll be worth it. I promise."

"But—"

"I'll be back in an hour," she said with a big smile and a little wave of her fingertips. She turned and walked away, the hip pockets of her jeans swaying back and forth as only Liz's hip pockets could. Mark turned back to Eddie, who was staring at him with the tight, narrow-eyed expression of a very short, very intense Henry Higgins.

"Time to get started," he said, with a single clap of his hands. "We have a lot of ground to cover."

Mark cringed. The more ground they covered, the more it was going to cost him. "A suit. That's all I really need."

"Nonsense. I promised Liz a new man from the inside out, so first things first. Boxers or briefs?"

LIZ WANDERED AIMLESSLY through the mall, weaving in and out of Abercrombie & Fitch, then Garden Botanika, then browsed a store that sold nothing but purple stuff. She stopped for a while at the indoor ice rink to watch the skaters, which was a pretty surreal experience considering the temperature outside had topped the hundred-degree mark. Then she spied a coffee shop on the other side of the rink and headed for that. She wished she could have hung around the men's department, but she knew

Eddie too well for that. He had a flair for the dramatic. For maximum effect, she knew he wanted to dress Mark from head to toe, then display his artistry in one grand, high-fashion moment when she returned.

Liz got in line behind a guy at the coffee counter, who was practically threatening to sue if his coffee had a molecule of caffeine in it. She had no idea why people drank coffee if not for the buzz, but saying so in a place like this would be an unspeakable offense to Starbucks, god of the coffee bean.

The guy took his caffeine-deprived beverage and stepped aside. Liz approached the register. She asked for a cup of coffee. Not latte, not cappuccino, not espresso. Just coffee.

The perky little yuppie-in-training cocked her head and gave Liz a vacuous smile. "Sure. Plain coffee. Would you like Royal Raspberry Rum, Hawaiian Macadamia, Decadent White Chocolate Mint or Creamy Amaretto Delight?"

None of the above. What she wanted was a big ceramic mug full of hot, black coffee flavored with nothing but caffeine, served up by an over-the-hill waitress with a beehive hairdo and a pink polyester uniform who'd never even heard of macadamia nuts.

Liz sighed. Since Royal Raspberry Rum seemed to have the fewest syllables, she went with that one. She sat down at a table, grabbed a few sections of the *Dallas Morning News* that were lying on an adjacent table and tried to read, but she couldn't stop thinking about Mark.

What if he didn't like what Eddie picked out for him? What if he flipped over the price? What if he resented her horning into his life in the first place?

And why was it so important to her how he felt about it?

Because helping people was her destiny. Okay, maybe she was taking it a step or two further than her mother and grandmother by actually implementing her own advice, but Mark was a special case.

Ever since she'd left his apartment last night, she hadn't been able to stop thinking about what incredible potential lay just beneath his surface, if only he realized it. She didn't know his whole story, of course, but he was clearly hung up on the fact that he was from a small town where he'd grown up poor, and judging from his modest apartment, the clothes he wore, and the car he drove, he'd never gotten over it. She'd overheard enough conversations at Simon's to know that a manager at one of those big accounting firms pulled down a substantial amount of money, but none of it was reflected in Mark's lifestyle.

He was a rarity—a guy who had money but didn't flaunt it. A guy who had a position of professional responsibility but didn't yammer endlessly about it, trying to impress people. If he hadn't blown up last night and given himself away, she might never have known how successful he really was. He'd mentioned money markets and stock and thrift plans. She liked that about Mark. A lot. And he didn't seem to be nearly as stuffy as she would have assumed when she first saw his business card, either. His only negative trait seemed to be his poor taste in the opposite sex.

Why would he want a cold woman like that, anyway? Living with Gwen would undoubtedly mean he'd have to wear a smoking jacket around the house, drink beer out of a glass and eat pizza with a knife and fork—if Gwen would allow him to drink beer and eat pizza at all. What kind of fun was that?

Wait a minute. Pizza.

All at once she remembered Mark's invitation. *If we were to go out for a pizza after shopping…*

She swallowed hard, her heart suddenly racing. Had he been asking her out on a date?

No. That was silly. It had been just a friendly gesture.

Any man who went ga-ga over a woman like Gwen Adams would never be interested in a woman like her. Nor would she want a man who would want a Gwen Adams. But the more Liz tried to picture him with Gwen, the harder it was to imagine. He just didn't seem like the kind of guy who'd enjoy being around a woman like that.

Liz sighed and took another sip of coffee, admitting the truth to herself. Gwen was well-dressed, educated, and icy-perfect, and Mark was a professional man. Despite his small-town origins, he'd moved up the corporate ladder. Way up. Men like that looked for their female counterparts. But still he struck her as the kind of guy who wouldn't mind sitting in a brown vinyl booth at a truck stop diner, sipping thirty-weight coffee and chatting the night away.

No. That's exactly the kind of image he wants to escape. And he's counting on you to help him do it.

Exactly fifty-three minutes after she'd left the men's department, Liz returned. Eddie greeted her with a smile of supreme satisfaction, then sat her down in an overstuffed chair in a large, plush-carpeted room outside the men's dressing area. Soft classical music floated through the room, imparting an air of quiet sophistication. Eddie handed her a glass of wine.

"Relax, darling. You're going to love the show."

Then Mark came out of the dressing room.

5

LIZ BLINKED to clear her eyesight, because for a split second she wasn't completely sure that the man who walked out of the dressing room was actually Mark. She tried to reconcile the man she'd first seen in Simon's a couple of nights ago with the man she saw before her now, but there was such a disjunct between the two images that her brain was having a tough time putting them together. She blinked again. It was Mark, all right.

And he looked *gorgeous*.

He wore a dark navy double-breasted suit, a cornflower-blue shirt, and a tie in brilliant jewel tones. The cut of the suit showed off his body in a way his other suits never had, making him appear taller, trimmer in the waist and even broader in the shoulders. Eddie had removed his glasses and Mark's face had come alive, defining his cheekbones, sharpening his chin and adding a surprising touch of power and sensuality. And those eyes. Why hadn't she noticed his deep, dark eyes when he'd taken off his glasses the other night in the parking lot at Simon's? It had been nearly dark and they were in the midst of committing an act of vandalism, but even that shouldn't have mattered.

"The suit is Tallia Umo," Eddie said. "Mark's got such height and such an athletic build that the Versace and the Austin Sandoval I tried just weren't right. The tie is Bruno Westphal. He's one of the few designers holding on to bright colors right now, thank God. Mark's dark hair and eyes absolutely *demand* contrast, so I simply could not allow him to wear the drab brown tones everyone is so indiscriminately fond of this season.''

His running commentary went in one of Liz's ears and out the other. The designer names were meaningless to her, the color analysis nothing but white noise. All she knew was that the clothes had come together to create a man so attractive, she couldn't breathe.

Mark shrugged a little, giving Liz a look of apprehension, as if he were waiting for a bomb to drop. ''Well? What do you think?''

Liz just stared at him. Not only had he taken her breath away, but her speech had gone with it, as well.

Mark shook his head with disgust. ''I knew it. The tie's too loud, isn't it? I feel like a traffic light. And I've never worn a suit that *fits* like this before.'' He tugged at a button on the coat, then walked across the room to a three-way mirror, examining himself from all angles. ''It'll probably look even worse when I put my glasses back on and can actually see.''

Eddie leaned over to Liz and whispered, ''You'd better tell him how wonderful he looks, darling. He'll listen to you.''

''To me?''

''Oh, yes. Every time he tried something on, he asked me if I thought you'd like it. He values your opinion.''

Liz stared at Eddie, dumbfounded. Mark valued her opinion? Up to now she assumed he thought of her more like a prison guard leading him to his execution.

She set the wineglass down on the table beside her chair, then stood and walked over to Mark. With him in dress shoes and her wearing flip-flops, he towered over her by a good seven inches. When she looked into those deep-brown eyes—eyes she felt she was seeing for the first time—it struck her that he'd wasted ten years of his life being ordinary when he could have been spectacular.

She smoothed her hands down his lapels and gave them a gentle pat, then looked up at him.

"Mark, I'm saying this from the bottom of my heart, so I want you to listen up. I don't remember the last time I saw a man who looked as handsome as you do right now."

He stared at her blankly for a moment. Then his lips quirked up in a wary smile, as if she'd told him a joke and he wasn't quite sure he'd caught the punch line.

"You're kidding, right?"

His question told Liz this wasn't some thinly disguised self-deprecating attempt to hide an enormous ego. He genuinely didn't know how wonderful he looked.

Liz maintained her somber expression. "I've never been more serious in my life."

He turned back to the mirror, narrowing his eyes, as if to get a different perspective on the man looking back.

"Maybe I'm just not used to it," he said, his voice still unsure, as if the realization of how good he looked was coming to him in tiny pieces that he couldn't quite fit together yet.

"I told you, Mark. You look fabulous."

He stood up a little taller, pulled his shoulders back, then raised his chin a notch, until finally he was displaying the confident bearing that made the look complete—a successful man from head to toe. All at once she felt a strange, fluttery feeling in her stomach.

You're attracted to him.

It had been so long since she felt that deep-down reaction to a man that she froze, then told herself, *No, you're not.* He wasn't her type. She wasn't his. And that was that.

"I've helped him pick out other things, too," Eddie said. "Two more suits, slacks, shirts, ties, accessories. Everything he needs to make a spectacular appearance anywhere he goes."

Mark frowned, a look of uncertainty settling in again. "Look, Eddie. I know you went to a lot of trouble, but I'm not sure I really need—"

"Tell you what," Liz interrupted. "Why don't you go change, and while you're gone Eddie can ring everything up. Okay?"

Mark closed his eyes, then took a deep breath and let it out slowly. Reality had struck again. But Eddie had done wonders for his image, and she couldn't let him back out now.

"I'll give you the final tally," Eddie said. "After that you can still make adjustments if you want to."

To Liz's relief, Mark finally nodded. He disappeared into the dressing room. Eddie headed for the cash register, tossing Liz a sly smile over his shoulder.

"Go ahead, darling. Tell me. I outdid myself, yes?"

"Yes, Eddie," Liz said, joining him at the counter. "You outdid yourself."

"You never did say. Why the sudden need for a make-over? He looks smashing now, to be sure. But you don't usually go for the sophisticated look in your men."

"That's because he's not my man."

Eddie's brows arched. "Oh? I just assumed—"

"No. Actually, he's just a friend who decided he needed a new look."

"How long have you known him?"

"Not long. Just a few days, really."

Eddie beeped a hand-held scanner across a tag on one of the ties. "Very attractive man. Not classically so, exactly, but there's something about him...."

"Yes, I know."

"He seems to like you. Are you sure he's just a friend?"

"Don't start, Eddie. He's not my type. He's a CPA. All that corporate stuff. When's the last time you saw me date a guy like that?"

"Why not? He doesn't strike me as the snobbish type."

"He's not. He's just a really successful guy who wants to look the part. And he wants the women he dates to look the part, too."

"Perhaps he doesn't know what's good for him," Eddie said.

"But he knows what he wants, whether it's good for him or not. Trust me. It's not me."

She meant every word of that. Any man who had wanted a woman like Gwen would never be happy with a woman like her. Up until ten minutes ago, that hadn't mattered. Did it now?

Eddie beeped the scanner over several more tags. "Does he know how you feel about him?"

Liz's mouth dropped open. She lowered her voice to a whisper. "I don't *feel* any way about him!"

Eddie raised a single eyebrow. "Oh?"

"Cut it out, Eddie. You're way off base here."

Eddie dropped three dress shirts into a bag, then gave her a knowing smile. "I think you're protesting too much."

Eddie was a hopeless romantic. That was his problem. He saw what he wanted to see—true love blossoming before his very eyes. Sure she found Mark attractive—she wouldn't deny that—but that's as far as it went, and as far as it would ever go.

"Oh, sure, Eddie. Can't you just see me being one of those fluffy, picture-perfect little corporate wives? It gives me hives to even think about it."

Eddie merely shrugged, as if washing his hands of the issue, but his smug expression said he hadn't changed his mind.

A moment later Mark came out of the dressing room wearing his old clothes. He gave Eddie the suit and accessories he'd been wearing, and Eddie added them to the others. When he showed Mark the final tally, his face literally went white.

"Oh, boy." He breathed the words in such a shaky voice that Liz knew they weren't out of the woods yet. "I thought I was adding it up as we went along, but I— I had no idea."

"Mark? Are you okay?"

"Yeah. I'm fine. Really. It's no problem. I'll just pay this bill and then declare bankruptcy."

He closed his eyes, his jaw tight, and despite his sarcasm she could see how truly painful it was for him to spend this much money. It went beyond being frugal, or even miserly. She knew it touched something deep inside him that he'd never really reconciled, and it hurt like hell to face it.

"It's worth every penny," Liz said, dropping her voice so she was talking just to him. "Every penny. Do you understand me?"

He turned his gaze back to meet hers. She lay her hand against his arm and gave it an encouraging squeeze. He swallowed hard, and for a moment she truly thought he was going to call the whole thing off.

"Okay," he said finally. "If you say so."

Liz felt a surge of relief. He laid the charge slip on the counter and signed it, then tucked the receipt into his wallet. He sighed.

"Thanks, Liz."

"For what?"

"For making me do something I should have done a long time ago. Of course, a long time ago I'd have had to rob a bank to pay the bill."

He smiled, and that fluttery feeling struck Liz again. It wasn't as if she felt *that* way about him, as Eddie had suggested. She just hadn't expected such a drastic change. That was all. She certainly wasn't shallow enough to be attracted to a guy solely because of the way he looked.

But was it that he looked so handsome, or that he didn't know it?

She saw nice-looking men every day of her life at Simon's. Some absolutely *dazzling* men. But those good looks were always accompanied by a huge ego—the prettier the face, the bigger the conceit—and not one of them had ever made her feel the way she did right now when she looked at Mark.

Not to mention the way she felt when he looked at her. Lord have mercy. Could Eddie be right after all?

THEY LEFT Bergman's and took a trip to the optical shop, where Mark let Liz talk him into getting a long-overdue eye exam, then contact lenses. He'd anticipated having to spend days getting used to them, but he was surprised how comfortable they really were. Unfortunately, the new lenses put him back to twenty-twenty again, so the bottom line on the bill was so crystal clear he couldn't pretend it was anything less than what it was. But Liz's admiration for the way he looked without his glasses made him feel as if the contacts, like the clothes he'd just bought, were worth every bit he'd spent.

They walked back through the mall, and as he gazed around at the extravagant surroundings, he thought back to when he was a kid. The only place his mother could afford to shop had been in the thrift store in Mason, Texas, twelve miles down the road from Waldon Springs. His clothes had always been too big or too small and had always belonged to somebody else first. Back then he never could have imagined shopping in a place like this and having the means to buy the things he'd bought today. But that was exactly why he'd left Waldon Springs and worked his tail off all these years—so he could become wealthy and successful enough that he could forget that kid had ever existed. Thanks to Liz, that memory had faded more this afternoon than it had in the past ten years.

"Are you ready for that pizza now?" Liz asked as they headed to the mall exit.

"Yeah. I'm starving, and you're buying. It doesn't get any better than that."

Gino's Pizzaria turned out to be one of those funky holes in the wall on Lower Greenville, with plastic red-checkered tablecloths, rough plank floors and garage-sale art. A waitress led them to a table close to a big screen TV, where a baseball game was in progress—the Texas Rangers versus the Yankees in Dallas. He would have loved to watch it, but he figured it would be rude to stare at the game all through dinner and ignore Liz. So to alleviate temptation, he circled the table and sat with his back to the big-screen TV.

Liz looked down at him quizzically. "Why are you sitting there?"

"Why not?"

"Because you can't see the game, silly." She turned the table around a little and pulled two rickety wooden chairs together that faced the TV. "There. Now we can both see just fine."

Mark blinked with surprise. "You watch the Rangers?"

"My dad took me to a lot of baseball games before he died. I was kind of a pudgy little kid, and I think it was because of all the hot dogs I ate at the ballpark." She nodded toward Mark. "I assume you like baseball, too, or you wouldn't be wearing that shirt."

Mark looked down at his Texas Rangers T-shirt. Good point.

After they ordered a large deep dish with everything and a couple of beers, Liz leaned over to an elderly man at the table next to them. He held a cigar between his stubby fingers, its smoke twirling toward the ceiling.

"What inning is it?" she asked.

"Bottom of the fourth," he said, in a New York accent

so thick his aging vocal cords could barely eek out the words. "Score's one-zip, New York."

"You really keep up with the Rangers?" Mark asked Liz.

"Uh-huh. And the Cowboys, and the Stars, and the Mavericks. With luck, Dallas will get the Olympics in 2012."

All at once a roar went up from the crowd at the restaurant, and Mark spun around to the TV. A ball sailed over the left field fence and the batter rounded the bases to tie the score.

Liz let out a whoop, then turned to Mark with a smile of delight. "This is going to be a great game! And it's so much better on the big screen. I'm glad we came here."

So am I, Mark thought, even though he wasn't completely sure it was only because of the game.

They finished off the pizza, then ordered two more drinks and settled in to watch the game. Every time the network flashed one of those baseball trivia questions on the screen, Liz had an answer, and she never missed. It wasn't long before she garnered the attention of people at the surrounding tables, the vast majority of whom were men. They seemed to be a die-hard group of sports fans, but it was impossible to miss the sidelong glances they cast at the flamboyant redheaded Ranger's fan. Once a couple of guys even came over and asked her to settle a bet—something about lifetime batting averages Mark couldn't have answered in a million years. The answer rolled right off her tongue.

All Mark could do was sit back in amazement. He'd never known anyone like Liz. She was smart, sassy, flamboyant, fun and *alive,* and she'd never met a stranger in her life. And people liked her. A lot. She had a kind of glow about her that warmed a room the moment she stepped into it. Just being with her made him see how secluded his life had been, how work-intensive, and above all, how god-awful boring. And he hadn't even realized it.

He thought back to this afternoon. Eddie had assured him that the clothes were exactly right for him, but Mark now realized that all the time Liz had been gone, he'd been holding his breath, waiting for her to return so he could see his reflection in her eyes. He remembered the surprise on her face when he walked out of the dressing room. For a minute he'd thought she didn't like the way he looked and his chest had tightened with disappointment. Then she'd told him, with that warm, wonderful smile of hers, how handsome he looked. Handsome. He couldn't remember a time in his life when he'd *ever* felt like that.

Out of the corner of his eye, he watched Liz enjoying the game, and suddenly he was hyperaware of everything about her—the strands of auburn hair that cascaded around her face, her warm, musical laughter, the feel of her hand against his arm whenever she wanted his attention. She'd lean toward him and point out something on the screen, and she'd be so close that he could smell the faint remnants of the perfume she wore. It was a quirky scent he couldn't quite place, but it suited her perfectly.

"So how are you feeling after the shopping trip?" she asked him. "Are you getting over the sticker shock?"

All at once he realized that, for the past hour, he hadn't been thinking about the money he'd spent at all. He'd been thinking about Liz.

"I'm fine. Another beer and I'll forget all about it." He paused. "Until the credit card bill comes."

"Want me to come by for moral support when you open the envelope?"

"Good idea. I'll need someone to call the paramedics."

"Who needs paramedics? I know CPR."

Mark was suddenly blindsided by an image that sprang

to his mind—an image of Liz's lips meeting his and bringing him back to life.

"I want you to come by Simon's Monday night after work," Liz said, "so you can tell me how your day went. You're bound to get a thousand compliments on your new look, and I want to hear all about it."

"I don't know about the compliments," he said, "but I can drop by."

She smiled. "I'll be waiting."

Simon's. That meant he could see Liz again.

That thought warmed him so much that he held on to it far longer than ever he should have, finally shoving it aside and concentrating on the real reason he needed to go to Simon's again: his company function was coming up in less than three weeks, and it was a gathering place for just the kind of woman he needed.

Then, out of nowhere, an image of Gwen flashed through his mind. He saw her sitting on that bar stool, aloof and icy-perfect, holding a glass of white wine that was almost as chilly as the look she'd given him when she'd handed back his suit coat and said, in so many words, that he just didn't measure up. A small shiver actually slithered down his spine, as if a wisp of cool air had suddenly swirled through the restaurant.

Liz touched his arm again, running her hand from his wrist to his elbow and back down again. "Hey. You okay?"

He turned to meet her eyes, and the imaginary Arctic air instantly disappeared, replaced by a balmy Caribbean breeze.

"Mark?"

"Uh, yeah. I'm fine. Why?"

"You were frowning."

"Sorry. Didn't mean to be."

"Having a good time?"

He smiled with contentment. "Yeah. I am."

Liz nodded toward the screen, where the Rangers were

retiring to the dugout after holding the Yankees to a tied game in the top of the ninth.

"Think they can pull it out in the bottom of the ninth?" Liz asked.

"Depends on how loud you cheer for them."

That's when he found out Liz could whistle through her fingers.

A minute later she rose from her seat. "I've got to go to the little girls' room," she said. "Don't let the game start again without me."

As Liz headed toward the rest room, Mark felt a tap on his arm. Cigar Man.

"That little redhead sure does remind me of my wife when she was her age," he confided, with the raspy voice of a guy who'd smoked for approximately seventy-one of his seventy-two years.

"Your wife?"

"Yeah. Mildred knew more about the Yankees than I did. We had season tickets for thirty years. Some of the best times we ever had were at ball games." He leaned closer to Mark. "Let me tell you something. Having stuff in common like you and your girl do—that's what it's all about. And a pistol like that one," he said with a grin, "is gonna keep you entertained for the rest of your life." He clapped Mark on the shoulder. "You're a lucky man. Hang on to her."

Liz? His girl?

It amazed him that a total stranger had watched them together and assumed they were a couple. He started to tell the man that Liz wasn't his girl at all, but somehow the words got lost between his brain and his mouth. Finally he just smiled and nodded.

His girl.

For some reason, Mark couldn't get those words out of his mind. He thought about how easy Liz was to be around, and what an incredibly good time he had when he was with her. And just for a moment he found himself wishing that the ideal corporate wife was a curvaceous bartender with a headful of auburn hair and an outrageous wardrobe, who loved to watch baseball and could whistle through her fingers.

LIZ LEANED against the bathroom wall, her eyes closed, trying to get a grip on herself. When had it happened? When had she stopped looking at Mark as just a friend? Or as a person she'd promised to help? Or even as a nice guy who was fun to hang out with? When had she started looking at him the way a woman looks at a man she's attracted to—physically, mentally and every other way there was?

For the last hour, she'd used every excuse in the world to touch him because it felt so wonderful. She'd watched furtively for signs that he objected to that, but she hadn't seen any. In fact, the longer they were together, the better he seemed to like it. And as the evening had worn on, she'd inched closer to him, as if trying to make it easier for them to talk with all the noise around them. Had he noticed, though, that the restaurant really wasn't all that loud?

The last thing you need is an uptight accountant.

That argument might have held water when she first met Mark, only she'd discovered he really wasn't all that uptight. At least, he hadn't been once they left the Galleria. He seemed right at home here, having a beer and cheering for the Rangers along with her.

She went back to their table and slid into her chair just as the Yankee pitcher threw the first ball to start the bottom of the ninth. She settled in to watch game, but she was so fixated on Mark, she barely noticed when the Rangers put a man on base. A few minutes later a batter knocked a ball deep into right field, allowing the man on base to score. The moment he crossed home to win the game, everyone in the restaurant came to their feet cheering. Liz leaped up along with everyone else, and in a reflex action, she threw her arms around Mark's neck and gave him a hug. He circled his arms around her waist, lifted her from the floor and swung her around in a circle in celebration. Then, when he set her down again, something changed.

Their gazes locked, their arms still wrapped around each other. He should have let her go by now. Why hadn't he?

Driven by some force she couldn't control, Liz's gaze fell to Mark's lips. It lingered there a moment, then rose to meet his eyes again. In the span of a single heartbeat, she imagined him slipping his hand around the back of her neck, pulling her close, meeting her lips with his—

"So what do you think?" Mark said, as he released her and moved away. "Will the Rangers go all the way to the play-offs?"

Liz blinked herself back to reality. Had she imagined those few seconds between them that had held so much potential? It had been silly, of course, to think he would kiss her while they were standing in the middle of a crowd of sports fans. But just for a moment, she could have sworn...

Collecting herself, Liz looked at Mark.

"The play-offs? They'll go all the way to the World Series."

"Such optimism," he said. "I like that in a woman."

What else do you like in a woman? Do I even come close?

As Mark smiled down at her, Liz felt the possibilities blossoming between them. He was coming to Simon's on Monday night, and the thought of seeing him again made her entire body tingle. Maybe they weren't so different after all, and something could happen between them.

One way or the other, she intended to find out.

6

AT SEVEN FORTY-FIVE on Monday morning, Mark rode up the elevator to the offices of Nichols, Marbury & White. He'd spent all day Sunday worrying about what his co-workers' reactions to his new look might be. And now, as he stared into the elevator's mirrored wall, he still felt uncertain about the guy looking back.

He'd messed with his hair for a good twenty minutes this morning, but no matter what he did, it still stuck up funny. The suit looked pretty good, though, and he was finally getting used to looking at his face without glasses. But how would people react to such a radical change? Would they think he looked sharp and professional, as Liz seemed to think, or would they think he look like some pitifully unsophisticated guy trying for sharp and professional and missing by a mile?

When the elevator doors opened on the seventh floor, he took a deep breath and strode across the lobby past the receptionist, who was engrossed in a phone conversation and didn't look up. He went down the hall toward his outer office. He strode past Tina's desk, where she sat tapping away at her computer.

"Morning, boss," she said, giving him the same quick glance and smile of greeting she always did before returning to her work. He returned the greeting and kept on walking.

"Stop!"

Mark's heart leaped to his throat. He ground to a halt,

then turned around to find Tina gaping at him. She walked over to him, circled him slowly, then came back around to face him, swallowing hard.

"Wow," she said. "What did you do to yourself?"

Tina's startled reaction made Mark wish he had a great big rock to crawl under, until he saw her huge smile of delight.

"You…look…*fabulous!* How did you…? What did you…?"

"I just did a little shopping, that's all."

"That's *all?* New suit, new haircut… Oh, God, your glasses are gone! So who picked all this stuff out for you? No offense, Mark. But guys are usually clueless, and up to now, you—" She paused. "I didn't mean that as an insult. It's just that—"

"I know, Tina. It's different. But you're telling me it's good different?"

"Are you kidding? If I could get my husband to dress like this, I'd think I'd died and gone to heaven."

Mark felt a flush of relief. The apprehension he felt when he came into the office vanished. If everyone reacted the way Tina had, his new look could be just the boost his career needed.

"Hey, McAlister. I need to talk to you about—"

Mark spun around to see Jared Sloan standing in the hallway. The man's eyes widened, and then his mouth dropped open, but nothing came out. Neither Mark nor Tina said a word. In silent, mutual understanding, they let Sloan clear his throat and cough a little in that phony way people always did when they had no clue what to say next.

"Uh, the Dixon Pharmaceuticals account. We need to talk. When, you know, you have a minute."

The whole time he stuttered and stammered, his gaze was glued to Mark. Mark felt a rush of satisfaction. It was the first time he'd ever seen Sloan stumble around, searching for words. Mark didn't dare hope it was because he finally looked the part of a successful professional man on the verge of a partnership. But what else could it be? Could it be that for the first time Sloan sensed a little competition?

"Dixon Pharmaceuticals? Tina, check my schedule, will you? Let Mr. Sloan know when I'm free today?"

"Certainly," Tina said, raising her nose a notch and returning to her desk for his calendar. She traced a long, pink fingernail down the page in that distracted, slightly annoyed manner that said, *We'll see if we can work you in.* Mark wanted to kiss her for it.

"Hmm," she murmured. "I suppose we could squeeze you in around one-thirty."

"Okay," Sloan said. "Come down to my office, and—"

"No," Mark said, determined not to be one-upped by that power play Sloan loved to use. It was time he was the one who sat in his executive chair behind a big desk while they discussed business, instead of him squeezing into one of Sloan's guest chairs and looking like a subordinate. "We'll meet in my office." He turned to walk away in a gesture of dismissal, then turned back. "And Sloan? I've got a full schedule today. Don't be late."

Sloan nodded and left the office. It didn't escape Mark's notice that that his rival's usual arrogant swagger was strangely absent.

Tina peered around the corner until Sloan was out of earshot, then spun back around. "Ha! Did you see the look on his face? That was *so* cool!"

Mark couldn't help smiling himself. And all he could think was, *Liz was right. I don't look outrageous. I look...successful.*

Work on the outside, and the inside will follow.

"Here's what we'll do," Tina continued. "When he comes back here at one-thirty for your meeting, you stay in your office with the door closed, and I'll make him wait out here. Maybe ten minutes or so. Just to irritate him."

"That won't be necessary, Tina."

"Why not? He does it to you every time you go to *his* office, doesn't he?"

"I know. That's why we're not going to do it."

Tina looked supremely disappointed. "How about I give him a cup of regular coffee and tell him it's decaf? You know how he spazzes out if there's caffeine in his coffee."

"Sorry, Tina. No sabotage."

"Can I make nasty faces behind his back?"

"You do that already."

"True." Tina sighed. "Damn. I hate professional workplaces. No room for genuine creativity."

After Sloan left Mark's office, his day only got better. He got compliments all over the place, from his co-workers to the owner of the deli on the fourth floor to the UPS delivery girl. Then after lunch, the managing partner, Edwin Nichols, came down to his office, which he rarely did, for a reason that seemed flimsy. He even stayed around to shoot the breeze, which was even more unprecedented, since he believed that every moment of every business day should be consumed with doing business. As usual, he wore his toupee—a mass of hairlike material a blind man could spot at a hundred paces. Considering he had more money than Midas, his choice of hair augmentation was a mystery that nobody at Nichols, Marbury & White had ever been able to solve.

"A personal visit from the man himself," Tina mused after Edwin left. "That's a good sign."

"Now don't go reading anything into it."

"Oh, I wouldn't think of it," she said, but he could already see her wheels turning as she plotted her next entry into the company grapevine. Then she assumed a thoughtful expression.

"I wonder if Edwin knows a weasel fell asleep on top of his head."

"Now, Tina. You're not supposed to malign Edwin's hair."

"You're right. I'm being heartless. I mean, maybe that really is his hair, and he has some obscure genetic disease. *Hairus hideousus*. Suppose we ought to get a telethon together to help eradicate that?"

Mark knew he should make a better effort to curb Tina's running commentary on office life, but since entertainment around here was so hard to come by his heart really wasn't in it.

Later in the day, Tina stuck her head into his office and asked him if he'd received the invitation to the company dinner dance. Mark couldn't believe he'd forgotten all about it. He had only a little over two weeks until that function and he still hadn't found a date.

"You are coming aren't you?" Tina asked.

"Uh…yeah. I'll be there."

"With a *date* this time?"

Mark gave her an admonishing look. "Did I ever tell you how nosy you are?"

"I'll take that as a compliment. So will you be bringing a date or not?"

Trying to sidestep Tina's questions was like trying to sidestep the Grand Canyon. "Yes, Tina. I'll be bringing a date."

"Anyone I know?"

"No. It's no one you know."

And it was no one Mark knew, either. Yet.

"Well, it's about time." Tina grabbed the contents of his out box and headed for the door. She tossed a grin back over her shoulder. "I'm looking forward to meeting her."

So am I.

LIZ CHECKED HER WATCH. Ten until six. She wished she knew what time Mark got off work. Five o'clock? Five-thirty? How long would it take him to get here? And the later it got, the more she wondered if he were coming at all.

Liz put four margaritas on a tray and slid it over to one of the waitresses. She wiped up some spilled lime juice, and for the hundredth time, her gaze wandered to the door. When she finally saw Mark walk in, her heart leaped, then settled into a crazy rhythm. She thought she remembered how handsome he looked on Saturday, but as he walked into the club she had a hard time catching her breath. Again.

It wasn't just the clothes. It was the way he walked, his chin up, gazing around the room as if he owned it for a switch, rather than trying to remain anonymous. She remembered the first night she'd met him, how he'd blended right into the wall. Well, he wasn't doing a heck of a lot of blending now. As he walked through the club, heads literally turned, and almost every woman in the place gave him an appreciative up-and-down look. Mark seemed oblivious to all of it. He came to the bar and slid onto a stool. He gave Liz a big smile and a cheerful hello, and she practically melted right into the floor.

How had this happened? How had she gone from helping him catch a woman to wishing she were the woman he wanted to catch?

"So how was your day?" she asked, though the smile he wore made it no mystery at all.

"It couldn't have been better."

"Compliments?"

"All over the place. I couldn't believe the number of people who said something to me. You were right, Liz."

She grinned. "Told you so. Can I get you something to drink? Scotch?"

"Sounds good."

Liz moved down the bar to pour him a drink, hoping the crowd was light tonight so she and Mark would have time to chat some more. But she was *not* going to get all weird about this. She was not going to give in to some adolescent schoolgirl infatuation and hyperventilate every time she saw him, even though she hadn't stopped thinking about him since they parted on Saturday night. She wasn't going to stare at him when he wasn't looking, even though it was sure to make her feel all light-headed and giddy. And she was *not* going to think about them maybe going on an actual date, even though she'd had such a wonderful time with him at Gino's. After all, he probably still thought he wanted a woman like Gwen, and it might be an uphill battle to convince him otherwise.

Calm, cool and collected. That's what she was.

She fixed a Scotch and water, then turned back around, and all her calm, cool collection went right out the window.

In the time it had taken her to make the drink, a young woman had slid onto the stool beside Mark. She wore a red suit with a neckline that dipped far too low to be conservative, along with so much gold jewelry she probably rattled when she walked. She swept her chemically enhanced blond hair away from her shoulder with a preening flick of her hand and gave him a dazzling smile.

"Hi, there."

Mark smiled back at her. Liz set the Scotch and water down in front of him. He smiled and thanked her. When the blonde touched his sleeve and he turned back to her, that thing that had fluttered around in Liz's stomach for the past two days curled into a tight little ball and lay there like a rock.

She walked back down the bar and took a few drink orders, trying to pretend nothing was going on behind her back, but still she had the urge to yank Mark aside and spell out a few facts. Did he know that little hussy's glowing blond hair was mouse-brown in disguise? Did he know that anyone that thin was clearly anorexic? Did he know she probably still remembered all her high-school cheerleading routines? Did he *know* these things?

Liz glanced down the bar at Mark, and by the unassuming smile he wore, she knew he didn't. He wasn't used to looking as handsome as he did right now, and therefore he was totally ill-equipped to deal with a sexually overblown little hussy with the wardrobe of Business Barbie and the come-hither stare of a two-bit tramp.

"So is he here yet?"

Liz spun around to see Sherri standing at the bar.

"Who?"

"Mark. You know. The guy you wouldn't shut up about earlier? The guy who looks *wonderful* now?"

Liz refused even to turn around and subject herself to that blonde. "Uh, yeah," she said, nodding over her shoulder. "He's here. Down at the end of the bar."

"Where?"

"Talking to that blonde."

Sherri stared for a moment, then turned to Liz with a skeptical look. "That's the same guy who was so intimidated by the Shark Woman last week? The one you couldn't blast off the bar stool with a nuclear bomb?"

"Yeah."

"Wow." Sherri blinked, then blinked again. "You weren't kidding. He looks great."

"I know."

"So what's with the blonde?"

Liz shrugged, then grabbed a drink order and started pouring a couple of vodka tonics, telling herself she was *not* going to turn around to monitor the situation. But Sherri's expression as she watched them said it all.

"Wow!" Sherri whispered. "She's really coming on to him, isn't she?"

Liz slapped the drinks onto a tray. She grabbed her purse, ducked under the bar, and headed down the hall to the ladies' room. She shoved the door open and went to the sink, feeling a swell of irritation, or anger, or *some-*

thing she couldn't exactly identify, but it was driving her nuts just the same.

A few moments later, the bathroom door swung open and Sherri came in. "Liz? What's the matter?"

"Who's watching the bar?"

"Allison. Are you mad about something?"

"No. I'm not mad about anything."

For lack of anything better to do, Liz pulled the pins out of her hair because some of it was falling down anyway, then took a brush from her purse.

"That sleazy little blonde," Liz said, raking her brush through her hair. "She was practically sitting in Mark's lap!"

"Yeah, I saw."

"I swear, Sherri, she might as well have Wanna Go to Bed? tattooed across her forehead. I can't believe Mark is even talking to her. I'll bet there's not a single inch of her that hasn't been chemically, mechanically or surgically altered."

Liz took a few more swipes at her hair, then pulled it up into a ponytail, yanking it so hard she winced.

"Liz? Are you...jealous?

Liz froze for a moment, then tucked her ponytail into a knot at the crown of her head and pinned it securely. "Of course not!"

"Yes, you are. You're jealous!"

Liz jammed her brush back into her purse. "I am *not* jealous!"

She squeezed her eyes closed, then put her hand to her forehead, hating the feeling of all those mixed emotions scurrying around inside her head.

"Oh, all right!" She zipped her purse shut and plunked it down on the counter, trying to get a grip on herself and failing miserably. "It was the weirdest thing, Sherri. On Saturday it was as if there was this really nice guy there, and then all the sudden there was this really nice, *handsome* guy. But it wasn't just his looks. It was everything about him. We had such a good time together, and...and now I don't know what to do about it."

"Do you think he likes you?"

"Sure, he *likes* me. But anything more—I don't know. I'm hardly the kind of woman he's looking for."

"That blonde is no competition, Liz. She's a walking, talking stereotype. If he's halfway smart, he'll see right through her. In fact, I'll bet he's looking for an excuse to get away from her right now. Why don't you go give him one?"

Liz felt that stupid fluttering in her stomach again, and she wondered if it would *ever* go away. This was exactly what she'd told herself she wasn't going to do, and here she was doing it.

"I'll be out in a minute," Liz said. "Will you go check on Allison? She thinks Johnnie Walker is a country-western singer."

"Sure."

Sherri left the bathroom, and Liz turned back to the mirror. She dug in her purse and put on a little lipstick, wondering if Mark really did want that blonde to go away. After all, he certainly was a smart man, and smart men didn't like brainless bimbos. Then again, that blonde was offering her body, not her brain. What difference did it make whether or not she could answer the questions on "Jeopardy"?

Liz had to see what was happening.

She left the bathroom and walked back down the hall. When she came around the corner and glanced at the other end of the bar, she felt like cheering. The blonde was nowhere to be seen. Mark was alone.

She breathed a huge sigh of relief. Okay. Now she could take it easy. Be nonchalant. Just chat with him. It had been easy the first night he'd come in here. Why wasn't it easy now?

Because you didn't feel about him then the way you feel about him now.

She ducked under the bar and came up behind it, and the minute she did, Mark turned. He met her gaze. She stopped and stared at him, her breath catching in her throat. He never took his eyes off her. It was as if he'd specifically been waiting for that blonde to leave and for Liz to return. Then he gave her a brilliant, welcoming smile.

She smiled back, and all at once it was like in the movies, when a man's and a woman's eyes meet across a crowded room. Everything else around them fades into the background, and at that moment they're the only two people left on earth. All at once Liz had that musical comedy kind of feeling—the one that told her roses were blooming, birds were singing, life was full of a thousand possibilities and dreams really did come true. Something was happening between them. She just knew it.

Then she saw Gwen Adams walking toward the bar.

Liz ground to a halt, her heart suddenly in her throat. For a moment she held out hope that Gwen had simply been taking a roundabout route to the bathroom and had gotten lost. But to her dismay, the Paragon of Perfection slid onto the bar stool beside Mark. She touched his sleeve to get his attention, and when he turned she smiled at him as only an impeccably gorgeous woman can, with flawless lips and perfect teeth and eyes that made her whole face sparkle. Liz wouldn't have thought that arrogant face of Gwen's could express actual warmth, but that's sure what it looked like right now.

Then Liz shifted her gaze to Mark. He stared at Gwen with an expression of dumb disbelief, which slowly melted into a smile of utter delight.

At that moment, Liz wanted to die.

7

FOR THE NEXT thirty minutes, Liz watched Mark and Gwen out of the corner of her eye. She waited on other customers and filled drink orders, still trying to make some sense of the adoring expression she saw on Gwen's face when she gazed at Mark. Worse, though, was that Mark was gazing at her with equal adoration.

Well. So much for singing birds and blooming roses and all that other nonsense. How dumb and deluded had that been? As euphoric as she'd felt before, that's how depressed she felt now. What had ever made her think there could be something between her and Mark, even for a minute?

Wishful thinking. That's what.

"Oh, my God," Sherri whispered, coming up beside Liz, giving Gwen and Mark a sidelong glance. "What's going on there?"

"I don't know."

"It's the Shark Woman. Talking to Mark."

Liz was silent.

"If you want him, go after him."

"I can't do that."

"Why not?"

"Because he wants *her*," Liz said with a dejected sigh. "He's wanted her since the first night he walked in here."

"They sure do seem chummy, don't they? Wow. It's amazing what a change of wardrobe will do."

That had to be it. It was the only thing about Mark that

had changed since the night he'd helped Gwen with her tire. To Liz's surprise, that crinkly, constipated look Gwen wore most of the time had given way to an actual bit of animation in her expression. And her body language—her casual shifting toward Mark, the way she touched his sleeve every once in a while, and the way she tossed her head back to laugh softly at something amusing he said—were all hallmarks of someone who was highly interested. Sadly, Mark was returning her attention, giving that wonderful smile of his to a woman Liz didn't even know, but was absolutely sure she hated.

Sherri leaned closer to Liz and dropped her voice. "Want me to dump a drink in her lap?"

Liz liked the sound of that, but what would it accomplish? When it got right down to it, she knew what Mark wanted, and it wasn't her.

She tried to concentrate on her job and not look toward the end of the bar, but after twenty minutes her eye muscles were worn out from trying to be inconspicuous. Then she saw Gwen rise from the bar stool and give Mark one last smile, dragging her fingertip over his shoulder as she walked away. Mark turned on his bar stool in sync with Gwen's departure, moving around 180 degrees so he could watch her leave.

When he came back around, Liz turned away quickly so he wouldn't see her staring.

"Hey, Liz!"

Liz froze, trying to ignore him.

"Liz! Come here!"

Finally she turned around and walked to the end of the bar. Mark leaned toward her, lowering his voice. "You're not going to believe this. I have a date with Gwen."

His words were matter-of-fact, but she could hear the undercurrent of excitement in his voice, and her heart fell to her toes.

"You do?"

"I can't believe it. She came up and started talking to me, thanking me for changing her tire the other night. Before I knew it, we were talking about going to dinner together."

"That's great."

"It has to be the clothes, Liz. I look different. I *feel* different. She was so easy to talk to this time, as if I'd known her forever."

Liz mustered up a smile, wishing she could be genuinely glad that he was getting what he wanted. But she wasn't. No matter how sweet Gwen was being tonight, she was a barracuda at heart. Anyone could see that. Anyone, it seemed, but Mark.

"There's still a problem, though," Mark said.

Liz's heart leaped. "Oh? What's that?"

"It's where she wants to go to dinner. Rosario's."

Liz couldn't believe it. That was one of the most expensive, exclusive restaurants in Dallas, and Gwen had suggested it?

"Wow. I hear it's pretty expensive."

"I can deal with that part. I mean, I'll choke when I see the bill, but I'll deal with it. You've convinced me that I'm going to have to get used to spending money."

Me and my big mouth.

"The problem is that I've never been to a restaurant like that before. If I walk in there cold with Gwen, I'm bound to screw something up."

"So go someplace else."

"She suggested it."

"Don't you think that's a little presumptuous?"

"No. She probably eats there a lot. Maybe it's her favorite restaurant. It's kind of like you suggesting Gino's."

Liz cringed at that comparison. She was beer and pizza. Gwen was crystal, silver and six-course meals. And it was pretty clear which he preferred. It made her feel not just in second place, but out of the running altogether.

"You'll be fine, Mark. It's just a restaurant. How different could it really be?"

"I don't know, but I don't want to take any chances. If I'm going to screw something up, I don't want to do it in front of Gwen. I'm going there before our date to check it out."

"I guess that couldn't hurt."

"I want you to come with me."

Liz looked at him with astonishment. "What for? I don't know any more about fancy restaurants than you do."

"Because it's just not the kind of place you can go by yourself."

The irony was just too much for Liz to bear. She was going to be nothing more than a warm-up act. His practice date. And then the real woman he wanted would step in and take over.

"I'll call for reservations. Gwen's going to be out of town until Friday, so I have a little time to play with."

"Mark—"

He reached out and took her hand, enveloping it in both of his. The initial shock she felt at his touch was displaced by her sudden awareness of how warm and strong his hands were. A shiver raced up her arm, then took a sharp right turn and headed straight for her heart.

"I shouldn't be asking you to help me when you've helped me so much already. But it's so important that I impress Gwen."

"I don't get it. If you have to work so darned hard to impress her, is she really worth it?"

"Yes."

He answered so unequivocally that Liz was taken aback.

"She's the woman I need, Liz. I know this makes no sense to you, but I have to make this work, and I have to do it now."

Mark's intensity when he spoke about Gwen was even greater now than the first night he'd come to Simon's. How was she supposed to fight that?

She'd said once that she'd never be interested in a man who would want a woman like Gwen. No matter how down to earth Mark seemed, it was clear now that they'd never be compatible if he was still that intent on having the Ice Princess. Finding that out now beat obsessing over him for weeks only to discover the hard way—*after* she'd fallen for him—that he really wasn't the man for her. Besides, this was a good lesson for the future. Once she got her psychology degree, was she going to get all emotionally involved and fall for every person she tried to help?

She still wanted to say no. But Mark was looking at her with such a hopeful expression, and with the feel of her hand still tucked inside his, she just couldn't make the word come out.

"Okay," she said. "Just tell me when you want to go."

Mark grinned. He patted her hand, then released it. "Great. I'll try for reservations sometime in the next couple of days, and then get Saturday night reservations for Gwen and me."

At that moment, Liz made a decision. Chasing after a man who was so clearly interested in another woman was pitiful, so she was not going to look at Mark as if he were anything but a friend. She was not going to wish their "date" were the real thing. She was not going to pray that Gwen would contract a weird tropical disease that turned her face purple and made all her hair fall out.

No. She was going to do what she'd promised Mark in the beginning. She was going to do everything in her power to get him a shot at his dream woman.

And that would be that.

THREE DAYS LATER, Mark drove down Collins Boulevard, the main thoroughfare that ran through Morrison Heights, an eclectic part of town with strange little antique shops, quirky restaurants and semirenovated apartment buildings, all steeped in the art deco of the 1930s. He saw a secondhand store, a turn-of-the-century church, an ethnic bookstore, then turned into an apartment building parking lot at the address Liz had given him.

He pulled into a parking space beside the red brick building with green-and-white awnings over the windows, most of which were coming loose and flapping in the night breeze. He shut his car door, double-checking to make sure it was locked. Sandwiched between a rusty Camaro and a vintage Volkswagen that was a lovely shade of pea-green, his Volvo practically screamed "Steal me."

Thank God for car insurance.

Mark went up the steps and into the building, where he was immediately assaulted by a cataclysm of color. The walls were a few shades lighter than a ripe peach. Woodwork that should have been natural oak had been painted forest-green, with the ceiling awash in turquoise and sponged with blobs of white that he figured were supposed to be clouds. On the wall by the stairs, a bizarre floor-to-ceiling mural of a jungle appeared to have been painted by someone in the throes of an LSD flashback.

Mark made his way up the wide oak staircase, a little nervous at the persistent creaking beneath his feet. He headed for the numberless door with the eucalyptus wreath, just as Liz had described when he'd called to tell her he'd gotten reservations.

He rapped on the door.

"It's open! Come in!"

He opened the door cautiously. "Liz?"

"Make yourself at home!" she shouted from the bedroom. "I'll be ready in a minute!"

He came in and shut the door behind him, making a mental note to chastise her for being way too trusting and leaving her apartment unlocked. Then he turned around and got an eyeful of Liz's living room. The visual effect almost knocked him off his feet. As a man used to only the sparse necessities of life—sofa, bed, TV, stereo, microwave—her decor put him right into sensory overload.

Nothing matched. Nothing even came close. A huge, overstuffed sofa sat against one wall, its big red flowers clashing like crazy with the lime-green velvet chair along an adjacent wall. The end table and coffee table probably hadn't been made in the same century. And photos were everywhere—amateur shots of people who couldn't possibly all be relatives—in a weird assortment of frames that lined the walls, the tables, and every shelf of a bookcase next to the window.

All in all, it looked like an explosion at a flea market.

"Hi."

Mark spun around, and he discovered that the visual effect of Liz's living room was nothing compared to the visual effect of Liz.

A strapless electric-green sheath of clingy fabric hugged her body, staying in place by some unseen force Mark couldn't fathom. It shimmered with every breath she took, clinging to her breasts like cellophane, breasts he was pretty sure weren't laboring within the confines of a bra. His gaze followed the path of the dress as it slithered south, outlining her waist and hips, then covering *maybe* six inches or so of her thighs. On the average woman, a dress that short would have definitely revealed too much, but the average woman didn't have Liz's magnificent legs. In his unbiased opinion, the more the world saw of those, the better. And her hair. For the first time since he'd known her, she'd taken it down and let it fall free over her shoulders—a mass of wavy auburn tresses that shone like a copper penny. Add a wristful of silver bracelets, big silver hoop earrings and stockings so shimmery they looked as if they'd been dipped in diamond dust, and she was positively *dazzling*.

But how would the stuffy maitre d' at Rosario's take it? Would he suggest that perhaps madam would like to go home and put on something less…spectacular?

Liz's smile faltered. "Mark? Is something the matter?"

Mark opened his mouth to speak, but nothing came out. He cleared his throat. "That dress is really…something."

Liz beamed. "Thanks." Then her smile faded again. "You don't think it's too short, do you?"

He could have done a whole essay on that question: "The Pros and Cons of Diminutive Dressing." And there would have been more pros than cons, except they weren't going disco dancing. They were going to a high-class establishment that was undoubtedly very conservative. But knowing Liz, this could easily be the most conservative thing she owned.

"No. You look great." And he meant every word of it, as long as he was talking from a man's point of view. He only hoped the restaurant staff didn't measure skirt length at the door.

Liz grabbed a silver purse off her dining room table. "Okay. I'm ready."

Liz was ready for Rosario's. But was it ready for her?

8

FIFTEEN MINUTES LATER Mark pulled up in front of Rosario's, a beautifully restored turn-of-the-century red brick mansion in the heart of Turtle Creek. Everything Morrison Heights was to the eclectics in Dallas, Turtle Creek was to the rich.

"Wow," Liz said. "This place is really something."

Evening was slipping into night, and the lamps that lined the brick driveway glowed through the twilight. Mark stopped his car in front of the valet stand, where three white-coated valets, who looked to be in their early twenties, stood talking among themselves. One of them opened Liz's door, and when she stepped out, their talking abruptly ceased. As they stared at her, Mark thought their eyeballs were going to pop right out of their heads and go rolling down the driveway.

Liz responded with a cheery wave. "Hi, fellas!"

They all grinned, and Mark felt a flash of dread. Liz was, after all, Liz. He wanted to blend into the surroundings tonight—to observe, to prepare, to learn—but he had the feeling she was going to render anonymity pretty much impossible.

After passing his car off to one of the valets, Mark led Liz to the door of the restaurant, where a short, balding man in a tuxedo greeted them. The guy played it cool, but Mark still noticed his moment of hesitation as his gaze traveled along Liz's dress from top to bottom. It was a short trip.

"Good evening." He swung the door open and invited them to enter with a sweeping motion of his hand.

"Good evening to you, too," Liz said, giving him a big smile. Then she stopped short. "Oh, look!"

Mark froze in disbelief as she reached up to the man's tuxedo jacket. She picked something off his coat, then rubbed her fingers together to send it floating away.

"There you go. It was just a little piece of lint."

She gave him a friendly smile, then patted his lapel. The man's astonished expression said he was accustomed to being ignored most of the time, and for a moment he didn't say anything. Finally he cleared his throat.

"Uh…thank you, madam."

"Anytime."

Mark's feeling of foreboding grew stronger. It was one thing for Liz to act so friendly when they were sitting at Gino's, but it was another thing to do it at a place like this.

They went into the foyer of the restaurant, a two-story expanse of marble and mahogany that glittered beneath crystal chandeliers. The maitre d' confirmed their reservation and led them through the restaurant to a table for two near a window. After seating him, he informed them their waiter would be by momentarily.

"Look at this place," Liz said. "It's beautiful, isn't it?"

Mark had to agree. The restaurant was decorated in warm hues of red and gold that blended with table linens the color of cream. Ornate silver and crystal sparkled like jewels on every tabletop. The sun had slipped below the horizon, and the dim lighting in the restaurant cast an ethereal glow around the room. At one end of the restaurant was a parquet dance floor, along with chairs and music stands that told him a band of some kind would be playing.

A waiter came to their table. He looked to be in his

early thirties, with dark, slicked-back hair and exactly the arrogant, nose-in-the-air attitude Mark had expected.

"Good evening. My name is Ricardo. I'll be your waiter this evening."

"Hi there, Ricardo," Liz said. "Nice place you've got here."

Ricardo blinked with surprise, his uppity facade crumbling a little. "Thank you, madam."

Ricardo handed them menus, then gave Mark a wine list. He recited the specials for the evening, which included items Mark had never even heard of, but he nodded as if he understood.

"I'll return in a few minutes to take your order," Ricardo said, then strode to the next table.

"Did you catch all those specials?" Liz asked.

"Nope."

"Did he actually say one of them was *ostrich?*"

"That's about the only one I did catch."

"Wow. Can you imagine the Colonel frying up one of those?"

"Don't worry," Mark said. "It looks like there's normal stuff on the menu."

"Wait a minute. Something's wrong with my menu."

"What?"

"There aren't any prices." Her eyes widened. "Oh, boy. Do you suppose this is one of those places where if you have to ask, you can't afford it?"

A little panicked, Mark glanced at his menu again, noting that it suffered from no such deficiency. In fact, there were prices all over the place. Even bigger prices than he'd anticipated.

"Maybe they only put prices on the man's menu," he told Liz.

She looked at him with disbelief. "What is this? The 1950s?"

"I'm buying," he said, his mind already at work, estimating the future damages. "So don't worry about it."

"Tell me how much this chicken thing is," Liz said, pointing to her menu. "The second one down on the right."

"Liz—"

"What? Fifteen bucks?"

"No."

"Twenty?"

"I said not to worry about it."

"Mark, if you don't tell me how much this stuff is, I'm going over to McDonald's and bringing back a Big Mac."

Unfortunately, where Liz was concerned, he couldn't automatically assume that was an idle threat.

"Thirty-two dollars," he said.

Liz's eyebrows shot up. "That's outrageous!"

"Will you keep your voice down? It's the cheapest thing on the menu."

Liz slapped her menu closed. "Then I'll have a side salad and a glass of water."

"No, you won't. You were right when you said I need to get used to spending money."

"On you! Not on me!"

"If you don't order something that's actually a meal," he warned, "then I'm ordering for you."

Liz rolled her eyes. "Oh, all *right*. I'll have the stupid chicken. But don't blame me if your credit card goes into cardiac arrest."

"Not a problem. You know CPR, remember?"

He gave her a smile, finally coaxing one out of her. Then he took a moment to survey the place setting in front of him. Of the nine pieces of silverware, everything looked familiar except the small fork at an angle across the bowl of the soup spoon.

"Do you know what that fork is for?" he asked Liz.

"I have no idea."

This was just the kind of thing he'd been afraid of—some strange ritual involving a utensil he knew nothing about. Then, before Mark knew what was happening, Liz leaned over, caught Ricardo's attention and motioned for him to come over.

"Yes, madam. Are you ready to order?"

"Oh, in just a minute. But about the silverware. We're pretty clear on what most of this stuff is for, but what about this little fork?" She pointed to it, then smiled up at him. "I mean, this is already *way* more hardware than a person needs to eat one meal, don't you think?"

Mark groaned inwardly. She might as well have plastered a sign on their foreheads that said they were best friends with Ronald McDonald. A vision flashed through his mind of the waiter showing them the restaurant's policy on table etiquette, then ejecting them from the premises.

But to his surprise, Ricardo's haughty expression faded, replaced by a smile. He leaned toward Liz and whispered, "It *is* kind of ridiculous, isn't it?"

Mark was stunned. Not only was the guy agreeing with Liz, but his voice had gone from waiter-perfect to nice-guy friendly with a touch of Texas twang.

"That's an oyster fork," he answered, pointing to the unknown utensil. "A lot of people order oysters as an appetizer, so we go ahead and set one out. If you skip the oysters, skip the fork."

"Thanks, Ricardo," Liz said. "You're a peach."

Ricardo gave her a furtive wink, then put his waiter face back on and headed to the next table to take an order. Mark stared at Liz with pure astonishment. Was there anyone she didn't talk to as if she'd known them all their life? And what was it about Liz that made people drop all pretense and talk back to her the same way?

Mark picked up the wine list. "Okay, Liz. What do you know about wine?"

"It's made from grapes."

"But you're a bartender."

"Well, I can tell a Chilean merlot from a California chardonnay, but as far as all that vintage and appellation stuff, I haven't got a clue." Liz slipped the wine list from Mark's hand and scanned it. "Well, okay. I now know one more thing about wine. Places like this mark it up even more than Simon's does."

Ricardo came back to their table to take their order. This time he lost his haughty waiter look as soon as he approached their table. Mark ordered the chicken for both of them.

"Will you be having wine with dinner?" Ricardo asked.

Before Mark could answer, Liz pointed to the wine list and said, "Let's make this easy. Which one of these tastes pretty good but won't break the bank?"

Again, Mark wished he could slide unnoticed under the table and crawl out of the restaurant. To his surprise, though, Ricardo smiled obligingly. "Try the pinot blanc, or maybe the Beringer chardonnay." He lowered his voice to a whisper. "Good wines, low price. Comparatively speaking, anyway."

"Thanks." She looked at Mark. "Chardonnay?"

Still in shock, Mark just nodded.

As it turned out, the wine and the meal were perfect. Mark thought he managed to use the right utensil with each course, but after a glass of wine, he loosened up a little and it didn't seem to matter so much anymore.

As they ate, they talked about everything from the state of current affairs to the latest movies they'd seen to the books they'd read, and Mark discovered Liz was well versed in a lot of subjects besides sports. But sometimes he didn't catch everything she said because he'd start looking at that gorgeous mouth of hers, or watching the way her eyes sparkled when she talked.

He was having a wonderful time, which would have been even more wonderful if Ricardo hadn't butted in. He stopped by the table so many times that Mark thought he was going to pull up a chair, prop his feet up and pour himself a glass of wine, particularly when Liz started asking him a ridiculous number of personal questions, which he seemed delighted to answer. After he left for the umpteenth time, Mark turned back to Liz.

"Okay, now that we know all about Ricardo's life history, how about yours? You said you went to high school in Big Fork. What did you do after that?"

"Not much. I wasn't ready for college." She laughed. "I wasn't ready for much of anything that required responsibility. See, I was a bit of a hell-raiser in high school."

"No! Really?"

Liz smiled. "I knew you'd be astonished. Anyway, I kind of hung on to that attitude for the next five years or so, and then I went to the Lone Star College of Bartending." Liz put a phony flourish on the words, her nose stuck in the air. "Pure class, it was. But since I really do like talking to people, it's been a great way to make ends meet. And now that I've finally grown up, I'm starting college next semester."

"Really? What are you majoring in?"

"Psychology."

Mark smiled. "Ah, that's right. I remember now. Good choice."

"You really think so?"

"You're already smart about people. Remember?"

Liz smiled. "I remember."

"You're smart about a lot of things, Liz."

The longer they sat there, sipping their wine and listening to the soft music provided by a quartet of tuxedoed musicians, the more Mark felt himself slipping into a zone of comfort he never would have anticipated. And he came to the realization that it didn't much matter where he was with Liz, he had a good time.

"Thank you, Mark."

"What for?"

"For inviting me tonight. I know you just needed someone to go with you so you wouldn't have to go alone, but—"

"No. If I made it sound like that, I'm sorry. I wanted *you* to come with me. You've done a lot for me in the past week. Liz. This gives me a chance to do something for you."

"I wasn't too sure about this fancy restaurant thing. But everyone seems so nice. I'm having a wonderful time." She paused, her smile fading. "I think Gwen will, too."

The words *Gwen, who?* popped into his mind. Not that he'd actually forgotten her, but he sure hadn't spent much time thinking about her, and wasn't that why he was here? To make sure things went perfectly when they went out on Saturday night?

"I've got to admit I'm a little nervous," he told Liz. "It's been a while since I've been out on a date."

"Me, too. Guys ask, but I'm past the point of going out just to be going out, you know? I'm not even sure I know how to behave on a date anymore."

"First dates are tough under any circumstances," Mark said.

"You know the worst part for me? Waiting for that first kiss. I mean, when it's a guy I really like, I can't enjoy the date because I'm wondering when he's going to kiss me, *if* he's going to kiss me. Screws up the whole evening."

"Hey, it's even worse for a guy. He's got to wonder all night if this woman wants him to kiss her or not."

Mark shook his head. "If he tries to and she doesn't want it, he looks like a jerk, but if she wants it and he doesn't do it, he looks like a wimp. Try figuring that one out."

"You're better off taking a shot at it whether you're sure or not."

"Oh, yeah?"

"Shows confidence. No matter what most women say about all that sensitivity stuff, they like men who know what they want. Audacity pays off. Now, I don't mean you should push a woman to do something she doesn't want to do. But a confident man who expects to succeed really gets a woman's blood rushing."

Mark pondered that for a moment. It was hard to believe he was sitting here talking with a woman about kissing. But for some reason, no subject seemed uncomfortable when he discussed it with Liz.

"So I should just do it," he said.

"Right. Knock her for a loop. Kiss her before she even realizes that you've mussed her lipstick or knocked a hair out of place. By the time she realizes what's happening, believe me, she won't care about any of that."

Mark tried to picture kissing Gwen the way Liz described, but it was an image that just wouldn't come together. She was so pristine that she was probably going to make him boil his lips for three minutes before they touched hers.

"Would madam like dessert?" Ricardo asked on his twentieth trip to their table, reverting to his waiter voice, but maintaining a conspiratorial twinkle in his eye.

"No, Ricardo, madam is going to pass on that, or madam's hips won't be able to fit through the door. But I do have one more favor to ask." Liz touched Ricardo's sleeve and he leaned closer. She nodded toward Mark. "My friend is bringing a woman he really wants to impress here on Saturday night, which is why we've been taking Fine Dining 101 from you tonight. Do you think you could help him out? Maybe make sure they sit at one of your tables and everything goes really well?''

Ricardo blinked. "You mean, you two aren't...?"

"No. We're just friends."

He raised his eyebrows hopefully. "Are all the other men in your life right now just...friends, too?''

"Right now, yes."

Mark couldn't believe the grin that spread across good ol' Ricardo's face. He turned to Mark with a magnanimous expression. "Sure, buddy. I'd be happy to help you out."

Mark read between those lines. The guy was so delighted that Liz was unattached that he'd have done anything for her. All at once it dawned on him that Ricardo was not a bad-looking guy, and Liz had smiled at him a lot tonight. And for reasons Mark couldn't fathom, it irritated the hell out of him.

Then Ricardo leaned in even closer to Liz and dropped his voice to just above a whisper. "Just for the record, my name's Rick. They make me use the Ricardo thing here. Image, you know."

He winked at Liz for about the tenth time that evening, then walked away. Mark noticed a spring to the guy's step that hadn't been there before, and that irritated the hell out of him, too.

"Nice guy," Liz said.

"Yeah," Mark said. "Nice."

As they sipped the rest of their wine, Mark found himself smiling when he focused on Liz, then frowning when he thought of Rick. And then he realized that too long a time had passed since he'd thought of Gwen.

Gwen. He yanked his thoughts back to her, wondering where they'd taken such a sharp turn in another direction. Thanks to Liz, he felt prepared. He was going to bring Gwen here for their date and everything was going to proceed smoothly. He'd have to remember, though, not to let his guard down. It was one thing to get a little lax around Liz and put his elbows on the table or drop his napkin on the floor, but it would be another thing to do it around Gwen.

"Let's dance," Liz said.

"Dance?"

"Sure. It'll be fun. You do know how, don't you?"

"Yes, I know how."

Dancing was no problem. What *was* a problem was that his head felt a little light from the wine, and he'd been enjoying Liz's company way too much. At a time when he needed to concentrate on the woman who could help him reach the number one goal he'd had for the past ten years, he did not need to think about a woman who offered him nothing but a good time, and he certainly shouldn't be holding her, touching her....

So why was he getting up and following her to the dance floor?

As Mark took Liz in his arms and began to move to the music, a distant warning bell went off inside his head, telling him to keep her at arm's length because prolonged, intimate contact was not a good thing. That slinky dress of hers felt way too soft and enticing beneath his hand, allowing him to feel her back beneath it as if the dress were barely there at all.

"You're a good dancer," Liz murmured.

"My mother taught me. It was one thing she really loved to do. She always told me that someday I'd have a girlfriend and I had to know how to dance."

Liz moved closer to him, so close her breasts brushed against his chest, and no matter how hard Mark tried to hold on to an image of Gwen in his mind, she faded away, like a dream that he couldn't quite remember. But he remembered with astonishing clarity how comfortable he'd felt with Liz at Gino's a few nights ago. And how comfortable he'd felt with her tonight. And how good it felt to hold her now. He felt as if he were getting bombarded by sensations from all sides, rendering his usually orderly mind into chaos.

"Liz?"

"Hmm?"

"Can I ask you a question?"

"Sure."

"It's about the kissing thing."

For a split second, Liz actually stopped moving. Then she recovered and followed his lead once again. Holding her as closely as he was, she was looking over his shoulder and he couldn't imagine what she was thinking.

"I'll admit it," he murmured. "I've been burying myself in my work for a very long time. It's been a while since I've even been out with a woman, much less kissed one."

It was as if his evil, sex-starved twin had suddenly taken over his body. He needed to be thinking platonic thoughts about Liz, yet here he was asking her to give him pointers on kissing. And why was he asking in the first place? Because he needed the pointers, or because he'd been staring at those soft, silky lips of hers all night and couldn't get kissing out of his mind?

"Exactly what is it you're unsure about?"

"Well...should I wait until I actually take her home, or take advantage of a moment earlier in the evening if it seems right?"

"Oh, if the right moment arises, you should *always* take advantage of it."

The tone of her voice had slipped into a lower register, lending it a seductive quality. She'd turned her head slightly, and because she was tucked so snugly in his arms, the soft, breathy words she spoke fanned his ear. The warning bells in his mind sounded a little louder, telling him he was playing with fire.

But still he turned up the heat.

"How should I go about...taking advantage of the moment?"

Words he'd never planned to say were coming out of his mouth—suggestive words that really had nothing to do with Gwen and everything to do with Liz—but he just couldn't seem to stop himself. When Liz responded, her voice was low and whispery, her breath warm against his ear again.

"When the moment is right," she said, "take her face in your hands. Stare at her intently for several seconds. Don't blink, and don't back down. Make her feel that your kiss is inevitable, and there's no way she could stop you if she tried." She eased her hand around his neck, her fingers teasing his hair just above his collar. "But trust me. She won't want to stop you."

Mark knew if he was smart, he'd shut up, push Liz away to arm's length as if he were dancing with his grandmother and pray the song ended quickly. Instead, he found himself pulling her so close that the length of her body was pressed against his.

He had no business doing this. No business at all. But the moment he'd taken Liz in his arms, he just couldn't seem to stop himself. The moment he'd taken Liz in his arms his common sense had evaporated, and the chances of regaining it now were just about nil.

"Okay," he murmured. "Then what?"

"Then kiss her," Liz said, "like you've never kissed a woman before. It's not a time to be chaste. Don't even let her come up for air. Make it so *hot,* so *exciting,* so *memorable* that she can't stop thinking about you for days afterward. Do you understand?"

"Yes. I understand."

"If you do that," Liz said, her voice dropping to a whisper, "she'll be yours. I absolutely guarantee it."

The music wound down, then came to an end. Couples all around them eased away from each other, applauding softly. Liz pulled away slightly and stared up at him, those soft, sweet lips beckoning him like a siren song.

If the right moment arises, you should always take advantage of it.

She slipped out of his arms. He caught her and pulled her gently back. She looked up at him, her eyes widening with surprise. He slid his hands up her arms until they were cradling her face. He didn't blink, and he didn't back down. He stared directly into those emerald-green eyes for several long, intense moments, until there was no way she could possibly mistake his meaning, until he was sure he'd impressed upon her that she couldn't stop him if she tried.

And then he kissed her.

9

THE MOMENT Mark's lips touched Liz's, a rush of desire swept through him that almost knocked him to his knees. He'd been adoring her lips all evening, and now he was kissing them, savoring their warmth. When he heard a tiny moan in the back of her throat that told him she wanted it as much as he did, he knew right then that kissing alone was never going to be enough. The feeling was so intense that it blocked out everything else around him. He slid one hand around her neck and laced his fingers through her hair, then wrapped the other one around the small of her back, pulling her toward him until her breasts were crushed against his chest.

Then she wound her arms around his neck and pulled *him* closer. When she kissed him back with an intensity that matched his own, the words *hot* and *exciting* and *memorable* spun through his mind, though he was surprised he could comprehend them at all since his brain wasn't doing much thinking while his body was feeling.

Couples were leaving the dance floor, but Mark barely noticed. He finally pulled his lips away from Liz's, but the spell wasn't broken. He was still mesmerized by the feel of her warm body beneath his hands and the sight of those beautiful green eyes staring up at him. Her cheeks were tinted bright pink and her breath was coming more quickly now, as if she'd forgotten to breathe for the past fifteen seconds.

He wanted to take Liz home with him. He wanted to

continue his exploration past her lips to the rest of her beautiful body, to spend the long hours of the night so close to her that nothing could come between—

Wait a minute. What was he thinking?

He awoke from his fantasy with a jolt of realization, finally comprehending the enormity of what he'd just done.

He'd kissed Liz.

In a fraction of a second, a mass of contradictory thoughts whipped through his mind. He'd finally kissed her because he'd wanted to so badly, and now here she was, looking up at him all flushed and breathy and beautiful, tempting him to toss her over his shoulder and carry her straight back to his apartment. But while she was fun and exciting and extraordinary in so many ways, she wasn't his future.

Gwen was. She could help him get that partnership, and wasn't that what he'd wanted since the day he walked into Nichols, Marbury & White?

But what about Liz, whom he loved to be with, who was warm and generous and funny, who could light up a dark room with a single smile? Why couldn't *she* be the one?

Because one look at her and his superiors would have a collective heart attack.

He'd lost sight of his goal somewhere along the line tonight, and because he'd been stupid enough to give in to the moment, he was going to end up hurting Liz.

Damn. How could he have done this to her? He'd kissed her, and she was going to think—had every right to think—

There was only one way out of this.

He turned away quickly so she wouldn't see his face change from ecstasy to apprehension. Taking her by the hand, he led her back to their table, careful not to look into those tempting green eyes of hers or he'd be lost all over again.

After they were seated, he managed an offhanded smile.

"So how did I do?"

She blinked with surprise, then swallowed hard. "Huh?"

Her confusion told him that she'd wanted the kiss as much as he had, which made the next words coming out of his mouth even more impossible to say.

"On a scale of one to ten. Come on, teacher. Give me my grade."

It took Liz a full five seconds before she realized Mark's meaning, and when she did, her stomach swam with that sickening feeling reserved only for the most heartsick moments of her life.

"I'm a little rusty," he said. "I hope it wasn't too awful."

Awful? *Awful?* Was he crazy? Somewhere along the line the poor boy from the dinky Texas town had learned how to kiss. If this was rusty, what would it be like when he got back in the swing of things?

Then it struck her: she'd never get the opportunity to find out.

She was his practice date. And he was practicing. And she'd been stupid enough to think it was the real thing. She'd told him exactly what to do, after all. And then he'd done it.

Excruciating disappointment swept through her. She was sure he'd meant it as so much more, that he wanted her as much as she wanted him, and now...

"Sorry, Mark," she said, struggling to keep her voice even. "You only get a nine. I'd give you a ten, but then you'd get conceited."

"Like I said, it's been a while."

"It's like riding a bicycle," she said.

"You never forget."

"Right."

He smiled. "So I passed?"

"Gwen will be...impressed."

Liz was so filled with disappointment and jealousy she could barely speak. Mark paid the bill, then tucked his credit card away and rose from the table.

"It's getting late," he said. "We'd better be going."

Liz looked at her watch automatically, but the time didn't even register in her mind. "Yes. I suppose we should."

The sinking sensation she felt as they left the restaurant was almost incapacitating. She'd fallen into her own trap—the man she'd created was the man she wanted. Only he wanted Gwen, not her, and after tonight, she'd be forced to step out of the picture. And the thought of doing that just about ripped her heart in two.

Liz tried to keep some light chatter going on the way home, but she couldn't, and finally the silence loomed between them. When they arrived at her apartment, Mark insisted on walking her to her door. She wished with all her heart that he'd think about the way he'd kissed her and want to repeat the experience, only this time for real.

The walk up to her apartment was excruciating for Liz. When they reached her door, she turned to face him.

"Good luck on Saturday," she said, forcing a smile, but feeling as if she were falling apart inside.

He looked at her questioningly.

"On your date with Gwen."

"Oh. Yeah. Gwen."

He paused, and it was all Liz could do not to grab him by his eighty-dollar tie, drag him into the apartment, lock the door behind them and make him forget all about that snooty, condescending woman he was so hell-bent on having.

"Thanks again, Liz."

Then he did kiss her, but it was nothing more than a soft peck on the cheek, one friend to another, a kiss that wasn't even in the same universe as the one he'd given her at the restaurant.

"I guess I'll see you around."

I'll see you around. In other words, *It's been fun, but now it's over. Surely you didn't think it was anything more, did you?*

He turned and headed for the stairs, and she thought for a moment that maybe he'd turn back, their eyes would lock and he'd realize what a fool he'd been and that it was really her he wanted and not Gwen.

He never looked back.

He walked down the stairs, his footsteps echoing through the building, then took a right turn and disappeared around the corner. She heard the lobby door open, then click closed, and realized that he'd left the building and probably her life for good.

She slipped into her apartment and shut the door behind her, tears filling her eyes, hating herself that she couldn't control them. She leaned against the door, wondering how her mother and grandmother would have handled this one.

Who was she kidding? Her mother and grandmother would have dispensed the advice, then stood back and let the advisee take it or leave it. They would not have tried to implement that advice by wading knee-deep into the situation, only to end up getting hurt by the advice they'd given. And above all, they'd have offered plenty of sound wisdom but never, ever, a piece of their own hearts.

MARK SAT in a lawn chair on his balcony, the nighttime Dallas heat surrounding him like a heavy shroud. He stared out at the city lights, hating himself for what he'd done to Liz.

She wanted it as much as you did.

He had to stop thinking about that. He'd just gotten

caught up in the moment. That's all. It had been way too long since he'd been on a date, and he'd lost his head. As soon as he swept Gwen into his arms on the dance floor on Saturday night, he'd forget all about the way he felt right now about Liz. He'd forget all about her sweet, tantalizing lips, the way her hair smelled and the way she'd felt beneath his hands as they moved together to the music. He'd have Gwen instead, and wasn't that what he'd wanted since the first moment he walked into Simon's? She was the kind of woman who could make him look like partner material, so she was the woman for him.

Liz wasn't.

He could just imagine the look on Edwin Nichols's face if he found out he was keeping company with a woman who worked as a bartender, lived in Morrison Heights and wore dresses so hot they set off fire alarms. Those bushy eyebrows of his would rise all the way up to his artificial hairline, and then he'd make sure Mark's career stayed on a back burner for the rest of his life.

But you made her believe you wanted her....

He yanked himself up out of the lawn chair and went back inside, frustration still eating away at him. Heading for his bedroom, he told himself for the hundredth time that he'd done the right thing. He'd ended his relationship with Liz before it had even gotten started.

Why, then, when he went to bed and closed his eyes, could he not see Gwen's face because Liz's kept getting in the way? Why did he dream that night about Gwen at a baseball game eating hot dogs from a linen-covered tray with nine pieces of silverware, while Liz led the waiters at Rosario's in a chorus of "Take Me Out to the Ball Game"? And why, when he awoke the next morning, did he stare at the empty pillow beside him and imagine long red hair fanned out across it and beautiful green eyes staring up at him? He'd done the right thing.

So why did it feel so wrong?

LIZ DREADED Saturday night, and when it finally arrived, it was all she could do to keep her mind on her job and her thoughts focused somewhere else besides on Mark and Gwen. She hadn't seen Mark or heard from him in the last two days, but why should she? He had a date with his dream woman. What did he need with her?

Maybe if she told him how she felt about him, he'd see her in a different light. Things would change. He'd reconsider his overwhelming attraction to The Most Perfect Woman on Earth and realize whom he really belonged with—

No.

She couldn't say a word to him about how she felt, because he didn't feel the same way about her. His kiss that really wasn't a kiss had proven that. If he had any feelings for her at all, he would never have been able to kiss her like that and then walk away as if it had meant nothing. Anything she said to him at this point would only make her look like a fool.

She glanced at her watch. Well, it was all a moot point now, anyway. Undoubtedly Mark was with Gwen, heading for Rosario's. And by the time the evening was over, Gwen would know what a wonderful man she had her hands on, and she'd never let him go.

Sherri came up beside her. "Look, Liz! Isn't that Mark?"

Liz whipped around. Mark and Gwen were coming into the club and taking a seat at a table by the window, evidently stopping by for a drink before dinner.

Liz thought she was going to be sick. If Mark had looked wonderful before, he looked spectacular now. And Gwen, she had to admit, looked positively radiant. They looked good *together*. The picture was so right that Liz wanted to cry. A stunning sophisticated woman and a handsome professional man. How could she argue with that?

"Sherri, watch the bar for me, will you?" Liz asked.

There must have been a catch in her voice or something because Sherri got a worried look on her face. "Are you okay?"

"I'm fine. I just need to go to the bathroom." *So I can fall apart in private.*

Sherri gave Liz one of her rare sympathetic looks, and Liz wondered if she really looked that despondent. When she went into the bathroom, she saw herself in the mirror and had to agree with Sherri. And if she looked at her pitiful self for one more second, she was probably going to cry. It would accomplish nothing, of course, except make her mascara run, but she wasn't running high on logic right about now.

When she felt that telltale burn behind her eyes, she slipped into one of the bathroom stalls and closed the door behind her. She dabbed at her eyes with a square of toilet paper, trying to keep the tears from falling. How could he want that awful woman? Liz trembled as she dabbed, then sniffed a little, determined that her emotions were *not* going to get the better of her.

Then all at once she heard the bathroom door open, accompanied by the click of heels and women's voices.

"You're right, Gwen. He does look good. A whole lot better than he did last week. What prompted his sudden change of wardrobe?"

"I don't know, but it'll save me the trouble of dressing him right."

Liz recognized Gwen's voice, along with the voice of the woman who came here frequently with her. They had to be talking about Mark. She peered out the gap between the stall door and its frame. Gwen was standing at the mirror, pulling a small makeup bag from her purse.

"Attractive, well-dressed and a six-figure salary," Gwen's friend said. "Nice package."

"It's not six figures yet. But it will be when he gets that partnership he's up for at his accounting firm."

Partnership? Mark was up for a partnership? He'd never told her that. But then again, he wasn't one to go around tooting his horn about how rich and successful he was, either.

"How did you find out about that, anyway?" Gwen's friend asked.

"My assistant knows someone who works at the firm. I had no idea the first time he came on to me what potential he had. I mean, you saw him last week. Would you have thought—"

"Good heavens, no!"

"But now that I do know—" Gwen raised an eyebrow and gave her friend a conspiratorial smile "—it suddenly makes him *so* much more attractive."

Liz's mouth fell open with disbelief. Then she narrowed her eyes angrily. So that was it. It wasn't the fact that Mark suddenly looked so handsome. That was merely icing on the cake. Gwen was after his money.

"I'm telling you," Gwen said, "there's nothing more *tiring* than trying to motivate a man into being successful. It's so much easier to find one who's on the edge, then—" Gwen held up a finger and flicked it in the air "—*push* him over."

"Sounds like a plan to me. This is your first date, right?"

"Yes. But now that I know what potential I'm dealing with, I can assure you it won't be our last." Gwen gave her lips a practiced swipe with a tube of lipstick, then capped it and tucked it back into her purse. "Tonight we're going to Rosario's."

"Ahh. The test."

"He's not the most sophisticated man I've ever met, so this should be interesting."

"Think he'll pass?"

"With money like that on the horizon, as long as he doesn't drink from the finger bowl I'd say there's hope."

It was all Liz could do not to stomp out of that stall and shove that tube of lipstick right up Gwen's nose. Why had she gone to that stupid restaurant with Mark to help him learn exactly what to do? Was it too late to tell him that the liquid in that little bowl was actually very weak soup?

"And the best part," Gwen continued, "is that he seems to be a very nice guy."

"Hmm. I never thought you considered that much of a selling point."

"Why, of course I do. Nice men are so much easier to manipulate."

"And if he doesn't get the partnership?"

Gwen smiled. "There are a lot more fish in the ocean. I'll just have to throw this one back and catch another one."

Forget shoving the lipstick up her nose. Liz wanted to send her face first into the toilet. The worst part was that Mark had everything that little gold digger was looking for. Not only was she getting an attractive man with money, she was also getting a man who could send her to heaven with a single kiss. Once Gwen realized the package deal was *that* sweet, no force on earth would be able to pry her claws out of him.

After the two women left the bathroom, Liz ripped the stall door open, fury bubbling inside her. What should she do now? Could she tell Mark the truth? Would he believe her?

She pictured the hurt expression that would fall over his face when he realized his confident new image had nothing to do with Gwen's interest, but his bank book did. Then she pictured his *really* hurt expression when he found out the same thing a month or two from now.

She had to stop him from spending another minute with that woman.

She marched out of the bathroom and up the hall toward the bar, but every step she took was slower than the last. Finally she stopped completely, overcome with indecision. What was she going to do? Confront Gwen right now in a crowded club and humiliate Mark in the process?

She glanced toward their table. Mark was rising to escort Gwen out of the club. Even at this distance, she could see the expression on his face, as if heaven had decided to send an angel to earth and he was the lucky recipient. She wanted desperately to scream at him. *Mark! Don't go! She'll never love you for you! She's only after your money!*

Instead, her feet remained fused to the floor and her mouth stayed shut. In the end, she just couldn't do it.

And then they were gone.

Liz drew in a couple of deep breaths. After a few shaky moments, she went back to the bar.

Mark had never even looked at her. Never glanced toward the bar, never come over to say hello. Nothing. She felt as if she'd lost something very precious, but she had to admit it was something she'd never really had in the first place.

She picked up a drink order, drew two beers, then placed them mindlessly onto a tray.

Just try to put him out of your mind.

A couple at the end of the bar ordered two of her signature margaritas, but as she held the bottle of tequila over one of the glasses, she found she couldn't remember how much to put into a drink she'd made approximately half a zillion times. She stared at the glass, blinking dumbly.

Don't think about Mark. Think about work.

Finally she remembered and finished the drinks. Unfortunately, she put salt on the rims when they'd asked for no salt. She dumped out the margaritas and started over, finally getting them right, then made a martini for another customer, which she spilled immediately after plopping the olive into it. The glass clattered against the bar, sloshing gin right into the woman's lap. The olive rolled along with the alcohol wave, coming to a squishy stop at the edge of the bar.

Enough was enough.

Liz apologized profusely to the woman, cleaned up the mess, took off her apron, then told her supervisor she felt lousy and wanted to go home. That didn't please him since it was Saturday night and the place was hopping, but she'd told the truth. She really *did* feel lousy, and she didn't expect to feel better any time soon.

Once she got home, she went to her bathroom and filled her clawfoot tub. She soaked for half an hour, trying to wash away thoughts of Mark, but every time she closed her eyes to relax, she saw that overpriced restaurant with its glowing candlelight and soft-ivory table linens and glittering crystal, and that horrible woman smiling at Mark over a glass of chardonnay, her devious little mind making plans for their future that undoubtedly involved his platinum credit card and a very large joint checking account.

She got out of the bathtub and put on an old pair of shorts and a T-shirt. Walking into the living room, she plopped down on the sofa, grabbed her cordless phone and hit One on her speed dial. A few seconds later she heard her mother's voice.

"Hello?"

"Hi, Mom. It's me."

"Hi, baby! How's it going?"

Liz sighed. "Lousy."

"Uh-oh. Is this gonna be a long story?"

"Probably."

"Okay. Hold on. Let me grab my cigarettes."

Liz heard some shuffling around, then the muffled sound of the fridge door opening and closing. If she knew her mother, she'd just pulled out a Bud Light to go with her Virginia Slims. Liz heard a kitchen chair scrape across the linoleum floor, then her mother plopping down with a comfortable sigh and a flick of her Bic.

"Okay, baby. Shoot."

She told her mother the whole story, starting with the first night she'd tried to help Mark meet Gwen, and ending with the fact that the same woman was about to snag him for all the wrong reasons, emphasizing the fact that this particular woman was the most vile creature who'd ever lived. Liz left out the part about how she felt about Mark, because she still wasn't sure exactly how she did feel, and that wasn't the issue now anyway. The issue was saving Mark from Gwen.

Her mother listened, with only an occasional "Uh-huh" to encourage Liz to continue.

"He's on a date with her right now," Liz said, when she'd gotten to the end of the story. "What should I do?"

She heard her mother take a long drag on her cigarette and blow it out slowly. "Nothing."

"But Mom, she's so *wrong* for him!"

"Let him figure that out for himself."

"I just don't think—"

"Baby, sometimes the best thing you can do for people who desperately want the wrong thing is to let them have what they want so they can realize they don't want it after all."

"But he doesn't know what a rotten, underhanded woman she is!"

"Is he a smart man?"

"Well, yeah, but—"

"You think he can't figure out what kind of woman she is, so he needs you to tell him?"

"Well, of course, he *could* figure it out—"

"Then let him."

"But—"

"What can you do right now, anyway? Call him while he's at the restaurant? Tell him what a god-awful woman his date is? That'd go over *real* big."

"Maybe tomorrow—"

"No, baby. It's time for you to butt out. If she's really wrong for him, he'll know it. And he'll dump her."

"But what if he doesn't?"

"Don't worry. If he's the man for you, he'll come to his senses."

"The man for me?"

Her mother was silent.

"I didn't say *anything* about wanting him for myself!"

Her mother laughed softly. "Baby, you may be able to fool the rest of the world, but you've *never* been able to fool your mother."

Liz sighed with disgust. "Oh, all right! I'm crazy about him. Does that make you happy?"

"Don't make me one way or the other. But it looks like it's making you miserable."

"Yes! Because he doesn't want me. He wants her!" Liz leaned her head against the back of the sofa and closed her eyes. "Mom, what am I going to do?"

"I told you what to do. Nothing."

"But what if he doesn't figure it out?" Then Liz had an even more terrible thought. "Or what if he knows, and he doesn't care?"

"Nah. It won't be anything like that. He's a wonderful man."

"How do you know that? You've never even met him."

"Because you wouldn't be so crazy about him if he

wasn't. Next time you come home, you bring him along, you hear?''

With that, her mother hung up. Liz stared at the phone in disbelief. Bring him along? Her mother was only fifty-seven. Senile dementia couldn't possibly have set in. But evidently her hearing was going fast, because she obviously hadn't heard her say that Mark *wanted another woman.*

Liz sighed heavily. As right as Laura Lee Prescott had been all her life about everyone else's problems, why did she have to choose this moment to be so wrong?

Her mother was right about one thing, though. There wasn't anything she could do about it tonight, even if she wanted to. All she could do is get a quart of Ben & Jerry's out of the freezer, drop back onto the sofa and add a few inches to her hip measurement, while she spent the rest of the evening picturing the man she wanted with the woman she hated.

Did it get any more pitiful than that?

10

No doubt about it, Mark thought as he stared across the candlelit table at Gwen Adams. She was everything he'd expected, and more.

She blended into Rosario's like a jewel blended into a crown. She wore a powder-blue dress in a silky fabric that stopped a modest two inches above her knees. Her hair was put up in one of those intricate twists that was probably the result of hours in a beauty shop. She walked with the grace of a duchess and displayed manners that said there was a headmistress glowing with pride out there somewhere. It was as if every quality he needed in a woman had come together in one highly attractive package.

The table they'd been given was perfection, too. It sat beside a huge picture window that looked out on a garden full of flowering shrubs and trees strung with tiny white lights. Pale evening light shone through the window and mingled with the glow from the candle on their table, lending a celestial quality to Gwen's already impeccable beauty.

Gwen was perfect. The setting was perfect. His nervousness eased a bit.

So far, so good.

Rick sauntered up to their table, doing his very best stuck-up waiter imitation. Knowing what he knew now, Mark almost laughed at the phony expression of arrogance the guy wore. Gwen, however, didn't seem to find it the least bit suspect.

"Mr. McAlister. It's a pleasure to see you this evening."

"Ricardo."

Out of the corner of his eye, he saw Gwen glancing back and forth between him and Rick. *The waiter knows you?*

Mark smiled to himself. True to his word, Rick was going to make this an evening to remember. Evidently he hoped Mark would put in a good word for him with Liz. Mark frowned at that thought, then brushed it aside.

They'd made better time from Gwen's apartment to this part of town than he anticipated, making them early for the reservation, so she'd suggested stopping off at Simon's for a before-dinner drink. Mark had hoped it would be Liz's night off, but then he glanced over and saw her working behind the bar. All at once he remembered the way she'd felt in his arms, and it was all he could do not to go over there and repeat the experience.

Instead, he chose a table across the club and sat with his back to the bar, hoping she wouldn't see him. He didn't know whether she had or not, but he'd been acutely aware of her presence nonetheless. Even now she popped into his mind, distracting him from the task at hand.

Rule number one: Do not think about Liz tonight.

Rick handed them menus and Mark the wine list, and when he returned, Gwen ordered an appetizer of smoked salmon and a salad of spinach and radicchio with a raspberry vinaigrette dressing. Then she went for the lobster. He checked the price of it and just about choked. Would she have chosen that if she knew how incredibly expensive it was? Probably. Women like Gwen expected the finer things in life.

When it came Mark's turn to order, he decided to go with the same things Gwen had chosen, figuring he couldn't go wrong with that no matter how much it rattled his bank account.

"Would you like wine with dinner this evening?" Rick asked.

Mark skimmed the wine list, then handed it back to Rick. "Bring us the Beringer chardonnay, 1995."

"Excellent choice. It should compliment the lobster nicely."

Mark turned to Gwen. "I assume that's all right with you?"

She seemed shocked that he'd actually chosen a wine, and that his choice had the waiter's blessing. "Of course."

"Very good, sir." Rick nodded and headed to the next table. A few minutes later, he brought their wine. Mark went through the wine testing procedure, feeling perfectly confident. Rick poured them both a glass, then stepped away from the table, and he and Gwen talked while waiting for their food to arrive.

To Mark's relief, conversation came easily. Gwen's favorite topic, for some reason, seemed to be his job, because she asked him every question in the world about it. He told himself that was a good thing. If she was interested in his work, didn't that translate into being interested in him?

As they ate their appetizers, Gwen told Mark they weren't quite chilled enough, and their salads, she said, were a bit on the wilted side. She didn't seem thrilled with the lobster, either, and told Rick so. He apologized profusely, and she asked him to inform the chef that while it was edible, it was quite overcooked. Rick nodded, but as he strode away from the table out of Gwen's sight, he glanced back at Mark and rolled his eyes.

They continued with dinner, which Gwen consumed with surprising gusto considering her distaste for overcooked lobster. They talked about various things—the current trends in the stock market, the benefits of one mutual fund versus another, the value of investing in real estate. Actually, Gwen asked a lot of questions, some generic in nature, some personal, and Mark answered them. His responses seemed to please her greatly, which he guessed was a good thing. Aside from the entrée glitch, everything was going better than he'd expected.

He thought about his company dance. Before the evening was over, he could ask Gwen if she'd like to come with him, and he had all the confidence in the world that she would accept. Basically, everything was perfect.

And now he knew just how irritating perfect could be.

As the meal wore on, Gwen's soft, cultured voice started to drone like a mosquito buzzing around his ear, and he really had to concentrate to catch what she was saying. Those icy-blue eyes of hers were stunning, but whenever he met her gaze, he felt as if he were looking into…well, *nothing*. Rick had looked at Gwen a lot, too, but every one of those looks had been full of distaste, unlike the complete and total adoration he'd shown for Liz.

Liz.

No matter how hard Mark tried to devote his attention to Gwen, thoughts of Liz kept crowding his mind, kicking and shoving their way in, until finally they plopped themselves down and refused to go away. Every word Gwen spoke in that beautiful, lilting voice of hers made him realize just how desperately he wished he were here with Liz instead, having fun instead of just having dinner.

Now, pay attention, McAlister. This is a quiz. Which woman should you be interested in? Which woman will help secure your future? Which woman will impress your superiors and make them finally see that you're partner material?

As a logical, rational man Mark knew he should listen to the answer his head was giving him. Unfortunately, his heart was screaming so loudly he couldn't hear a word his head said.

When they finished dinner, Mark's attempts to concentrate on Gwen had failed miserably. It wasn't for her lack of trying to keep his attention, though. She prattled on as if she were a talking doll and somebody kept pulling the string. On and on and on…

Damn it, would she shut up already about his job? Why did it fascinate her so much? Sometimes his job even bored him, and he was the one doing it. He wondered vaguely if this was what life with Tiffany was like. If so, for the first time ever, Mark actually felt sorry for Sloan.

Then, as Gwen rattled on, turning the conversation to 401-K accounts and then asking him how he'd fared in the recent stock market decline, something slowly shifted in Mark's perception. He couldn't put his finger on exactly what it was—just something that cast a shadow across her perfect features and sent a feeling of unease creeping through him.

"I'd love to dance," Gwen said.

Mark barely heard the words. "Excuse me?"

"I said I'd love to dance."

He realized the band had started to play and couples were moving to the dance floor. He knew he should be jumping at the chance to have a socially acceptable way to get his hands on the woman he supposedly wanted— so why wasn't he?

Finally he got up and led her to the dance floor. But when he took her in his arms, he decided he should keep her at a respectable distance because, after all, they really didn't know each other very well.

"My assistant knows someone at your company," Gwen said. "I heard some interesting news about you."

"Oh?"

"You're up for a partnership. Is that right?"

Gwen knew about his potential promotion?

"Yes. That's right."

"Interesting. I hear a move like that can be very... lucrative."

Gwen purred the words like a satisfied cat, smiling up at him with an odd, calculating expression that baffled him.

"I suppose so."

"Well, then. Good luck. I'll be pulling for you."

It didn't hit Mark all at once. As they danced, though, bits and pieces of their evening started to come together to form a picture that was becoming clearer with each passing moment. She hadn't shut up about his job all night. She'd moved the conversation into discussions about every financial issue there was, easing personal information out of him so artfully he hadn't even realized he was giving it to her.

That's essentially all they'd discussed. Money.

Then another thought struck him. When had she found out about the partnership? Sometime at the beginning of last week, when she'd suddenly found him oh-so-attractive?

As the final piece fell into place, Mark felt like the biggest fool alive. And he thought Gwen's sudden interest in him was because he'd become so damned irresistible. He almost laughed out loud. She didn't want him for *him*. She wanted him for his *money*, and that positively astounded him. Growing up in Waldon Springs, he never could have imagined that he'd ever have a financial portfolio of sufficient size to be of interest to *anyone*.

But there it was, as clear as the upturned nose on Gwen's face. Her calculating expression hadn't faded. She had a veneer of beauty and refinement, highlighted by a heavy dose of lethal charm, and if she played her cards right, some poor unsuspecting guy would eventually make her rich.

But it damned well wasn't going to be him.

At the same time, though, he realized that he hadn't been much better than Gwen. He'd wanted her for her cool sophistication, for her social skills and for what she could do for his career. He hadn't given a single thought to whether they'd even *like* each other or not.

And then there was the way he'd treated Liz.

How could he have led her on the way he had the other night, then shoved her aside for another woman? And he hadn't even spoken to her at Simon's tonight, ignoring her as if she meant nothing to him. How could he have done that to her?

As he continued to dance with Gwen, he realized he was holding her so far away from him that a truck could have driven through the space between them. He remembered how he'd deliberately maneuvered Liz so close to him when they were dancing that he could practically feel her heartbeat, and all at once a longing swept through him that was so great it threatened to tear him apart. He had a huge void in his life right now that he'd never even recognized before, an emptiness that clawed at him, begging to be filled.

He stopped in the middle of the dance. Gwen looked up at him questioningly, but he merely took her by the hand and led her back to their table.

"Is something the matter?" she asked.

He pulled out her chair and motioned for her to sit. "I have to make a phone call. I'll be back in a moment."

As he walked away, Gwen called after him, saying something about letting him use her cell phone, but he never looked back. There was one thing on his mind now, and one thing only.

He had to talk to Liz.

LIZ FELT as if she'd achieved at least a small victory when she held herself to only half a quart of Ben & Jerry's. Then she collapsed on the sofa to watch some dumb old movie on TV. Every once in a while she'd get caught up in the show and realize that a whole fifteen seconds had passed since she'd thought of Mark, and then she'd feel depressed all over again.

She lay the remote on her chest and closed her eyes, wishing tomorrow would come, then the next day and the next, because after a while, like maybe in a hundred years or so, she'd quit thinking about him and get a life again.

Then the phone rang.

Liz picked up the cordless phone that was lying on her coffee table. "Hello?"

"Liz. It's Mark."

Liz blinked with surprise. "Mark?"

"I tried you at Simon's. They said you'd gone home."

She sat up suddenly and swung her legs around, her heart striking up a sudden wild rhythm. She picked up the remote that had fallen to her lap and switched off the TV. "Wait a minute. Aren't you at the restaurant with Gwen?"

"Yes. Forget that for a minute. I have a question for you, and I want you to answer me truthfully."

Liz's heart skittered. What could he possibly want to ask her? "Of course."

"The other night when we were out together and I kissed you, what did you think? I mean, right at that moment?"

Liz sat stock-still, her heart beating her chest to death. Why was he asking her that? Did he want her to tell him that she didn't feel a thing for him? That going out with Gwen was the right thing to do? That he was a wonderful pupil, but that's where their relationship ended?

Or did he want to hear something completely different?

"Liz," he prompted, his voice barely above a whisper. "What did you think? *Tell me.*"

She felt as if she were tossing her heart out to be trampled on, but in the end she couldn't make anything but the truth come out of her mouth.

"I thought," she said, "that if your kissing me was a dream, I never wanted to wake up."

Silence.

Liz squeezed her eyes closed, berating herself first for speaking the truth, then for speaking it in a way that sounded so incredibly dumb. But his sudden call had muddled her brain so much she couldn't think straight, and his lack of response told her she'd given him exactly the answer he didn't want to hear.

"The reason I'm asking, Liz, is that I was having the same dream."

A second or two passed before his words sank in. When they did, Liz felt the air rush out of her lungs, making it hard to catch a good, solid breath.

"What I said after kissing you was a lie," Mark continued, "because I thought it was the wrong thing to do. It wasn't the wrong thing to do. It was the best thing I've ever done."

Liz pressed the phone tightly against her ear, hanging on to every word he spoke. A wave of desire swept through her that was so powerful she had to take a deep breath to control it.

"I'm coming to your apartment," Mark said.

"But what about Gwen?"

"I'm taking her home."

"How long will you be?"

"Thirty minutes—tops."

Then his voice became soft and seductive, like moonlight and roses and all those romantic things that Liz wanted to wrap both of them in forever.

"The whole time I've been with Gwen tonight," he said, "all I've been able to think about is you."

Liz sank back on the sofa, feeling a surge of elation that obliterated all the sadness and uncertainty she'd felt before. She didn't know why he'd changed his mind about Gwen, and right now she didn't care. All that mattered was that before the night was out he'd be kissing her again, and this time there would be no doubts—it would be the real thing.

"I have so many things I want to say," he continued. "I don't even know where to start."

"It's okay. We've got all night."

"All night," Mark echoed softly. "I like the sound of that."

"So do I. So will you hurry? Please?"

"I'll be there as fast as I can."

11

MARK FUMBLED to replace the receiver on the hook, fighting the urge to drop the phone and race out of the restaurant. He felt so electrified he could have *run* all the way to Morrison Heights.

We've got all night.

Those whispered words held so much promise that his knees weakened. As soon as he'd heard Liz's voice on the phone, all the reasons he shouldn't go to her apartment and sweep her into his arms flew right out of his mind. To hell with Gwen, to hell with his job, to hell with keeping up with the Sloans of the world. Once he got within touching distance of Liz he was going to make certain she didn't sleep for two days.

He returned to the table, barely able to think. While he saw Gwen, he really didn't see her at all. It was as if she had shifted to some other dimension he could no longer relate to.

"Is there a problem?" Gwen asked.

"Yes. Something's come up. I have to go to the office."

"The office? At nine-thirty on a Saturday night?"

"I phoned an associate, and it was just as I suspected. A crisis with one of my clients. I'm afraid I'm going to have to cut our evening short."

He was surprised at how easily the lie rolled off his tongue. But then again, Gwen hadn't exactly been up front with her motives, either.

She smiled seductively. "But we were having such a nice time."

"It can't be helped."

She gave him another one of her long-suffering sighs. "Well, I suppose with the level of responsibility you're getting ready to assume, this could become a common occurrence." She gave him a phony smile. "I guess I'll just have to get used to it, won't I?"

No, you won't, because we'll never be seeing each other again.

All at once Mark realized just how terribly misguided he'd been. He didn't need to bring the right woman to his company function to show the management he was partner material. His new wardrobe and his new attitude around the office had already worked wonders in that direction. In just the last week, Edwin Nichols had consulted with him personally on a few management issues he never would have discussed before, and Mark noticed co-workers deferring to him more often. And Tina had become his self-appointed personal publicist, using the company grapevine to boost his image every chance she got. *This is a new Mark McAlister you're dealing with,* she'd said in so many words. *So look out.*

But it was Liz who'd given him the confidence to look like a sharp professional and to act like a man who expected to win, and when it came right down to it, that's all he'd ever really needed.

Liz sat paralyzed on her sofa. Had Mark really said what she thought he said?

I'll be there as soon as I can.

She glanced at her watch. He'd said thirty minutes, max. That's all the time she had before he'd be here. She closed her eyes and tried to get a grip on her jangled nerves, still unable to believe he was leaving Gwen in the lurch and coming here to be with her. She held up her hands. They were actually shaking.

If he's the man for you, he'll come to his senses.

Her mother, without a doubt, was the smartest woman alive.

Then Liz looked down at herself, at the ratty gym shorts she wore, along with a T-shirt that was more hole than shirt.

This would never do.

She went to her bedroom and flipped madly through her closet. Seeing nothing remotely attractive, she dug through her dresser drawers, flinging clothes left and right. Why wasn't she one of those women who had drawers full of sexy underwear and a closet full of exquisite things just made to seduce a lover? She wanted to look beautiful. Alluring. Desirable. But how was that going to happen when she had nothing but happy-face panties and Looney Tunes nightshirts? After several minutes of wardrobe analysis that led to nothing but frustration, she made a decision.

If she had nothing to wear, she'd have to wear nothing at all.

FORTUNATELY, Gwen's apartment was on the way to Liz's, and Mark made good time. He could tell Gwen hated being brushed off, but he couldn't have cared less. He walked her quickly to her door. She angled for a kiss, so he relented and leaned in to give her a quick peck on the cheek. She shifted at the last moment, though, and turned his quick kiss into a lengthy mouth-to-mouth experience that he wouldn't have thought Miss Prim and Proper capable of. But it did nothing for him. Absolutely nothing.

He couldn't believe this was the same woman he'd have once sold his soul to go out with. All he could think about now was checking himself in his rearview mirror

to make sure he didn't walk into Liz's apartment with
lipstick where it didn't belong.

"Call me," Gwen said in a breathy voice, then slipped
inside her apartment and closed the door behind her.

Not a chance.

Mark leaped back into his car and pulled out of the
parking lot as quickly as he could without burning rubber.
He swung his car onto Porter Avenue and proceeded to
run three yellow lights in a row. After nearly sideswiping
a minivan, he stepped on the brake until he was going
only ten miles per hour over the speed limit instead of
twenty. In just a few minutes he was going to be holding
Liz again, kissing her—making love to her, if he had his
way—and this time it was the real thing. If she wanted
to grade his performance, that was all right by him, because tonight he intended to move right to the top of the
class.

When he got to Liz's apartment building, he parked
quickly, then hurried inside, his heart beating like crazy.
He climbed the squeaky oak steps and approached Liz's
door. To his surprise, it was standing slightly open. He
pushed it open farther, heard nothing, then came inside
and closed it behind him. The living room was dark. Investigating further, he saw that the bathroom door was
ajar, with a pale, unsteady light shining through the crack.

"Liz?"

No answer. Slowly he opened the door. On the edge
of the sink three candles flickered, casting an ethereal
glow around the room. A huge clawfoot tub overflowed
with bubbles. And in the midst of them, like an earth-
bound angel, sat Liz.

She stared up at him, her hair swept into a loose knot
at the crown of her head, with slender red tendrils spiral-
ing down her cheeks that shimmered in the candlelight.
Bubbles clung to her chest like a sparkling white evening
gown, dipping low into the tantalizing hollow between

her breasts. She met his gaze with a sweet, vulnerable smile that was more enticing to him than any come-hither stare could possibly have been. He couldn't move. He couldn't speak. All he could do was stare at her as a slow, dreamy desire built up inside him that left him speechless.

Then her smile faltered. She folded her arms over her breasts and sank lower in the tub until the bubbles grazed her chin.

"Mark?" she said weakly. "Say something."

He blinked, but the rest of him stayed put. He felt as if his feet had been fused to the bathroom tile.

"Mark, I'm starting to feel a little silly here, so I'd really appreciate it if you could kind of think about getting in here with me."

As Mark continued to stare at her, Liz suddenly felt…naked. Then it struck her that all he'd said was that he wanted to be with her, not that he wanted to be, well…*with* her. While she was thinking hot sex in a bathtub, he was thinking pizza and a movie rental. How could she have been so stupid?

He blinked again, as if waking from a trance. "I'm sorry, Liz. It's just that—"

No. Don't say you don't want me. Please don't say it.

"It's just that you look so *beautiful.*"

At those few heartfelt words, Liz's insides melted into a warm puddle that settled somewhere in the region below her waist. In the dim, flickering candlelight, Mark removed his suit coat and tossed it on the floor beside him, the buttons clicking softly against the tile.

Oh, God.

With his eyes never leaving hers, he reached up and slowly pulled his tie from around his neck and dropped it. She trembled as he unbuttoned his cuffs, then his shirt, and when he pulled it off and tossed it aside, too, she got a beautiful view of a broad, muscled chest dusted with dark hair.

He unbuttoned his slacks, then paused. "Don't laugh."

Liz froze. Those were not words a woman wanted to hear when a man was removing his pants.

Finally he took them off, and it was a good thing he'd warned her not to laugh. He wore a pair of silky boxers in a kaleidoscope of rainbow hues, their color so bright that even in the dim light Liz practically needed sunglasses just to look at them.

"They were Eddie's idea," Mark said with disgust. "I think he needs to stick to the outer man."

"Very nice," Liz said, smiling. "Can I see how they look on the bathroom floor?"

He took them off and added them to the pile of clothes he'd already discarded. Liz saw what lay beneath, and there was *nothing* funny about that. She knew he was tall and broad-shouldered with big, strong hands, but she hadn't known the rest of him was so…proportional. As gorgeous as his body looked inside his clothes, it looked a hundred times better out of them, and just the sight of him made her heart beat so wildly she seriously wondered if her body could withstand the assault.

She curled into one end of the large tub to give Mark room to join her. Once in the water, he shifted around until the length of his body was stretched out beside hers. Beneath the water his hand slid across her back and curled around one side of her rib cage. She yielded to the pressure he exerted there as he pulled her buoyant body around to align with his. As he drew her closer, the bubbles billowed up between them in glittery white mounds.

"I saw your face when you came in," she murmured. "I was afraid you didn't want to do this."

"You just surprised me a little, that's all."

"Was it a good surprise?"

"Liz, for future reference, anything that involves us naked together, I'm there."

All at once she realized this was real, Mark was here,

and he wasn't going to disappear in a cloud of her own wishful thinking. She put a tentative hand against his shoulder, then ran her palm down the length of his arm, watching as the candlelight shimmered across the damp, bubbly trail she left behind. She stroked her fingertips along his cheek, then moved them upward to brush a lock of dark, steamy hair away from his forehead. She stared at him with wonder, astonished that she was finally free to touch him however she wanted to. Then he curled his hand around the back of her neck and drew her into a long, passionate kiss.

Oh, *yes*.

He urged her lips apart and kissed her deeply, twining his tongue with hers, and she thought back to the kiss he'd given her at Rosario's. If that had been wonderful, this was spectacular. She wanted to know how a shy, unassuming guy from Waldon Springs, Texas, had learned how to drive a woman crazy with lust, but maybe that was a question for tomorrow, because if he told her now his wonderful, talented mouth would occupy itself with speech, and that was the *last* thing she wanted to have happen.

He kissed her for what seemed like forever, his hands caressing her beneath the water, exploring the curves of her thighs, her hips, her waist, then moving upward to her breasts, sending hot ripples of pure sensation washing over her. He teased his lips along her neck, sending a flurry of warm shivers down her spine. "I could kiss you all over."

A jolt of pure desire shot through her.

"But I'd get a mouthful of bubbles."

Liz smiled at him, then reached around to pull the plug. As the water gurgled down the drain, they came to their feet, mounds of bubbles drifting down their bodies. She pulled the shower curtain into the tub, then turned on the shower.

They stood beneath the spray together, kissing and caressing each other until the bubbles had washed away completely. For first time in her life Liz didn't have the urge to cover herself when a man looked at her naked. She'd always felt as if she'd been cursed with a body that was way too round and about ten pounds too heavy. But there was something about the way Mark looked at her, as if he couldn't get enough of her, that made her feel more beautiful than she ever had in her life. He wrapped his arms around her, and with his hands and his mouth everywhere at once and the steam from the shower billowing up around them, she felt as if heaven wasn't in the clouds at all, but in a clawfoot tub with the man she loved.

Loved?

No. She couldn't think about that now. She'd think about it tomorrow, when her mind wasn't lost in the feel of Mark's body, so warm and solid, against hers and his hands working such magic. Tomorrow, when she had her head on straight and she could be absolutely certain that the *L* word was really *love* and not *lust*.

She put her lips next to his ear. "Do you remember?"

"Remember?"

"The kiss-you-all-over thing."

"Oh, sweetheart, I could never forget a thing like that."

Mark turned off the shower and they stepped out of the tub. He grabbed a towel and wrapped her in it. Then pulled her to him, tucking her into the crook of his elbow and kissed her—a wild, demanding, breathless kiss that set her on fire again.

She pulled away just long enough to drag him into her bedroom, where he stretched out beside her on the bed and kept his promise, exploring her body with his hands and his mouth in a way that was at once giving and demanding, tender and wild. In the midst of it all, she reached for him, curling her hand around him, touching him, stroking him. Then she touched his cheek with her other hand, drawing him toward her for yet another kiss, loving the feel of his lips against hers, while at the same time, his velvet hardness pulsed beneath her hand.

Then he broke their kiss abruptly, clasping her hand with his, stilling its movement. He bowed his head and let out a harsh breath.

"Liz, if you keep doing that—"

"I want you *now*," she whispered.

The words barely escaped her lips before he pushed her gently to her back, moved between her legs and rose above her, pausing only a moment to stare down at her. The intensity of his gaze told her how much he wanted her, and Liz practically lost it right there.

Finally he slid into her, and she gasped at the feeling of their bodies joined together. Slowly, he began to move inside her. He filled her so completely and the sensations were so intense that she thought she'd die from the pleasure of it. She wrapped her legs around him, tilting her hips to meet his, wanting him so much her heart overflowed with it. She felt a hard pulsing deep inside that grew more intense with every thrust, pushing her toward the peak of ecstasy. She teetered on the brink, suspended in time for a long, excruciating moment. Then Mark groaned softly, and that small sound of pleasure was all it took to send her plunging over the edge. He thrust harder, faster, then clung to her tightly, breathing her name over and over in wild release. He fell against her, and together they spiraled back to earth, his breath hot against her neck and his arms wrapped around her, holding on to the intimacy between them until the last tremors of pleasure faded away.

After a while Mark slid away and fell to his back, sighing with contentment. He pulled Liz into his arms and they lay together in satisfied exhaustion, bathed in the light of the moon whispering through the curtains.

"A bubble bath," he murmured. "That was a *very* nice surprise."

"Uh…yeah. Bubble bath." She paused. "Will you remind me tomorrow that I'm out of Ivory dishwashing liquid?"

Mark groaned painfully, but the smile that followed told her that making like a dirty dish tonight had pleased him immensely.

"You think I'm crazy, don't you?" Liz said.

"Yes." He brushed the wispy hair away from her temple, then teased his thumb over her cheek. "And I never knew how wonderful crazy could be."

12

MARK'S FIRST THOUGHT when he woke the next morning was that his eyes were open but he was still dreaming, because his arms were wrapped around Liz and she was snuggled right next to him, her back pressed against his chest and her backside pressed against...other things. Then he realized it wasn't a dream at all, that they'd actually slept together. The sheets were in tangled disarray, proof positive that they'd done a whole lot more than sleep.

Mark had never felt this way about a woman before—this overwhelming hunger that made him want to wake up beside her not just on this morning, but on many mornings to come. Still half-asleep, his mind drifted into uncharted territory, producing loose, fragmented thoughts about what it would be like to spend his days with Liz as well as his nights, to integrate their lives, to plan forever together....

She stirred beside him. He kissed her shoulder, then ran his hand along her waist to her hip, loving the feel of her skin. And when his gaze followed the same path, he couldn't believe what he saw.

Positioned just below the curve of her back near her left hip was a dime-shaped tattoo in the shape of a daisy. He'd imagined she had one just like it the first day he met her, and now he smiled at how right he'd been. But unless she wore an extremely teeny bikini, no one but her, her doctor or a lover would ever see it, so the fact that he was seeing it now positively delighted him. And then he got to thinking that maybe he should check out the rest of her body for any other identifying marks he might have missed last night.

He brushed his fingertips against her breast, then kissed her neck just below her left ear. She let out a soft moan of pure pleasure. Slowly she rolled over and smiled at him, her green eyes blinking sleepily.

"Hi," she murmured, and kissed him. Soon, she was in his arms and they were making love all over again.

Later, after a shower for two that used up most of the water supply of the city of Dallas, Mark watched Liz make breakfast. He offered to help cook, but she sat him down at the table, gave him a ceramic mug that had real coffee in it with real caffeine, and told him to stay put. She wanted him to save his energy, she said with a wink and a quick kiss, then started buzzing around the kitchen like a bee around a hive. She moved pots and utensils and various food items in a way that seemed haphazard, but somehow eggs were cooking, along with bacon and biscuits and gravy, and he was basking once again in the joy of being with a woman who genuinely liked to eat, who didn't toss a dried-up bagel on a plate and pronounce it breakfast.

Actually, he was basking in the joy of a lot of things right now, such as what they'd done together last night, and again this morning, and just might do again a couple of times today if he had his way. He'd do his best to use up all that energy she was allowing him to save. Just watching her move around the kitchen with that wild auburn hair tumbling over her shoulders and those gorgeous long legs of hers flowing out from beneath that short little robe made him want to forget breakfast altogether and drag her straight back to the bedroom.

After breakfast, he pulled her from her chair and into

his lap. "I don't know about you, but I've got absolutely nothing to do for the rest of the day."

"Except be with me?"

"Exactly."

Liz gave him a sparkling smile. "Sounds wonderful."

"Why don't you get dressed, and then we'll go to my apartment and I'll put on some clothes that didn't spend the night on the bathroom floor."

She gave him a quick kiss, then went to get dressed. Mark sat at the kitchen table, finishing off the rest of his coffee, this time basking in the feeling of having a whole day ahead that, for once, he wouldn't be spending alone. It wasn't until Liz came out of the bedroom, dressed as only Liz could dress, that he felt a twinge of foreboding, suddenly reminded of the reason he'd resisted falling for her in the first place.

She wore a minuscule pair of faded denim shorts with frayed cuffs and a pair of shoes with heels so stratospheric that she stood a good four inches taller than usual. She'd pulled her bright auburn hair up into a scrambled ponytail, with curly strands already trickling down around her face. She'd replaced one set of star earrings with a pair of silver dolphins dangling from her earlobes, and her T-shirt read, I Don't Need Your Attitude. I've Got One of My Own.

He let his gaze travel down those incredible legs of hers and back up again, cruising along her hips, her waist, her breasts. Then he met her sparkling eyes. She smiled at him, that broad, beautiful smile that lit up a room, and any concern he felt about the consequences of her unusual dress and behavior flew right out the window.

They drove to his apartment. He went into his bedroom to change clothes while Liz relaxed on his sofa, her feet up on his coffee table. A few minutes later he came back out, comfortable now in jeans and a sports shirt, already thinking that his sofa might be a dandy place to take those outrageous clothes right off her again. Then he saw what she was holding, and a wave of apprehension swept through him.

"You're having a company party!" Liz said, waving the invitation to his company dinner dance.

"Uh...yeah."

"It says here you're supposed to bring a guest. Can we go?"

We?

His own attendance was not just requested, it was required. But—oh, God—could he take Liz with him?

He remembered the dress she'd worn to Rosario's the other night, that hot little number that had made him sweat just to look at it. If she showed up looking like that...

But it wasn't just the way she dressed. What if she brushed lint off Edwin Nichols's lapels? What if she brought a hand-held TV and caught the last few innings of the Rangers-Mariners game? What if there was an unfamiliar piece of silverware at dinner and she asked the waiter for a supplementary lesson in table etiquette? What would happen then?

He'd be ostracized by his superiors for his questionable taste in women. With him and Sloan neck and neck the way they were, that's all it would take to tip the scales in Sloan's favor. Then he could kiss the partnership goodbye.

"You wouldn't like it," he said, trying to keep his voice light and offhanded. "Believe me."

"Are you kidding? I love parties!"

He sat down beside her. "This isn't a party. It's more like business. It's a group of stuffy, boring people who spend all their time talking about accounting. And I know how you hate stuffy, boring people."

"But it says here that it's at a country club. I've never seen inside one of those. I bet it's really something."

"No. These things are so dull. Everybody dresses up

like they're going to a ball at Buckingham Palace. You'd hate it.''

And you'd give my superiors a collective heart attack.

"Now, you know me better than that," Liz said with a wave of her hand. "I can have a good time wherever I go. It'll be fun."

It'll be fun. Why did those three words coming out of Liz's mouth strike fear in his heart?

Because trying to keep her personality under wraps would be like trying to douse a forest fire with a squirt gun.

He shook his head. "It's really just a business thing, Liz. Dull as dirt. So I don't think—"

"I'll get to meet the people you work with. And there'll be dinner, probably a lot like the one we had at Rosario's, and since we both like to dance, it'll be—"

"Liz!"

He spoke sharper than he intended. He softened his voice, but he wasn't sure he softened the message.

"I think it'd be best if I went to this one by myself."

Liz stared at Mark a long time, trying to understand his reluctance. It was just a party, after all, and she was a party expert. Then, for some reason, Gwen popped into her mind, and slowly everything started to make sense.

She's the woman I need, she remembered Mark saying after he made a date with Gwen. *I know this makes no sense to you, but I have to make this work, and I have to do it now.*

Gwen was exactly the kind of woman Mark could bring to a company function and impress the conservative management who was making the decision about his partnership.

Everybody dresses like they're going to a ball at Buckingham Palace. You'd hate it.

That's what Mark had told her. But that wasn't what he meant.

The men dress in tuxedos and the women dress in formal gowns. You'd never fit in.

That's what he'd been trying to tell her.

As reality of the situation hit Liz full force, she thought she was going to be sick. It wasn't that she'd hate his coworkers.

It was that they'd hate her.

Her heart sank so low it practically tumbled onto the ground. For the first time in her life, she wished she were somebody else. Mark needed a woman who could glide through a room with social competence, radiating sophistication and grace, a woman who would be a positive reflection of his own professional image. Instead, he was getting an unsophisticated nobody who worked as a bartender, whose only claim to fame was that she made the best margaritas in town.

She turned to face him. "Mark, I want you to tell me the truth. You're uptight at the very thought of taking me to one of your company parties, aren't you?"

He glanced down at his hands. "Uptight? Why would I be uptight?"

"Because I'm not like Gwen."

"And I'm very thankful for that."

"Still, she'd fit in real good at Buckingham Palace, don't you think?" She paused. "I'd fit in better in the servants' quarters."

Mark looked at her a long time, and the silence between them seemed to stretch on forever. Finally he shook his head. "It's just these people I work with, Liz. And the big bosses. They think the only reason you have a relationship is to gain money, prestige or power. If they knew I was dating—"

He stopped short, then let out a harsh breath, leaving the sentence dangling.

"If they knew you were dating a woman like me," Liz

said, "and a *bartender* at that, your career would come to a screeching halt."

She waited through a long, miserable silence, wanting desperately for Mark to deny it. Instead, he said nothing. Her chest tightened with disappointment.

"Okay," she murmured. "At least I know where I stand."

"It's not me, Liz! I don't care what you do for a living!"

"But you have to care. Because *they* care. Right?"

Mark closed his eyes for a moment, his jaw tight. "I'm up for a partnership, Liz. It's something I've wanted since I started working for that company. I'm in competition with another guy, and right now it could go either way. I can't afford to…"

His voice trailed off, but Liz got the picture. He couldn't afford to make any mistakes because he wanted this so badly. And showing up with the wrong woman might be just the mistake that would make him lose out.

"Do you regret what you did last night? Leaving Gwen to be with me?"

"No! She's not the one I want!"

"But she's the one you need, right?"

"Don't you understand? She's the one *they* think I need!"

"So where does that leave me?"

Mark opened his mouth to respond, then closed it again. He stared at her a long time, and her heart beat frantically as she imagined the words he was getting ready to say. *Well, it was fun while it lasted, but it's time to get real. We don't belong together.*

Instead, to her surprise, he reached out and lay his hand over hers, caressing it gently.

"It leaves you with me, I hope."

Liz blinked with disbelief. He smoothed the hair away

from her forehead with his fingertips, then kissed her gently.

"I'm sorry, Liz. I don't know what I was thinking. I want you to come with me."

She felt a rush of relief. "You do?"

"Yes. Of course I do. It's just this partnership thing. It's made me a little crazy." He shrugged. "It's just one party. It really isn't all that important."

In spite of his easygoing manner, Liz saw the little worry lines around his eyes and heard the hesitancy in his voice, and she knew he was lying. This party was clearly *very* important. Still, he cared enough about her to ask her to come in spite of the consequences he thought he might face, and she loved him for that.

Yes. She loved him. She hadn't meant for it to happen, but it had happened just the same. She was falling in love with Mark. But still, that tangled-up feeling in her stomach wouldn't go away, the one that reminded her that she just didn't measure up to the kind of woman he was expected to associate with. No matter how he felt right now, how long would he want her if he thought she was going to be a detriment to his career?

Not long. And that's why she was determined not to let him down.

"I can do this, Mark. As long as you help me."

"Help you?"

"I'll get Eddie to dress me, and I swear I'll study up on Emily Post and Miss Manners. But you need to tell me about all the people you work with so I'll know whose you-know-whats I'm supposed to kiss."

He smiled. "No problem. I'll point out all the proper posteriors. I promise."

Liz grinned. "How many *P*s were in that sentence, anyway?"

"I have an affinity for alliteration."

She rolled her eyes. Mark pulled her back toward him

and kissed her again. The second his lips met hers, she knew she was doing the right thing, even if it involved being somebody she wasn't.

One week. That's all she had to make herself into the kind of woman he needed, or they had no future at all.

A WEEK LATER, Mark climbed the stairs to Liz's apartment, walking up slower than he ever had before. He'd never sweated anything the way he'd sweated the last seven days.

He had no idea what was going to happen tonight. Liz said she could handle this, but could she really? He didn't know. All he knew was that when he'd seen that look of hurt on her face when he'd suggested that she might not fit in with the crowd at his company, he'd have done anything to erase it—including inviting her along.

How had this happened? How could he be falling in love with a woman who made him deliriously happy yet at the same time could be a wrecker's ball to his career?

He took a deep breath and knocked on her door. A moment later she opened it, and he was so stunned he couldn't move. If he lived to be a hundred, he would never have imagined seeing Liz dressed like this.

She wore a long black gown that exposed her skin only from her wrists down and her neck up, with a satiny skirt that fell in soft folds all the way to her feet. The top part of the dress was formfitting, but subtly so, the high neckline dipping only slightly toward her breasts, enhancing her figure without drawing undue attention to it. She wore a necklace that looked like a simple strand of diamonds. Matching diamond earrings occupied only *one* set of her many ear piercings. Her hair was swept up in a style so sleek and proper that it was hard to remember just how wild and curly her hair really was. She held a simple black satin handbag against her waist and smiled up at him with an aura of calm composure.

"Hello, Mark."

Her whisper-soft voice drifted across her threshold, mesmerizing him. It was Liz, but it wasn't. It was as if the body snatchers had landed, taken the real Liz and put a polished, cultured, ultraconservative version in her place.

She stepped aside, and he entered her apartment. He heard the soft swish of her skirt, then caught the scent of a dainty floral perfume that was totally different from the quirky scent she usually wore. She placed a hand against his shoulder and gave him a gentle kiss of greeting on his left cheek.

Okay. Now it was definite. This was not Liz. Liz would have dragged him through the door by his shirt collar and given him a kiss so hot he'd feel it all the way to his toes. It was time to call out the National Guard. Earth had definitely been invaded and the body snatchers were taking over.

He was absolutely speechless. How could she have changed so drastically? How?

Every bit of his apprehension about how she would present herself in a social situation suddenly vanished. He'd worried for nothing. Her manner was subdued, which wasn't like the Liz he knew at all, and her dress was a little boring compared to what she usually wore, but both were absolutely correct for the occasion, and he found himself thinking, *She makes Tiffany Sloan look like a cheap hooker.*

A smile inched across his face. "You look absolutely *beautiful.*"

"Thank you. Shall we go?"

Mark breathed a sigh of relief. Maybe tonight was going to work out after all. They headed for the door, and Liz turned and tossed him a wink and a smile over her shoulder.

I'm still Liz, that gesture told him. *But I'm going to*

play this part just for you. And I'm going to do a bang-up job of it.

Mark didn't know whether to love her for that or cringe in fear. She may look like a socialite, but the real Liz still lurked beneath the surface.

As they drove to the country club, he gave Liz a primer on the people she'd be meeting that night.

"Edwin Nichols," he said. "Managing partner. Pompous and self-important. Thinks appearances are everything and lives to work. His wife's name is Margaret. She looks like Edith Bunker and acts like her, too. She's not the sharpest knife in the drawer, but she's friendly and talks up a storm. You won't have any problem with her."

"The big boss and his wife."

"Right."

Liz nodded, as if absorbing the information.

He went on to tell her about the other partners and their wives, then filled her in on Jared and Tiffany Sloan.

"Basically, Sloan's a jerk, and Tiffany's got her nose so far in the air if an indoor thunderstorm blows through, she'll drown. They're both insufferable."

"And this guy's your competition?" Liz looked at Mark as if he were nuts to think so.

"He talks a hell of a good game. You'd be surprised how far you can get in the business world on a good line of bull."

"Anybody else?"

"Yes. Steven Millstone."

"*The* Steven Millstone?"

"Yeah. Boy wonder of the computer world. There'll be a few other prospective clients there tonight, but Millstone is the biggie. If you're looking to kiss a you-know-what, you might consider his."

Liz nodded studiously, as if committing everything he said to memory. He had to stop worrying. She looked great. All she had to do was stand there looking classy and smile a lot, and the evening would be a success.

Briarwood Country Club sat in the heart of North Dallas, the clubhouse surrounded by acre upon acre of groomed landscape, and beyond that the rolling hills of the golf course stretched as far as the eye could see. Mark drove through the iron gates, then crept along the road leading to the clubhouse. The evening sun cascaded over the live oak and crepe-myrtle trees, casting long shadows across the manicured lawn.

Mark pulled up in front of the clubhouse and brought the car to a halt. A valet took his car, and he escorted Liz toward the clubhouse, stopping short when he saw the man himself, Edwin Nichols, standing at the door greeting guests.

"That's Edwin Nichols," he whispered to Liz.

Liz blinked with surprise. "The guy with the bad toupee?"

"Uh...yeah. But we don't talk about that."

"It looks like—"

"I know. A piece of shag carpet stuck to his head."

"All that money, and yet—"

"Yet he still looks like a electroshocked Pekingese. I know. Just try to focus on his face instead of his scalp."

They walked up the short flight of brick steps to the door of the country club. "Hello, Edwin," Mark said. He shook the man's hand, then turned to Liz. "I'd like you to meet—"

"Elizabeth Prescott," Liz said, extending her hand. "It's a pleasure to meet you."

Elizabeth?

"It's a pleasure to meet you, too," Edwin said. He introduced his wife, Margaret, to Liz, then turned to Mark. "I had no idea you were seeing such a lovely young woman."

"Why, thank you, Mr. Nichols," Liz said. "What a nice compliment."

"Please. Call me Edwin."

Liz nodded her assent, and Edwin's wall-to-wall grin, so different from his usual sourpuss expression, told Mark that she'd sailed over the initial hurdle and made a smashing first impression.

Maybe he'd worried for nothing.

Edwin turned to greet another couple, and Margaret caught Liz's eye.

"So tell me, dear," she said, with that vacuous smile that said she'd lost her brain somewhere along the line and didn't even miss it. "What is it that you do?"

Liz blinked. "What do I do?"

"Yes. What is your profession?"

13

MARK JUST ABOUT CHOKED. It couldn't be. They hadn't been here two minutes, and already their backs were against the wall. He'd been so swept up in how Liz looked and the manner in which she behaved that he'd forgotten all about who she really was. He wanted to say something to ward off the inevitable, but his mind was frustratingly blank.

Liz raised her chin a notch. "I'm a mixologist."

Mark blinked. What did she say?

Margaret looked confused. "A mixologist? I'm afraid I don't know what that is."

"Well, it's quite complicated," Liz replied, "but suffice it to say I deal mainly in the interaction between ETOH and various natural compounds taking into account the effect of CO_2 and $NaCl$ on the chemical processes."

Mark's heart all but stopped. He couldn't imagine anyone on earth who wouldn't translate that into exactly what it was: alcohol, fruit, seltzer and salt. But chemistry clearly wasn't Margaret's long suit.

"That sounds fascinating!" Margaret gushed. "What college did you attend to get such a degree?"

"Lone Star College."

Margaret's eyebrows pulled together. "I don't believe I've heard of that."

Liz gave her an obliging smile. "It's a small, but exclusive private college. They offer a limited number of degree programs. But what they do, they do *very* well."

Mark felt as if every nerve ending were suddenly on red alert. It was exclusive, all right. Exclusively for people who want to tend bar for a living. And as far as the limited number of degree programs…yes, *one* was pretty limited.

"Well," Margaret said. "A professional woman. How nice."

Mark excused them, putting his hand against the small of Liz's back and turning her in the direction of the ballroom before any more questions could pop out of Margaret's mouth.

"Mixologist?" Mark said, once they were out of earshot. "Where did *that* come from?"

"Would you rather I'd have told her the truth?"

"No! I mean, yes, but—" He exhaled sharply. "It's not me, Liz. I told you before. I don't care what you do for a living. It's them. They care. They shouldn't, but they do, and with me right on the verge of this partnership…"

Liz turned away. He saw the wounded expression on her face, and a wave of guilt spread through him. He had no business wanting her to be something she wasn't just so he could get the job he was after. But when it came right down to it, what choice did he have?

"Just promise me one thing," she said.

"What?"

"Once you get that partnership, you'll unstuff some of the stuffiness at the top."

Mark nodded. "I will."

"And if the question of my profession comes up again," Liz added, "I'll just tell them I'm a hooker."

"*What?*"

"That way when I tell them I'm really a bartender, it won't sound so bad."

She smiled, but he could tell this whole thing hurt her more than she was letting on, and the only reason she was going along with it was to help him. It struck him once again what a lucky guy he was that a smart, sexy, beautiful woman like Liz would even give him the time of day.

Don't screw it up, his brain was telling him, at the same time it was also shouting, *Get that partnership no matter what.*

"Don't worry," Mark told her. "Chances are it won't even come up again, and you won't have to tell anyone anything."

After saying hello to a few of Mark's friends, he and Liz moved into the ballroom. It was a spectacular place, with towering ceilings dripping with chandeliers, walnut paneling and polished marble floors. Couples stood talking to one another, the low hum of conversation filling the air. Mark saw Sloan across the room.

He touched Liz's shoulder and whispered, "Jared Sloan at twelve o'clock."

Liz turned and scanned the crowd. "The guy with his chest all puffed out?"

"That's the one. You'll have to meet him sooner or later."

Liz smiled. "Well, then. By all means, let's do it now."

He led Liz over to where Sloan stood guzzling a glass of Scotch and monopolizing yet another conversation. Sloan turned, and when he caught his first glimpse of Liz, his eyes widened with surprise. He gave Tiffany a nudge. She turned, and her expression dissolved into a comical reprise of her husband's.

"Sloan, I'd like you to meet Elizabeth Prescott. Elizabeth, Jared and Tiffany Sloan."

They made nice all around, and it was all Sloan could do to keep his eyeballs in his head when he looked at Liz.

"So, McAlister," Sloan said, staring at Liz. "I didn't know you were seeing anyone."

He slid his hand around Liz's waist. "No one but Elizabeth."

Liz looked up at him adoringly, and he wanted to kiss her right then and there.

"That's a lovely dress, Elizabeth," Tiffany said, then crinkled her nose. "I wasn't aware black was in this season."

Liz smiled indulgently. "You know, that's *exactly* what I told my wardrobe consultant. But he insisted that the runways this season were positively overflowing with it." She gave Tiffany a self-deprecating smile. "What can I say? I'm a slave to fashion."

Tiffany blinked dumbly. Apparently she didn't know *what* to say to that.

"If you'll excuse us," Mark said, "there are a few more people I want to introduce Elizabeth to."

Mark swept Liz away, in awe of how she'd scored a direct hit on Tiffany but had done it so sweetly that the woman barely knew she'd been fired on. And that pleased him immensely.

He introduced Liz to the other partners, their wives and to his co-workers. Everywhere they went, she made a wonderful impression. She chose her words carefully, speaking slowly and evenly, punctuating her conversation with pleasant little smiles doled out at just the right time.

This is working, Mark thought, after they'd made it through most of the cocktail hour. *She's exactly what I need her to be.*

"Mark?"

He turned to see Edwin standing behind him.

"Dinner is in five minutes. Why don't you and Elizabeth join Margaret and me at our table?"

Mark's confidence level about the promotion shot straight through the roof. "Thank you, Edwin," he said calmly, feeling anything *but* calm. "We'll do that."

Edwin strode away, and Mark whispered to Liz.

"That's a *really* good sign." He ran his hand down her arm and took her hand in his. "Did I tell you that you look absolutely beautiful tonight?"

"Yes. I think you did. How am I doing?"

"You're doing great. Everybody loves you." He kissed her hand, then offered his arm and escorted her to the dining room. Once there, Mark glanced toward the table where Sloan and Tiffany sat with Richard White and his wife. All the partners had a say in the decision, but as the newest partner, White wouldn't have as much pull as Edwin, and Sloan knew it. Then Sloan turned and saw Mark, and if his eyes had been rifles, Mark would have been dead.

Mark smiled. This was definitely going to be a night to remember.

LIZ TOOK THE SEAT Edwin offered her at the round table for six, which put Mark on her right and Margaret on her left. Edwin sat on the other side of Mark. Oh, joy. Evidently they were going to get grilled from both sides by the Top Dog and Mrs. Top Dog. One of the remaining chairs, she discovered, was for Steven Millstone.

"He's been delayed," Edwin told them. "But I spoke to him a moment ago and he'll be here soon."

Liz took a deep, furtive breath. A client. Mark had to make a good impression, which meant *she* had to make a good impression.

Mark's admiration a moment ago had pleased her immensely, but still, she couldn't ignore the funny twinge she felt inside. A part of her had wanted him to reject this image of her, to ask her why she'd go to this much trouble and this much expense when he liked her just the way she was. But judging from the smile he'd worn all evening, along with the compliments he'd given her, right now this was clearly the woman he preferred.

She straightened her spine and raised her chin. No matter how hard it was to be all proper and perfect, she was going to do it. Was it really such a big deal to hunt for the right fork to use or wear a dress so conservative that it aged her ten years just to look at it? Later, when she and Mark were alone, she could eat with her fingers and wear nothing at all if she felt like it. But for now, if she loved him and wanted to have a future with him, she had to at least give the impression that she could fit in with this crowd.

Fortunately, as they ate dinner, Margaret held up her end of the conversation so well that Liz was able to smile, nod and say very little. On the other hand, Mark and Edwin seemed to be carrying on a fairly intense discussion. Liz kept her eyes on Margaret as she prattled away, but tuned her ears toward the men.

"...and you've always had the technical ability," Edwin was saying, "but now it seems that you finally understand what it takes to become a partner at this firm. The right look. The right attitude." He paused. "And now, it appears, the right woman. Tell me. Are you serious about her?"

"Very serious."

"Margaret tells me she's a chemist."

Liz nearly choked. Is that what Margaret's addled brain had done? Turned "mixologist" into "chemist?"

"She's quite a catch," Edwin continued. "You know how I value intelligence in a woman."

Oh, sure he does. That's why he married Margaret.

Liz could sense Mark freezing up, and she wondered what he was going to say in reply. Fortunately, Edwin kept talking, making a reply unnecessary, then dropped his voice so low Liz could barely make out his words.

"As far as the partnership is concerned, I've decided you've got my vote. And I think I can persuade White and Marbury to see it my way, too."

"Thank you, Edwin," Mark said calmly, but Liz could

hear the undercurrent of excitement in his voice. "I appreciate the endorsement."

"Millstone will be here shortly. Let's see what you can do toward getting his signature on the dotted line."

THE MOMENT he and Liz finished dessert, Mark excused them from the table and escorted Liz from the dining room, a wild flurry of emotions stirring his brain into chaos. It looked as if the partnership was going to be his. Unfortunately, he was going to be able to keep it only until the people at Nichols, Marbury & White discovered that mixology had nothing to do with chemistry.

Once they were outside the door, he took Liz's arm and pulled her behind a potted palm, his apprehension escalating with every second that passed.

"We're in trouble now," he told her. "Edwin thinks you're a chemist!"

"I heard. But I never said that, and neither did you. Margaret made it up."

"But I didn't correct him, either!"

"I know. But you never lied. That's all that matters."

"That's *not* all that matters! It's appearances, Liz. If it even *looks* as if I lied—"

He swiped a hand through his hair, trying to combat the tension building up inside him. Steven Millstone could show up at any moment, and if this thing with Liz's job got any more out of hand, damage control would be impossible. Somebody would figure out the truth, and he'd be a laughingstock.

"Hey, boss."

Mark spun around to find Tina standing behind him, holding a drink and giving Liz the once-over. He collected himself as best he could and pasted on a smile of greeting.

"Tina. Hi. Uh…this is Elizabeth Prescott. Elizabeth, this is my assistant, Tina."

Liz extended her hand. "Tina. It's a pleasure."

Tina shook Liz's hand, eyeing her up and down. "Nice dress, Elizabeth."

"Thank you," Liz said, with a gracious smile. "It's a Geoffrey Allen."

"Geoffrey Allen, huh?" Tina raised an eyebrow. "You know, I was going to wear my Geoffrey Allen, but it was in the wash. So I wore my Sam Walton instead."

Mark knew the WalMart reference hadn't gotten by Liz, but she didn't bite. "Well, it's simply lovely. Fuschia is the perfect color for you."

Tina gave Mark one of those nose-crinkling looks that said she knew social insincerity when she heard it, and Liz was feeding her a truckload of it.

Liz turned to Mark. "Will you excuse me for a moment, darling?"

She gave his arm a gentle squeeze, then headed toward the ladies' room. Tina watched her walk away, then turned back.

"Interesting," Tina said. "How long have you been seeing her?"

"Not long."

"I've been watching her. She's beautiful."

Mark smiled. "Yeah, I know."

"And that dress really is something."

"It is, isn't it?"

"She has nice manners. And she seems smart, too. I hear she has a master's degree in chemistry."

A master's degree?

Mark stared at Tina with total disbelief. This couldn't be happening. Apparently Margaret had shared her mixologist interpretation with everyone she talked to, and now some big-mouthed gossip had upped the ante and given Liz an advanced degree. What would she be promoted to next?

"Yeah," Tina said. "She seems pretty much perfect. Is that why she's so stuck up?"

Mark physically recoiled and stared at Tina. "Stuck up?"

"Yeah. She walks like Miss America and talks like the Queen of England. And her nose is so far in the air I'm surprised she can see where she's going. No offense, Mark. But she doesn't seem like your type."

Mark just stared at her, unable to believe what he was hearing.

Tina tapped her drink glass. "Look, boss. Jack Daniels and I are having a close, personal relationship here tonight, so I'm getting ready to say something I *know* I'll regret on Monday morning. But a woman like that will only make your life hell. You want another Tiffany? Stick with her, and that's just what you're gonna get."

Tina walked away, leaving Mark standing in shocked silence. She'd just expressed something that, until this moment, he hadn't thought possible from any member of the human race.

She didn't like Liz.

He wanted to rush after Tina, to tell her that this wasn't the real Liz, and that she'd like her a lot if only they could go out for pizza or something, instead of being around people like the ones here tonight.

No. That's not the Liz you need. The Liz you need is the one the big boys like, not Tina.

A moment later Liz came back across the ballroom. Mark met her halfway and pulled her aside again. "You'll be pleased to know you've just earned your master's degree in chemistry."

Liz's mouth fell open. "You've got to be joking."

"It's no joke," he said, trying to stay calm and failing miserably. "That's what's going around now. How are we ever going to explain it?"

"Take it easy, Mark. It's going to be okay."

"It's *not* going to be okay! This could ruin everything!"

She stared at him a long time, her face drifting into a melancholy frown. "Is it really so bad what I do for a living?"

He let out a harsh breath of frustration. "I told you, Liz. I'm not the one who feels that way. It's them."

"But you're part of *them*. Aren't you?"

Mark stared at her wordlessly as the truth of the situation hit him right between the eyes. She was right. He *was* part of "them," now more so than ever before. He was dressing right, acting right, talking right, which had pleased the hell out of the managing partner, who was now prepared to clear the way for his rise to the top. But it wasn't until this moment that he realized just how much of a stranglehold his job had on his life. His job *was* his life.

Or, at least it had been until Liz had come along a few weeks ago and turned things upside down.

Suddenly he felt as if he were wearing an invisible straitjacket made up of the firm's unwritten rules of life inside the office *and* out. But all those dictates were nothing new. He'd been wearing this same straitjacket for ten years. So why was it suddenly squeezing the breath out of him?

"Uh-oh," Liz said, glancing around Mark's shoulder. "Edwin's coming over here. And he's got somebody with him."

Mark spun around, and the tension he'd felt escalated into full-fledged panic. That somebody was Steven Millstone.

"Mark," Edwin said, with as much joviality as a man of his sour nature could muster. "This is Steven Millstone."

"Of course," Mark said, shaking his hand. "It's a pleasure to meet you."

"You'll be getting to know each other quite well," Edwin told Steven. "Mark will be the one overseeing your account."

"*If* I decide to go with your firm," Steven said, looking a little annoyed.

"Of course," Edwin said. "But I'm quite sure you want the best. And we *are* the best. Particularly with men like McAlister here on the job."

Steven looked wholly unconvinced of that. A millionaire at age twenty-six, he hadn't gotten there by wading through a lot of bull. Mark got the impression he didn't appreciate Edwin's you'd-be-a-fool-not-to-go-with-us approach.

Edwin turned to Liz. "And this is Mark's lady friend, Elizabeth Prescott. I was quite impressed to find out that she has a doctorate in chemistry."

Doctorate? *Doctorate?*

Mark felt as if the walls were closing in on him, squashing him so he couldn't breathe. He saw Liz struggling to keep her panic under wraps, too. At the rate the gossip was flying, it wouldn't be long before she was a Nobel prize-winning scientist conducting experiments aboard the space shuttle.

"I'm delighted to meet you," Liz said to Steven, her voice a little shaky.

Steven eyed her carefully. "Have we met before?"

Wait a minute, Mark thought. She *knew* Steven Millstone?

No. That was impossible. He was just confusing her with someone else.

"No, I don't believe we have," Liz replied.

Mark glanced at Steven, then back to Liz. What was going on here?

Then Sloan and Tiffany approached their group and edged into the conversation. Under normal circumstances that would have irked the hell out of Mark, but now he was glad to see anyone who would take Steven's attention away from Liz. They all engaged in small talk for a few minutes, Sloan occasionally shooting Mark looks that said, *You think you've got it all sewn up. But it's not over till it's over.*

Then Steven glanced at Liz again, his head tilted in that way people do when they're trying to remember something that's just beyond their grasp. "I *know* I've seen you somewhere before."

"Perhaps you went to college together?" Edwin said.

"I doubt that, Edwin. I didn't go to college."

Steven looked at her several more seconds. Then a smile spread across his face, his eyes lighting with recognition.

"Now I remember where I've seen you. You're a bartender at Simon's."

14

MARK FELT AS IF the high-dollar oriental rug beneath his feet had just been yanked out from under him. He glanced at Liz and saw the shock on her face, which probably matched the shock on his. Every muscle in his body tightened as he waited for the ax to fall.

"No," Liz said, her voice even shakier than before. "I believe you have me confused with someone else."

Steven looked unconvinced. "Hmm. I could have sworn—"

"Wait a minute," Tiffany said. "I think I've seen you in there, too. I went there a few times with friends.... Yes! It was you! Working behind the bar!"

Tiffany had a glazed, triumphant look in her eyes, as if she'd just solved one of the greatest crimes of the new millennium. Edwin looked all red and flustered, Sloan was grinning like a hyena, and Mark felt as if he were dying.

Edwin laughed nervously, glancing back and forth between Steven and Tiffany. "A bartender? I'm quite certain both of you must be mistaken. Ms. Prescott is a professional woman."

Steven smiled at Liz. "Maybe so, but she also makes one hell of a margarita."

Edwin turned to Mark, his expression shifting from anxiety to anger. "May I see you for a moment, please?"

He stepped aside, pulling Mark along with him until

they were out of earshot of the rest of the crowd. Then he wheeled around, his eyes narrowed with anger.

"Am I to understand that the woman you purport to be serious about works behind a *bar?*"

Edwin's reprimand felt like a slap in the face, and for a moment Mark was speechless.

"With all due respect," Mark said, "you thought she was perfectly charming when you weren't aware of that fact."

Edwin's mouth twitched. "That's hardly the point. The very idea that you'd consort with such a woman, and then try to pass her off as *educated*—" His face turned red with fury. "A Ph.D. in chemistry. Did you expect to be able to pull that off forever?"

"It wasn't him! It was me!" Liz came up beside Mark, a pleading expression on her face. "I'm the one who lied! Mark had nothing to do with it!"

"I had high hopes for you these past few weeks, McAlister," Edwin went on. "Very high hopes. It's unfortunate that you've disappointed me."

"Listen to me!" Liz said. "Please! It wasn't Mark's fault!"

Edwin didn't so much as glance in Liz's direction. It was as if she'd suddenly become a nonentity, a nobody who didn't warrant so much as a second glance.

"I thought you finally understood what it took to be a partner in this firm," Edwin went on, "but evidently it has escaped your attention that we cater to a very-high class clientele and such a woman would be a hindrance to your career."

Mark was shocked by the echo of his own thoughts. That's exactly what he'd been afraid of these past few weeks, but hearing it come out of Edwin's mouth now, he couldn't believe how petty it sounded. He'd been so apprehensive about how Liz would affect his job that he'd never bothered to acknowledge the truth.

His job was just a job, but Liz was his life.

A sly, calculating expression came over Edwin's face. "This isn't insurmountable, Mark. We'll tell Steven that you were just as surprised as the rest of us to discover that this woman was *not* who she claimed to be."

Mark felt a burn of anger start in the back of his throat and spread to the rest of his body. His hands tightened into fists, and it was all he could do not use them.

"Let me get this straight," he said. "You're condemning me because you think I lied about her profession, yet it's perfectly all right for you to fabricate a story to placate a big client?"

"Damage control. That's all we're talking about." Edwin edged closer and dropped his voice. "Just assure me that you'll see no more of this woman, I think I can still persuade the other partners to make you the top candidate."

For a moment all Mark could do was stand there in utter disbelief. This was what he'd wanted for ten years? To play these kinds of games? To lie on purpose? To treat a sweet, wonderful woman like Liz as if she didn't even exist, just because she didn't meet the expectations of people he thought he wanted to emulate, but had just discovered he didn't give a damn about? If this was what life at the top was like, he wanted no part of it.

Mark inched closer to Edwin, skewering him with a look of pure malice. "Listen to this, you pompous ass. For the past ten years, I've sweated blood for this company. It's been my whole life. I've come in early, I've worked late, I've given up everything for your bottom line. I've let it rule my life, and that's the biggest mistake I've ever made. I've got a life of my own, Edwin, and I'm not letting the company get in the way of it anymore."

"McAlister! Keep your voice down!"

"I'll talk as loud as I want to. And I don't care if the whole damned world hears me!"

"Now, listen here—"

"No. You listen. I'm not going to let *anyone* else stand here and tell Liz she's not good enough for me. Because the truth is that I'm the one who's not good enough for her. I just hope I can get a ring on her finger by the time she figures that out."

Liz stared at Mark in complete awe. He was throwing his career away. He was telling the managing partner to go to hell, and it was all because of her. He was going to regret this. Maybe not now, maybe not next week, but eventually, and when he did—

Wait a minute. What was that he said about a ring?

"That's *enough,* McAlister." Edwin's voice was low and intense, full of rage. "You've embarrassed me, and you've embarrassed the firm in front of a very important client. I can't overlook this."

"You won't have to. You'll have my resignation Monday morning."

Liz felt a rush of panic. "No! Mark, don't do this—"

He grabbed her hand. "Come on."

He pulled her toward the door. She looked back over her shoulder and saw Edwin turning ten different shades of red. Steven Millstone watched them go, and Liz could have sworn she saw him smile. Mark led her out of the club, right past the valet, then strode through the parking lot directly to his car.

"Mark. Stop. You can't do this."

He kept walking, pulling her along.

"You've worked there almost ten years!" Liz protested. "You can't just throw that away!"

Still he ignored her. He unlocked her door and motioned for her to get inside.

Liz couldn't stand this. She couldn't stand the fact that he went into that country club tonight thinking he was on the verge of a partnership, only to come out unemployed because of something she'd done. Or something she *was*, which was even worse.

The moment Mark got into the car, she said, "You can't give up that partnership for me, Mark. You can't!"

He shut the door and turned to her, taking her hands in his.

"Liz. Listen to me."

"I never wanted this to happen!"

"Neither did I. But I'm glad it did."

"You're glad? You're glad you no longer have a job?"

"I'm glad I no longer have *that* job." He tightened his hands against hers. "I've changed in the past few weeks, Liz. I don't like the person that firm made me. But the person I've become since I met you—I like him a whole lot more."

"Mark—"

"No, listen. I went a little crazy there for a while, thinking I knew what I wanted when I really didn't. But I've wised up a lot tonight."

"I guess I went a little crazy, too." Liz sighed heavily, holding out her palms and looking down at the dress she'd never wanted to buy in the first place. "This isn't me, Mark. This dress, this hair, this *life*. I was only kidding myself to think I could be somebody else." She hated to speak the truth, but what else could she do? "You know the real me. And I'm afraid that's all you're ever going to get."

She held her breath after she said that. Maybe he wasn't thinking straight before, and he'd wake up and realize the horrible mistake he'd made and want to take it all back.

"You're all I'll *ever* want," he said. "The real you. Not the made-up you."

"But your job," she said, "your future—"

"My job isn't my future, Liz. You are."

For a moment Liz was speechless, so overcome with

happiness that she didn't know what to say. Mark drew her close and kissed her, a soft, gentle kiss that was full of the promise of even better things to come, and it made her heart soar. Then she remembered.

"Mark, when you were yelling at Edwin in there, you said something else. Something about a—"

She stopped short, afraid to bring it up again because he'd said it in the heat of the moment, and she wasn't sure he really meant it.

"A ring?" Mark said.

"Yes."

"I meant every word of what I said. The question is, how do *you* feel about it?"

She saw tension on his face as he waited for her answer, his gaze fixed on hers as if he were trying to read her response in her eyes. She smiled to herself. How could he not know how desperately she wanted him?

"You'd better be very careful if you put a ring on my finger," she told him. "Because once it's there, it's never coming off again."

He gave her a brilliant smile. "Then we have a lot to talk about, don't we?"

She nodded and kissed him again, her heart so full it was about to explode. Despite a few glitches here and there, this had turned out to be the very best day of her life.

Mark glanced at her hair. "How many pins do you suppose are in there?"

"About three or four thousand. The stylist almost had to use Super Glue to get it to stay up."

"When we get home, I'm going to pull all of them out. One by one. And you're never putting your hair up like that again."

"Okay."

"And if I ever hear the name Elizabeth again, there'll be hell to pay. Got that?"

"Got it."

"And while we're at it, I hate that dress."

"This dress cost me three hundred dollars!"

"I'll give you four hundred if you promise never to wear it again."

Liz smiled. "Since when did you become such a big spender?"

"Since I found a reason to be. I love you, Liz. And I'm never letting you go."

MARK TOOK his leave from Nichols, Marbury & White the following Monday. It took him most of the day to close out his responsibilities, to say good-bye to the people he was genuinely going to miss, and to do the obligatory exit interview in personnel. Sloan made himself scarce, which was a good thing, and he never saw a hair of Edwin Nichols's bad toupee, either, which was even better.

He came out of his office for the last time to find Tina sitting on the edge of her desk.

"No, you don't," Tina said. "You turn around and go right back into that office. You do it right now, or I'm going to cry. And you'll be sorry about that. I don't look pretty when I cry."

They stared at each other for a long, painful moment. Then Mark gave her a bittersweet smile, and she slid off her desk and wrapped her arms around him in a heartfelt hug.

"It's going to be terrible, Mark. I just know they're going to reassign me to some nasty, demanding jerk who I hate and I'm going to end up getting fired. You're the only one here who would put up with me."

"I'll call you the minute I get settled in a new job," Mark said. "If there's any way I can, I'll bring you along."

"Warn them first. I'm hardly your average secretary."

"You're right. You're not average. You're the best I've ever had."

She sniffed a little and wiped her eyes, then backed away. Mark left the office, giving her one last smile over his shoulder.

Some passages in life were easy. Others weren't. As he headed to Simon's to see Liz, though, Mark found himself looking forward rather than looking back. No matter what the future held, there was no question in his mind that he'd done the right thing.

He came into Simon's, spied Liz behind the bar and headed toward her, excited at the very thought of seeing her again. She leaned over the bar and gave him a quick kiss. It wasn't until he sat down on a bar stool that he realized who was sitting next to him.

Steven Millstone.

Mark blinked with disbelief. "Steven?"

"Hi, Mark. Liz said you'd be here soon. I wanted to talk to you."

"What about?"

"Edwin told me you'd been fired."

"I resigned."

"Yeah, Liz finally gave me the straight story on that."

"It doesn't matter now," Mark said. "The firm will handle your account just fine without me. Jared Sloan—"

"Jared Sloan is an idiot. And who says they'll be handling my account at all?"

Mark stared at him. "I just assumed—"

"Look, Mark. I grew up in a lower-middle class family, where my dad worked two jobs just to make ends meet. If I hadn't been such a computer geek, I never would have made all this money, and it makes me uncomfortable to give my business to people who are used to dealing with the rich folks. I've just got a little software business that happened to get big. I don't want someone to feed me caviar and champagne and all that other crap, and then bill me an outrageous amount of money so they can cover all those expenses. I just need someone who can keep half my profit from going away to Uncle Sam. That's all."

The more this guy talked, the more Mark liked him.

"So are you interested?"

Mark blinked. "Excuse me?"

"Ever think of starting your own accounting firm?"

Mark stared at him, dumbfounded. He couldn't say that he'd ever thought about that at all. There were a lot of unknowns there, and he'd never been a big risk taker. But something had changed in the past few weeks, something that told him he was ready to take a chance.

"Yeah," he said. "The thought has occurred to me."

"Good. When I saw you stick up for Liz the way you did, I knew you were the kind of guy I was looking for. Can we get together tomorrow and discuss it?"

Mark couldn't believe it. The million-dollar kid wanted to hand him an account that other people would saw off a limb to have. He glanced at Liz. She was all smiles.

"Yes," Mark said. "Let's do that."

Steven glanced at his watch. "I've got to go right now. My son's baseball game starts in half an hour, and it's going to be tough for them to play if the coach doesn't show up."

"Baseball?" Liz said. "We *love* baseball."

Steven smiled. "Then why don't you come along?"

"Why not? My shift's done."

It was a beautiful, breezy evening at the Little League ballpark, with the smell of freshly cut grass warmed by the evening sun. Mark and Liz got corn dogs for dinner at the concession stand and watched a nail-biter of a game that Steven's team pulled out in the last inning. At the same time Liz had the opportunity to chat with Steven's wife, and they hit it off so well that he and Steven finally had to drag them apart long after the players and their parents had gone home.

That night Mark was so excited he couldn't sleep. The longer he and Liz talked about the possibilities, the more enthusiastic he became. By the time the clock inched past midnight and he finally pulled her into his arms to make love to her, he'd made his decision. In both his personal life and his professional one, it was time he stepped off that cliff, because Liz had given him all the confidence he needed to ensure he wouldn't fall.

With her in his life, he'd sprout wings and fly.

Epilogue

FIVE MONTHS after opening the doors of McAlister & Associates, Mark was bringing in new clients almost every week. Steven Millstone's account was the largest by far, but with his recommendation, several smaller companies had also signed on. Mark's only "associate" so far was Jeff Miller, a kid with outstanding potential that he had hired right out of college, but he was also interviewing a couple of experienced accountants on Monday to help take on the increased workload.

In the beginning, he'd gotten office space in Morrison Heights because it was cheap, but with their new house close by, a deli next door that made the best sub sandwiches in town and enough oddball things going on in the neighborhood to keep life interesting, Mark wondered why he'd ever want his office anywhere else.

"It's five-thirty, Jeff," Mark said, late on a Friday afternoon. "Go home."

"But there's plenty of work. And I don't mind staying."

"It's not necessary."

"I'll only be here an hour or so."

Mark started to protest again, but then he looked past Jeff and saw Liz at the door of his office. She wore a long purple knit dress with a slit up the thigh and a row of buttons from her neck to her navel. She held a bag from the nearby deli.

Mark had never seen his wife look more beautiful. Then again, he thought that every time he saw her.

"But I don't mind staying, Mr. McAlister," Jeff said.

"It's Mark. Remember?"

"Mark. Right." He opened the file. "See I was looking at this client's tax liability for last year, and—"

"I just made a new rule, Jeff. Nobody works late on Friday."

Liz winked at Mark, then rattled the deli sack a little. Jeff whipped around. When he saw Liz, he stood quickly, nearly spilling the contents of the file he held.

"Mrs. McAlister. I—I didn't see you standing there."

Liz gave him a thousand-watt smile, one that would send even the most experienced ladies' man to his knees. Mark just hoped the poor kid didn't wet his pants.

Jeff swallowed hard. He dropped the file to Mark's desktop. "Uh, I guess I'll see you Monday, Mark," he said, scurrying out the door. Liz watched until he disappeared from sight, then came into the office and closed the door behind her.

"Why, I do believe that poor boy is afraid of me."

"He's in awe of you." Mark led her over to his sofa and pulled her down beside him. "So am I."

"Eager little thing, isn't he?"

Mark edged the slit in Liz's dress aside, then ran his hand up her leg. "Yeah. And smart as he can be. I've gotta teach him to take it easy, though, or he might get to age thirty and have nothing but a job to turn to."

"Unlike his boss."

"No. *Like* his boss, until his boss met you."

Mark kissed his way along Liz's neck, his fingers finding the first of those many tiny buttons.

"I thought you had to work late tonight," Liz murmured, her eyes dropping closed.

"Didn't you hear the new rule I made?"

"But I brought dinner."

"Later." He unfastened two buttons, then three.

Liz laughed softly. "Did I ever tell you that for a stuffy, boring accountant you're not so stuffy and boring?"

"A time or two. Did I tell you Randall Pearson is signing with us tomorrow?"

Liz turned around suddenly. "Oh, Mark! That's wonderful!"

Wonderful pretty well summed it up. Pearson Paper Company had revenues in the millions, and he was going to have to do some fast hiring just to take on the extra business.

"After we had dinner with him and his wife the other night, Pearson said you were 'a breath of fresh air.' He told me any man who was smart enough to persuade a woman like you to marry him deserved his business."

Liz's eyes got a little misty when Mark said that, and he was amazed at how he could love her more with every minute that passed.

Then all at once she gave him a wicked grin. "Wait a minute. If we got Pearson, that means—"

"That Sloan didn't."

"Yes!" Liz threw her arms up in victory, then wound them around Mark's neck and gave him a kiss that resonated through every nerve in his body. "So how many more clients are you going to steal right out from under his nose?"

"Now, I'm not stealing anyone from Sloan," Mark said. "I'm just using my secret weapon."

"Your secret weapon?"

"You."

Liz cuddled against him with a satisfied smile. "You can use me any old time you want to."

"So how was your final this afternoon?" he asked her.

"Tough, but I think I did okay."

"That's it, then. Your first semester is over." He undid

another button and teased his lips over her ear. "We have lots to celebrate, don't we?"

Suddenly the door to his office swung open, and Tina barged in. Mark and Liz sat up suddenly. Mark glared at Tina.

"Tina! I thought you'd gone home!"

"I left my car keys on your desk."

"Have you *ever* considered knocking?"

"Can't say that I have." She nodded back over her shoulder. "I saw Jeff in the hall. When are you going to get him to lighten up? He's still calling me Mrs. Boyd." She grabbed her keys off Mark's desk. Then her gaze shifted to Liz.

"Ooh, Liz! I love that dress!"

Liz grinned. "Thanks."

"Where did you get it?"

"At Second Hand Rose. That resale shop on Collins Boulevard."

"I went over there the other day, but I didn't see anything that cute."

"If you dig around a little, you'll find all kinds of things. Do you want to go over there with me sometime? If you do, I can—"

From behind, Mark clamped his hand over his wife's mouth. Her eyes widened, then shifted back and forth Lucy Ricardo style. He leaned over and put his lips a scant inch from her ear.

"I like the dress, too," he whispered softly. "And if you'll kindly shut up, Tina will leave, then I'll unbutton every one of those buttons, take it off you, hang it up on the back of my *locked* door, and then I can admire what's under it for the next hour or so. How would that be?"

Slowly he removed his hand from her mouth.

"Tina," Liz said. "Go home."

Tina grinned. "He whispered something dirty, didn't he?"

Liz just smiled.

"God, I *love* this place."

Tina gave a little wave with her fingertips, backed out the door and closed it with a gentle click.

Mark turned back to Liz and drew her into a long, lingering kiss, secure in the knowledge that everything in life happens for a reason, whether it's apparent at the time or not. He'd walked into Simon's in search of the perfect woman.

And he'd found her.

MAITLAND MATERNITY

Where the luckiest babies are born!

In April 2001, look for

HER BEST FRIEND'S BABY
by Vicki Lewis Thompson

**A car accident leaves surrogate mother
Mary-Jane Potter's baby-to-be
without a mother—**

and causes the father, Morgan Tate, to fuss over a
very pregnant Mary-Jane like a mother hen. Suddenly,
Mary-Jane is dreaming of keeping the baby…and the father!

*Each book tells a different story about the
world-renowned Maitland Maternity Clinic—
where romances are born, secrets are revealed…
and bundles of joy are delivered.*

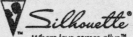

Silhouette®
Where love comes alive™

HARLEQUIN®
Makes any time special ™

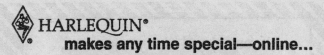

If you enjoyed what you just read,
then we've got an offer you can't resist!

Take 2 bestselling love stories FREE!

Plus get a FREE surprise gift!